P9-DGH-492

UNLAWFUL CONTACT

PAMELA CLARE

BERKLEY SENSATION, NEW YORK

THE BERKLEY PUBLISHING GROUP
Published by the Penguin Group
Penguin Group (USA) Inc.
375 Hudson Street, New York, New York 10014, USA
Penguin Group (Canada), 90 Eglinton Avenue East, Suite 700, Toronto, Ontario M4P 2Y3, Canada
(a division of Pearson Penguin Canada Inc.)
Penguin Books Ltd., 80 Strand, London WC2R 0RL, England
Penguin Group Ireland, 25 St. Stephen's Green, Dublin 2, Ireland (a division of Penguin Books Ltd.)
Penguin Group (Australia), 250 Camberwell Road, Camberwell, Victoria 3124, Australia
(a division of Pearson Australia Group Pty. Ltd.)
Penguin Books India Pvt. Ltd., 11 Community Centre, Panchsheel Park, New Delhi—110 017, India
Penguin Group (NZ), 67 Apollo Drive, Rosedale, North Shore 0632, New Zealand
(a division of Pearson New Zealand Ltd.)
Penguin Books (South Africa) (Pty.) Ltd., 24 Sturdee Avenue, Rosebank, Johannesburg 2196,
South Africa

Penguin Books Ltd., Registered Offices: 80 Strand, London WC2R 0RL, England

This is a work of fiction. Names, characters, places, and incidents either are the product of the author's imagination or are used fictitiously, and any resemblance to actual persons, living or dead, business establishments, events, or locales is entirely coincidental. The publisher does not have any control over and does not assume any responsibility for author or third-party websites or their content.

UNLAWFUL CONTACT

A Berkley Sensation Book / published by arrangement with the author

PRINTING HISTORY
Berkley Sensation mass-market edition / April 2008

Copyright © 2008 by Pamela Clare.
Cover design by Annette Fiore.
Interior text design by Stacy Irwin.

ISBN: 978-0-425-21762-7

BERKLEY® SENSATION
Berkley Sensation Books are published by The Berkley Publishing Group,
a division of Penguin Group (USA) Inc.,
375 Hudson Street, New York, New York 10014.
BERKLEY SENSATION and the "B" design are trademarks belonging to Penguin Group (USA) Inc.

PRINTED IN THE UNITED STATES OF AMERICA

10 9 8 7 6 5 4 3 2 1

This book is dedicated to the memory of Leah Rhiann Clifton, who died in her mother's womb in a prison cell.

ACKNOWLEDGMENTS

Special thanks to Christie Donner, Pamela Clifton, and the Colorado Criminal Justice Reform Coalition for their tireless work on behalf of prison inmates.

Special thanks to Sergeant Gary Arai for answering my many questions about police operations—and teaching me how to break out of handcuffs; to Sergeant David Murphy for his insights on SWAT operations and gear; and to my mother, Mary White, a registered nurse, for sharing her medical knowledge.

With deep gratitude to Cindy Hwang, my editor, and Natasha Kern, my agent and friend, for their patience and for believing in my stories.

Personal thanks to Michelle White, Timalyn O'Neill, Norah Wilson, Bonnie Vanak, Kally Jo Surbeck, Aimee Culbertson, Libby Murphy, Kristi Ross, Sue Zimmerman, Debbie Hoke, Dede Laugesen, and Amy Vandersall for their patience, support, and friendship.

And as always, thanks and much love to my family and to my sons, Alec and Benjamin, who do so much so that I can write. I love you deeply and forever.

PROLOGUE

Grand Junction, Colorado
June 9, 1996

SOPHIE ALTON WALKED through the party, wishing she'd stayed home. Heavy metal pumped from car speakers, blaring so loudly that she could barely hear herself think. Kids stood and sat among the cottonwoods, drinking beer, smoking cigarettes, making out.

She didn't belong here. She wasn't sure why she'd let Candy talk her into coming to this stupid graduation party. Did she really think Hunt was going to notice her?

She saw him through the trees, leaning against his car, talking with Dawn Harper and Kendra Willis. He wore a black T-shirt that hugged his broad shoulders and a pair of low-slung jeans. His thick brown hair looked like he'd just gotten out of bed, his square jaw covered with dark stubble. He was taller and bigger than the other boys, and though she couldn't see them from here, she knew his eyes were a deep green. He was by far the cutest guy in the graduating class. Just seeing him made her feel like she was melting.

But Sophie wasn't an idiot. A guy like Hunt wasn't about to waste time on a flat-chested sophomore when he could have pretty senior girls like Dawn and Kendra. Besides, he probably liked girls who partied, not nerdy girls who studied all the time.

He glanced in her direction, saw her watching him.

She gasped, looked away, and walked faster.

Her grandma had warned her that Hunt was trouble. She'd said his mother had gone to prison and that he would probably follow in her footsteps. It seemed unfair to blame him for things his mother had done, though he *did* seem to get into trouble a lot. He was the kid teachers blamed for everything, even things he hadn't done. Once during a school assembly, someone had pulled the fire alarm, and they'd blamed Hunt, even though he'd been sitting in the bleachers at the time. Sophie had known where he was sitting when the alarm went off because she'd been watching him. She'd told the principal this, but he hadn't listened.

Hunt had just shrugged his shoulders and grinned when they'd led him away, as if to say, "It happens all the time."

Sophie had felt sorry for him.

She glanced around, looking for Candy. Maybe she could talk Candy into letting her borrow her pickup truck so she could drive home. Or maybe one of the other kids would be heading back into town soon.

But how will you know if they've been drinking?

She wouldn't know. She'd have to trust them not to drive drunk, and she wasn't sure she trusted even Candy to tell the truth about that. And where was Candy anyway?

Realizing she was stuck at the party until Candy surfaced again, she walked toward the edge of the crowd, stepping over empty plastic beer cups, potato chip bags, and clusters of prickly pear cactus, looking for someplace she could sit down and be by herself.

A group of girls broke into giggles as she passed.

"She's such a nerd! I bet she studies all night."

"Do you think she's ever kissed a guy?"

"Are you kidding? She's a total virgin."

Sophie felt her face burn.

"I heard her parents are dead."

The breath left her lungs in a rush, and her step faltered, tears stinging her eyes. She wanted to run, but then they would know she'd heard them and she'd feel even more humiliated. She forced herself to keep her gaze straight ahead and to walk slowly.

Her parents *were* dead. They'd been dead for almost a

year, run over by a drunk driver while crossing the street in Denver. She and her little brother, David, had gotten the terrible news late one night and had found themselves on the way to their grandma's house in Grand Junction the next morning. Everyone told Sophie how she needed to think of the future, how she needed to become the young woman her parents knew she could be. But no matter how hard she fought not to be a big baby about it, she couldn't stop missing her mom and dad.

She saw an outcropping of rock and went to stand on the other side of it where no one could see her cry. But someone was already there.

"Fuck off, stupid bitch!"

A group of boys huddled together, putting something that looked like whitish rocks into a strange, little pipe. *Drugs.* They were doing drugs.

"Get lost!"

Momentarily speechless, Sophie took a step backward. "S-sorry!"

One of the boys grabbed her roughly around the wrist and dragged her forward, his sunburned face a wide grin. "Maybe we should keep her around. You know how horny this stuff makes me."

Shock became fear. She shook her head, tried to pull her arm free. "No!"

"Bad idea. How do we know she won't narc?" one of them asked. "Besides, you know you can't get it up on this shit."

A deep voice came from behind her. "Get your hands off her, Patrick, or I'll stuff your balls down your throat!"

The boy let go of her so fast that she stumbled backward and almost fell in the grass. "Sorry, Hunt. I didn't know she was here with you."

Astonished, Sophie turned and saw Hunt standing behind her, glaring at the group of boys, his jaw tight, his mouth a grim line.

His gaze met hers and grew softer. "Come on, Sophie. You don't want to hang around with these losers."

Sophie didn't need to be asked twice. She followed him to his car.

Hunt looked at the girl who sat in his passenger seat, feeling a strange tenderness in his chest. She'd put on her seat belt the moment she'd gotten into the car and now sat with her hands folded in her lap, her pretty face downcast and half-hidden by a fall of strawberry-blond hair. He'd always thought she was one of the prettiest girls in school, her eyes a deep blue, her skin pale and creamy, her mouth full and pink. She wasn't short, but she wasn't tall either, her slender build, her little nose, and the slant of her eyes making him think of a fairy sprite more than a human girl. But she was a smart fairy sprite, making honor roll despite what had happened to her. He had to respect that.

He'd heard what those stupid girls had said about her, and he'd watched her hurry away from the party, looking like she might cry. He'd realized she was headed straight for Patrick and his meth-head buddies, but he hadn't gotten to her fast enough to keep her away from them. He'd wanted to beat the shit out of Patrick for grabbing her and scaring her like that.

"You okay?" He tucked her hair behind her ear, unveiling her face.

Her cheeks wet with tears, she nodded. "Thanks."

He stuck his key in the ignition of his '55 Chevy Bel Air, turned it, and gunned the engine once just to feel its power. It had belonged to his grandfather, and Hunt had mowed a lot of lawns to earn the money to fix it up. "This isn't exactly your scene, is it?"

She sniffed, shook her head. "No."

"Where do you want me to take you?" He kicked the car into drive and steered through the trees and partiers toward the dirt road that headed through the adobes back to town.

"I guess I should go home, but . . ."

"But what?"

"If my grandma sees I've been crying, she'll ask me what

happened, and then I'll have to tell her I was here. I'll probably get grounded. She's pretty strict."

Hunt was struck by her honesty. If he'd have been in her situation, he'd have solved the problem by telling a bald-faced lie.

That's why you're a loser and she's not, dumbshit.

"Then I won't take you home—not yet. Ever been up to the Monument?"

She looked up at him, and he could see the wariness in her eyes.

He pushed on the brake, reached under his seat, and pulled out his tire iron. "I'm not going to hurt you, Sophie. See this? If I do anything you don't like, just hit me with it."

Her fairy-sprite lips curved into a smile. "I don't think I could really hit you."

"You're not supposed to tell me that. It makes it hard for me to be afraid of you."

She laughed. "You're not afraid of me."

But a part of him was.

Sophie stared up at the stars, Hunt's arm around her shoulder, his voice a deep purr in her ear as he explained the constellations, his car radio playing some romantic old Elvis song.

"Over there is Leo." He pointed toward a configuration of stars just above the western horizon. "See that star, the brightest one? That's Regulus."

She looked where he pointed, tried to see a lion, and thought maybe she did. "Which is your favorite constellation?"

"I suppose my favorite is Orion, but he's not up yet. He's really easy to spot, though. He's got three bright stars for his belt."

"Why do you like him best?"

He smiled, looked straight at her. "He's the hunter."

She couldn't believe this was happening, one of the worst nights of her life becoming one of the best. He'd taken her to get sodas, then he'd driven her to Colorado National Monument, where they'd gotten out of the car and looked

over the guardrail at the vast expanse of desert and canyon beyond, the cliffs and rock outcroppings dark shadows against
the night. Then he'd driven her along a road made for tourists
until he'd found a place to park.

"Got that tire iron?" he'd joked as he'd killed the engine.

They had talked until their sodas were gone and then
talked some more. She'd found she could tell him anything—
about her school in Denver, about the loneliness she'd felt
since coming to Grand Junction, about missing her parents.

"You want them back again, and there's nothing you can
do to get them back," he'd said, pulling her against his chest
when her eyes had filled with tears. "I know."

Then he'd told her how his mom had gone to prison twice
and how he'd been placed in one foster home after another,
fighting with the social workers who wanted to put him up for
adoption, refusing to cooperate.

"Is that why you get into trouble so much?" she'd asked.

He'd looked at her, something like surprise on his handsome face.

"I guess so," he'd said, after a moment's silence. "If I'd
have been a good kid like you, they'd have found a new home
for me and taken me from my mom. No matter what she's
done, she's still my mom. She didn't deserve that."

They'd talked about school, about their favorite teachers,
about what they wanted to be one day. Sophie'd told him how
she'd always wanted to be a reporter so that she could travel
and meet people. He'd told her he liked science, especially astronomy and geology.

"I always wanted to be an astronaut," he'd said, shrugging
as if he'd just said something ridiculous.

"You could still try. Really, you could. Why not shoot for
the stars?"

He'd laughed, shaken his head—and dropped a bomb. "I
don't think any college would take me, at least not yet. I enlisted in the army. I'm leaving tomorrow morning."

"You're *leaving*?" The revelation had stunned her—and
left an ache in her chest.

She hated saying good-bye, hated being left behind.

He'd looked down at her and grinned. "Gonna miss me, sprite?"

And as he showed her the stars, opening up the sky to her, Sophie realized she *was* going to miss him. She'd spent only a few short hours with him, but she already felt like she'd known him forever.

"Up from Leo is Virgo. Can you see it there? And that really bright star is Spica. If you follow it to the south—"

"Hunt?" Sophie was afraid to ask him, was afraid to say it, but he was leaving in the morning. If she didn't say it now, she'd probably never get another chance.

"Hmmm?"

Heart slamming, she forced herself to speak. "I . . . I want you to kiss me."

For a moment he said nothing, but looked into her eyes as if trying to see inside her. Then he cupped her face with his left hand, ran his thumb over her lips, and ducked down.

Sophie had been kissed before, but she'd never been kissed like this.

He brushed his lips over hers again and again, soft butterfly caresses that made her whimper. Then he kissed the corners of her mouth, tasting her lips one at a time. And when she was sure she couldn't take it another second, he took her mouth in a scorching, full-on kiss.

The heat of it stunned her, stole her breath, made her brain go blank. She heard herself moan, her body turning to hot jelly. She clung to him, instinctively following his lead, opening her mouth to the velvet strokes of his tongue, so new and strange to her. By the time he pulled back, she was shaking.

"Hunt?"

"Yeah, sprite?" He sounded breathless.

"Do that again."

He groaned, fisted a hand in her hair, and crushed her against him, his mouth plundering hers, lips and tongue and teeth, until she was gasping for breath.

But all too soon he let her go and faced forward, his fist so tight around the steering wheel that his knuckles turned white. "I think it's time to get you home."

She scooted closer, still shaking. "No, Hunt, please!"

He looked down at her, his forehead furrowed, his lips wet. "If I don't take you home now, you're not going to get home till morning."

She took his face between her hands, felt the rough stubble of his whiskers against her palms. "But that's what I want! I want—"

"What?"

"You."

She heard the breath rush from his lungs, felt some kind of battle raging inside him, knew he didn't believe her.

"I heard what those girls said about you. You shouldn't feel bad about being a virgin. That's a beautiful thing. You should save it for a man who makes you feel special. You should save it for—"

"For you." She'd never been more sure of anything in her life.

He turned in his seat to face her once again, ran his knuckles down her cheek. "But I'm the kid who always gets in trouble, remember?"

"Not with me you're not."

Hunt couldn't believe what she was offering him. How could a smart girl like Sophie Alton see anything in him? "I'm leaving tomorrow."

She nodded, her eyes looking impossibly big in the dark. "That's why it has to be now."

He couldn't argue with that. Besides, if she wanted to have sex with him badly enough that he couldn't talk her out of it, he wasn't stupid enough to stop her. He wanted her—bad.

"Come on."

He grabbed the blanket he kept in his trunk, took Sophie's trembling hand in his, and led her to a secluded copse of piñon pine away from the road. Then he spread the blanket on the warm, sandy ground.

If he'd expected her to get cold feet, he was wrong. The moment he turned to her, she wrapped her arms around his neck, stood on her toes, and kissed him. His little fairy sprite was passionate. Well, that was fine by him.

He drew her down to the blanket beside him, kissed her until his mouth burned, until he'd tasted her lips in every possible way, until they were both breathless, her fingers digging into his shoulders.

"God, Sophie, you are so sweet!"

Slowly, he undid the buttons of her blouse to reveal a lacy white bra and two small but perfect breasts.

"I-I'm flat chested." She looked away.

"Who told you that?" He pressed his lips against the lace, felt her body tense, heard her gasp. "I think you're perfect."

Unable to suppress a hungry groan, he unfastened the clasp, lowered his mouth to a tight, pink nipple, and sucked.

"Oh!" She arched off the blanket with a cry, her fingers digging into his hair.

Soon she was twisting beneath him, her head turning from side to side, her silky hair a tangled mass, and he was so hard and so turned on from the sight and taste of her that it hurt. He knew he needed to go slowly, but he didn't think he could wait much longer. He ran his hand down the satin skin of her belly, unbuttoned her jeans, then tugged them off with her panties, exposing the soft curls of her muff and a pair of smooth, slender legs.

He'd expected her to be shy, but she wasn't. Instead of hiding herself from him, she tried to undress *him*, tugging his T-shirt out of his jeans and fumbling with the buttons of his fly.

"I want to touch you!" Her voice was a breathy whisper.

"Yeah." He liked that idea.

He yanked off his shirt, then guided her uncertain fingers, nearly coming undone when she slid her hands over the skin of his bare ass to push his jeans and boxers out of the way.

"Can I see?" she asked.

"See?" And then he understood.

She'd never seen a dick before, at least not a hard one.

He rolled onto his side, took her hand, and guided it to his stiff cock, his entire body tensing when her fingers closed around him.

Sophie hadn't thought an erect penis would be so big. Or so hard. Or so silky. "I thought it would be like a hot dog."

He gave a snort. Then laughed. "A hot dog?"

She stroked him, ran her thumb over the moistened tip, felt his body jerk, his laughter catching in his throat, becoming a moan. Hungry for him, she explored him with her hands—his erection, his belly, his chest with its mat of dark curls.

And then he was kissing her again, his lips burning a path over her mouth, down her throat to her breasts, his fingers seeking between her thighs, teasing that secret part of her until she felt damp and hot and achy.

"I want to taste you!" His breath was cool against the heat of her wet, tingling nipples, his hand persistent between her thighs.

Surely he didn't mean . . .

Oh, but he did!

Shocked to her core, she tried to stop him. "Hunt, no! You don't have to—"

"I want to." His hard thigh pressed between hers, nudged her legs apart. Then he kissed his way down her body, the heat of his mouth and the anticipation raising bumps on her skin.

When at last he kissed her there, he did it with the same attention he'd given her mouth, his lips and tongue unbearably hot, the sweet tug of his lips so intense it almost made her scream. Never had she felt anything like this. She bit her lip, held her breath, fought not to break apart.

"Mmm." He groaned, nipping her sensitive inner thigh. "God, you taste good!"

He took her with his mouth again, this time sliding first one finger, then two deep inside her, stretching her, stroking her, setting her body on fire.

Breath left her lungs in a low, keening cry—and the heat inside her exploded. Molten gold blazed through her, the sensation both scorching and sweet. Only when the pleasure had ebbed did he stop, his lips finding a path up her belly, over her breasts, to her mouth. He tasted wild and musky, and she realized it was *her* flavor on his lips.

"Are you sure you want to do this, sprite? We can just hold at third base if you want, and you can stay a virgin. I won't be angry."

She could see on his face that it cost him something to say those words, and it struck her as excruciatingly sweet that he would give her the chance to back out. Most guys probably wouldn't do that. But then he was special. Hadn't she always sensed that?

She pressed her fingers against his lips to quiet him, her decision made the moment he'd kissed her. "I want it to be you, Hunt. I want you."

"Thank God! I want you more than any girl I've ever known!" He stretched himself out above her, lifted one of her slender legs, and wrapped it around his waist. "But there's something you should know."

Sophie slid her shaky hands up the muscles of his chest. "Wh-what?"

"I've never done this with a virgin. I might hurt you." Then he nudged himself slowly into her, breath hissing from between his clenched teeth, his gaze locked with hers, his muscles tense.

She gave a surprised gasp at the pain, then felt him withdraw.

Had she scared him off?

She drew him closer. "Don't stop! It doesn't hurt—too much."

He gave her a lopsided grin, sweat on his forehead and chest. "I don't plan to stop, sprite. I'm just letting you get used to me."

She felt his hips shift, felt him slide slowly into her again, stretching her past the pain, the fullness both piercing and hot. "Oh! Oh, Hunt, yes!"

He groaned, his eyes closed. "God, Sophie! You feel so good! So wet and tight! I don't think this will last very long."

Then he began to move, his motions reigniting the fire inside her, the pleasure building thrust upon thrust, until the stars seemed to explode and rain down around them, leaving them both panting and sweaty in the cool summer night.

HUNT STROKED SOPHIE'S hair, staring at the star-strewn sky above, his senses filled with her. "It's different with you."

She lifted her head off his chest, looked at him through sleepy eyes. "What's different?"

"Everything."

THEY LAY TOGETHER on the blanket, dozing, talking, laughing. He made love to her twice more, holding her until the sun came up and turned the canyon walls pink. Then he dressed her, crooning an old fifties love song, his lips pressed against her hair.

"One starry night, I kissed your lips / One starry night, I held you tight / You and I under the starry sky."

But the happiness Sophie had felt through the night seemed to dim with the daylight. All too soon, she found herself sitting in his car just down the street from her grandma's house, fighting tears as silence stretched between them.

"What are you going to tell your grandma?"

"I don't know. That I just lost my virginity to the guy she warned me about." She laughed despite the heaviness in her chest and realized that something had changed. She no longer cared what her grandmother thought.

Hunt frowned. "She warned you about me?"

"Yeah."

"Well, she was right, wasn't she?"

Sophie shook her head, clasped his big hand tightly. "No, she was dead wrong."

More silence.

"I liked you from the first moment I saw you," he said at last.

"Really?" She found that hard to believe. "Why didn't you say anything?"

He reached over, ran a finger down her cheek. "I didn't think a guy like me would stand a chance with a girl as smart and sweet as you."

"That's stupid!" she snapped, feeling genuinely angry. But one look at his face and her anger was gone. He truly believed what he'd said. "I liked you from the first time I saw you, too. I'm going to miss you, Hunt."

"I'd promise to stay in touch, but I've never written a letter in my life."

She stared down at their entwined fingers. "I wish . . ."

"Me, too. But it's better this way. You have better things to do than hang around with a loser like me. You're going to go to college, become a famous journalist, and end up on the TV news. I'll be able to watch you and think, 'See that beautiful woman? She gave you the sweetest night of your life.'"

His words seemed to shoot straight through her heart.

Sophie squeezed her eyes shut, fought to keep her voice steady. "And what about you?"

He shrugged. "Who knows. Maybe I'll try to be an astronaut after all. Might as well shoot for the stars, right?"

She nodded, swallowed her tears, unable to speak.

"Stay away from Patrick and his gang. Promise?"

She nodded again.

"And don't listen to what anyone in this town has to say. You're beautiful, and one day the perfect man will come along and sweep you away. Tough luck for me, isn't it?" He gave a little laugh, then his voice grew tight. "I won't forget you, fairy sprite."

And as she watched him drive away in his blue '55 Chevy, tears streaming down her face, Sophie knew she'd never forget him either.

CHAPTER 1

Twelve years later

SOPHIE ALTON DROVE through the streets of Denver as quickly as she could in six inches of slick snow. She was running almost twenty minutes late on the one day in her journalistic career when she didn't want to be late. Today Megan Rawlings would be able to hold her baby girl for the first time since the baby's birth seven months ago. It was the day Megan had been living for, the day she'd been working so hard for, and Sophie didn't want to miss a single moment of it.

She'd told the publisher that she had an important interview this morning, but Glynnis Williams never let anyone's schedule interrupt her agenda. Glynnis had joined the paper three months ago and had made it abundantly clear that she cared more about advertising dollars than journalistic ethics. She'd interrupted the Investigative Team meeting to explain at great length why she wasn't going to oppose legislation that would weaken the state's whistle-blower laws, her reasons having everything to do with sucking up to big business and government interests and nothing to do with journalism.

Naturally, Tom hadn't taken this lying down. Tom Trent had the reputation of being the toughest, most brilliant editor in the state—and the most likely to be murdered by a member of his own staff. But today he'd seemed almost likeable. He taken Glynnis on, haranguing her for a good fifteen minutes about the importance of whistleblower protection laws and slamming her with the most inspired version of his "Watchdogs of Freedom" rant Sophie had ever heard. Glynnis had left the meeting looking gratifyingly angry, but that didn't change the fact that Sophie was now running late.

She took the exit at Federal, glanced at the digital clock on her dashboard, and pushed the speedometer up to thirty-five, weighing the benefits of speeding against the risk of totaling her car on the ice. "Dammit, Glynnis!"

She'd been reporting on Megan's struggle since last summer, when her investigation into the stillbirth of an inmate's baby had spurred her to look closely at the plight of women in prison. Megan had been seven months pregnant then, and something about her had tugged at Sophie's heartstrings. Perhaps it was Megan's vulnerability, a young woman going through the uncertainty of pregnancy and childbirth in a world of cold steel and indifferent strangers. Perhaps it was Megan's brave struggle to overcome her addiction. Or maybe it was Megan's sweetness and lingering innocence, qualities one didn't often encounter among repeat offenders.

Sophie had visited Megan every week for months. She'd reported on the drug charges that had landed Megan in prison, six weeks pregnant. She'd bitten her fingernails in the hospital hallway while Megan, shackled by one ankle to the delivery table and denied pain relief by an indifferent obstetrician, had endured eighteen long hours of labor. She'd watched when Megan had kissed and cuddled her newborn. She'd tried not to cry when Social Services had taken little Emily away, her heart breaking at Megan's tears and grief.

But today there would be tears of a different sort. Today, mother and child would finally be reunited for a two-hour supervised visit. Just thinking about it put a lump in Sophie's throat.

She turned left onto Acoma—and pressed on the brakes. Five police cruisers sat in front of New Horizons, lights flashing. It wasn't unusual to see a cop car parked there. After all, New Horizons was a halfway house, and every so often one of the residents screwed up—broke the house rules, tested hot for drugs, lifted something—and landed back in prison. But never during the months she'd come here had Sophie seen this kind of police response.

Someone was in deep trouble.

She made her way around the bottleneck created by the police cars, nosed her little Toyota into the parking lot, and turned off the engine. Then she grabbed her notebook and purse and stepped out into the frigid February morning. The sky was a brilliant blue, but the sunshine held no warmth, an icy wind blowing off the jagged white mountains to the west. She pulled her coat tighter and, chin down, hurried to the front door.

Joaquin Ramirez, the paper's best shooter, was already waiting for her in the lobby, his camera ready. He grinned when he saw her. "Told you I'd get here first."

"You cheated." Sophie fished out her press card, glanced toward the reception desk. "Lucky for you every cop in Denver was here. One of them might have pulled you over."

He rolled his dark eyes. "Don't blame me if you're chicken to drive in snow."

She glanced toward the reception desk. "Did you check in?"

"Nope. I was waiting for you."

Sophie crossed the lobby, signed in, and held out her press card. "Sophie Alton and Joaquin 'Speedy' Ramirez here to see Megan Rawlings."

The receptionist glanced down at Sophie's press ID, then met her gaze, a strange look on her face. "You'll have to wait in the lobby."

Sophie's stomach knotted. "Is something wrong?"

The police couldn't be here for Megan. They couldn't be.

"Wait in the lobby."

Too nervous to sit, Sophie walked back into the lobby and stood by the window, looking out at the police cars. "They can't be here for her, Joaquin."

He set his camera bag down on one of the chairs, gave her arm a reassuring squeeze. "You've really gotten attached to her, haven't you?"

There was no way to deny it. "Yeah."

They'd waited almost thirty minutes—a half hour that seemed an eternity—when a squat, balding police officer came round the corner accompanied by a tall, dark-haired man with a fat moustache who was wearing a charcoal gray business suit. Sophie could tell by the way the jacket bulged on one side that the man was carrying a firearm. A detective?

Her heart sank.

"Ms. Alton?" The cop had a notepad and a pencil in his hand.

"Yes."

"I'm Officer Reed. This is Officer Harburg."

Officer Harburg held out his hand. "I'm Megan Rawlings's parole officer."

Feeling almost sick, Sophie shook the man's hand. "Please tell me Megan and Emily are all right."

Officer Harburg gave a sad smile. "I wish we could, but Ms. Rawlings seems to have taken her baby and disappeared."

"WHEN THEY CATCH her, they'll charge her with possession of a controlled substance, skipping parole, and kidnapping." Sophie tossed back the last of her chocolatini, chasing her misery away with the one-two punch of booze and best friends. "The stuff they found in her room field-tested positive for heroin."

"I'm sorry, Sophie." Tessa Darcangelo, a former member of the I-Team, rubbed her pregnant belly, her blue eyes filled with sympathy, her long blond curls hanging down the back of her chair. "I know how much she and her baby meant to you."

Sophie knew that Tessa really *did* understand. Last year, Tessa had witnessed the murder of a teenage girl and had nearly lost her own life trying to expose the human trafficker who was responsible. Sophie suspected Tessa carried the girl's dying screams with her to this day.

"How can they accuse her of kidnapping her own daughter?" Holly Bradshaw, one of the entertainment writers at the paper, popped an olive in her mouth. Tall, platinum blond, and model-gorgeous, she rarely ate food that contained calories. "Doesn't she have a legal right to be with her baby?"

"Not if she doesn't have custody." Kara McMillan, who'd once been the I-Team's star reporter, set her empty margarita glass aside and tucked a strand of long, dark hair behind her ear. With a hunky senator for a husband, three adorable kids, and a successful freelance and nonfiction book career, she was everything Sophie hoped to be one day—wife, mother, star journalist. "I'm guessing the baby is a ward of the state."

Sophie nodded. "A family of Mennonites has been caring for her—really sweet people. I bet they're worried to death."

Sophie had met them and interviewed them—a kind, older couple who'd raised nine children of their own and somehow had energy left to lavish love and attention on the kids of women in prison. Emily was the sixth foster child they'd taken. It had been plain to see that they adored her.

Tessa flagged down the waiter. "Another boring herbal tea for me and another chocolatini for her. Drink your brains out, Sophie. I'll take you home."

"That's the nice thing about having pregnant friends." Sophie smiled, fighting the sense of gloom that had dogged her all day.

"Designated drivers," they all said in unison, laughing.

One hour and two drinks later, Sophie felt tipsier, but not more cheerful. Katherine James, the I-team's environmental reporter, arrived late and ordered a mug of hot chocolate. A mixed-blood Navajo with long dark hair and unusual hazel green eyes, she never drank alcohol. Sophie had originally found her distant and aloof, but she'd realized that Katherine, or Kat as everyone called her, was just naturally reserved. Maybe it was a cultural trait.

They'd quit talking about Megan and her baby and had moved on to a discussion about virginity, prompted by Holly's tale of the Saudi Arabian prince she'd met and slept with while skiing at Aspen last weekend. "He was surprised to discover I wasn't a virgin, but he didn't see anything wrong with the fact that he wasn't a virgin."

"Ah, the good old double standard!" Kara smiled. "Somehow I think the two of you aren't meant for each other."

"Hardly! Though the prince thing *was* très glam." Holly ate another olive. "So how old were you when you lost your virginity?"

Kara was the first to volunteer. "I was nineteen. We did it at his apartment—lots of candles and Bon Jovi playing in the background. It seemed romantic at the time, but compared to sex with Reece, it was pretty silly."

"I was at college, and we did it in his dorm room." Tessa shook her head at the memory. "I thought he was the one, but afterwards he told me he'd just wanted to have sex with a natural blonde. It was so humiliating! I didn't go near a man after that until Julian."

"How about you, Kat?" Holly was obviously enjoying the conversation, sex being her favorite topic and natural habitat.

Kat looked down at the table. "I haven't done that yet."

"Really?" Holly looked so stunned that Sophie almost laughed.

Kat shrugged. "There was no way to hide birth control living with nine other people in my grandmother's hogan, and I didn't want to get pregnant and miss out on college."

"Okay." Holly seemed to be thinking it through. "But what about during college?"

"Not everyone makes sex their top priority, Holly," Kara said.

But Holly was still staring at Kat.

"I never met anyone who was worth it," Katherine answered simply.

"I was fourteen." Holly smiled conspiratorially. "He was the brother of my best friend. It was so lame! We did it in his bedroom while his parents were downstairs watching TV."

As Holly went on to share too much information, as she always did, Sophie found her thoughts drifting back to the night she'd spent with Hunt so long ago. She could almost hear his voice explaining the stars, oldies tunes drifting over his radio, his arm around her shoulder.

It hadn't been silly or humiliating or lame.

It had been romantic and passionate—and beautiful.

I want you more than any girl I've ever known!

He'd said it, and she'd known he meant it.

No man had come close to matching his intensity—or his sweetness. Not the egocentric attorney she'd gone out with a few years back. Or the self-absorbed rock climber she'd dated briefly after that. Or the reporter from the *Post* she'd gotten together with last year.

She'd thought of tracking Hunt down, but then she'd imagined how it would feel to knock on his door—and come face-to-face with his lovely wife and their three kids. The thought had stopped her cold.

"How about you, Sophie? Your turn."

Sophie sipped her chocolatini, swallowed the rush of emotion that lingered around that bittersweet memory. "I was sixteen, and he was the hottest guy in the senior class—and the school bad boy. We had sex on a blanket under the stars in the desert, and it was perfect."

Four pairs of eyes stared at her, blinked.

"Really?" Holly looked incredulous.

Sophie tossed back the last of her drink. "Really."

"What happened afterwards?" Tessa asked.

"He enlisted in the army, and I never saw him again."

With that, the conversation shifted once more.

Tessa shared her determination to get through her baby's birth without drugs, provided she could have a vanilla latte the moment the baby was born. "Nothing can equal the agony of going without coffee for nine months."

Kara assured them they had nothing to worry about with the whistle-blower bill. "Reece says the bill will die in committee." Kara always had the inside scoop on events at the state capitol because her husband, Reece Sheridan, was president of the State Senate. "There's no way it will even reach the Senate floor."

"That's good to hear," Kat said. "If it were to pass—"

"Why the hell did she do it?" The words burst out before Sophie could stop them. "Megan was close—*so close*—to having her life and her baby back!"

For a moment, none of her friends said anything.

Then Tessa reached over, took Sophie's hand, and gave it a squeeze. "God only knows why people do the stupid things they do."

"You know, Sophie, maybe this is so hard for you because

of what happened with your own parents." Kara spoke quietly, almost hesitantly. "It must be hard for you to see a mother and child torn apart like that."

The ache that had been sitting in Sophie's chest all day grew sharper. "Yeah. I'm sure that's part of it."

She'd been fifteen when her parents, who'd owned a popular restaurant in downtown Denver, had been hit and killed by a drunk driver. Everything about her life had changed overnight. She and her younger brother, David, had gone from living with a doting mother and father in a wealthy Denver suburb to living with their maternal grandmother in Grand Junction, a smallish Colorado town on the edge of nowhere. The sense of loss and the shock of separation had been staggering. Her parents had gone out—but they'd never come home.

And yet somehow she and David had gotten through it. David was studying in California to become an equine reproductive vet, and she was living her dream of being an investigative reporter. They'd gotten over it. Mostly.

Sophie wiped her tears on her napkin, voiced the secret thought she'd been carrying all day. "If I'd gotten to New Horizons on time—"

"Don't *even* start!" Holly glared at her. "I don't want to have to take you out in the alley and kick your butt, because it's too damned cold. But I'll do it if I have to. It's *not* your fault."

Then Sophie remembered *why* she'd been late. "That's right. It's Tom's fault for raving at Glynnis about the whistleblower bill."

"There you go." Tessa nodded with apparent satisfaction. "Blame Tom."

"Not to defend Tom," Kara said, sounding like she was about to do just that, "but the only person to blame for Megan's situation is Megan herself. No one forced her to start using drugs again or to take off with her baby."

Holly fished a silver tube of lipstick out of her purse. "You just say that because your mom is living with Tom."

"Holly!" Tessa scolded.

"No." Kat met Sophie's gaze. "She's saying that because it's the truth. It takes a strong heart to defeat addiction."

Sophie's heart felt anything but strong. "Can we go now, Tess?"

A half hour later she sat in the parking lot of her own apartment building in Tessa's snazzy Thunderbird, her head throbbing.

"Promise me you'll call if Julian hears anything, okay?"

Julian Darcangelo, Tessa's husband, had been an undercover FBI agent, but now worked as a detective for the vice unit of the Denver Police Department. Nothing much happened on the streets of Denver without him knowing about it.

"You know how Julian is. Just because he knows something doesn't mean he'll tell me. I'll make a point of prying, okay?" Tessa gave her a hug. "Now are you going to make it to your front door walking on that ice, or am I going to have to carry you?"

ONE HUNDRED TWENTY-ONE. *One hundred twenty-two. One hundred twenty-three.*

Marc Hunter counted the reps, his third set of push-ups for the night, his mind focused on maintaining form despite the burn in his arms, shoulders, and chest. He barely heard the animal howls coming from the cell upstairs or the shouts of "Shut the fuck up!" that echoed through the cellblock or the throbbing din of angry fists and feet pounding on steel doors—an attempt to force the guards to silence whoever it was who'd bugged out. His mind was as focused and clear as it would be if he were back in Afghanistan, eyes on tango. He'd realized six years ago that surviving in prison meant keeping both his mind and his body disciplined and fit. He'd already lost his future. He wasn't about to yield his sanity.

One hundred thirty-seven. One hundred thirty-eight. One hundred thirty-nine.

He kept his breathing controlled and even, sweat beading on his chest and forehead, his muscles shaking. He pushed himself past one-forty, maxing out, forcing his body where it didn't want to go. He grunted through the last several reps, his arms and chest barely able to lift his weight, then sat back against the cold concrete wall, breathing hard.

What time was it? He had no idea. There was no window in his nine-by-nine cell, no break in the gray concrete wall to let in daylight and show him whether it was morning or night. In the Colorado State Penitentiary, day broke at 5 A.M. when the fluorescent lights came on and ended at 11 P.M. when the lights went out.

He closed his eyes, imagined the moon rising over the plains, its pale light making yesterday's snow glow silver, Orion setting over the mountains, his belt of stars gleaming. It had been six long years since Marc had seen the moon, six years since he'd glimpsed the stars, six years since he'd set his eyes on the mountains. It might as well have been an eternity.

It was strange what he missed. Not just the night sky, but sunrises, rainbows, lightning. Not just fresh fruit and vegetables, but birds singing, the bright colors of flowers, the change of the seasons. Not just sex, but the softness of a woman's skin, the wild taste of female arousal, the sweetness of a feminine voice.

His life was a monotony of steel and concrete, recycled air and canned food, isolation and masturbation—sterile, cold, and empty. That's how it would be until the day he died. No house in the mountains. No wife. No chance to be a father.

And whose fault is that, dickhead?

It was his own fault, of course.

He'd thought the deprivation would get easier, but it hadn't. It seemed go grow sharper with each passing year, until he was afraid that he, too, would be reduced to shrieking and howling in his cell like some wild thing desperate to get out.

But that wasn't going to happen. He couldn't let it happen.

Megan still needed him. Even from behind bars, he'd been able to help her, trading cigarettes, favors, and secrets to make her life easier both in prison and out, using money from his 401(k) to get her into the best halfway house, working through his attorney to secure little Emily's future. His life might be fucked up beyond hope, but Megan and Emily still had a chance, and he intended to be there for them as much as a man serving a life sentence could be.

In the cellblock beyond, the din of stomping feet and pounding fists reached a crescendo. Any moment now the lights would flash on, and guards would march down the hallway to remove the screamer. They'd haul whoever it was down to psych, strap him to the board, and pump him full of sedatives. Then the noise would finally stop, and everyone would be able to get some sleep.

He heard the checkpoint down the hall click open and clang shut, quick footsteps hurrying down the tile floor. Hard soles. A guard.

Instantly on his feet, Marc drew himself up against the wall to the right of the door and waited. He wasn't about to be taken by surprise. His conviction for killing a federal agent hadn't made him popular with guards, and his status as former DEA had made him an object of hatred among the inmates, particularly the ones he'd put behind bars. He'd already survived more than a few attempts to off him—and worse.

The footsteps stopped outside his cell, and the tray slot on his door slid open.

"Hunt! You awake?" came a whisper. "It's Cormack."

Marc let himself relax. "Yeah, Cormack, what you got?"

Cormack was one of the few guards he trusted. When Cormack had been new and green, Marc had pulled him away from a mob of lifers who'd been about to blade him up. Naturally, Cormack had been grateful—grateful enough to become one of a network of people who kept Marc informed about the world outside.

"It's about Megan," Cormack whispered.

Marc felt his pulse skip. "Go ahead."

"They say she bolted from the halfway house and took the baby with her. When they searched her room, they found a couple unused syringes and a half ounce of shit."

The breath rushed out of Marc's lungs, and he sank slowly down the wall to the floor.

He couldn't believe it. He didn't want to believe it.

Goddamn it! Goddamn it!

Megan had worked so hard to get clean. She'd been clean since the moment she'd realized she was pregnant and had promised both him and herself that she wouldn't use again. She'd told him in the letters Cormack had smuggled to him how she wanted to be a good mother to Emily, how she planned to give her baby a home and not abandon her to foster care as their mother had done. Her last message had seemed so full of hope and determination. How could she have broken so quickly?

She'd been out for only a week. One goddamned week!

He fought to find his voice. "When?"

"Yesterday morning."

That meant Megan had been on the run for almost twenty-four hours. She wasn't an experienced mother, didn't know much of anything about babies. She had no money, no place to sleep, no way to take care of Emily—to feed her, change her diapers, keep her warm. The newspapers said it had gotten to ten below last night.

If Megan had Emily out on the streets . . .

Rage burned in his gut, tangled with the sense of helplessness he felt every time his sister did something to fuck up her life. Only this time it was worse. This time she had an innocent baby with her. He fought the urge to slam his fist into the wall, fought to clear his mind of anger and disappointment and worry. He needed to think—and fast.

He reached for the photo of her that he'd taped to the wall beside his bunk. It had been taken in the hospital the day she'd had the baby. She sat in the hospital bed, holding a bundled Emily in her arms, her ankle shackled to the guardrail of the bed. She looked exhausted, her brown hair in a disorganized ponytail, her eyes holding both happiness and heartbreak.

What the hell had she been thinking? Was she out of her fucking mind?

Maybe seeing Emily again had made it too hard for her to turn the baby back over to Social Services. He knew his sister was emotionally fragile. Or maybe she'd been strung out and had bolted without thinking of the consequences. She'd have to have been high as a kite to leave behind that much smack. What kind of addict left their stash to the cops and . . .

"Did you say a *half ounce*, Cormack?"

"Yeah. That's what the police report says. It was laced with fentanyl."

Christ!

That shit was deadly.

But a half ounce was a hell of a lot for anyone who wasn't a dealer or a rock star. Either she'd come into some connections he didn't know about—or it wasn't her heroin.

And in a single heartbeat her disappearance took on a more sinister meaning.

One day I'll just disappear, and you'll find me dead!

Marc felt the cold hitch of fear in his gut. "Did she have any visitors yesterday morning or the night before?"

"I knew you were going to ask that." Cormack sounded pleased with himself. "Just that lady journalist who's been writing about her. What's her name?"

"Sophie Alton."

"Yeah, Sophie Alton."

Marc glanced at the pile of articles he'd torn out of the *Denver Independent*, a plan forming in his mind. "I feel like giving an interview, Cormack. Get in touch with Ms. Alton and let her know I have information that could lead her to Megan Rawlings."

"You think she'll want to talk to you?"

Marc lifted one of the articles, glanced at the byline. "I know she will."

CHAPTER 2

SOPHIE FILLED HER water bottle at the watercooler, trying to gather whatever thoughts were in her aching head for the I-Team meeting. Worried about Megan and Emily, she'd found it hard to sleep last night despite the alcohol in her system. She'd finally given up at five, shuffling into the kitchen for water and aspirin when her hangover had kicked into full gear. Outside her kitchen window the thermometer had read fifteen below.

"Any word?" Kat's soft voice came from beside her.

Sophie capped her bottle. "No. I checked with police dispatch this morning, and they hadn't found them yet. I don't know what scares me more—what will happen if the cops don't find them or what will happen when they do."

Kat gave her arm a squeeze. "All you can do is keep them in your prayers."

Sophie managed a smile. "Thanks."

She walked back to her desk, downloaded her e-mail, and checked her voice mail. A call from an activist group that was hoping to halt the building of yet another private prison. A long rant from a woman who wanted to know why Colorado's prison system wouldn't let her have conjugal visits with her husband like the California prison system had. A quick word from Officer Harburg, Megan's parole officer, who praised her article and suggested they meet for lunch to talk about some of the subtleties of the parole system.

Was that male interest she detected in his voice?

Would it bother her if it was?

No, it wouldn't. He was an attractive man—tall, dark,

masculine. So what if he was several years older than she was? He might have some insights on Megan that would help all of this make sense. Besides, she hadn't had a date for months.

She'd just written down his number when her phone buzzed with an incoming call. She was tempted to let the caller go to voice mail, knowing she had only a few minutes until the I-Team meeting, but then she'd just have another message to wade through.

She picked up the line. "Sophie Alton."

"Are you looking for information about Megan Rawlings?"

Sophie's adrenaline picked up a notch. She hit the record button on her phone. "Yes. Absolutely. Who is this?"

"I'm just calling to let you know that you should request an interview with Marc Hunter, an inmate in Cañon City. He's her brother. He can help you out."

The caller rattled off a DOC inmate number and then, before Sophie could ask him any other questions, hung up.

Momentarily forgetting the I-Team meeting, Sophie opened her Internet browser, logged on to the DOC's website, and filled out the online interview request form, using the information the caller had provided. Hadn't Megan mentioned once or twice that she had a half brother who was also in prison? Yes, she had. Her brother had stayed with their mother, while Megan had been placed with Social Services for adoption. Despite the fact that they must have grown up apart, Megan had seemed to feel real affection for him.

Sophie wondered who the caller had been. It couldn't have been Marc Hunter himself. Prisoners could only make collect calls, and this hadn't been a collect call. Perhaps the caller was a friend, someone on the outside. Or maybe he was a CO—a correctional officer—someone who did Hunter's business from the inside in exchange for bribes. In either case, Megan's brother had to have illegal connections.

What kind of information could he have? He wasn't supposed to be in communication with his sister. Megan's parole prohibited her from having any contact with other felons. She wasn't even allowed to write letters to her brother. Of course, parolees broke that rule all the time, and some went back to prison for it.

Sophie had just placed a request with the Colorado Bureau of Investigation for Hunter's criminal record when she glanced at the clock. "Crud!"

She grabbed her notepad and pencil and hurried down the hallway to the conference room, where the rest of the I-Team sat around the table waiting for her.

Tom sat at the head of the table, notepad and a stack of newspapers in front of him, one pencil behind his right ear and another in his hand. More than six feet tall and built like a linebacker, he was an intimidating man. If he hadn't been such a brilliant journalist, Sophie might have left the I-Team a long time ago. Tom had hired her from the *News*, where she'd worked boring GA—general assignment—and had taught her more about journalism in a month than she'd learned in four years of J-school.

And if he was sometimes a jerk and ran the newsroom as if it were a sweatshop?

Well, she didn't always have to like him to respect him.

He looked up at her and frowned, a shock of gray curls half covering his eyes. "Glad you could make the time, Alton. Harker, what's the latest?"

Matt Harker, the city reporter, sat to Tom's left. Freckle-faced with short reddish hair, he always looked like he'd dressed out of his laundry basket, wearing the same wrinkled tie every day with a different wrinkled shirt. He glanced up from his notes. "The mayor and city council are going at it again—this time over the fire department budget. Council wants to freeze it, but the mayor is holding with the union and wants a substantial increase. Can you tell we have a municipal election coming in the fall?"

Syd Wilson, the managing editor, looked at Matt over her new reading glasses—the reading glasses no one was supposed to notice. Small and wiry, she wore her salt-and-pepper hair short and spiked and didn't like to think of herself as nearing fifty. "How much?"

Matt shrugged. "Probably no more than ten inches."

Tom nodded, glanced at Joaquin. "I'm sick of the mayor's mug shot. Get something fresh from one of the fire stations. Benoit?"

Natalie Benoit was the newest member of the I-Team, hired to take Tessa's place on cops and courts. From an old Cajun family, she had relocated to Denver after her family lost everything in Hurricane Katrina. Tom had hired her on the spot when he'd learned she was the journalist who'd stayed in Community Medical Center rather than evacuating, helping to care for the sick and dying. Her coverage of the tragedy there had made her a Pulitzer finalist.

With long dark hair, big aqua eyes, and a charming New Orleans accent, she'd put the libido of every heterosexual man at the paper into overdrive but rarely seemed to date or socialize. She never talked about her ordeal during Katrina, and no one dared to pry.

"I can probably do with ten inches, as well. A couple of animal rights activists claim they were beaten up by police at last week's antifur protest. An observer has come forward with a digital recording that seems to support their allegations—pretty rough stuff. They've lawyered up and are seeking damages. Chief Irving has promised an internal investigation."

"Oh, good." Tom sounded anything but impressed. "Another one."

Syd punched numbers into her calculator. "Any chance we can get stills off the recording?"

Natalie smiled. "I've already turned it over to production."

"What's on your plate, James?"

Kat kept her gaze on her notes. She rarely looked anyone in the eyes, something Sophie had come to understand was cultural. "I got a tip that someone in the Department of Wildlife has been distributing eagle parts illegally."

"Eagle parts?" the room said in unison.

Kat nodded. "When an eagle is accidentally killed or found dead, there's a process wildlife officials are supposed to follow for distributing feathers, claws, and other ceremonial body parts to Indian spiritual leaders. Apparently, someone has been selling parts off to non-Indians. I'm meeting with the whistle-blower today, but I doubt I'll have anything by dead-line."

And just like that Tom was off again, ranting about what would happen if state lawmakers weakened protections for whistle-blowers.

Sophie's mind wandered to Megan and her baby. Had she found a safe, warm place to spend the night? What was she feeding the baby? How far did she think she could get before the police found her and sent her back to prison?

"Alton!"

Sophie snapped back to the present. "I'd like to do a follow-up to yesterday's piece and see how many parents on parole kidnap their own children. This was supposed to be a supervised visit, after all. I want to find out if this has happened before. Unless I find something big, I'm guessing no more than six inches."

Syd punched the numbers into her calculator. "Do we have any photos of the baby?"

"Not recent ones." Sophie glanced down at her notes. "I got an anonymous tip this morning from someone who wants me to request an interview with Megan's brother, who also happens to be in prison."

"What is it—a family business?" Matt shook his head, rolled his eyes. "Does she have any relatives on the outside?"

For some reason, Sophie didn't find Matt's comment funny. "I've already put in a request for an interview with the brother and asked CBI for a copy of his criminal record. I have no idea what kind of information this guy might have."

Tom leaned back in his chair. "Sounds like there's only one way to find out."

SOPHIE MET OFFICER Harburg for lunch at her favorite downtown sushi joint.

"We try hard to keep women out of prison, because many are mothers and most are nonviolent offenders. Those who end up behind bars tend to be hard-core."

Sophie set her notepad aside to make room for her miso

and edamame. She met Officer Harburg's gaze and knew without a doubt that he was interested in her. She could see it in his eyes—light blue eyes—and hear it in the warm tone of his voice. For a moment, she let herself imagine what it might be like to kiss him.

OK, so it wasn't fireworks, but it wasn't a repulsive idea either.

"More hard-core? I thought men were more difficult."

"Oh, yes, they are." He picked up his chopsticks and stirred his miso. "Men are absolutely more violent and dangerous. The vast majority of violent crimes both in prison and out are committed by men, but women are harder to rehabilitate."

"How so?" She dipped her spoon into the soup and sipped.

"Most female inmates are what we call dual-diagnosis—they have mental-health issues on top of drug or alcohol addiction." He paused to pop a chunk of tofu into his mouth and chew. "Unfortunately, there are few treatment programs for female felons."

"Don't they get treatment in prison?"

"The state doesn't have the money to give them the therapy they need. Besides, most of them are poor. Prison offers better food and housing than they'll get on the outside. No pimps to beat them up. No kids to feed. No job to find."

"That's true for male inmates, too, isn't it?"

"Yes, but there are more treatment programs for men, more jobs, better pay. Men are generally more assertive and more independent. Fewer men raise their kids alone. And—this is important—men are different emotionally. Women tend to form close friendships with other women in prison and have a hard time surviving without the support system offered by those relationships. Men don't face that obstacle."

Sophie tried to imagine life without the support system her friends offered—and found it stark. But her friends weren't felons. "Did Megan have close friends in prison?"

"She's been in and out of state custody since she was a teenager. I assume she does, though she never talked about personal things with me. I represent 'The Man,' you know. Based on what I've read of your articles—which are very good, by the way—I'd say she was much more open with you."

"We mostly talked about her plans and how much she wanted to raise Emily."

Officer Harburg nodded, a sad look on his face. "I doubt she'll get that chance now."

Sophie knew it was the truth, but it still hurt to hear him say it. "I hope you're wrong, Officer Harburg."

"It's Ken." He smiled, revealing a bit of seaweed that had gotten caught in his front teeth. "Call me Ken."

Definitely *not* fireworks.

"Okay, Ken." She forced herself to look into his eyes and not at his teeth. "What else do you know about Megan?"

SOPHIE RETURNED TO the office to find that the DOC had approved her interview with Megan's brother for four o'clock on Friday. It was the speediest green light she'd ever gotten. She hadn't expected to hear back from DOC until next week at the earliest.

Clearly Marc Hunter was hooked up and had pulled some strings.

ON FRIDAY AFTERNOON, Sophie made the familiar two-hour drive down to Cañon City while listening to the BBC on her car radio. More violence outside Banda Aceh in Indonesia. An increase in the value of the Euro. AIDS orphans in South Africa.

Her mind wandered off during a report about flooding on Denmark's Jutland coast. Traffic was sparse for late on a Friday afternoon, the highway wet and icy in places. In front of her and to the west, Pikes Peak loomed jagged and white against the horizon, snow blowing from its summit like a frosty pennant. The sky to the east was clear and blue, but a bank of dark storm clouds rose ominously behind the mountains.

There was a winter storm warning for Colorado's Front Range tonight—twelve to eighteen inches expected just in time for Sophie's commute back to Denver. If she'd had money, she would have reserved a hotel room in Colorado Springs and waited till morning when snowplows would have cleared most of it away. But she was trying to save money to help David with his next tuition payment, and a hotel room seemed like a frivolous expense, especially since she'd already spent almost four hundred dollars on studded snow tires.

Just deal with it, Alton.

She found herself thinking through the questions she wanted to ask Megan's brother. Did he have any idea where his sister had gone? Did he know of anyone who might be helping her, giving her money or shelter or food? Had Megan ever contacted him about wanting to take Emily and run? Had he heard from his sister since her escape?

Last night, she'd read through her notes from Megan's interviews, looking for anything Megan might have said about her brother. She'd been surprised to find that Megan had mentioned him almost every time—how he'd gotten a message to her every day when she'd been going through heroin withdrawal, how he'd had his attorney deposit money into her commissary account so that she could buy an extra pillow when her pregnancy made it hard for her to sleep, how he'd worried that she wasn't getting good enough prenatal care.

Sophie had tried to reconcile Megan's blindly heroic image of her brother to the cold reality of the arrest report CBI had e-mailed to her. Six years ago the man who cared so much about his drug-addicted sister and her baby had taken a high-caliber handgun and shot a fellow DEA agent, at point-blank range. Not just once, but three times. He'd put John Cross, a husband and father of four, in his grave in order to cover up his own drug dealing. Investigators had found two kilos of cocaine spread out between his house and car and had concluded that he'd killed the other agent to silence him. It was a violent act, heartless and brutal.

How did he square those two parts of himself in his own mind?

"God only knows why people do the things they do," she said aloud, echoing Tessa's words of a few days ago.

She exited I-25 and wound her way to US-50, arriving ten minutes early at the Colorado State Penitentiary—a hulking zigzag building of red brick surrounded by high fences, razor wire, and guard towers. She parked in the visitors' lot in a space reserved for the press, then refreshed her lipstick and checked her hair in the vanity mirror. Not that her appearance really mattered. She wasn't going to meet Mr. Right in this place.

She sorted through her purse, transferring everything into her briefcase except for her digital recorder, her press card, and a couple bucks in change for the vending machine in case there were delays and she got thirsty. Having covered the prison beat for four years, she knew she'd speed things up and make it easier on herself and the guards if she took with her only the things she needed for her interview. It cut down on the time the guards had to spend searching her and prevented her from having to rent a locker.

DOC regulations for visitors were very stringent, an attempt to preempt human ingenuity when it came to smuggling contraband and perpetrating violence. Postage stamps could carry LSD. Pens and pencils could be used as weapons. Cell phones could be used to communicate with criminals outside prison walls. And almost anything—cigarettes, weapons, drugs—could be hidden inside the human body. Once inside the walls, something as simple as a cigarette butt could be used to control, to manipulate, to dominate.

Sophie locked up her car, dropped her keys in her purse, then picked her way through the icy parking lot. She knew it was stupid to wear heels in the snow, but big snow boots just didn't look professional. Then again neither did lying sprawled on her butt in the snow. But once she got inside it wouldn't matter what was on her feet.

On the other side of the fence, a group of inmates in four-piece shackles and orange uniforms was being herded out of a van. She barely noticed the way their heads turned as she passed or the chorus of catcalls that followed her. It happened every time she came here.

She stepped through the entrance and walked toward the front desk. A mother with two young children sat in the lobby, probably waiting to visit her husband. A young woman with tattoos on her arm sulked in the corner. A man in a suit—probably a lawyer—chattered in legalese on his cell phone.

"Hey, Ms. Sophie." Officer Green smiled and handed her a clipboard. "Whose sob story have you come to hear today?"

Like most COs, Officer Green was open about his low opinion of inmates.

"Some guy named Marc Hunter." Sophie took the clipboard, filled out the Consent to Search form, and handed it back with her press card.

Officer Green gave a snort. "Mr. Badass himself. Your readers will love him."

Her curiosity piqued, Sophie couldn't help but ask. "Is he trouble?"

Officer Green handed her press card back and gave her the sort of knowing look that promised inside secrets. "Depends on how you define *trouble*. He keeps his nose clean, follows the rules—till someone tries to fuck with him. His first week here, he put five guys in the infirmary."

It was on the tip of Sophie's tongue to ask what the five guys had done, but she knew Officer Green would talk for hours if given half a chance. She put her press card back in her purse. "Thanks."

She crossed the room, passed through the metal detectors, then watched while Officer Russell searched her purse. A big, beefy man with a crew cut, he was a teddy bear.

"Here you go, Ms. Alton." He handed her purse back, then reached for the ink pad.

Sophie held out her hand, watched as he stamped the back of it with an ultraviolet marker. Visible under a black light, it would have to be verified before she could leave. It seemed like a silly thing to do, given that this was a men's prison and she was demonstrably not male. But rules were rules.

"Be sure not to wash that off." Officer Russell chuckled.

"Thanks for the reminder." Sophie laughed at his joke—the

same joke he always made when she came through—then headed down the labyrinthine hallway.

She knew many of the officers who worked the entrance by name, and most were friendly to her, even if they sometimes disagreed with the tone of her articles. Every once in awhile one of them called her with a news tip, making them valuable to her as potential sources, as well.

Around the corner, Officer Hinkley and Officer Kramer staffed a thick steel gate that marked the entrance to the visitation area.

"So the bastards had him in the shower and went after him with a broom handle. It took the ER doc an hour and a half to stitch up—" Officer Hinkley saw her and broke off. He straightened up, grinned. "Hey, it's Lois Lane."

"Hi, guys. How's it going?" Sophie flashed them a smile, pretended she hadn't heard, making a mental note to check the incident reports on the way out.

They buzzed her through, and a minute later she was seated in the assigned visiting room. She glanced at her watch, realized she was a few minutes early. Rarely did guards bring the inmates on time. There were so many variables. More than once she'd arrived only to find her interview canceled because of some unforeseen event—fighting on a cellblock, shakedowns, inmate transfers. She sat back in her chair and settled in for the wait.

CHAPTER 3

"LET'S GO, HUNTER." Cormack stepped back from the open cell door, his voice gruff to disguise any hint of favoritism. "Move your ass!"

Marc held out his wrists, relieved to see Cormack was putting him in standard-issue police cuffs instead of a four-piece. Marc had pleaded male pride, telling Cormack that the idea of being seen by a pretty woman while wearing full restraints was humiliating.

"I haven't been near a chick in six years, man," he'd said. "I don't want to shuffle in there like some fucking loser."

"I'll see what I can do, but you're classified red, you know. They can't do nothing to you they ain't already done, but *me* they can fire." Cormack had pointed a thumb at his own chest. "You hurt that lady, and it's *my* ass that'll be on the line. I got kids to feed."

It was too bad about the kids, but Marc had people depending on him, too.

He'd allowed himself to look insulted. "I'd never hurt a woman. Besides, why would I do anything to her? I need her help finding Megan."

Obviously, Cormack had believed him.

Cold steel touched Marc's skin, the handcuffs closing with a series of metallic clicks. Then, sandwiched between Cormack and another guard, he walked down the long hallway and through the first checkpoint, ignoring the shouted warnings, obscenities, and threats that followed him.

"You think you the big bitch, don't you, Hunter?"

"Better watch your back, Hunter! I'm gonna kill you before I kill my number!"

"Check it out! Hunter's going to lay some pipe. Is she pretty?"

Marc felt his pulse pick up as they left the maximum-security wing. He tried to tell himself it was just the thought of what he was about to attempt that had his adrenaline going, but he knew there was more to it than that. It was also the thought of seeing Sophie again.

What would she think when she saw him? What would she think of the man he was now? Truth be told, he didn't want to know.

It had been twelve years since that night at the Monument, twelve years since they'd sipped sodas and shared their dreams, twelve years since she'd made what had probably been the biggest mistake of her young life and given him her virginity. He'd always wondered how she felt about it afterward, whether she'd had regrets. He certainly hadn't. Memories of that night had helped him get through boot camp, sustained him through the freezing cold of Afghanistan, and brought him back to Colorado when his term of enlistment was over.

No, he hadn't forgotten her.

I'm the kid who always gets in trouble, remember?

Not with me you're not.

That night had changed his life—for a while. He'd gone into the army with a different sense of himself, had pushed his way up through the ranks, becoming a Special Forces sniper and earning the rank of sergeant first class before giving up the green. He'd parlayed that experience into a post with the DEA, hoping to put away the kind of scum who'd sold drugs to his mother and sister. Some part of him believed he'd overcome his past, that he'd become a man worthy of a woman like Sophie. But in the end, it hadn't mattered. He'd ended up exactly where everyone had known he would.

Why not shoot for the stars?

Marc had shot—and missed.

Tension drew to a knot in his gut as Cormack led him through the last checkpoint and into the visitor's area. He was lower than a snake's ass for even thinking of putting Sophie through this. But she was his only ticket out of this place, and Megan and Emily needed him. Hopefully, the fact that Sophie knew him would give her some measure of trust and keep her from becoming too afraid—or putting up a fight. Then again, if she reacted too strongly to seeing him or was friendly, the guards would get suspicious.

And then he'd be fucked.

"You taking it from here, Kramer?" Cormack motioned Marc through the next gate and stepped aside.

"Yep." Kramer adjusted his leather belt with its Glock 21 .45 caliber and looked at Marc with obvious disgust. "Why anyone wants to talk to this piece of shit is beyond me."

Some of the tension inside Marc settled. He liked Cormack and hadn't been looking forward to roughing him up. But he had no qualms about kicking Kramer to hell and back. In fact, he'd probably enjoy it. Kramer was a cold bastard who got off on breaking inmates' balls.

"Over here, Hunter." Kramer led him toward one of the visitation rooms. "You got thirty minutes. And just in case you got ideas about putting your hands on that sexy bit of gash, just remember I'll be standing right behind you."

Bit of gash?

Yes, Marc was going to enjoy this. He met Kramer's gaze and smiled, the edges of the little shim he held in his mouth sharp against the inside of his cheek.

I'm counting on it, asshole.

Then through the Plexiglas window, he saw her.

He quit breathing. His step faltered. His mind went blank. He didn't notice Kramer opening the door or ordering him inside or shoving him into a chair, one beefy hand on his shoulder. He was oblivious to the heavy click of the locking door, Kramer's hulking presence behind him, the weight of the handcuffs on his wrists.

He was aware only of Sophie.

She was even prettier than he remembered—not a teenage

girl, but a woman. Her strawberry-blond hair was still long, and she wore it up in a style that was both feminine and sophisticated. Her gentle curves seemed fuller, softening the professional cut of her navy blue blazer and skirt. Her face seemed even more delicate, her cheekbones higher, her lips more lush, her eyes impossibly blue.

Fairy sprite.

He bit back the words and drew in a deep breath to clear his mind.

A mistake.

Her scent slammed into him, subtle and fresh and so very female, igniting every drop of excess testosterone in his blood. How long had it been since he'd smelled anything but the sweaty bodies of other men? If his hardening cock was any indication, too goddamn long.

Jesus H. Christ!

He fought to clear his mind, to think, to relax. He needed to focus, to rein in his hormones, to control his emotions. Anything else would get him killed.

She seemed to study him, her expression detached, her hands folded in her lap. She wore no rings—no engagement ring, no wedding band. She reached to shake his hand. "I'm Sophie Alton from the *Denver Independent*. Thanks for agreeing to meet with me."

That's when it hit him.

She didn't recognize him.

She has no idea who you are, Hunter.

The realization came like a fist to the gut, cutting short his breath, the force of it taking him completely by surprise. It had never occurred to him that she might not remember him. It didn't seem possible, but he could see in her eyes that it was true.

He willed himself to speak, took her small hand in his, tried not to look like a man whose world had just imploded. "My pleasure."

Helluva blow to the ego, isn't it, dumbass?

But it was more than that.

It meant that she would be terrified.

He looked at her sweet face, saw the girl he'd made love to—and wondered how he was going to bring himself to do this to her. Then he thought of Megan, alone and running for her life, Emily in her arms, and he knew he had no choice. He'd already lost his sister once. He wouldn't risk losing her again.

Sophie pulled her hand back, feeling strangely uncomfortable. There was something about the tone of the inmate's voice, something in the way he looked at her . . .

She set her digital recorder in the middle of the table, cleared her throat. "Since I can't have my notebook or pens here, I need to record our conversation. I hope that's all right with you, Mr. Hunter."

He nodded, his gaze focused entirely on her. "Whatever you want."

Marc Hunter wasn't what she'd expected. She'd known he'd be tall because his sister was tall. But Megan was also fragile and out of shape, the result of heroin addiction, a sedentary life, and years of prison food. There was nothing fragile or out of shape about Marc Hunter.

At least six foot three, he was athletic and well built, his orange prison smock stretched across a broad chest, the sleeves of his white undershirt rolled up to reveal powerful, tattooed biceps, the U.S. Army's eagle and shield on his right arm and a Celtic band on his left. His brown hair hung to his shoulders, thick and wavy. A dark beard covered the lower half of his face, concealing most of his features, emphasizing the hollows in his cheeks and his high cheekbones, and giving him a threatening look that was lessened somewhat by a full mouth. His eyes were a piercing green that seemed to see beneath her skin.

Even if she hadn't read his criminal record, Sophie would have known he was dangerous. He had an air about him— intimidating, menacing, aggressive.

A killer.

She pushed the record button and struggled to compose her thoughts. "Um . . . As I'm sure you know, I've been following Megan's situation since—"

"I've read the articles," he said, adding, "obviously."

She hadn't revealed to DOC officials that her interest in this interview had originated with an anonymous caller sent by the inmate, sure they'd refuse to grant her request under those circumstances. She wasn't going to acknowledge that fact now, either, not with Lieutenant Kramer listening. Mr. Hunter might not care whether he aroused their suspicions, but she did.

"What you might not know is that I care very much for Megan and Emily and haven't been able to think of anything else since they disappeared. I was hoping you might have some idea why Megan vanished or where she's gone."

His lips curved in a slow smile. "And here I thought you might be able to tell me."

Confused, Sophie stared at him. He had contacted her, hadn't he? The man who'd called had told her that Marc Hunter would be able help her find Megan. And yet Hunter was sitting here saying that he hoped *she* had information. It made no sense.

His smile faded, and his expression grew serious. "Megan is a very troubled young woman, Ms. Alton."

And you're a model citizen!

Sophie kept her expression neutral and waited for him to say more.

"She's been fighting drug addiction since she was a teenager, and every time I think she's made it, she relapses."

No news flash there. Sophie had already reported this in her articles. "Are you saying you think that's what has happened this time?"

"That's what your article led me to believe." He stretched out, his muscular leg brushing against hers beneath the table.

She sat up straighter, tucked her feet beneath her chair, wondering if the contact had been accidental. The guy had been in prison for six years, after all. He wouldn't be the first inmate she'd interviewed who'd tried to make physical contact. "I know Megan was in touch with you. Did she say anything to make you think she'd started using heroin again?"

"I haven't had contact with Megan for years. We're not

allowed to communicate with one another, as I'm sure you know. What did she say to you?"

Growing annoyed by this purposeless, circular conversation, Sophie found herself glaring at him. What kind of game was Marc Hunter playing? She glanced up at Lieutenant Kramer, who looked like his mind was a thousand miles away, then back at Hunter. "Is there anything about Megan you'd like to tell me, Mr. Hunter?"

He started to speak, his words cut off by a coughing fit. He raised his cuffed hands to cover his mouth, croaked out, "Can I get . . . some water?"

Lieutenant Kramer nodded, and Sophie realized he expected her to get it.

"All right." Biting back a retort about middle-aged men and sexism, she stood, crossed the room to the watercooler, and filled a little paper cone.

Why had Hunter wanted her to come down here? If he had something to tell her about Megan, why didn't he just tell her? He'd known a CO would be present during the interview, that he wouldn't be able to speak with her privately.

She carried the water back and held it out for him.

It happened all at once. The splash of cold water against her wrist as he exploded out of his chair, hands somehow free, feet flying. Her own scream as Lieutenant Kramer fell, unconscious or dead, his weapon out and in Hunter's hands. Hunter's iron grip as he grabbed her wrist and yanked her roughly against the hard wall of his chest.

Their gazes collided, his green eyes as hard as jade and unreadable.

Light-headed, her body shaking, her pulse frantic, she gaped up at him, tried to jerk away. Then her splintered thoughts drew together, formed one word. "N-no!"

"Don't fight me, Sophie!" He wasn't even out of breath. "I don't want you to get hurt."

From outside in the hall came shouts and the shrill peal of an alarm.

They knew. The guards knew. They would stop him.

They would protect her.

Stay calm, Alton. Stay calm.

Even as the words entered her mind, she found herself spun hard about, her back crushed against his ribs, his arm locked around her shoulders. She heard him rack the slide on the gun, felt the cold press of steel against her throat, and then she *did* understand.

You're his hostage, Alton. He might kill you. He might kill everyone.

She shuddered, felt her knees turn to water.

This couldn't be happening. It could *not* be happening.

Marc felt Sophie's heart pounding, saw her lips go white, and hated himself for doing this to her. Then she did something that made him hate himself even more.

"Pl-please don't! I-I h-helped your s-sister!"

It was nothing less than a plea for her life, a desperate appeal to his conscience.

Too bad he no longer had one.

"I know." He pulled her toward the door, almost lifting her off her feet. "And now you're helping me."

He heard a key in the lock, and every muscle in his body tensed, ready for whatever came through the door. He knew he had one chance—one chance to convince the guards he was serious, one chance to escape, one chance to find Megan. He was ass betting on this one. If he fucked up, if the guards didn't buy it, his sister would pay the price.

The door flew open.

Russell, Hinkley, and Slater filled the doorway, weapons drawn.

"Drop the steel and back off, or I'll blow her the fuck away!" Marc yelled it like he meant every word of it.

Russell's nostrils flared, and a muscle clenched in his jaw. "Ain't going to happen, Hunter. You might as well let her go and drop—"

"Do it!" Marc's shout made the guards jump and drew a terrified shriek from Sophie, who trembled, almost legless, in his arms. "Do it now!"

"P-please do what he says!" Sophie's voice quavered, barely audible above the harsh blare of the alarm. "I-I don't want any of you t-to get hurt!"

A knife twisted in Marc's gut. He ignored it. "Listen to the pretty lady, boys! You don't want to make this harder on her than it already is."

Russell glanced at Sophie, and Marc could see that the old man was fond of her, a weakness that would make him easier for Marc to control. Marc watched the shifting emotions in Russell's eyes as the guard weighed his options—and broke.

"You win, Hunter." Russell bent down, put his weapon on the tile floor, then backed away, shouting over his shoulder. "You heard him! Lay down your weapons! Clear the hallway! We've got a hostage situation!"

The other officers followed Russell's example.

But Marc knew he hadn't won—not yet. "Get on your radio and have them order the snipers out of the towers. I don't want to see a single uniform between here and the highway. If I do, she pays the price. And have someone kill that fucking alarm!"

Russell did as he asked, conveying Marc's demands via the radio clipped to his shoulder. "Done. No one is going to stop you. But if you hurt her, so help me God . . ."

The alarm fell quiet, the silence almost startling.

Marc nudged Sophie forward, took a step toward the door. "You're a good man, Russell. You may have saved her life. Now back up, lie facedown, head toward the wall, hands behind your head. You know the position."

Russell stepped backward, got down onto the floor. "Think about this, Hunter. You don't want to hurt her. Let her go. Take one of us instead."

"Are you kidding? No offense, but she makes a much prettier hostage than any of you. Mmm—she even smells good." Marc took another step, Sophie moving unsteadily with him.

"You'll pay for this, you son of a bitch!" Hinkley lay down, his face a red scowl.

Marc laughed, a harsh sound that echoed in the hallway.

"What are you going to do? Lock me in prison for the rest of my life? That'll suck."

"There's still time to rethink this." Russell lay on his stomach now. "Let her go. You'll still have the weapon, and we're unarmed now."

"When I'm safely away, I'll let her go, but not until then." Marc glanced out into the hallway, saw no one. He reached down, grabbed a second Glock off the floor. "Come on, sweetheart. Visiting hours are over. And don't forget your purse."

CLUTCHING THE ARM that imprisoned her, Sophie struggled to keep up as Hunter pushed her down the empty, silent hallway, gun near her cheek. Her mouth had gone dry, and her heart beat so hard it hurt, her sense of unreality growing with each forced step.

This couldn't be happening. It couldn't be real.

It was only too real.

His breath hot on her temple, his hold on her never letting up, Hunter half dragged, half carried her toward the security checkpoint where only thirty minutes ago she'd overheard Sergeant Hinkley saying something to Lieutenant Kramer—she couldn't remember what.

Dear God, what if Lieutenant Kramer is dead?

They reached the gate, found it locked.

"Crappy hospitality." Hunter hit a button on the control panel with the butt of the gun, and the gate clicked open. "I guess we'll have to show ourselves out."

"They'll catch you sooner or later." She barely recognized the sound of her own voice.

"I'm hoping for later." He didn't sound worried in the least. "Now hush your pretty mouth, and keep moving."

It seemed to her she watched from outside herself as he drew her through the checkpoint, down the hallway, and through Lieutenant Russell's station with its metal detectors, ink pad, and black light scanner. She felt an absurd impulse to hold out her hand and run it under the scanner as she always did on her way out.

You're in shock, Alton.

That must explain why she couldn't think straight, why she was stumbling along with Hunter like a puppet, why she hadn't tried get away from him. Well, that—and the fact that he'd threatened to kill her and had a gun to her head.

And to think she'd come here to help his sister.

Rage, hot and sudden, burned through Sophie's panic and fear. She twisted, kicked, scratched, brought her knee up hard. "Let . . . me . . . go!"

"Son of a—!" His curse became a grunt as her knee met his groin.

In a heartbeat, Sophie found herself pinned up against the wall, the hard length of his body immobilizing her, her arms stretched over her head, his forehead resting against hers.

His eyes were squeezed shut, breath hissing from between his clenched teeth, his face contorted in obvious pain. He drew a deep breath, then opened his eyes and glared at her, his expression shifting from pain to fury.

"I'll give you that one because, God knows, I deserve it. But *don't* try to play rough with me, Sophie! You'll only end up getting yourself hurt!"

He seemed to hesitate for a moment, then his gaze dropped to her mouth.

For a split second, she thought he might try to kiss her, and a completely new fear unfurled in her belly. "Don't!"

He thrust her in front of him and pushed her down the hallway. "I'm a convicted murderer, not a rapist! Besides, now isn't the time. Move!"

Her rage spent, she did as he demanded, trying not to trip, trying not to cry, trying not to throw up. Just ahead lay the lobby and beyond it the front entrance and visitors' parking lot.

When I'm safely away, I'll let her go.

His words came back to her, and she latched onto them, clinging to the hope they offered, repeating them in her mind like a mantra.

I'll let her go. I'll let her go.

They passed the abandoned registration desk where

Sergeant Green had checked her in and hurried through the now vacant lobby. And then they were outside.

Sophie barely noticed the cold wind or the fat snowflakes that had begun to fall or the fact that the sun had set, her thoughts riveted on Hunter and what he would do next.

He surprised her by stopping just outside the door and drawing her back against the brick wall with him. "Give me your keys! Which one is yours?"

"Wh-what?"

"Which car?"

"The blue Toyota. But you can't—"

"There's no time for this!" He covered her mouth with his hand. "Listen close, Sophie. The moment we step away from this building, a dozen snipers with high-powered rifles will sight on my skull. Perhaps that idea pleases you, but it makes me a little nervous. I don't have time to call a cab, so we're taking your car. Understand?"

He lifted the hand from her mouth.

She nodded, her pulse skyrocketing. "Y-yes."

He was *kidnapping* her!

No! No! Please, no!

She swallowed a sob and fumbled in her purse for her keys.

Marc heard Sophie's breath catch, felt her body jerk, and realized she was crying.

Goddamn it! Goddamn it!

He fought the urge, so instinctual, to reassure her. He couldn't afford to think about what she was feeling. Not now. Not yet. One mistake out here, and he'd be a dead man.

She drew her keys from her purse and held them out for him, metal jangling. "P-please just take my car and leave me!"

"No can do, sweetheart." He grabbed the keys from her hand, glancing from the parking lot, which was flooded by searchlights, to the lobby, where a dozen COs had gathered, waiting for him to slip and offer them a clear shot. "Go!"

He realized his mistake as soon as they hit the parking lot. Dressed in those ridiculous heels, she could barely walk on the ice and snow, much less run. She skittered and slipped, more than once nearly toppling them both to the ground. If she fell, she'd give the snipers the clear line of fire they were waiting for.

"Jesus Christ! It's winter, woman, or hadn't you noticed!" Marc lifted her off her feet, held her hard against him and ran, his prison-issue tennis shoes offering little more in the way of traction, the skin on his back prickling with the imagined heat of red lasers. He'd worked the other end of the rifle for too long and could almost hear the snipers' thoughts in his mind.

Slip. Drop the girl. Raise your head up just an inch, you bastard!

Her car was parked nearby—the first space in the second row. He fought for footing, skidded into the door, his knees crashing against metal as the first shot rang out.

Sophie screamed, and for one terrible moment Marc feared she'd been hit. Then he felt it—searing pain in his shoulder.

"Shit!" He slipped the key into the lock, jerked the door open, then shoved Sophie through the door and piled in behind her. "Scoot over!"

An explosion of weapons fire.

A barrage of bullets.

The driver's side window and mirror shattered, glass spraying through the air as rounds shredded the door where he'd been standing a split second ago.

Keeping low, he slammed the door, slid the key into the ignition, and gunned the engine. Then, both hands on the steering wheel, he fishtailed out of the parking lot and toward the highway. "Put on your seat belt, sweetheart. This ride is likely to get rough."

CHAPTER 4

TRAPPED IN A nightmare, Sophie sat, shivering, a prisoner in the passenger seat of her own car, barely able to breathe as her kidnapper sped west on Highway 6 through the darkness and swirling snow. Freezing air blasted through the shattered driver's side window, blowing away the warmth of the car's heater and carrying in fat flakes that melted on her skin and clothes, leaving her damp and chilled to the bone.

The road behind them was a river of squad cars—state patrol, county sheriff, city police—their red and blue lights flashing through the storm and glinting off the rearview mirror. They'd long since cut the banshee shriek of their sirens and were running silent. From overhead came the choppy beat of a helicopter, its searchlight flooding both the road and the car's interior, illuminating the whirling snow and turning night into surreal day.

The highway was eerily empty, no headlights coming toward them, no taillights ahead of them. Had the state patrol closed the highway? They must have. They were trying to clear the way, to prevent an accident, to keep people safe.

She glanced at the speedometer again and felt her stomach lurch.

He was going *sixty-five*. In her car. In a fricking blizzard. At night.

How could this man be the brother Megan loved so much? If he was afraid, he didn't show it, his face expressionless. He wasn't even shivering, though he ought to have been much colder than she was. After all, he was right next to the window.

His face and beard were beaded with moisture, his prison smock damp.

He isn't human, Alton. He has ice for blood.

The car slipped, its rear wheels skidding as the road curved to the north.

"Oh, God!" She squeezed her eyes shut, gripped the door handle tighter, her heart kicking against her breastbone.

But as quickly as he'd lost control, he regained it. "Relax, Sophie. It's not time to start praying—not yet."

"Re-relax?" She opened her eyes and gaped at him, fighting the hysterical laughter that bubbled up inside her. "H-how about y-you slow d-own?"

"Why?" He glanced at the rearview mirror, then back at the road. "Do you think they'll give me a speeding ticket?"

Ass! Bastard! Son of a bitch!

She wished she were brave enough to shout all the four-letter words she was thinking. Did he really think he would get away with this? What did he possibly stand to gain?

He's LWOP Alton. Life without parole.

Unless he murdered someone, they couldn't do anything to him beyond locking him in solitary in the maximum-security wing. He could steal, maim, rape and be no worse off when they eventually caught him. Every moment of freedom would be a holiday for him, a vacation from the boredom of prison, a reward for breaking the law.

He had everything to gain and nothing but a life of misery to lose.

Terror settled like a block of ice in her stomach, the full extent of her peril suddenly horrifyingly clear.

A chill that had nothing to do with the weather skittered down her spine.

Ignoring the bitter cold and the pain in his shoulder, Marc glanced into the rearview mirror and was almost blinded by the chopper's searchlights. They were pacing him, watching him, waiting for him to spin out of control, run out of gas, or give up. But it wasn't going to happen. Too much was at stake for him to fuck up.

"Y-you might not m-mind if you d-die tonight, b-but I do!"

He heard the barely suppressed panic in Sophie's voice and realized she was trembling. Was she *that* afraid of him? He thrust aside his sense of guilt. "I had no idea you cared."

"I-I meant *I* don't w-want to die tonight! Y-you can g-go to hell f-for all I c-care!"

And then it hit him. She wasn't trembling out of fear. She was shivering.

He glanced over at her, saw that she was shaking almost uncontrollably. He'd thought that, seated on the passenger side with the heater on, she'd be spared the worst of the cold and wet, but he could see droplets of icy moisture on her face and realized her clothes were almost as saturated as his. But she had a much smaller body mass than he did. She wouldn't be able to withstand the cold as long as he would.

"Do you have a blanket?"

"A s-space blanket. In the t-trunk."

"That won't do you any damned good. Don't go fucking hypothermic on me."

Behind him, the cops slowed their pace and began to fall back.

What the fuck? Were they giving up?

"Y-you don't c-care what h-happens t-to me! Y-you threatened to k-kill me!" She glared at him. Then her eyes flew open wide. "Y-you . . . y-you're b-bleeding! You've b-been shot!"

He glanced down, saw that he'd bled through his shirt and down his arm. "I know this will come as a disappointment, but I'll live."

"N-not if y-you pass out behind the whe—"

"It's not as much blood as it seems. It's just a deep graze." That's what he hoped, anyway. He hadn't had time to check it.

"I h-have a first-aid k-kit in the b-back, too."

But he didn't hear her, his gaze fixed on the road ahead. "Shit!"

At least a dozen squad cars blocked the highway, creating a barricade of steel where the road forked off into Clear Creek Canyon. They were trying to keep him from doing exactly what he'd planned to do—use the narrow canyon walls and lack of visibility to lose the chopper before eluding the squad cars in the mountains.

So that's why the cops had slowed down.

If he was going to avoid crashing into them, he needed to downshift now and start braking. But he'd be damned if he'd give up yet. He weighed his options—or, rather, his lack of options—and made up his mind. "Okay, Sophie, it's time to start praying."

Eyes wide, she had already braced her hands against the dashboard. "Oh, God, no! Pl-please don't do this!"

Marc pressed on the accelerator, hurtling them toward the flashing lights.

Beside him, Sophie whimpered. "N-no!"

A hundred yards. Sixty. Thirty.

He jerked the wheel to the left, fighting to keep control of the little vehicle as it swerved off the road and hurtled toward the vacant tourist parking lot that marked the entrance to the canyon. The car fishtailed, jumped the curb, caught air.

He heard Sophie scream, her cry cut short when the car came down with a bone-jarring crunch. Breath knocked from his lungs, Marc fought to get the car out of a spin.

Shouts. The drone of the chopper. A blinding spray of snow.

"Hang on!" He gunned it, straightened the wheel, made for the dark slit of the canyon.

The car skidded, studded tires chewing ice, fighting for traction.

And they were away.

SOPHIE HUDDLED IN the emergency blanket Hunter had retrieved from her trunk, praying he would stop and let her out, praying someone would see them and call the police, praying the nightmare would end. As far as she could tell, they were now high above the casinos of Central City and Black Hawk, the car nosing through the dark and snowy streets of some nameless little mountain town, the police left far behind.

The helicopter hadn't followed them into the canyon, probably because the wind, low visibility, and high, narrow rock walls made it too dangerous to navigate. But the squad cars had stuck with them—until Hunter had cut the lights and plunged her car down a small side road. Tears of rage and helplessness blurring her vision, Sophie had watched the flashing lights disappear around the bend and had realized she was alone—with a killer.

In that moment, she'd known it was up to her to protect herself, to escape, to survive.

If only she weren't so afraid. And tired. And cold.

More of the heat generated by the heater stayed in the car now that they had slowed down, and the blanket helped her retain some warmth. But she was still freezing, her soggy clothes holding in the chill. Outside, the temperature continued to plummet, the wind howling, the snow blowing in gusts around them, making it almost impossible to see beyond the muted glow of the headlights.

Somehow, Hunter seemed to know where he was going. He turned a corner, then pulled into an empty parking lot, drove around to the back of a building, and killed the lights. It was a sporting goods store, one of those "last chance for ski rentals" places that were the winter mainstay of so many small Colorado towns.

"I need to get a few things." He put the car in neutral, set the brake. "You stay here."

He was leaving her in the car?

"Okay." She avoided meeting his gaze, tried to hide her surprise.

As soon as he was inside, she would call the police on her cell phone and make a run for it. They'd passed a string of houses just down the street. Surely someone would be home. Someone would help her. Up here everyone owned guns.

He turned off the engine, pocketed her keys, and reached behind his back. "I hate to spoil the little plans you're making, but I can't have you running off just now."

Before she could react, he'd handcuffed her to the handle of her door.

"No!" She stared at her wrists in astonishment, adrenaline and outrage temporarily burning away her chills. "You *bastard*! You said you'd let me go as soon as you got away!"

He leaned in close, his face inches from hers, his voice silky, icy amusement in his eyes. "Do you believe everything convicted murderers tell you?"

Then he fished her cell phone from her purse, climbed out, and slammed the battered driver's side door behind him.

Sophie watched him disappear into the swirling storm, desperation and rage swelling in her chest. Well, she'd be damned if she'd just sit here like some subservient little captive waiting for him to come back and shoot her in the head—or worse.

She jerked on the cuffs, twisted them, looked for some kind of emergency release. After all, he'd broken out of them in a heartbeat. There had to be a way.

"Come on, Alton! If he did it, you can do it!"

But if there were a quick way out, she couldn't find it. Heart hammering, she stopped, closed her eyes and took several deep breaths.

"Think! Think! Think!"

The door handle!

If she could pull it off at one end or the other, she could slip free that way.

She shifted her position, braced one knee against the door, and yanked on the cuffs with all her strength.

The steel bit painfully into her wrists, but the handle didn't budge.

"Damn!" She glanced into the storm.

No sign of him.

Knowing she might never get another chance, she tried again, this time pulling on the door handle itself, but still it held.

"Oh, come on!"

What she needed was room to maneuver, more leverage. If she could put her foot against the door and push with the much stronger muscles of her leg . . .

Sophie unlocked her door, opened it, and was almost

jerked out of the car when the wind caught it and blew it back on its hinges. Forced by the handcuffs to bend down, she stepped out into the icy gale, sinking deep in cold powder, the wind sucking her breath away, snow biting her damp skin. She kicked off her heels, pressed one foot against the door, pushed with all her might . . . and slid feet-first beneath the door, her knees hitting steel, her cheek slamming the side of the car on her way down.

For a moment she lay flat on her back in the snow, the breath knocked out of her, her cheek throbbing, her arms stretched painfully over her head. Then she forced air back into her lungs, tried to draw herself upright and get back to her feet. But the snow was deep and slick, and she couldn't get her footing, even without her heels. Again and again she tried, until she was panting for breath and painfully cold, her wrists raw and aching, her body shaking, her skirt riding up to her hips.

Good job, Alton. Any other brilliant ideas?

It was only then that she realized she was in real trouble.

If Hunter didn't come back soon, she wouldn't have to wonder whether he planned to kill her. She would already be dead.

MARC GRABBED AN internal frame pack off the wall and began to fill it. There'd been no alarm on the store, which had made breaking in a piece of cake. But he couldn't waste time. He had to get back to the car before Sophie got too cold. He could have brought her inside with him, but then he'd have been distracted by her inevitable attempts to run off or get to the phone or spear him with a ski pole. Better to get what he needed quickly and hit the road. He still had a long night ahead of him.

Head lamp. GPS receiver. Batteries. Waterproof watch. Pocket knife. Ice ax. Cook pot for water. Bivvy bag. Subzero sleeping bag. Rope. Instep crampons.

He'd been debating for most of an hour whether he should tell her who he was. She didn't *need* to know. She could get through this without knowing. But some part of him *wanted* her to know. She might be less afraid of him if she knew, and he fucking *hated* scaring her. Besides, no matter how much he tried to pretend otherwise, it galled the hell out of him to think she'd forgotten him when he'd spent years carrying the memory of her with him like some kind of goddamned jewel.

How many nights had he reached for that memory to keep himself from going over the edge? How many times had he fought back desperation and loneliness by remembering what it had been like to talk with her, to hold her hand, to see her smile? How many times had he banged one out while imagining he was burying his cock inside her sweet, tight body?

No woman before or after had come close to touching him the way Sophie had, and she didn't even remember him.

Snowshoes. Polypro glove liners and socks. Men's and women's long underwear. Thermal hat. Boots. Down mittens. Ski pants. Turtleneck. Merino sweater. Jeans.

So what was stopping him from telling her? Why hadn't he just come out with it? Why hadn't he forced her to remember him?

He knew the answer as soon as he asked the question.

He wasn't sure he wanted her to know the man he'd become.

Emergency hand warmers. Waterproof matches. Candles. MREs. Power Bars. Instant coffee. Iodine tablets. Biodegradable shampoo and soap. Disposable razors. Bottled water. Duct tape. Wilderness first-aid kit.

He'd put her through hell today. He'd made her believe he was both willing and able to kill her. He'd risked her life along with his own at the prison and on the highway. He'd put terror in those pretty blue eyes of hers. And he'd done it knowingly.

Please don't! I helped your sister!

The regret he'd been trying so hard not to feel edged into his gut. He quashed the emotion, ruthlessly forcing his feelings aside. He'd only done what he'd had to do.

Out there, somewhere, Megan and little Emily needed him.

He walked over to the cash register, pulled out forty dollars plus change and stuffed it into one of the backpack's many pockets. Then, on a hunch, he lifted the cash drawer and found another two hundred in twenties stashed beneath it. "That's more like it."

He moved to a display of winter parkas, grabbed one off the rack, slipped into it. Then he lifted the heavy pack onto his back, wincing as the padded strap scraped over the wound on his right shoulder. With one last glance around the store, he grabbed a parka for Sophie, then made for the door, impatient to get moving.

He would tell her who he was once they were back on the road. After what he'd done to her, he owed her at least that much.

He stepped outside, sucked cold, fresh air into his lungs, savoring the shock, the chill, the scent of it. Wind-driven snow pricked his cheeks and forehead, caught in his beard, sand-blasting the lingering stench of prison from his skin. He couldn't have gotten better weather if he'd asked for it. The storm would delay the cops, cover his tracks, make it almost impossible for search teams to pick up his trail. By sunrise to-morrow, he'd be free and clear.

Of course, anything could happen.

He rounded the corner, stopped in his tracks. "Oh, for fuck's sake!"

Sophie lay sprawled in the snow beside the open car door, struggling clumsily to get upright, arms stretched over her head, her wrists still cuffed to the door handle.

He reached her in two long strides, dropped the pack on the ground, and knelt beside her, fear kicking him hard in the gut. "How in the hell did you manage this?"

Apart from a fresh bruise on her cheek, her face was deathly pale. She shivered violently, snowflakes on her skin and lashes, her wrists badly bruised, her fingers bloodless. But when she looked at him, her eyes spat fire. "B-bastard!"

At least she was conscious and aware and cussing.

"Save the name-calling for later, sweetheart." He covered her with the parka he'd stolen for her and shoved a hat over her head to preserve whatever body heat he could, then dug in his pack for the pocket knife, knowing he had to get her warm if he wanted to save her life. "Right now, you have bigger problems."

He flipped to one of the attachments on the pocket knife—a thin metal blade—and jimmied it into the tiny space beside the teeth of the handcuffs, forcing back the internal locking mechanism, freeing first her right wrist and then her left. Then he slipped his arm beneath her shoulders and eased her to a sitting position.

Furious with her, even angrier with himself, it was all he could do not to shout. "Do you realize how fucking stupid this was? Jesus, Sophie! Are you trying to kill yourself?"

She tried to push him away, her motions sluggish and weak. "I-I forgot. K-killing m-me is y-your job."

"Don't tempt me!" He stuffed her arms into the sleeves of the stolen parka, then dug in the pack for one of the emergency hand warmers. "Can you stand?"

"Y-yes." But she didn't budge.

"Damn it!" He lifted her off the snowy ground, buckled her in the passenger seat, then activated the emergency warmer and slipped it inside her parka. "Stay awake, do you hear me? Watching you die is not on my list of things to do tonight!"

CHAPTER 5

"EASY, SOPHIE. I'M not going to hurt you."

Sophie heard a man's voice, felt hands move over her, tugging off her bra, unzipping her skirt, ripping off her panties. A spark of panic ignited in her belly, moved sluggishly to her brain. She tried to push the hands away, but couldn't seem to move. "N-no!"

"That's right, sweetheart. Get angry. I'd love nothing more right now than for you to wake up and hit me."

But she couldn't hit him. She couldn't even open her eyes.

Then strong arms surrounded her, precious heat enfolding her, soothing her, chasing away her shivers. And she drifted.

Sometime later—she couldn't say how much later—gentle fingers tested the pulse at her throat, pushed back the hair from her face, brushed over a sore spot on her cheek. Then she felt her head being lifted. A cup nudged her lips.

"Come on, sweetheart. Drink. That's it." The man's voice was deep, comforting, somehow familiar.

Coffee.

Warmth slid down her throat to her stomach, spread through her belly and into her limbs, rousing her, driving the terrible cold away, bringing her slowly back to herself.

The crackling of a fire. The scent of wood smoke. The soft warmth of skin against skin. An arm around her waist. The steady thrum of a heartbeat.

She opened her eyes, found her face pressed into a bare chest.

A man's bare chest.

Her heartbeat picked up as she tried to remember, her mind strangely fogged.

Had she met someone? Had she gone home with someone last night? Had she been so drunk that she'd forgotten? She'd never done that before—ever. That was Holly's MO.

But here she was. And here *he* was.

They lay as close together as a man and woman could without having sex, her head resting on the hard mound of his bicep, one of her legs tucked intimately between his, her breasts squashed against his rib cage. As close as she was, she couldn't see much of him. But she could *feel* all of him—the coarse hair on his hard thighs, the prodding outline of his testicles and penis, the ripped muscles of his chest and abdomen.

She was in bed with Adonis, and she couldn't remember how she'd gotten here.

She drew her head back to get a better view of him. The firelight revealed some kind of tattoo on his right arm, which lay possessively around her waist. She tried to make out what it was—an eagle?—but most of it was concealed by a dark band of duct tape and something that looked like—

Dried blood.

Her memories flooded back, riding on a surge of fear.

It was *him*.

Marc Hunter.

The man who'd held a gun to her head. The man who had kidnapped her. The man who'd . . . oh, God! Had he *raped* her?

"No!" She pushed, kicked, tried to shove him away.

"Calm down, Soph—!" He gave a grunt, then a growl, then rolled her beneath him, the length of his naked body holding her motionless on the mattress, his hands pinning her arms above her head. "Oh, Christ!"

Some part of her registered the pain in his voice, but she was too afraid, too panicked, too damned angry to care. "Get off—"

"Not till you promise to keep your knees away from my balls!" He groaned through gritted teeth. "Damn, woman, you're hard on the manberries!"

It took a moment for him to catch his breath.

Then he raised his head and scowled down at her. "Listen to me, sprite! I'm sure this is confusing as hell, but it's not what you think. Nothing violent or X-rated happened. You were hypothermic, and I spent the past few hours trying to keep you alive. We're in a sleeping bag together to preserve body heat."

But Sophie barely heard him.

Only one person had ever called her that.

She stared up at him, almost too stunned to breathe. But even as she tried to deny it, she knew it was true, recognition dawning in a bittersweet rush.

She drew in a shaky breath, then let it go. "Hunt?"

The scowl on his face softened to a frown. "So you don't recognize me till I'm lying naked on top of you? I guess I'll take that as a compliment."

Through the havoc of her feelings, she tried to explain. "Y-you called me 'sprite.' "

His dark brows drew together. "I did?"

"Yeah." The word came out a whisper.

For a moment, they lay there in silence, skin to skin, the weight of his body pressing down on her, their gazes locked. At an emotional edge, she forgot all the big things—like the fact he'd held a gun to her head—her mind catching only the details.

The rapid beat of his heart against hers. The rasp of his chest hair. The hard ridges of his abdomen against her belly. The heat of his skin. The strength of his grasp. The dark length of his lashes. The unreadable emotion in his eyes.

Slowly, he released her wrists, his hands shifting until they pressed palm to palm with hers, his gaze never leaving hers.

Somehow her fingers twined with his, locked.

Then he groaned—and kissed her.

It was a deep kiss, full and scorching, his lips pressing hot against hers, his tongue probing the recesses of her mouth with skilled strokes, his body moving against hers in a slow grind as if he were kissing her with every fiber of his being.

A bolt of heat ricocheted through her, unexpected and

overwhelming, making her shudder. Unable to think, she arched against him, her tongue seeking his, her body driven by raw instinct. And for a moment she was lost in him—in the male feel of him, in the intensity of his kiss, in the erotic pressure of his erection against her hip.

Then she caught it—the coppery scent of blood.

His blood.

Reality crashed in on her like an avalanche.

Drop the steel and back off, or I'll blow her the fuck away!

She was kissing a cold-blooded killer, the man who'd held a loaded gun to her head, the man who'd almost gotten her killed.

In a heartbeat, the fire inside her became fury. She wrenched her head to the side, tried to twist away. "N-no! Stop!"

"God, Sophie!" He sounded breathless, his voice strained. "Jesus!"

"Don't touch—"

He clamped a hand over her mouth, glared down at her. "Believe it or not, I didn't mean for that to happen any more than you did! Now, I'm going to unzip the sleeping bag and get out, and you're going to leave my nuts intact, got it?"

HER BODY TREMBLING, Sophie pulled the sleeping bag tighter around her, struggling to come to grips with all that had happened and watching as Hunt, still naked as a Greek statue, fed his prison garb to the fire, one piece at a time.

Marc Hunter was Hunt.

Strange to think she'd never known his real name. She'd thought Hunt *was* his real name. She'd never heard anyone call him anything but Hunt, not even teachers. She hadn't known he had a younger sister, either. So much for teenage intimacy.

She ought to have recognized him at the prison. True, he had a beard and much longer hair, and he was taller now, more muscular, his rangy frame filled out. But those green eyes, those lips, those high cheekbones were the same. In retrospect, it seemed so clear. Hadn't she had a strange feeling about him? God, she felt stupid!

But then prison was the last place she'd expected to see him. All these years she'd imagined Hunt serving his time in the army, going to college, and setting out for the stars, a wife and three kids at home. Instead, he'd been rotting in a prison cell.

The teenager who'd secretly wanted to be an astronaut—the young man who'd taken her virginity and given her the most romantic night of her life—had grown up to become a cold-blooded killer.

The pain of it cut through her like a razor, her anguish made sharper because he'd clearly known who *she* was from the beginning—and he'd put a loaded gun to her head anyway.

Drop the steel and back off, or I'll blow her the fuck away!

She swallowed, forced down the rush of emotions that welled up in her chest, unwilling to let him see how much he'd hurt her.

And if he'd also saved her life?

She'd been unconscious for part of the time, but she remembered enough—hands tearing away her wet clothing; a voice urging her to wake up, to open her eyes, to drink; strong arms holding her close, enfolding her in warmth.

Easy, Sophie. I'm not going to hurt you.

Could an act of compassion make up for cruelty?

She didn't know.

She raised a hand to her mouth, pressed her fingers against her tingling lips. Why had she let him kiss her like that? Why had she kissed him back? And how could his kiss have affected her so much after all he'd done?

It was shock, Alton.

Or nostalgia. Or exhaustion. Or adrenaline.

She came up with a quick list of excuses, none of which appeased her conscience. All she knew for certain was that she'd never felt anything like the surge of emotion that had taken her the moment she'd realized who he really was—relief and joy and grief and anger twined so tightly that she hadn't been able to tell them apart.

At least she knew he wouldn't rape or kill her.

He stood, watching the fire burn, his hair hanging between his shoulder blades, the muscles of his back narrowing to his waist, his butt tight and round. How he'd stayed in that kind of shape during six years in a nine-by-nine cell was beyond her. But there was no doubt in her mind how he'd managed to pull so many strings from behind bars. He positively *exuded* dominance. He gave off a vibe that said, quite distinctly, "Don't fuck with me."

But, clearly, someone had tried. A thick scar at least six inches long curved down the left side of his back. She didn't have to be a doctor to know it had been made with a crude and vicious weapon and that he'd come close to being killed.

He bent down and reached for the stolen backpack, giving her a brief glimpse of the body part she'd supposedly abused, scattering her thoughts.

She looked quickly away, found herself gazing around a one-room cabin. Log walls. A pine table and chairs that matched the bed. A chest of drawers. Antlers above the fireplace. One shuttered window. One door, its lock broken, a chair tucked beneath the knob to keep it from swinging open. He must have kicked it in when he'd brought her indoors. Had he carried her inside? He must have. She had no memory of arriving here.

"If you're thinking of running, you'd best think again." His voice startled the silence. He turned toward her, still naked, and tore into what looked like a package of long underwear. "We're miles from anywhere, and the snowpack is almost six feet deep. You'll exhaust yourself post-holing and will probably be dead before you reach the main road."

She forced herself to look at his face, not the heavy planes of his chest or the silver scar near the dark circle of his right nipple or the shifting tattoos on his biceps or his six-pack or the trail of dark hair that led to . . .

Her mouth went dry.

And he wasn't even hard.

Something clenched deep in her belly to think that *that* had once been inside her.

She jerked her gaze back to his face, hoped he hadn't noticed, and was relieved to see he was looking down at the long johns in his hands. She swallowed—hard. "I want my clothes."

"Forget it. They're soaked." He stepped into the bottoms, pulled them up, tucking himself inside, the stretchy material seeming to accentuate, rather than hide, his penis. Then he ducked down and grabbed something else from the backpack. "But if you're done staring at my crotch, you can put these on."

Sophie felt her cheeks burn—and got a face full of long underwear.

Pink long underwear.

"Hope you like the color." He turned his back to her, picked up a piece of firewood, and dropped it onto the blaze. "Got it on sale."

She pulled the stolen garments inside the sleeping bag and put them on, her mind filling with questions as it always did if given a few seconds. "Does this place belong to you?"

He gave a snort. "Are you kidding? The feds confiscated everything I owned, even before I was convicted—my house, my old Chevy, my computer. This is a vacation rental. I used to come up here with my buddies during elk season."

"So you kill animals, too."

"Elk make good eating. Lots of lean protein. Besides, bringing down a seven-hundred-pound animal with a hunting bow takes skill."

"That's very manly man of you." She tried to mask her surprise with sarcasm. "How much skill does it take to shoot another man at point-blank range?"

He ignored her, tugged at the duct tape on his right shoulder, sucked in a sharp breath as it pulled free of the bullet wound, fresh blood trickling down his arm from a deep gash.

Irritated with herself that she should feel any sympathy for him, she said the first angry thing that came to her mind. "That wasn't very smart, was it? You should have put a real bandage on it."

"There wasn't time." He wadded the bloody tape, threw it

into the corner, then met her gaze, his green eyes hard. "I had to cover it quickly so I could save your life."

AWARE SOPHIE WAS watching him, Marc turned his attention to his bleeding shoulder. It was worse than he'd imagined. He'd only gotten a glimpse of it before he'd slapped duct tape over it, and his mind had been on something else at the time. But now, with Sophie no longer critical, he examined it and found not a graze, but a furrow. The round had carved a half-inch-deep groove through skin and muscle.

Shit.

He grabbed a bottle of water and the first-aid kit he'd stolen, sat down at the table, and washed the still-bleeding wound as best he could in the half-light of the fire. He needed stitches, but he couldn't just stroll into the emergency room even if there'd been one nearby. No doctor could mistake this for anything other than a bullet wound, and his mug shot was probably all over the evening news. Besides, he didn't have time to play sick. He needed to get his ass in gear. He'd already lost three precious hours stabilizing Sophie's core temp.

Not that holding her naked body had been a chore.

You're scum, Hunter.

Yes, he was.

He'd known the moment she'd realized who he was. She'd quit struggling, her body suddenly pliant, her blue eyes wide, a look of stunned disbelief on her sweet face. His heart had nearly broken through his chest, his pulse thundering in his ears, his brain buzzing. He'd forgotten that he was a convicted murderer and that she was his hostage. He'd forgotten the police that were on his trail. He'd forgotten what a fucked-up mess his life had become.

For a moment, it had been just the two of them—him and Sophie.

And he'd kissed her.

One taste of her, and he'd lost it. After six years of isolation, of surviving on memories, of living without human contact, feeling her beneath him, soft and female, had been more than he could take. And when she'd reacted by kissing him back . . .

It had been twelve years of sexual fantasies coming true in an instant.

How he'd managed to stop he didn't know. He'd felt her stiffen, her rejection taking a moment to register through his raging hormones. It had cost him every ounce of willpower he possessed to rein himself in, to take his hands off her and crawl out of that sleeping bag. If she hadn't demanded he stop, he would have fucked her hard and fast without sparing a single thought for cops or condoms or consequences.

His heart was still beating too fast, his groin heavy and aching, his body's need for her overwhelming. He could still taste her, feel her breasts against his ribs, smell her—the scent of her skin, of her perfume, of her hair. And her little whimper . . .

At least you'll have something new to think about once you're back in your cell, Hunter.

Or maybe his balls would explode first.

He gave up trying to wash the blood off his arm, swabbed the wound with Betadine—and spent the better part of a minute trying not to cuss.

He had just pressed down on it with clean gauze when he heard the squeak of bedsprings and looked up to find Sophie walking unsteadily toward him, her long hair a tangled mass, a look of weary resignation on her bruised face.

"I'll do it."

He shook his head. "You need to stay where it's warmest. Your body temp is still low. Get back in the sleeping bag."

"I'm done being your obedient little captive—"

"Obedient?" He almost laughed.

"—so quit telling me what to do."

She reached into the first-aid kit, pulled out a pair of latex gloves, and tugged them onto her hands. Then she pushed his hand out of her way and lifted the gauze square he'd been using for direct pressure, her touch striking sparks against his skin. How long had it been since another human being had touched him out of concern or by choice? The nurses in the infirmary had been paid for what little compassion they'd shown him.

Sophie didn't flinch or say "eww," but examined his shoulder as if caring for bullet wounds was something she did every so often between deadlines.

He'd always known she was strong.

"Well, at least the bullet didn't lodge in your arm. I guess you can be grateful for that."

He was. "I'm even more grateful it didn't hit you."

She frowned, her delicate eyebrows knitting together, and he could feel her anger. "You need stitches."

"Probably. Too bad I left my sewing kit in my cell."

It was hard to think with her standing close like this. The Polypro long johns fit her like they'd been painted on, every sexy curve of her body highlighted in detail—her delicate breasts, the flare of her hips, her round ass, the soft curve of her belly. He could see her belly button, a little indentation he'd love to explore with his tongue. Her nipples, with their puckered areolas and hard tips, stood out against the cloth, making him want to kiss them, taste them, tease them. He could even see the cleft that divided her labia.

"I guess I'll have to butterfly it somehow. But we need to stop the bleeding first." She took a clean square of gauze and pressed down hard.

He sucked in a breath, the pain helping to clear his mind.

"So are you going to tell me what this is all about?"

CHAPTER 6

MARC CONSIDERED HOW he should answer. Sophie deserved an explanation. She deserved to know why he'd done it, why *she'd* ended up being his hostage, why she'd just suffered one of the most traumatic days of her life. But she was a reporter. Anything he told her would go straight to the cops —and to the press. The less they knew, the better for Megan and Emily.

"I'm guessing this has to do with Megan—at least I hope it does." She lifted the gauze to check for bleeding, then pressed it down again. "I'd be pretty upset if all of this drama and mayhem were just a case of lockdown ennui—some kind of lifer's joyride."

He looked up at her, saw the dark circles beneath her eyes, the bruises, the exhaustion and emotional strain. *He'd* done that to her. "You think I'd do this for kicks?"

"Then why *did* you do it? Wait—let me guess. You could tell me, but then you'd have to kill me, right?"

He hesitated. "Megan's running from someone, Sophie."

"Yeah. Social Services and the police."

"No, I mean she's really running—for her life. She needs my help."

"Hold this." Sophie took his hand, guided it to the patch of gauze, then took a small pair of scissors from the first-aid kit and started cutting a piece of duct tape into little strips. "Who would want to hurt Megan?"

"If I knew that, he'd be dead."

It was the truth, and not even the shocked look on Sophie's face could change it.

"You're pretty casual about this murder stuff, aren't you?"

She stuck the tape strips on the edge of the table one by one as she cut them. "You shot John Cross three times point-blank in the chest—a bit excessive, don't you think?"

Marc ignored the sarcasm in her voice. "He raped Megan."

She stared at him, scissors motionless in her hand. *"What?"*

"Promise you won't print this in your paper."

She hesitated. "Okay. Off the record."

"He raped Megan repeatedly when she was locked up at Denver Juvenile. He was a guard. She was fifteen. If I'm right, she's running from the man who helped him—his accomplice."

For a moment, Sophie watched him in silence, those eyes of hers seeming to measure him, then she set the scissors aside. "Lift the gauze out of the way."

Marc did as she'd asked and saw that the bleeding had slowed to an ooze.

"This will probably hurt." She pinched the edges of the wound together, then stretched strips of duct tape over them to hold them in place.

It did hurt, but being close to her was like a drug. "It's not bad."

"This isn't sterile, but I don't know what else to do. If you keep it clean, disinfect it every day—" There was genuine worry on her face. How could she care about him after what he'd done today?

"It'll be fine."

She finished quickly, covering the improvised butterfly bandage with thick squares of gauze and taping the gauze in place. "That ought to last for a while."

Marc flexed his arm, shrugged his shoulder. The bandage held. "Thanks."

"If you thought Megan's life was in danger, why didn't you tell the DOC and have them go to the police?" She pulled off the gloves and tossed them into the corner.

He gave a snort. "Come on, Sophie. You know better than that. Even if the good folks at DOC had believed me, do you think they'd have gone to the cops to report one of their own, especially since I have no idea who he is? Besides, if the bastard was once a CO, he's probably still working in law enforcement somewhere. The last thing I wanted to do was give away what I know or lead him to my sister."

"You know where Megan is?"

"No."

"Oh." She took a step, swayed on her feet.

Marc caught her around her waist as her knees gave. "You should've stayed in the sleeping bag. You're shivering again."

She tried to shrug him off. "Let go of me."

"And let you fall on the floor? Not a chance." He guided her to the bed and helped her get back into the sleeping bag, irritated with himself for accepting her help. Was he so desperate for human contact that he'd let her endanger herself?

He didn't want to know the answer.

"Don't fall asleep. I'll make more coffee."

Sophie watched Marc while he poured coffee grounds and bottled water into a small aluminum coffeepot and set it on the edge of the fire, her mind reeling, struggling to make sense of everything he'd told her.

You're a journalist, Alton. Think!

She took a steadying breath, tried to break down what he'd said the way she would in a complicated interview. Marc admitted to killing John Cross and alleged that Cross, with the help of an accomplice, had repeatedly raped Megan when she'd been in juvenile detention. He claimed it was some kind of threat from this unknown accomplice that had driven Megan to take Emily and run. He said that he'd broken out of prison to help his sister.

Was there any chance that a single word of it was true?

Well, he'd murdered Cross. That much was certain. And Megan *had* spent time in Denver Juvenile, though she'd never said anything about being raped when Sophie had interviewed her. Then again, rape wasn't a topic most women felt comfortable discussing with the press, and Megan was more emotionally fragile than most women. And although Sophie couldn't imagine a CO getting away with repeated acts of rape, she knew abuses did happen.

Hunt's story wasn't *probable*, but it was *possible*.

And then it hit her. "You never really wanted to be interviewed, did you?"

"No." He turned away from the fire, pulled a pair of blue jeans out of the backpack, and bit off the tag. Then he stepped into them and pulled them over his long johns. "You'd been interviewing Megan and seemed to care about her. I knew you'd come."

"So the interview was just a pretext for luring me down there, for getting yourself out of the maximum security wing and into a less guarded part of the facility. It was just a way of getting your hands on a hostage and nothing personal."

He met her gaze, zipped his fly. "Nothing personal."

She wasn't sure whether she should feel relieved, angry, or hurt. "Well, I sure fell for it, didn't I? Stupid me."

"You're not stupid." He pulled a black turtleneck over his head and tucked it inside his jeans.

"I've never gotten approval for an interview from DOC that fast. I should have known something was screwy. You must be pretty connected on the inside. Maybe you can make this up to me by using your influence to get me an interview with someone who *does* want to talk—*after* they catch you and let you out of solitary, that is."

"*If* they catch me, they'll probably bring me back in a body bag."

Hearing him speak so nonchalantly about being killed jarred her, made her temper spike. "How can you joke about that?"

"I'm not joking. I'd be dead right now if someone had been a better shot."

Sophie remembered the crack of the rifle and the explosion of gunfire that had followed. At the time she'd been sorry they'd missed. And now?

She shivered. "Can you tell me one thing?"

"Maybe."

She forced herself to meet his gaze straight on. "Would you have pulled the trigger if things hadn't gone the way you'd planned? Would you have killed me?"

He shook his head. "No. Never."

She let out a shaky breath. "So what happens now?"

"I get my shit together and get out of here. Once I'm away, I'll contact the cops and give them your location. You'll be back in Denver before sunrise."

She pulled the sleeping bag up to her chin and watched as he finished dressing for the outdoors and organized his gear. Wearing normal clothes instead of prison orange, he no longer looked like a dangerous convict, but a dangerously sexy man—an outdoorsy type, the kind who climbed mountains, skied black diamonds, and thought Class IV rapids were fun.

He walked back to the fireplace, filled a little metal cup with coffee, and carried it over to her. "Drink, but be careful. The cup is aluminum, so it's hot."

She sipped, then felt like she'd slipped into some kind of surreal dream when he pulled out the guns and began to check them. They looked at home in his big hands—hands that had killed. "If you commit another murder, they'll go for the death penalty."

He didn't even glance up. "I don't plan on killing anyone unless I have to."

When he was finished, he tucked the guns in the waistband of his jeans, then reached toward the table for something that looked like a GPS receiver. He was getting her position, she realized. When he'd taken the reading, he tossed the receiver aside, then dug out a few energy bars and set them on the bed beside her, together with bottled water.

"I'll get help to you as fast as I can." He pulled out the handcuffs.

"Please don't!" She was too exhausted to do more than protest.

She might as well have saved her breath.

He took the coffee from her right hand, put it in her left, then gently cuffed her right wrist to the bedpost, leaving it loose. "I don't want the cops to get the wrong idea and accuse you of aiding me in any way."

"Oh." She hadn't thought of that.

He ducked down, brushed his lips over hers, his green eyes filled with some emotion that might have been regret. "Take care of yourself, sprite."

Her throat suddenly tight, she looked away. There was so much she needed to say to him, so much she needed to ask, so much she wanted to know. She fought to keep her voice steady. "If you find Megan, tell her how sad I am that she didn't make it."

He put on his parka, shouldered the backpack, and walked to the door. There, he stopped, seemed to hesitate, then looked back at her. "I'm sorry, Sophie. I never wanted to hurt you."

Then he walked out of the cabin and into the Rocky Mountain winter.

THE CABIN DOOR flew back on its hinges, hit the wall with a *crack*, the suddenness of it making Sophie scream.

"Freeze! Police!"

They'd gotten here faster than she'd imagined they would, streaming through the door with a burst of frigid air, guns drawn, a familiar face in the lead.

Relief surged through her, strong and warm. "Julian!"

Dressed head to toe in SWAT team black, his Kevlar jacket emblazoned with yellow letters that spelled POLICE, Julian Darcangelo swept the room with his gaze, making eye contact with her for the briefest moment as he and the rest of the team secured the cabin.

"I promise I'll come quietly." Sophie managed a smile, wiped the tears from her face with her free hand.

"Get medical in here!" Julian holstered his pistol and reached her in two strides, sitting beside her on the bed and pulling something from his pocket—a silver key. He uncuffed her, took her wrist in his hand, and rubbed it, his expression turning dark when he saw her bruises. "It's going to be all right, Sophie. The paramedics are right behind us."

Sophie sank into the hug he offered—and burst into tears.

She couldn't say why she was crying, exactly. Her emotions

were so jumbled she couldn't sort through them. Shock. Adrenaline overwhelm. Sheer exhaustion.

Heartbreak. Rage. Grief.

She buried her face in Julian's shoulder, unable to hold back her sobs, the weight of all that had happened crashing in on her.

"It's going to be all right." He held her tight, his Kevlar vest hard as steel, his voice soothing. "I'm going to stay with you till we get you to the ER. You're not alone anymore."

She soaked in the warmth of his friendship, felt him pull the sleeping bag more tightly around her, heard him issue a handful of orders, his voice quiet as if he were afraid of disturbing or upsetting her.

"Taylor, get out there and break trail so the Band-Aid boys can get through. And shut the door behind you. We need to keep her warm. Wu, you're stepping on evidence. King, you're in charge. I'm taking myself off duty as of this moment—oh-three-twenty hours."

And suddenly she felt silly.

She drew back, sniffed back her tears. "I-I'm sorry."

"You have nothing to apologize for, Sophie. None of this is your fault." He brushed his thumb over the bruise on her cheek, a muscle clenching in his jaw. "No matter what happened, no matter what he did to you, we're going to help you through it."

And then she saw the situation through his eyes—her crying, the handcuffs, her bruises, her clothes lying wet and torn on the floor.

"He didn't hurt me, Julian. I'm okay, really."

He frowned. "Like hell you are."

"The bruises are my fault. I tried to get away and—"

The look on his face told her he wasn't buying it. "How long ago did he leave you here?"

"About two hours ago, I think."

Julian passed the info on to his men, then pulled out his cell phone and typed in a quick text message. "I promised Tess I'd let her know when you were safe. She's waiting this out with the rest of the gang at Reece and Kara's place."

The thought of her friends gathered together, worrying about her, made fresh tears sting her eyes. She realized that Julian was here not so much because it was his job—he was vice, not SWAT—but because she was Tessa's best friend and he cared about her. He'd been willing to risk his life to save hers.

She swallowed her tears. "Thanks, Julian."

He brushed her thanks aside. "I didn't do anything. I'm ashamed to say it, but if he hadn't called to tell us where you were, you'd still be sitting—"

The door opened, and two men stepped inside, one carrying a folded stretcher, the other what looked like a large blue toolbox.

"Finally." Julian stood and made space for the paramedics, his hand strong and reassuring on her shoulder.

The one carrying the toolbox knelt beside her. "Looks like you've had a rough day, but we're going to take good care of you."

"I'm fine now, honest."

But she was the only one who seemed to think so.

The paramedics took her vitals and told her she was still mildly hypothermic. They stuck an IV of warm fluids into the back of her hand, a process that hurt more than she thought it would. Then they lifted her onto the stretcher, covered her from head to toe with heated blankets, and, with Julian's help and that of another cop, carried her through the snow to the waiting ambulance, despite her protests that she could walk.

"Hush, Sophie." Julian looked down at her, his expression stern. "This is the part of the adventure where you quit being tough and let other people take care of you."

In short order, she found herself inside the brightly lit ambulance, Julian beside her, a body-length heating pad beneath her, a ton of blankets on top of her, warm oxygen flowing through a mask into her lungs. It was as if someone had given her a sedative. She couldn't keep her eyes open.

"Why . . . am I suddenly . . . so sleepy?"

"Your body has been fighting to normalize your core temp for hours," one of the paramedics told her. "Together with everything else you've been through today, I'd say you're exhausted."

Sophie barely heard him, her eyes drifting shut, her thoughts shifting to Hunt. He was out there somewhere. Out in the cold. Alone. What if they shot him? What if he froze to death?

She willed her eyes to open, sought out Julian. "He's still out there."

But Julian misunderstood. He leaned down, gave her hand a gentle squeeze. "He's not going to hurt you again, Sophie. We're going to find him. I promise."

Before she could explain, she was asleep.

COCOONED IN WARMTH, she slept as the ambulance wound its way silently down the canyon, the occasional bit of conversation reaching her, Julian speaking in hushed tones with the paramedics. Some part of her realized they were talking about her, but she couldn't summon the strength to open her eyes or respond.

"—looks like he hit her across the cheek with a crowbar . . ."

"—think he raped her?"

"—a man his age in prison for six years . . ."

"—pretty woman, alone and helpless, would be tempting . . ."

"—put him in solitary for the next hundred years . . ."

"—shoot him first . . ."

It was the siren that finally woke her, startling her from her sleep.

"It's okay, Sophie." Julian still held her hand. "We're trying to get past your colleagues into the hospital parking lot."

Her colleagues?

"You think they'd show a little more respect for one of their own," said the driver. "CNN. MSNBC. Fox. Geee-zus!"

A media feeding frenzy.

You're news, Alton. How do you feel about that?

She felt pretty cruddy, actually.

"Let's see if I can't give her some privacy." Julian pulled out his radio. "Eight-twenty-five."

A voice crackled back. "Eight-twenty-five, go ahead."

"Eight-twenty-five, I need a unit on each side of the ambulance to create a barricade and block the windows."

Sophie listened, fighting to clear the cobwebs from her brain, as Julian spoke in police code, using his position as one of the city's top cops to shield her. Touched by his thoughtfulness, she gave his hand a squeeze. "Thanks."

"Figured you didn't feel much like giving interviews right now."

The ambulance rolled to a stop. The door at Sophie's feet opened, cold air rushing in. And suddenly she was moving, the gurney sliding feetfirst out the door.

She gasped, grabbed the rail, the sensation more than a little strange as the paramedics pulled her over the edge and the wheels beneath her dropped to the ground with a loud clunk.

"Easy, Sophie." Julian leaned over the gurney and placed a hand on each side of her face, blocking her from view. "We're almost inside."

How unreal it all seemed. The blazing fluorescent lights of the ambulance bay. The bright white flashes from a hundred clicking cameras. The burst of shouted questions.

"What's her condition?"

"Is it true the perpetrator called in her location himself?"

"Is Marc Hunter in police custody?"

The question jolted her, made her pulse jump.

Had they caught him?

Then she realized it was only a question. It didn't mean anything. The reporter was just fishing for information.

You're not worried about him, are you, Alton?

Yes, she was. Despite everything he'd done, she was.

Be careful, Hunt.

Even as the words formed in her mind, she drifted off again.

CHAPTER 7

MARC TOOK A sip of coffee—his first real coffee in almost seven years—and tried not to moan. It was black and strong and perfect.

He took another sip, his mouth watering from the mingled breakfast scents that drifted through the small café. He'd ordered the special—ranch eggs, home fries, bacon, and toast—and the anticipation was killing him, his fatigue dissolving at the prospect of a meal cooked by someone whose skill with knives came from culinary school and not street fights.

"More coffee?" The waitress—a pretty middle-aged woman dressed in jeans and a T-shirt emblazoned with a marijuana leaf—held up a glass coffeepot, and smiled.

He set down his mug, then remembered his manners. "Please."

It felt strange to have someone ask him what he wanted, to smile at him, to take an interest in him. He'd almost forgotten people could be kind without being paid or having an ulterior motive.

She refilled his mug, the unmistakable glint of female interest in her eyes. "I don't think I've seen you around."

"Oh, I've passed through a few times. I come for the hunting. Bagged a couple of elk south of here."

"Staying at the Sundance? Need someone to show you around?"

How he wished he could take her up on the offer. God knows he could use a quick fuck. It had been almost seven years, after all. And although she was probably a good twenty years older than he, she was one flower child who hadn't completely lost her bloom. But he didn't have the time. Besides, his senses were still too filled with Sophie.

He shook his head. "Checked out this morning."

She covered her disappointment with another smile, topped off his cup, and sauntered back toward the counter, humming to a tune on the radio.

It had been a long eleven miles to Nederland. After calling in Sophie's location, he'd found Highway 119 and followed it north, keeping to the cover of the trees, the terrain, poor visibility, and deep snow at times slowing him to a near crawl despite his snowshoes. Yet, as rough as it had been, he'd savored every minute of it—the sweat, the strain, the burn in his lungs. He'd felt himself coming alive again, his senses awakened from six years of deprivation by the fresh air, the smell of snow and pine, the wide-open vastness, and deep silence of the mountains.

And for a short time, he'd been forced to think about his immediate situation, and not the wreckage of his life or Megan's—or the damage he'd just done to Sophie's.

He'd removed his snowshoes on the edge of town, dropping them in a Dumpster. Then he'd slipped into the bathroom at the Kwik Mart, where the clerk was distracted by a broken snowblower, and had shaved off his beard and pulled his hair back in a ponytail. By the time he'd reached the Pioneer Inn he'd looked like just another mountain hippie.

That's why he'd chosen Nederland. It was hard for anyone to stand out in a town where the biggest annual event was a festival called Frozen Dead Guy Days—a celebration that honored one man's decision to keep his deceased grandfather on dry ice in his Tuff Shed.

"Here you go." The waitress set his breakfast down on the table. "Want ketchup or hot sauce for the home fries?"

It was all he could do to keep from stuffing his face. "Hot sauce would be great. Thanks."

She grabbed two bottles off a nearby table and set them down in front of him. "Take your pick. I'll be back to warm your coffee."

He looked at the bottles and, unable to decide, shook both

Frank's RedHot and Cholula onto his potatoes and eggs. Then he grabbed his fork and dug in. And this time he did moan.

"Good, isn't it?" The waitress smiled, taking an order at the next table.

He nodded, trying not to look like a starving man.

He'd shoveled half the plate into his mouth when something on the radio caught his ear.

". . . Reporter taken hostage yesterday afternoon was found alive in the mountains above Black Hawk early this morning and was evacuated by ambulance to University Hospital. The reporter, Sophie Alton of the *Denver Independent*, was interviewing Marc Hunter, a convicted murderer, when Hunter reportedly became violent, assaulting a guard, taking the guard's weapon, and using Alton as a human shield."

The bite Marc had just swallowed stuck in his throat.

The radio announcer droned on.

"According to police reports, Hunter called nine-one-one himself and gave them Alton's location before abandoning her and disappearing into the mountains. Details about Alton's injuries or her ordeal are not yet available, but she is listed in good condition."

At least she was safe.

No thanks to you, dickhead.

"Mountain residents are asked to keep an eye out and report all suspicious persons to the police. Hunter is six foot four with shoulder-length brown hair, a beard, and green eyes. He is armed and considered extremely dangerous."

Shit.

He forced himself to keep eating, willing himself to go slowly, keeping one eye on his meal and the other on the waitress and her customers.

"I hope they catch that bastard!" the cook shouted from the kitchen. "I saw his mug shot on TV last night. He sure looks mean. Whatever he did to that girl, it can't have been good."

It hadn't been.

Please don't! I helped your sister!

Sophie's plea echoed in Marc's mind, breakfast sitting like lead in his stomach. He couldn't ignore it, couldn't shake it, couldn't forget it—the image of terror on her pretty face. Now that he was on the outside and it was over, he found it almost impossible to believe he'd put her through that. But he had.

God, she'd been brave! She'd fought him in the hallway, taking on an armed man who outweighed her by an easy eighty pounds, knocking his nuts into his throat. She'd done her best to escape, almost losing her life in her desperate attempt to save herself. And through it all her tongue had been sharp as barbed wire.

So you kill animals, too.

It had been harder than he could ever have imagined to turn his back on her and leave her there, alone, bruised, and still hypothermic. A part of him had wanted to tell her everything, to lay it all at her feet and ask for her forgiveness, but he knew nothing could make up for what he'd done. And so he'd made sure she was safe and comfortable, then he'd taken one last taste of her and walked out the door, ignoring the anguish in her eyes and the fist-sized hole in his own chest, knowing as the door shut behind him that he'd never see her again.

He took another bite, forcing down his growing remorse with a mouthful of spicy home fries. Regret was a luxury he couldn't afford right now. It was nothing but a waste of time and energy. It wouldn't save Megan and Emily, and it wouldn't fix anything for Sophie. The situation was what it was, and he couldn't change it.

And yet wouldn't he sell his soul right now if he could do just that?

Yes, he would. He'd give anything to be an ordinary man living an ordinary life. He'd give anything to have bills to pay, a lawn to mow, and a leaky faucet to fix. He'd give anything to be a real brother to Megan, an uncle to Emily, a husband, a father. He'd give anything to be able to look at Sophie and see his future.

Maybe in your next life—if you don't come back as a cockroach.

The best he could hope for was to find Megan and Emily and make it safely to Mexico, where he'd spend the rest of his life looking over his shoulder. And that's what he ought to be thinking about, not obsessing over a woman he'd fucked one night back in high school.

What a heartless son of a bitch you've become!

Yeah, he had.

He had six years of prison to thank for that. Six years of watching his back. Six years of being treated as subhuman. Six years of sleepless nights, violence, degradation. Or maybe that was just an excuse and he'd always been this way.

He finished his breakfast, tossed back the last of his coffee, and dropped a ten on the table. He needed to get into Denver and pick up Megan's trail. He wasn't the only one looking for her, but for her sake—and Emily's—he'd damn well better be the one to find her.

"HE DIDN'T GIVE you any hint where he was going—look at any maps, ask you about bus routes or directions?" The cop—Sergeant Gary King was his name—looked up from his notepad, his brown eyes bloodshot.

"No. Nothing." Sophie pulled the blankets tighter around her, grateful for their warmth—and the reassuring presence of her friends.

They were all there, crammed together in the little hospital room, encircling her bed. Tessa sat in the only chair, absently rubbing her pregnant belly. Kara stood next to the chair, Reece beside her, his arm around his wife's waist. Holly and Kat stood beneath the television in the corner next to Matt, who looked more rumpled than usual, a coffee stain on his blue shirt. Julian stood at the foot of the bed, still dressed in black SWAT gear.

They all looked exhausted, and it touched Sophie more than she could say that they'd spent the night together in front of CNN, worrying about her—all except Natalie, who'd been assigned to cover the story, and Julian, who had apparently pulled rank and put himself in charge of the team that had come after her.

Sergeant King looked back at his notes. "He just walked out the door and left you handcuffed to the bed?"

"Yes." She knew Sergeant King was just doing his job. Still, she couldn't help but wish the questions would come to an end. All she wanted was to sleep, and she'd already told him everything—or almost everything.

She'd left out the fact that she'd once known Hunt. And had given him her virginity. And had never completely gotten over him. She couldn't see how that was relevant to their investigation. After all, she hadn't realized who he was until hours after he'd taken her hostage.

Still, she couldn't shake a growing sense of guilt. Somehow not telling the entire story made her feel like she was lying, particularly when it came to Julian. He'd risked his life to save hers when it wasn't even his job. The least she could do was to tell the whole truth.

But what if the whole truth didn't matter?

You haven't told them he kissed you, either.

More than that, she hadn't told them about Megan.

Although the part about the kiss wasn't important—what difference could it make?—the part about Megan was. Investigators had already guessed that Hunt had broken out to join his sister, but they had no idea why. They'd definitely want to know the allegations he'd made about Cross and this mysterious accomplice.

But everything Hunt had told her about Megan had been off the record. She'd made a promise, and she couldn't betray that promise without betraying her entire profession. Besides, what if Hunt had been telling the truth and the man who was after Megan was still working somewhere in the system?

The last thing I wanted to do was give away what I know or lead him to my sister.

She glanced at Julian, saw him watching her, his gaze seeming to measure her. Did he suspect she was holding something back?

Sergeant King flipped to a blank sheet of paper. "Can you remember what he was wearing when he left?"

Of course she could remember—she'd watched him dress from the skin up. So why did she hesitate to answer?

I'm sorry, Sophie. I never meant to hurt you.

"You don't owe him anything, Sophie," Kara said, seeming to read her mind.

"Not a thing—except maybe another knee in the nuts," Tessa added.

Then Reece chimed in. "I know you're grateful that he saved your life and kept his word about calling your location in to police, but he didn't do it out of concern for you."

Julian nodded. "He did it to keep himself off death row."

Above Holly and Kat, a mug shot of Hunt filled the television screen beneath the words "Colorado Manhunt."

Sophie swallowed the lump that had formed in her throat. "He was dressed for Everest—backpack, down parka, ski pants, jeans underneath, a wool hat, gloves, snowshoes. I wasn't in the store with him, so I'm not sure what else he might have taken. He was still armed. He had two guns, I think."

And just like that she went from feeling guilty to feeling like a traitor.

If they catch me, they'll probably bring me back in a body bag.

What if they shot him? What if they killed him? After what he'd done, why did she care? The man was a murderer who'd held a gun to her head and kidnapped her.

God, she felt confused! Her mind and her emotions were running in circles. Clearly, she was in desperate need of sleep.

Sergeant King took notes, nodding as he wrote. "We found bloody gauze, latex gloves, and duct tape in the corner, as well as bloodstains on the sleeping bag. How badly was he wounded?"

She'd forgotten to mention that, too. "A bullet cut a pretty deep groove across his right shoulder. He used the duct tape to stop the bleeding while he took care of me. I . . . I bandaged it for him before he left."

She felt Tessa's hand close over hers, a gesture of support.

Sergeant King looked up from his notepad, his expression grave. "I understand that you refused to undergo a forensic exam, is that correct?"

A forensic exam was the official term for a rape kit.

"I told you he didn't hurt me. The bruises—all of it—was my fault. Even the hypothermia. If I hadn't fallen in the snow . . ."

Julian and Reece frowned.

Sergeant King went on as if she hadn't said anything. "I understand he removed your clothing as well as his own and got into a sleeping bag with you naked—"

"He was trying to save my life!"

"—while you were unconscious. Under those circumstances it might be advisable to have the exam just in case something happened that you don't remember."

There was a moment of awkward silence.

Matt shifted nervously. "Maybe we should leave the room."

Holly elbowed him in the ribs. "Maybe *you* should leave."

Julian took a step forward. "Sophie, I know this is hard. I know you're exhausted and overwhelmed. But I have to agree with Sergeant King. Marc Hunter is a remorseless killer who's been behind bars for almost seven years. He got skin-to-skin naked with you while you were unconscious, which constitutes unlawful sexual contact at the very least. How can you be sure he didn't do more than that when you were unconscious?"

Because he used to be a boy who protected girls. Because he once offered to stop at third base so I could stay a virgin. Because no matter what else he's done, Hunt isn't a rapist.

She met Julian's gaze. "Because I'm sure."

He watched her, his scrutiny almost uncomfortable. "Everyone out."

Matt shuffled out the door.

Everyone else stayed stubbornly put.

If she hadn't been so tired and upset, Sophie might have laughed.

"It's okay," she said. "You can say whatever you need to say in front of them. They'll all find out anyway. It's impossible to keep secrets in a newsroom."

Reece shrugged. "Reporters."

Julian's frown deepened. He reached out, rested his hand on the lump of blanket that was her knee, and took a deep breath. "All right. I don't know a tactful way to say this, so I'm just going to come out and say it. Even if you *let* him touch you, even if you said 'yes,' even if you did everything he wanted you to do without fighting back, it would still be considered sexual assault because you were his hostage. I saw the tapes. I watched him put a forty-five to your head and threaten to kill you. I saw how afraid you were. No one would blame you, Sophie."

Blood rushed into her cheeks, and she gaped at him. "You think—"

"I think you've just been through hell and are lucky to be alive. I'm asking you to help me make sense of it, and I'm telling you it's okay. Whatever happened, it wasn't your fault."

Face burning, Sophie forced herself to meet his gaze. "He kissed me. That's all. When I told him to stop, he stopped. He even apologized."

Julian studied her, seemed to relax. "Okay, then. If you change your mind . . ."

"I won't. He didn't hurt me."

For a moment there was silence, then Sergeant King nodded to Julian and left the room.

"I know it probably doesn't mean much right now, but I'm launching a legislative probe of the Department of Corrections," Reece said. "I'm going to find out how this happened and make damned sure it never happens again."

Sophie met his gaze, managed a smile. "There's a reason I always vote for you."

Then someone knocked at the door, and a man's blond head poked inside. "Sis?"

"David! How—?" Tears filled Sophie's eyes, made her throat tight.

But then her little brother was there, beside her, hugging her.

And she couldn't speak at all.

"RENT'S DUE IN advance by noon every Monday. Cash or money order only—no checks, no credit cards." The motel's owner, a balding man with a beer gut that protruded from beneath his white T-shirt, jerked his thumb toward a list of rules that was stuck to the wall with yellowed tape. "You don't pay on time, I toss your shit out. This ain't no charity."

"Got it." Marc counted out three fifties and slipped his fake ID back into his wallet, his gaze scanning the brightly lit parking lot outside while he listened to the television behind him.

He told himself the tight feeling in his chest was just sensory overload—the natural response of the human mind to the chaos of the real world after six years of living in an institution. For so long he'd been locked in a tiny cell. Now he found himself walking wide-open streets, surrounded by the rush of traffic, the press of people, a riot of lights, of sounds, of scents. He ought to feel exhilarated. Instead, he felt naked, exposed, tense, some part of him always watching, always waiting, always wary.

He heard his name, and Sophie's, and knew CNN had cut away to the update it had promised its viewers.

"Number seventeen. All the way on the end." The man slid a key across the counter, his gaze on the television. "Think they'll catch that son of a bitch?"

Careful to keep his expression neutral, Marc glanced over his shoulder, saw his own face staring back at him. The only difference between the man on the screen and himself was the beard he'd shaved off and the ski hat he'd pulled over his ponytail. "What do you think?"

"I bet he's already crossed state lines. Probably hightailing it to Mexico."

"Probably. And thanks." Marc took the key and walked back out into the cold, trudging across the snowy parking lot to unit seventeen, careful to keep his head down.

He'd taken the bus from Nederland into Boulder this morning, then headed straight for the U-Store place. The last time he'd been there had been shortly after his arrest. Still out on bail, he'd realized he was probably going to go down. The case prosecutors were building against him in the press had seemed invincible—dirty agent gets caught with drugs, panics, and blows the good agent away—and every instinct inside him had told him to take Megan and head for the border. He'd spent a rainy afternoon gathering whatever resources the feds and cops hadn't confiscated—clothes, cash, a fake driver's license from an undercover job—and moved them into a storage locker just in case he needed to head south in a hurry. He'd put the locker under his mother's name, then paid in cash for ten years of storage.

But he'd known that the moment he took off for Mexico, he'd be pegged as guilty. Even more, he'd known that if he and Megan were caught crossing the border together, Megan would be dragged into the nightmare, too. And so instead of listening to his gut and bolting, he'd stayed in Denver, hoping the jury would acquit him.

What a fucking moron he'd been.

At least he'd had the foresight to set up his secret little cache at the U-Store. It sure as hell had come in handy today. After he'd gotten a few hours' sleep on the concrete floor of his locker, he'd hopped the bus into the city and come here. A seedy motel on the edge of town, it offered everything he needed—a place to sleep, shower, and store his shit, neighbors who wouldn't ask questions, and a dirt cheap week to-week lease.

He slipped the key into the lock just as the door next to his opened and a young woman with bleached-blond hair stepped out. She wore a rabbit fur coat, tight jeans, and knee-high leather boots. He didn't have to ask what she did for a living.

Her gaze raked over him, and she smiled with bright red lips as she passed. "You look good enough to eat, honey. I might even do you for free."

Marc returned her smile, watched her pass, his gaze drawn to her bountiful ass. A few days ago, he'd have taken her up on her offer. Hell, he'd have been more than willing to pay—anything to get inside a woman. But even as heat rushed to his cock, he realized he didn't want her, free or otherwise.

He wanted Sophie.

You're never going to see her again, idiot. Take what you can get before you find yourself back in prison wishing you had.

That was his dick talking. Unfortunately, his dick was probably right.

He pushed open the door to his room, stepped inside, and flicked on the light, locking the door behind him. The place was musty, stinking of mildew and cigarettes. A single bulb hung from the water-stained ceiling. A bed draped in an orange floral comforter sat against one wall, an old television against the other. On the other side of the bed, a door stood ajar, revealing a toilet. The far wall held a closet and countertop with a sink and a hot plate. A single window, its yellowed blinds hanging askew, offered a scenic view of the alley.

Home, sweet home.

Compared to his cell, it was the honeymoon suite at the Hilton.

He dropped his pack on the bed, his mind off the hooker and back on CNN. He hadn't realized how intensely the media would focus on his escape. It made his situation more dangerous, increasing the risk that someone would recognize him, even without the beard. It meant he needed to cut his hair, maybe even bleach it.

He turned on the television, telling himself that he was only watching in order to keep up with the police. But he knew that was bullshit. He wanted to hear about Sophie. He needed to see her. He needed to know she was all right.

The sound came on first, the picture fading slowly into view.

A heavyset cop was mumbling into the mic, giving the reporters an update on what was now apparently the biggest manhunt in Colorado history.

How flattering.

The cop droned on about how many investigators had been brought in and how many agencies were involved. The FBI wasn't one of them. Apparently, the feds didn't see any opportunity for good publicity in this, or they'd have stolen the limelight by now.

"At the moment we're reviewing every possibility, including the increasing likelihood that the fugitive has fled the state or frozen to death in the mountains."

Frozen to death?

Hunter, you dumbshit, how'd you do that?

At least the police were looking in all the wrong places.

But there was nothing new on Sophie.

Ignoring his urge to channel surf in search of news about her, he turned off the TV and began to unpack, determined to put his mind where it needed to be—on Megan and Emily and the job that still lay ahead of him.

He'd left most of the gear he'd stolen from the sporting goods store behind in the storage locker, taking only what he'd need in the city—six grand in cash, more clothes, shoes, the first-aid kit, food, and, of course, the pistols DOC had so kindly provided. He needed to lay in some basic supplies, including a laptop computer, and then hit the streets. He would check out all of Megan's former hangouts, talk to everyone she'd known, try to find out where she'd gone—and who was after her. Someone would know something.

God, he wished he'd gotten the full story from her. All he knew was that Cross had raped her and gotten away with it—and that he hadn't been alone. Megan had been too hysterical to tell Marc more. With a dead man on his floor and afraid for her mental stability, he hadn't pushed her as hard as he should have. Then he'd found his ass in prison, unable to see her, unable to communicate except through a complex network of COs, some of whom he'd never met, none of whom he trusted with his sister's life or sanity. Now he'd have to figure it out without her help.

But first he needed to unpack and get a shower.

He stashed the cash behind a couple of loose ceiling tiles, tossed his old, dusty clothes in a pile for the laundry, and put the first-aid kit with the shampoo, soap, and razors in the bathroom. Then he stripped, turned the shower on hot, and stepped into the spray.

A familiar knot in his stomach, he worked quickly, efficiently, shampooing his hair, scrubbing sweat and the stench of prison from his skin, rinsing the wound on his shoulder. It was only when he reached down to turn the water off that he realized he didn't have to hurry.

There was no CO shouting at him that his four minutes were up. There were no catcalls, no raunchy propositions, no lewd glances. There was no gang of shower hawks waiting nearby hoping he'd drop his guard so they could finally take him down and pound him in the ass.

I'm going to make you scream, Hunter!

And it finally hit him.

He was no longer in prison.

He was alone. In a motel. In Denver.

He was *out*.

His body started to shake, his breathing suddenly ragged, his pulse thrumming against his eardrums. He closed his eyes, then rested his palm against the green tile wall, leaned into the spray, and let the hot water wash over him.

CHAPTER

8

SOPHIE SLID HER pawn forward one space. It seemed a harmless enough move. Then again, she'd never understood the rules of chess no matter how many times her dad and brother had tried to explain them.

David moved one of his pawns, a look of mild amusement on his face.

Having no idea what to do next, her heart not really in the game, she moved another pawn. He moved a knight. Then she moved a castle—and watched him snatch it up with one of his bishops.

"How can you do that? He was all the way over there!"

He rolled his blue eyes, pretending to be annoyed, a grin tugging at the corners of his mouth. "Bishops move diagonally any number of spaces, until either they kill something or hit the edge of the board."

"I think you just make these rules up as you go." Then Sophie saw her chance. She moved a pawn and captured his bishop. "Ha!"

He raised an eyebrow, picked up his king, and moved it onto the other side of his castle. "Let me know if you need a hint."

"No hints." She captured one of his pawns with one of her pawns.

He shook his head and moved his queen halfway across the board.

"I hate her." Sophie glared at the bit of black plastic, then moved another pawn forward.

He moved his queen again—one space. "Checkmate."

"Already?" She stared in disbelief. "How can it be checkmate already?"

From the kitchen came the beep of the oven timer—and the delicious scent of their special chipless chocolate chip cookies.

"I've never understood how you can be so damn smart and still suck so badly at a simple strategy game." He stood and walked off toward the kitchen, a smile splitting his face.

"It's only simple for you because you got Dad's math brains," she called after him as he disappeared around the corner.

He was flying back to California tomorrow morning. She didn't want him to leave. No matter the circumstances, she loved spending time with him. He was her only family, the only person left in the world who shared her memories of Christmas mornings, spring picnics, and lazy summer afternoons spent playing in the backyard.

She couldn't imagine this past week without David. He'd been her rock, doing all the shopping, cooking, and cleaning, insisting that she rest, even contacting her insurance agent about her poor, battered car and picking up her rental. He'd listened when she'd needed to talk, held her when she'd cried, and kept her mind occupied. He'd even given her a Valentine's card on Valentine's Day complete with a red rose and chocolate.

When had her little brother become a man?

She could remember the day he'd been born, looking in her four-year-old opinion more like a shriveled potato than a brother. She hadn't been any more impressed with him a few years later when he'd clunked around the house in cowboy boots that were too big for his feet, a dumb plastic fireman's helmet on his head. And when he'd gone through his dorky Power Rangers phase, it had been all she could do not to clobber him.

But now he was a good five inches taller than she was, handsome enough to turn women's heads, and on his way to being a horse obstetrician, not one whiff of dork lingering anywhere around him. It touched her more than she'd ever be able to say that he had flown back to Colorado, dropping everything the moment he'd gotten the news.

Mom and Dad would be proud of him.

She swallowed the lump in her throat, leaned back into the couch cushions, and pulled the blanket tighter around her. The heat in her apartment was cranked up to seventy-five, but it was still hard for her to stay warm. The doctor had told her it sometimes took weeks to recover fully from hypothermia.

The blanket—a silky soft chenille throw—had been a gift from Tessa. Like David, her friends had been there for her, calling to check on her, stopping by her apartment all week to visit, bringing her gifts. Reece was prepping the Legislative Audit Committee for its probe of the DOC. Julian had ordered extra patrols for her street and was coordinating with jurisdictions throughout the state in what was the biggest manhunt in Colorado history. The I-Team had even sent flowers.

"You missed deadline, Alton," the card read. "Get out of bed, and get in here.'"

She felt loved and protected—and horribly guilty.

Her brother and her friends were doing all they could to watch over her and help her get back on her feet, and she still hadn't told them the whole truth.

She hadn't told them about her previous relationship with Hunt. She couldn't. The night she'd spent with him had been her most treasured memory. Hunt had destroyed it, turning something precious into something painful. Sharing that memory—and admitting what had become of the man who'd been at the heart of it—felt somehow too overwhelming. Besides, nothing had happened at the cabin that would help police catch him. They knew as much about him as she did, maybe more. The fact that she'd had sex with him one night twelve years ago wouldn't impact their investigation at all.

Nor had she divulged what he'd told her off the record about his sister. She was a journalist. Once she agreed to keep information confidential, she was obliged to honor her word, even in extreme circumstances. She'd heard of journalists who'd gone to jail rather than betray their sources. Of course, Hunt wasn't the typical source. He'd been holding her hostage when he'd asked her to keep his secrets. For that reason alone, there probably wasn't a journalist in the country who would condemn her if she went to the police and told them everything.

And that was the crux of it, the reason her conscience wouldn't leave her alone.

She didn't *want* the police to catch him.

What was wrong with her?

One minute she felt depressed, the next irritable, the next anxious, as if something terrible were about to happen. She felt sluggish all day, then lay awake at night remembering the way Hunt had kissed her, thinking through the things he'd told her, worrying about him and Megan. Had he found her? Were they safe? What if he'd frozen to death like police believed? Was someone really after Megan? What if the bad guy found her first?

Sophie tried to hide it, but, of course, she wasn't fooling anyone. Tessa and Kara blamed her moodiness on trauma, and she supposed they were at least partly right. The whole hostage ordeal had been terrifying. She didn't think she'd ever been more afraid in her life. For a time, she'd truly believed he might kill her.

But that wasn't the worst of it.

"Do you want milk?" David called from the kitchen.

"With warm, gooey cookies?" she called back. "Are you kidding?"

If Hunt had just been some random psycho—just some crazed murderer who'd held a gun to her head and dragged her into the mountains—she'd have been able to hate him and forget him. But, sadly, every terrifying moment had been brought to her by a man she'd once adored. A man she somehow still cared about. How else could she explain her reaction to his kiss?

God, she felt used. And stupid. But more than that, she felt . . . brokenhearted.

What happened to you, Hunt?

His name was Marc, she reminded herself—Marc Hunter. She'd spent the past two days running it all through her mind again and again, trying to understand, trying to put the pieces together, trying to find a way to think about what Hunt had done that made it less painful. But there was only one thing that could even remotely excuse the hell he'd put her through, and that was if he'd been telling her the truth.

And yet how could she take comfort in that?

If what he'd told her were true, it meant Megan had suffered unimaginable abuse while in state custody—and that her life was now in danger.

Either way, Sophie was going to do everything she could to get to the bottom of it starting Monday morning when she was back in the office.

She glanced at the clock on her DVD player, saw that it was almost ten. She reached for the remote, turned on the television, and surfed to CNN. Julian had promised to call her if and when they caught Hunt, but that hadn't stopped her from obsessing over the news, watching every broadcast and weather report, reading every newspaper online, putting Google on alert for the name Marc Hunter.

David reappeared carrying a tray with two glasses of milk and two plates heaped with cookies. He set the tray down on her coffee table, a frown on his face. "Are you sure that's good for you? Maybe you shouldn't watch the news. Give yourself time to recover."

She looked away from the screen, saw David watching her. She knew what he was seeing—her pale face, the yellowing bruise on her cheek, the dark circles beneath her eyes. She'd seen them herself every time she'd looked in the mirror and had felt like she was looking at a stranger. "Not watching it doesn't make it go away."

He sat down beside her and for a moment said nothing, seeming to study the coffee table. "When the police called and told me you'd been taken hostage, I thought it was a joke at first. Then, when I realized it wasn't . . . All the way to the airport and on the plane, I kept thinking, 'What if he rapes her? What if he kills her? What if she's already dead?' Jesus!"

Tears blurring her vision, Sophie reached out, took her brother's hand.

"I lost Mom and Dad." David looked up at her, his voice breaking. "I couldn't bear to lose you, too, Sophie."

She swallowed the lump in her throat. "You didn't lose me."

"Thank God!" He gave her fingers a squeeze. "But it makes me damned angry to think of how badly this bastard frightened you. You're trying to hide it, but I know you're afraid. It can't be good for you to keep watching these news reports."

"I'm a reporter. How can I avoid the news?"

"By turning your TV off, for starters." He picked up the remote, and the screen went dark. "I know you're afraid, but they *are* going to catch him. I just hope for his sake he *has* left the state. If your friend Julian finds him, he'll end up in pieces."

And then it hit her—a terrible possibility.

Marc and Julian facing one another.

Both armed.

Both trained to kill.

Her blood ran cold.

MARC FOLLOWED HIS quarry through the chilly darkness, stepping into the cover of an alley when the guy stopped to do a deal. A quick conversation, a show of cash—and the exchange was made. The guy moved on down the street, still clearly unaware Marc was tailing him.

Donny Lee Thompson was a hustler, a small-time pusher who sold whatever he didn't use himself. He was also Emily's father and Marc's best lead. He looked to be in his late thirties, maybe five-eleven, one-fifty—a skinny son of a bitch. His dirty blond hair was beginning to thin, and his skin had the sallow tone of a habitual drug user. Marc had wondered what Megan could possibly have found attractive about him—and then he'd remembered.

Drugs.

Ahead of him, Donny crossed a small side street, his pace suddenly quickening. For a moment Marc thought the bastard had realized he was being followed—and then he saw it.

A squad car.

A single black-and-white rolled slowly down the side street toward them.

Shit.

But even as adrenaline hit Marc's bloodstream, urging him to fight or run, some part of him realized they weren't here for *him.* They were just *here.*

He willed his feet to move—one casual step after the next. He'd once been an agent. He knew from his own experience that the best way to attract a cop's attention was to rabbit. If he just kept walking, they would see what they expected to see— just another pedestrian.

Left. Right. Left. Right.

He crossed the side street, the squad car not ten feet away from him and drawing nearer, its tires crunching heavily in the snow. He hunched his head between his shoulders as if huddled against the wind and kept walking, the Glock heavy in the waistband of his jeans.

If they stopped him, if they searched him . . .

Red-blue-red-blue-red-blue.

Lights flashed. The siren chirped, then wailed.

He was about to break into a dead run when the car accelerated around the corner—and disappeared down the street behind him.

Breath he hadn't realized he'd been holding left his lungs in a gust, his heart slamming against his ribs.

Jesus Christ!

He sucked in cold air, steadied his step, kept walking.

Get a grip, dumbass!

Marc had been in Denver for almost a week now, the rhythm of the streets slowly working its way back into his feet. He no longer looked over his shoulder at every approaching car, no longer felt quite as exposed, no longer jumped out of his skin every time someone shouted or honked their horn or slammed a door. Still, he couldn't seem to shake his sense of wariness, the instinct that told him to watch his back, the itchy feeling that never let him rest.

He'd spent every almost every waking hour this past week

on the streets looking for information about Megan. So far he hadn't found anything. Not one damned thing.

Megan wasn't in any of her old hangouts. She wasn't in any of the shelters. None of her old friends had seen her, and though some of them knew she'd skipped parole, they claimed to have no idea where she'd gone. They might have been lying, of course, but he didn't think so. It wasn't like hard-core addicts to turn down cash, and he'd flashed plenty of it. If anything ought to have made them talk, it was money they didn't have to steal—or earn on their backs.

His frustration and sense of urgency growing, he'd come back to his motel room each night and logged onto the Internet, first scanning newspapers nationwide for reports of unidentified female bodies or abandoned babies, a knot of dread in his chest. Then, once he was reasonably sure Megan and Emily hadn't been found dead in a ditch, he'd spent a few hours trying to crack the DOC database. Unfortunately, the latter was far beyond his pathetic IT abilities. He'd looked into hiring a real hacker, but he would've had to rob a bank first, and that went beyond his criminal ambitions, at least at this point.

Although he could certainly use his fake ID to request the records under state open-records laws, it would take weeks, maybe months, before he had what he needed. He knew from experience that the only requests the state took seriously were those filed by people with credentials—legislators, police detectives, attorneys, journalists.

Don't even think about it, Hunter.

He had thought about it, of course. He'd thought a lot about it—about her. But no way was he going to ask Sophie to help him. How could he after what he'd done to her? Besides, he didn't want her involved in this. He wasn't even sure what he was up against, and that made it too damned dangerous.

Ahead of him, Thompson turned off East Colfax onto Race Street, heading up the walk of a shabby house halfway down the block on the west side of the street. Marc closed the distance between them. He'd spent the past ten hours tracking Thompson down, following him, waiting for the right moment to hold a little surprise get-together. They were practically family, after all. It was time they got acquainted.

He came up behind Thompson just as Thompson stepped through the doorway.

"Donny Thompson?"

Thompson whirled about. "Who the fuck are you?"

"I'm looking for Megan Rawlings."

"Never heard of her. Besides, I don't talk to narcs." Thompson tried to slam the door.

Marc forced his way inside and dropped Donny to the floor with an old-fashioned punch in the face—not the most sophisticated move, but satisfying. Then he slammed the door behind him. "I'm not a narc, asshole. I'm Megan's brother—uncle to the baby *you* put inside her."

"Her *brother*? Oh, man! Fuck!" Donny groaned, sat up, hand on his face. "Like I told the other guys, I don't know where she went. I haven't seen her since they arrested her!"

"The other guys?"

"The cops who came looking for her." Donny rubbed his newly blackened eye. "Man, did you have to hit me like that?"

"Probably not, but I enjoyed it." He'd enjoyed it so much he wanted to do it again. "Tell me about these cops who came looking for her."

"What can I say? They were cops, you know? They asked me if I knew where she was."

Marc glanced around. Whoever those cops had been—if they really had been cops—they must not have had their eyes open for Thompson to still be roaming the streets. There were signs of drug dealing everywhere. The little mirror and razor blade sitting in the middle of the floor. Plastic sandwich bags strewn out across the sofa. The set of scales on top of the coffee table.

"Mind if I have a look around?"

Donny staggered to his feet. "She's not here, man. I told you that."

"I heard you, Donny. I just don't believe a damned word you say."

There wasn't much to the place. The living room. A filthy

kitchen piled high with dirty dishes, beer cans, and take-out boxes. A bedroom buried in dirty clothes, drug paraphernalia, and porn magazines. A bathroom that reeked of mildew.

"Jesus, Donny! You need to fire your housekeeper."

But nowhere did he see any sign of a woman or a baby—no diapers, no bottles or jars of baby food, no women's clothing.

She wasn't here.

Marc's stomach sank. This had been his last remaining lead, and it had gotten him nowhere. Fear for his sister and her baby churned in his gut, making him want to hit something.

Megan, where the hell are you?

If there was no evidence of Megan, there certainly was evidence of the addiction that had ruined her life—used needles and syringes, makeshift tourniquets, blackened cookers. Making an educated guess, Marc entered the bathroom and reached to lift the lid off the toilet tank. From behind him, he heard a little metallic click.

"Get the fuck out of here, asshole!"

He turned to find Thompson holding a knife, a look of fury on his face.

"Is that a switchblade, Donny? You're boring me." Marc shook his head, pretended to turn his back on Thompson—then pivoted and aimed his Glock at the bastard's head. "Get down on the floor! Hands behind your head!"

Thompson blinked, dropped. "You *are* a cop."

"Used to be DEA. Now I'm just a pissed-off brother." Keeping one eye on Thompson, Marc lifted the porcelain top off the tank and found what he'd known he'd find. "Look at this—a bag of white stuff! Can I borrow your little knife?"

He bent down, grabbed the switchblade from Donny's sweaty fist, and sliced the plastic, spilling what was probably an ounce of heroin carefully into the toilet.

Donny's face turned red, a gratifying look of horror in his eyes. "Christ! Oh, man! Do you know how much that's worth? Oh, God!"

"You want to dive in after it? Be my guest." Fighting the urge to beat the shit out of Thompson, Marc flushed and watched the drug that had enslaved his sister disappear in a swirl of milky white. "It's time you and I had a heart-to-heart, Donny."

He left the apartment after grilling Thompson at gunpoint for an hour—and after dumping a nickel bag of weed and a few grams of crack down the crapper. He knew it wouldn't put Thompson out of business, but it would slow him down.

Out on the streets, a cold wind blew in from the mountains, sucking the breath from Marc's lungs, calming some of his rage. Above, stars winked in a black velvet sky, dimmed by the lights of the city. A waxing quarter moon rode high, surrounded by a glowing halo of ice crystals. Farther to the west, Orion strode toward the mountains.

Megan was out there, somewhere.

And something told him her time was running out.

"COME ON, BABE. You know how it goes."

Panic turning her stomach, Char bent over the smelly janitor's sink, biting her cheeks to keep herself from screaming. Even if someone heard, no one would believe her. She was nothing but an inmate to most of them, nothing but a drug addict, a thief, a liar.

In the end, she'd only suffer more.

She heard him unzip his pants, heard the plastic condom wrapper tear, every muscle in her body clenching against the violation she knew was coming.

"You should thank me for wearing these, you know. Not every man would. At least I haven't knocked you up." He jerked down her pants and panties, kicked her feet apart, and nudged himself into her with a groan.

I hate you! I hate you! I hate you!

She screamed the words in her mind, repeating them each time he rammed himself into her, wishing to God he'd just hurry up and finish. She should have stayed in her cell instead of going to the stupid Narcotics Anonymous meeting. She should have stuck close to the NA leader. She should have found some way of getting back to the unit without walking past him.

Tears burned her eyes, the steel rim of the sink biting into her forearms, wooden mop handles only inches from her face, the reek of ammonia almost choking her.

He gave a deep groan, and it was over.

"You needed it as much as I did." He patted her bare butt, withdrew, tossed the condom into a nearby trash can. "Cover up."

She pulled up her underwear and pants, tears streaming down her cheeks.

He grasped her chin, forced her to look at him. "Oh, come on! It wasn't that bad. I didn't hurt you. You've got nothing better to do. Besides, I've got something for you."

He reached into his pocket, pulled out a little green balloon that was knotted to hold what looked like a white, powdery substance.

She stared at it, her heart pounding.

"Coke. Your favorite."

She shook her head, her blood tingling at the very mention of cocaine. "You're trying to get me in trouble."

"You just got me off. I figure I owe you one." He held out his open palm, the balloon sitting in the middle. "Besides, what's the worst that will happen to you if you're busted? A week in lockdown?"

But her heart was beating so hard she wasn't listening. There was nothing like the shimmering high of cocaine. It took away all her doubts and worries, made her fearless, turned the world into a place that was perfect and bright and beautiful. And even as she reminded herself she'd been clean for almost a year, she felt herself reaching for it.

"You'll have to swallow it," he said. "They're doing a shakedown this afternoon."

Her pulse drumming, she took it, popped it into her mouth, gagging as the foul-tasting rubber dragged against her throat and wrestled its way into her stomach.

He smiled. "Now you're one shit away from the best high of your life."

It was only after she was back in her cell that she knew

something was wrong. Euphoria surged like a tide of molten sugar through her veins.

"No!"

Realizing the balloon had broken, she fought to get up, tried to call for help, knowing she'd die if she didn't get to the infirmary right away. But this wasn't the heart-pounding, lightning rush of cocaine. It was too sweet, too pure, too seductive.

Heroin.

She struggled to rise, tried to shout for the guards, but found herself staring at the same patch of ceiling, silence coming from her mouth instead of screams.

Help me, someone please! I don't want to die!

Then her fear was gone, and there was only bliss—sickly, suffocating bliss.

CHAPTER 9

SOPHIE DRAGGED HERSELF out of bed and into work early Monday morning, hoping to do some digging on Hunt and Megan before the I-Team meeting. She planned to read through the old news articles about Hunt's arrest and trial, as well as the original police reports. She also wanted to file an open-records request with Denver Juvenile asking for all incident reports pertaining to sexual abuse during the period of Megan's detention. If she could piece all of that together, she'd have some idea whether the things Hunt had told her at the cabin were true.

Sparing a quick hello for Natalie and Kat, she booted up her computer and immediately checked CNN to see whether Hunt had been found.

You're being ridiculous, Alton. You checked before you left home twenty minutes ago.

Yes, but that was twenty minutes ago. The entire world could change in twenty minutes.

She clicked on the "Colorado Manhunt" link to find . . . nothing.

No updates. No new news. Nada.

She took a deep breath, her sense of relief at war with the growing fear that he might have frozen to death in the snow.

From across the room, Matt called out to her, "Hey, Alton, good to have you back."

She answered without really hearing him. "Hi, Matt."

She quickly sorted through a week's worth of e-mail. Most were old messages about Hunt's escape sent out by the DOC's Public Information Office to their general media Listserve. It felt strange to read about her ordeal written in the controlled language of the public relations trade, to see the most terrifying moments of her life reduced to the sterile term *incident*.

"Inmate takes reporter hostage, escapes Colorado State Penitentiary."

"Department of Corrections investigates recent incident."

"Inmate still at large."

But there were also e-mails, cards, and letters from concerned readers, community leaders, and colleagues, some touching, some sweet, some funny.

"I'm a retired U.S. Marine," wrote one man. "You've just broadened my understanding of the word *courage*."

"We learned about hypothermia in Cub Scouts," wrote a boy named Bobby, age nine. "Always wear a hat is what I learned. I have a extra hat if you need one."

"Just between you and me, they should have given that bastard the death penalty when they had the chance," wrote Christine, the mayor's executive assistant.

She sifted through her messages—including a very thoughtful message from Ken Harburg—and had just begun to write her open-records request for Denver Juvenile when Tom called them into the I-Team meeting.

"Welcome back, Alton." He looked down the length of the conference room table at her, his gaze passing over the yellowed bruise on her cheek before settling on her eyes. "We missed your contributions."

For Tom, it was tantamount to a group hug.

"Thanks." Sophie smiled, remembering the bouquet. "And thanks for the flowers, too. I especially liked the card."

Matt frowned. "I suppose this means I have to return the AP style guide I borrowed."

"You stole my style guide?" Sophie glared at him in pretend anger.

Tom pointed at Matt with his pencil. "Since you're so industrious, Harker, you go first."

Matt sat up straighter, smoothed his rumpled tie. "City Councilman Richard Pierce was busted last night when a bouncer caught him snorting coke in a downtown club. The arresting officer claims that Pierce tried to bribe him. I'm guessing fifteen inches."

"Well, his political career is over." Tom turned to Kat. "James, what's on your plate?"

"Representative of several Plains nations—Lakota, Cheyenne, Arapaho, and Kiowa—are staging a protest at the Department of Wildlife today over the missing eagle parts. They're demanding that DOW fire the program director. I should be able to do it in ten."

Tom turned to Joaquin. "Think you can get something for the front page out of that?"

Joaquin grinned. "Absolutely."

"Alton?"

Sophie glanced down at her notes. "I've got a couple of things. There's another rally at the Capitol to protest prison expansion. That should be no more than four to six. Also, an inmate was found dead in her cell of a heroin overdose. She was apparently acting as a mule for someone, and the balloon broke. I've got an autopsy report, so I'm guessing a solid ten inches."

Tom swiveled his chair, looked at Natalie. "Benoit?"

"I thought I'd do an update on the search for Marc Hunter." Natalie looked over at Sophie, her aqua eyes filled with concern. "I got a tip this morning that a correctional officer named Gil Cormack has admitted to calling you on Hunter's behalf to lure you down there. He also admits he placed Hunter in handcuffs instead of full restraints at Hunter's request, but he claims he had no idea Hunter was planning to take you hostage or to escape. Of course, DOC fired him. I thought I'd put together a reaction story, see what the talking heads have to say about that bit of information."

Tom nodded. "Let's get to work."

MARC WATCHED THE sleek silver Lexus SUV turn into the driveway and disappear into the spacious three-car garage. "It's about damned time."

He'd been waiting all morning. Where in the hell could

they have been early on a Monday? The tennis club? Couples' Botox? He waited five more minutes, then stepped out of the shadows where he'd been hiding and walked up the long sidewalk to the front door, catching his reflection in the sparkling clean glass of their windows.

Short hair. Ray-Bans. Black suit. Tie. Tan trench coat. He looked like a damned spook or some kind of missionary—which was perfect.

He rang the bell, waited.

A tall man with a white crew cut and a ruddy complexion opened the door. "Yes?"

"Mr. Rawlings?" Marc held out his hand.

Mr. Rawlings shook it. "Yes, sir. Can I help you?"

"I'm Detective Mike Chambers with the Denver Police Department." He held out a fake business card he'd ordered off the Internet. "I'm here to speak with you about your daughter, Megan Rawlings."

Rawlings took the card, glanced down at it, frowned. "Come in."

Soon Marc was seated on a beige-colored sofa in the sitting room, drinking tea from gold-trimmed china. The place looked like a Christian bookstore—various bibles and interpretations of the Bible on the bookshelves, a cross on one wall, a set of cheesy porcelain praying hands on another. Mr. and Mrs. Rawlings, it seemed, wore Jesus on their sleeves.

But there was no sign that they'd ever raised a daughter.

No family portraits. No school pictures. No snapshots.

"We've already shared all we know with investigators, Detective Chambers." Mrs. Rawlings, a slender, well-dressed woman, sat stiff-backed in an armchair, her manicured hands folded in her lap, her lips pressed into a frown. "I'm afraid we have nothing new to offer."

Marc's dislike for her was instant—and strong. He buried his contempt and gave her his most reassuring smile. "When a case gets old or goes cold, sometimes we reassign it. My job is to find what others might have missed. I realize you've already answered these questions, but I need to start at the beginning."

Mr. and Mrs. Rawlings glanced at one another, then Mr. Rawlings nodded.

"Go ahead, detective."

Marc ran through his questions one by one, taking notes on a pad of paper he'd picked up at the convenience store. Had they heard from Megan? Did they have any idea where she might have gone? Had she maintained contact with any friends from her school years? Did they have any family friends or relatives who might have taken her in? Were they aware of anyplace she'd liked to spend time as a teenager, anyplace she might think of as her own special place?

In each instance the answer was no.

No, they hadn't had any contact with Megan since they'd kicked her out on her eighteenth birthday. No, they had no idea where she might have gone. No, she'd had no close friends as far as they knew. No, she couldn't be staying with anyone in the family because everyone knew they'd renounced her. No, they couldn't think of a single place she might be.

With each answer, it became more apparent to Marc that Mr. and Mrs. Rawlings didn't give a damn about their adopted daughter. Megan had told Marc this herself during the few months she'd lived with him seven years ago, but he'd thought she was exaggerating. Now he could see she had downplayed the problem.

"You have to understand, Detective Chambers." Mrs. Rawlings leaned forward, lowered her voice. "Megan isn't really our daughter. We adopted her when she was four years old after Social Services took her away from her drug-addicted prostitute mother."

Marc felt blood rush to his brain, a blistering surge of rage. He fought to keep his expression—and his voice—impassive. "According to Megan's file, her mother was an alcoholic and a drug user, but not a prostitute."

Mrs. Rawlings gave a delicate and dismissive wave of her wrist. "She had two children by different fathers, and she was never married. We might not call it that today, but that's what it is when a woman is promiscuous."

"She wasn't a fit mother," Mr. Rawlings said with a decisive nod.

"We did our best to raise Megan. We took her away from poverty, gave her a home, offered her firm guidance, raised her in our faith, and she rejected all of it. I warned her many times that she was in danger of following her mother's path in sin, and I was right."

What about love, bitch? At least her real mother loved her.

Marc looked down to hide the anger he knew was in his eyes—and discovered he was gripping his pen so hard that his knuckles were white. He forced himself to relax, looked up again. "That must have been very disappointing."

Both Mr. and Mrs. Rawlings nodded.

"If we had adopted her earlier, things might have turned out differently," Mr. Rawlings said. "As it was, she never seemed to appreciate what we'd done for her. She ran away when she was fourteen and was arrested for shoplifting. She even managed to get into trouble in juvenile detention."

Marc pinned Mr. Rawlings with his gaze. "I heard she was raped."

From the uncomfortable looks on both their faces, they'd heard this, too.

Mrs. Rawlings cleared her throat, obviously embarrassed. "I'm not sure where you got your information, detective, but Megan was never raped. She and a few of the other delinquent girls used their bodies to win favors from a couple of the guards, then blamed the guards. That's what the investigators concluded."

Marc's pulse picked up another notch, a mix of outrage and interest. He hadn't known there'd been other victims—or an official investigation. "Do you have the report from that investigation?"

Mr. and Mrs. Rawlings exchanged a puzzled glance.

Marc realized his request must seem strange. He worked for the police department, after all. He was supposed to have all of this information at his fingertips. "I'm sure I could find it if I wanted to spend a day digging through the archives, but if you have a copy somewhere handy, it would save me both time and red tape. This isn't just about Megan, after all. It's about Emily, too—an innocent seven-month-old baby. Your granddaughter."

Mrs. Rawlings wrinkled her nose. "She's not our granddaughter! We didn't know a thing about her until that reporter contacted us and tried to interview us for her awful articles."

Mr. Rawlings seemed to consider the request. "I'm not sure what I did with that report. I might have kept it somewhere, or I might have tossed it out with the rest of her things."

Not only did they not care about Megan, they had purged her from their lives.

Marc stood, knowing it was time to leave. He no longer trusted himself to be anywhere near these two. "I appreciate your time, Mr. and Mrs. Rawlings. I'm sorry if my visit reopened old wounds today. I can show myself out."

But whatever Mrs. Rawlings lacked in warmth and motherly love she made up for in perfunctory manners. "Nonsense! We'll see you to the door."

Marc followed them, taking the time to suss out their security system—a simple open-circuit system with the control box mounted a few feet down the main hallway. Cheap and easy to neutralize should he feel the need to return. "Thanks again," he said when he reached the front door. "I'm sorry to have disturbed your morning."

"Another day and you'd have missed us," Mr. Rawlings opened the door for him. "I don't tolerate this cold weather very well. We're leaving for our house in Florida tomorrow morning and won't be back until mid-April."

This was interesting news—and it gave Marc a few ideas.

"Is there any chance that Megan might have gone there?"

"To Florida? Oh, no!" Mr. Rawlings said. "We bought that house after she left. I don't think she even knows about it."

"I'm relieved to hear that." He waited a beat. "I'd hate for you to run into her now that her brother is out."

Mr. and Mrs. Rawlings exchanged another glance.

"Her brother?" they said in near unison.

"He escaped from prison last week. Took some reporter

hostage. You probably heard about it on the news." Marc saw from the looks on their faces that they had. Then he lowered his voice like a cop about to share the inside scoop. "The guys working the case think he broke out to be with Megan, so the two of them have likcly hooked up somewhere. He's a convicted murderer—armed and dangerous. It's probably a good thing you're leaving town."

He stepped outside, took three steps down the sidewalk.

"What about our house?" Mrs. Rawlings called after him.

Marc stopped and turned to face them. "You should ask your neighbors and your housekeeper to report anything suspicious."

"Our neighbors are in Costa Rica, and we let our housekeeper go till spring." Mrs. Rawlings's voice had taken on a whiny tone.

Marc pretended to hesitate. "I suppose I could order extra patrols and look in on the place myself from time to time if that would give you some peace of mind."

"We'd appreciate that very much, detective," Mr. Rawlings said. "Thank you."

Marc smiled, already looking forward to his new home. "Don't mention it."

AN INMATE AT Denver County Jail was found dead of an apparent heroin overdose in her cell early Sunday morning. Charlotte Martin, 25, was found at 5:24 A.M. by a guard during morning count. No attempts were made to resuscitate Martin, who had cloarly been dead for several hours.

Sophie typed the words, then glanced at the clock. A half hour till deadline. She was never this far behind. Then again, she'd spent half the day rescarching Hunt's background, studying old news articles about his arrest and trial until she had the details memorized.

He'd spent six years in the army, becoming a decorated Special Operations sniper and serving eighteen months in Afghanistan, where he'd set a record both for confirmed kills and long-distance marksmanship. Then he'd returned to Colorado and taken a post with the DEA, working narcotics. He'd owned a home, a couple of cars, including the old '55 Chevy, and, according to his superiors, seemed the model officer.

But on the afternoon of August 12, 2001, Hunt had called 911 to report that he'd just shot and killed a friend. Police had rushed to his house in Westminster to find him sitting in his living room near the body, his unloaded weapon lying on the coffee table. He'd told the cops that he and Cross had argued and that he hadn't realized what he was doing until it was too late. News stories had discussed Hunt's flawless service record and had speculated that the stress of serving in Afghanistan had played some role in whatever had caused him to snap. The district attorney had hinted that he was inclined toward leniency—and a possible plea bargain.

Then police had found the drugs.

Drugs.

Heroin overdose. Denver County Jail. Deadline.

Crud!

Sophie forced her mind off Marc and back onto the article she was supposed to be writing.

Toxicology tests showed high levels of morphine . . .

She glanced quickly through her notes.

. . . and the anesthetic fentanyl in Martin's blood, as well as trace amounts of codeine in her bladder. Together with fragments of rubber found in Martin's stomach during the autopsy, the tests support the coroner's conclusion that Martin died quickly of an overdose after swallowing a balloon of fentanyl-laced heroin. Fentanyl is a fast-acting drug that when mixed with heroin offers an unparalleled but often deadly high. The combination is called fefe *on the streets and has earned nicknames like* flatliner, executioner, *and* drop dead.

A week after the shooting, police had found two bricks of cocaine in Marc's crawl space and a few ounces in his car. Marc had vehemently denied the drugs were his, claiming it must have been a setup, but they'd charged him with possession of a schedule I controlled substance with intent to sell. Then phone records had proved that Marc had called Cross the morning before the shooting, and Cross's widow had told investigators that he'd asked her husband to come over that afternoon. And abruptly, the tone of the news coverage had changed. Articles now depicted him as a corrupt agent who'd killed a friend to cover up his double-dealing. The DA had quit talking leniency and upped the charge to first-degree murder.

Sophie's phone beeped, jerking her back to the moment.

"How's that second story coming?" Syd sounded stressed, but then Syd was always stressed out.

"I'm getting there." Sophie flipped through her notes and popped in a quote from the DOC flack.

We work hard to keep contraband out of prison," said Allyson Harris, DOC spokeswoman. "Sometimes inmates on work release smuggle it in. Other times staff are to blame. Sometimes they take to selling drugs or other contraband during a financial or personal crisis."

As a DEA agent, Marc must have seen the human toll that hard drugs inflicted on society. He'd certainly seen what addiction had done to Megan. But somehow cocaine had found its way into his house and car. Tests proved it had been stolen from the evidence room. In the end, it had damned him because it created a clear and powerful motive for murder.

But what could have made Hunt betray his badge to sell drugs when drugs had destroyed his sister's life? Why would he admit to killing a man but steadfastly deny dealing coke unless it was the truth? And why hadn't he told the cops that Cross had raped Megan when surely that would have shaved decades off his prison sentence?

Not once had Hunt mentioned his sister—not during his trial when the prosecutor had tried to insinuate that Hunt and Cross had argued about the cocaine, not even prior to his sentencing when the judge had asked him for any reason to show leniency.

It made no sense.

In the end, he'd barely escaped lethal injection.

"It is the hope of this court, Mr. Hunter," the judge had said at Hunt's sentencing, "that you will die behind bars."

If he was caught, that's exactly what would happen. Unless

the police shot him first. Or he'd already frozen to death in the mountains.

Where are you, Hunt?

Sophie's phone beeped again and her gaze flew to the clock. Ten minutes.

"I'll have it to you in five, Syd."

Her blood spiked with deadline adrenaline, she pounded out the rest of the article, finishing with a minute to spare. She felt guilty that she'd put so little effort into the piece. A woman had died, after all.

You're obsessed with him, Alton. Admit it.

Okay. So she was obsessed with Marc Hunter.

Happy now?

What did she think she stood to gain by digging into Hunt's case? Could anything change the fact that he was a convicted murderer or that he'd held a gun to her head? Why did getting to the truth matter so much to her?

You're a journalist. Getting to the truth is your job.

And the truth was that some part of her—some really stupid teenage part of her—still cared about him.

"OH, GOD! OH, God!"

"Yeah, fuck me, baby!"

Thunk. Thunk. Thunk.

The hooker next door—Angie was her name—was giving some happy guy a little bang for his buck, the bed knocking against the wall, the throaty groans more than a little distracting. It would have been hard to ignore even if Marc hadn't spent the past six years in a cage with only his right hand for company. As it was, just the *idea* of sex gave him a hard-on. He didn't need Sex Surround Sound.

Trying to tune out the noise, Marc stared at the lightbulb on his ceiling, raw sexual frustration mixing with leftover rage from his visit with the Rawlingses. It had been hard enough to listen to their sanctimonious bullshit about his mother, the same sort of crap he'd heard all his life, but seeing their utter indifference to Megan and Emily had pushed him dangerously close to the edge. How could they have taken Megan into their home and yet feel nothing for her? How could they blame her for what Cross had done to her? How did they sleep at night knowing that the girl they'd raised from the innocent age of four was out on the streets with her baby?

Despites his mother's faults—and she'd had more than her share—he'd always known that she loved her children, even if she'd been too much of a mess to take care of them.

Your sister's gone to a better home. She's with people who will raise her right.

For so many years, Marc had fought off the guilt and grief of losing his little sister by clinging to the hope that his mother's words were true. While he'd drifted from one foster home to the next, he'd pictured Megan growing up with all the things a girl should have—doting parents to protect her from boys, pretty dresses, lots of friends. He'd assured himself that she was lucky because she didn't have to live with the shame of having a mother in prison. When he'd been in Afghanistan and their mother had fallen ill with advanced hepatitis C and liver cancer, he'd actually been *grateful* that Megan had been spared the ordeal of watching her die. He'd had no idea that Megan's life had been so miserable and lonely.

If he had known, if he'd had any idea . . .

Now another day had come and gone, and he was no closer to finding his sister than he'd been yesterday. Still, he supposed the day hadn't been a total waste. He now knew that Megan hadn't been Cross's only victim and that there *had* been an official inquiry and a report.

But how could he get his hands on that report?

He'd wasted a few hours tonight trying once again to crack the DOC database, hours that would have been better spent beating his head against the wall. Then he'd wasted another hour going through the online DOC staff directory, looking for anyone with past ties to the Denver Juvenile Detention Center. But there were hundreds of employees at dozens of facilities, and he couldn't be certain the information on the website was complete—or that the man he was looking for still worked for DOC.

Thunk. Thunk. Thunk.

"Oh, yeah! Oh, baby!"

His cock painfully erect, Marc was tempted to go with the flow and kill to another Sophie fantasy. But he was too pissed off for that. Besides, coming in his own fist had become noticeably less satisfying since kissing her in that sleeping bag, and he had other things to do.

It came down to this: he had to find Megan, and he had to find her now.

Easier said than done, buddy.

He needed that report. He needed someone whose credentials would force the DOC to open its file drawers. He needed someone who cared about Megan enough to spend hours looking through old records.

He needed Sophie.

But this wasn't something he could force Sophie to do. There was too much at stake for her if she were caught. If she agreed to help him, it would have to be of her own free will.

Thunk. Thunk. Thunk.

"God, yes!"

"Oh, for Christ's sake!" Sick of listening to the fuck fest, Marc rose from the bed, his body so tight he thought it might snap. He slipped into his boots, pulled on his jacket, and tucked one of the Glocks into his waistband. Then he stepped outside, locked the door behind him, and headed down the street, sucking cold night air into his lungs.

Would Sophie help him? Or would she call the cops?

He was about to find out.

CHAPTER 10

MARC MADE HIS way quickly through the cold streets of the city to Sophie's address on Gaylord Street in Cheesman Park. He'd expected to find her living in a stylish condo. Instead, she lived on the second floor of a small two-story apartment building that looked like it belonged on the bad side of town. The concrete stairs were uneven. The asphalt parking lot was pitted with potholes. The paint was chipped and curling. As he scoped out the place, he found himself wondering whether the address on her driver's license was out of date or whether reporters earned a lot less than he'd imagined. Surely, she could afford better than this.

He surveyed the front of the building—four apartments across the bottom and four on top—then made his way around to the back. Each of the apartments had either a little patio or a balcony, accessed with sliding glass doors. There were no security cameras, no floodlights, no gates or guards. Breaking in would be almost too easy.

Unless Sophie had a live-in lover who owned a gun.

Wouldn't it be a riot if some irate boyfriend lit you up, Hunter?

Yes, it would—a laugh a minute.

It had dawned on him on the way over that no rings on her fingers didn't necessarily mean no man in her life. For all he knew she was in the middle of a serious relationship with some guy who seriously wanted to kick his ass. It was only after he'd gotten good and pissed off, certain the bastard wasn't good enough for her, that he'd realized he was being ridiculous. He didn't even know for certain that she had a boyfriend.

If any man isn't good enough for her, it's you, dumbass.

Sophie had a right to do whatever she wanted with her life. If she had a live-in boyfriend, Marc wouldn't risk a confrontation. He'd just have to find some other way of reaching her—in the grocery store or at the gas pump.

He walked over to the patio beneath her balcony, grabbed a plastic lawn chair from her downstairs neighbors and shook off the snow. He positioned it carefully and stepped onto it. Then he reached up, caught hold of the iron bars, and pulled himself up. Five seconds later he was climbing over the railing.

He brushed the snow from his hands, flexed his chilled fingers, then stepped quietly up to the sliding glass door. Soft blue light flickered through a crack in the curtains, telling him she was there, on the other side of the glass, watching television. He peeked through, saw the top of her head resting on the arm of the couch, her hair spilling over the side.

She appeared to be asleep—and alone.

Quickly, carefully, he grasped the door and worked it out of its track, slowed only slightly by the wooden dowel she'd used to block burglars. He stepped inside and settled the door cleanly back into place, glancing over his shoulder at Sophie to see whether he'd woken her. On the television behind him, a man with an English accent was talking about medieval knights and chivalry.

Marc drew his Glock and moved silently from room to room, clearing the apartment, making absolutely certain she was alone. He couldn't help but notice the single toothbrush by her sink or the lack of man stuff in the shower or the pink and white quilt on her bed. Nor could he stop himself from feeling damn pleased by these discoveries.

Sophie lived alone.

Taking a few seconds to check that the front door was locked, he tucked the Glock into the waistband of his jeans and walked back to the living room.

She was still asleep, her face turned toward the television, the side of her throat exposed, her red gold hair fanned around her head like a halo. Her lashes lay dark against her cheeks, her lips slightly parted. Her bathrobe had come open to show the creamy swell of one breast, her chest rising and falling with each slow breath. A thick blanket hugged the curve of her hips and the slender length of her legs, her frosty lavender toenails peeking out the bottom.

Marc forgot to breathe, some emotion he didn't care to name stirring in his chest. She was the sweetest sight he'd ever seen—beautiful, feminine, innocently erotic. She slept so peacefully, so deeply, completely unaware that a man with a gun had just broken into her apartment and now stood beside her.

And suddenly Marc felt like an invader, a trespasser who'd violated something sacred. He didn't belong here. He shouldn't have come. If he left now, she would sleep through the night undisturbed, never knowing he'd been here.

But then he'd be no closer to finding Megan and little Emily.

He walked over to the sofa and knelt down beside her, drinking in the sight of her, wanting her, wanting to protect her. The bruise on her cheek was now a faint yellow stain, the deeper bruises on her wrists still purple in places—a reminder of what she'd gone through the last time he'd intruded into her life.

She stirred in her sleep, turned toward him, and gave a little sigh, her motions exposing a pink crescent of nipple, which puckered and grew tight even as he watched.

Marc's brain told him that she was just cold from the night air he'd let in, but his body read the signal as a personal invitation. Ignoring his growing erection, he ran his knuckles over her cheek, hoping to wake her without scaring her. "Sophie?"

Sophie was having the most delicious dream. Hunt was kissing her, and she was kissing him back. The kiss was perfect, romantic and sweet, the warmth of it melting her fears and worries away, stirring her sexual need. It felt so right being with him like this, and she wondered how she could have lost touch with him. She'd heard he'd been in prison, but that couldn't be true because he was here with her.

God, she loved the way he kissed, the way he—

"Wake up, sprite."

Sophie opened her eyes to find herself looking straight at Hunt—not some figment of her imagination, but the real, live man.

His face was inches from hers, his green eyes dark, his fingers pressed lightly against her lips. "Easy, Sophie. I'm not going hurt you. I just came to talk."

Confused, her dream still strong in her mind, she reached up, touched the stubble-rough skin of his jaw. "Hunt?"

"Yeah."

Confusion turned to a warm rush of relief. "You're alive!"

He gave a lopsided grin. "For the moment."

And then it hit her.

Hunt was a fugitive, and *he was really here*.

In her apartment.

In the middle of the night.

A jolt of alarm brought her fully awake, the truth of her situation crashing in. She sat up and stared at him, stunned.

It was then she noticed he'd cut his hair and shaved off his beard. Dressed in a fleece-lined denim jacket, a black turtleneck, and a pair of faded jeans, he looked more like the Hunt she remembered from high school than the Marc Hunter who'd held her at gunpoint. Except that he was quite obviously no longer a teenager, but a full-grown man—potent, hard-edged, and dangerous.

An image of him striding naked around the cabin invaded her mind, making it impossible for her *not* to think about the well-developed body beneath the clothes—smooth skin marred by scars, the shifting muscles of his butt, the hard planes of his chest, the trail of dark hair that bisected his abdomen, the heavy weight of his penis and testicles.

She swallowed, pulled her robe closer around her. "H-how did you find me? How did you get in here?"

He sat back on the coffee table. "I got your address from your driver's license when we were at the cabin. As for how I got in—let's just say that wooden dowel will only protect you from burglars if you use it to hit them."

The sliding glass door.

She jumped to her feet, hurried around him to the balcony

door, and found it unlocked, the dowel leaning up against the glass. Her face burned, the pent-up anger, grief, and worry of the past ten days breaking loose inside her. She turned on him, found him standing right behind her. "You son of a bitch! First you hold a gun to my head and take me hostage, and now you break into my home!"

"Would you have let me in if I'd knocked?"

"Of course not! You shouldn't be here!"

"You seemed happy enough to see me a minute ago."

Her palm stung as it struck his cheek, the sound of the blow sharp and startling. "I thought I was still dreaming!"

His eyes glittered, hard as jade, a muscle clenching in his jaw, a red palm print visible on his cheek. When he spoke, his voice held a low note of warning. "Sophie."

But Sophie was nowhere close to finished. Propelled by anger, she launched into him, pummeling the hard wall of his chest with her fists. "You want to hit me back? I wish you would, because then I could *hate* you! Besides, you can't do anything worse to me than you've already done! You ruined my most precious memory by growing up to become a loser!"

He caught her wrists, jerked her against him, a dark scowl on his face. "That's enough!"

For a moment, she glared up at him, breathless and trembling, shaken by the force of her own outburst. Had she just hit him?

His eyes narrowed, his lips curving in a slow smile. "So I'm your best memory? And you were dreaming about me?"

She realized what she'd admitted, felt her face flame. "I-I . . ."

And then he kissed her—or she kissed him. She couldn't tell. One moment they were standing there, looking at each other, the next she was crushed against him, her fingers clenched in his hair, one of his hands fisted at her nape, the two of them locked in a heated kiss. But this was nothing like the sweet kiss in her dream.

It was raw, feral, almost violent.

He nipped her lower lip, licked it, thrust his tongue deep into her mouth. She bit down, then sucked. He groaned, pulled her harder against him, melding her body to his, reclaiming control, his tongue doing things to the inside of her mouth that she felt all the way to her womb. She stood on tiptoe, arched into him, answering his intensity with the force of her own need.

Lost in him, Sophie forgot that he was a wanted man, that he'd held her hostage, that he'd just broken into her home, her awareness overcome by sensation—the heat and spice of his skin, the steel-hard feel of his body, the pounding of her own heart. There were probably a thousand reasons why she shouldn't be doing this, but right now she couldn't think of a single one. Then his hand slipped inside her robe to cup her breast, his fingers catching her nipple—and she couldn't think at all.

"Oh, yes!" Her knees turned to jelly, the floor tilting beneath her feet.

They stumbled backward, still kissing, and sank to the floor.

Somehow Hunt caught their fall, lowering her to the carpet, his mouth leaving hers only to find her throat. He trailed kisses down the sensitive skin beneath her ear, biting, nipping, licking. Then he shoved the silk of her robe aside, lowered his mouth to one aching nipple, and, with a hungry groan, drew it into the blazing heat of his mouth.

Sophie gasped, each tug of his lips making her belly draw tight, flooding her with arousal. She clenched her fingers in his hair, pressed his head closer, arching her back to feed him more of her. "Please, Hunt!"

Hungrily, he took what she offered, lavishing attention first on one receptive peak, then the other, flicking her with the roughness of his tongue, pulling on her with his lips, grazing her with his sharp teeth. "Jesus, Sophie, you taste good!"

He blew a cool gust of breath across her wet, distended nipples, making the nubs draw so tight they hurt.

"Oh, God!" she whimpered, impatient and aching for him, her hands feeling for his zipper, one of her legs instinctively wrapping around his waist to draw him—

Her calf pressed against something hard and cold.

A gun.

He was a convict. A fugitive. A killer.

Marc felt the pressure of the Glock against his back, felt Sophie stiffen beneath him. Some part of his brain that could still think realized this wasn't good. "Sophie, I—"

"No!" She twisted, tried to push him away. "Get off me!"

"Christ!" Marc raised himself off her and stood, testosterone pounding through his veins, his cock so hard he was surprised it didn't split his pants. He sucked air into his lungs. "Look, Sophie. I didn't mean to frighten you."

"You just broke in to say hello?" She ignored the hand he offered, stumbled to her feet and backed away from him, her arms crossed protectively across her chest. Even from six feet away he could see she was trembling.

"I came to ask for your help."

She glared at him, a look of outraged disbelief on her face. "My *help*?"

How did you expect her to react, dickhead?

"Sophie, I—"

"You held a *gun* to my head and let me believe you were going to kill me! Now you break into my home, take advantage of me, and ask me to *help* you?"

He didn't know whether to laugh or shout. "Take advantage of you? Correct me if I'm wrong, but you said 'yes.' Actually, I think you said, '*Oh*, yes,' and, 'Please, Hunt,' and then it was just, 'Oh, God,' and a few 'ooohs' and 'aaahs.'"

She glared at him, bright spots of pink in her cheeks, her coppery hair a tangled mass. She looked furious. Embarrassed. Sexy as hell. "I . . . I was confused."

But Marc didn't have the patience for this game. "Confused my ass! Was it confusion that had you grabbing for my fly? You might not want to admit it, but you still have feelings for me. You're sexually attracted to me."

Her expression went cold, a hint of sadness in her eyes. "Whatever I feel it's for the boy you were in high school, not the man you are now."

Damn! Well, he'd had that coming, hadn't he? Still, her words hit him like a second smack in the face. Something splintered in his chest, a sensation very much like emptiness settling behind his breastbone. It took him a moment to find his voice. "I'm not asking for me. I'm asking for Megan and Emily."

"That's not fair!"

"I don't give a *damn* what's fair! I'm trying to save my sister's life."

For a moment she watched him, the look in her eyes telling him to go to hell. But when she spoke, her tone was softer. "So you haven't found them?"

He shook his head. "Not a trace."

She glanced away, a worried look on her face, and he knew she was thinking it through, weighing the reality of the situation against her concern for Megan and Emily. A part of him wanted to use persuasion, to apply pressure by reminding her how helpless little Emily was, how vulnerable Megan was, to do all he could to influence her. But he knew the price she'd pay if she were caught, and so he kept his mouth shut.

This had to be her decision.

She met his gaze, and he could see she was still pissed off. "Helping you could constitute a felony, and I know enough about prison to know I never want to end up there."

"Smart woman." He bit back the other things he wanted to say, a tension rising in his body that had nothing to do with his pent-up lust or her outright rejection. She was his best, surest, fastest way of getting into DOC records and finding the son of a bitch who was after Megan. If she turned him down . . .

"I'll listen to what you have to say, but you're going to have to answer my questions, too. And no promises that I'll do anything. Got it?"

He released the breath he hadn't realized he was holding. "Got it."

"Just let me get dressed." She started toward her bedroom, then turned to look back at him, her anger still palpable. "And just to be clear—what happened a few minutes ago will *never* happen again. I understand you must be eager to get your hands on anything female after six years of having only men to play with, but—"

Before she could say another word, he had hold of her jaw, his face a hair's breadth from hers, rage pounding inside his skull. "Is that what you think? You think I spent the past six years fucking men?"

"I-I . . ." Her eyes flew wide.

"The truth is I spent the past six years protecting my own ass, and when I wasn't looking over my shoulder, I was thinking about *you*!"

Her face was frozen in an expression of shock.

Stunned by his own reaction, he released her and stepped back. "Get dressed."

She all but ran.

MARC PACED SOPHIE'S living room, furious with himself. He'd gone too far, given away too much. Worse, he'd acted like an asshole. She'd made a smart-ass comment because she was pissed off—understandable, given all that he'd done. Instead of letting it pass, he'd come unglued, grabbing her, dumping his guts, shouting in her face.

Whatever I feel it's for the boy you were in high school, not the man you are now.

Well, there was a good reason for that, wasn't there?

She'll help you now for sure. Good thinking, dumbshit.

Once again, he hadn't been thinking at all.

Christ!

He drew a deep breath, tried to slow his heartbeat, his body almost vibrating with the aftershock of his own anger. Her words had hit him where it hurt, unleashing something inside him that had taken him completely by surprise. But it wasn't her fault. She had no way of knowing what those six years had been like—six years spent watching his back, wondering when the next attack would come, knowing that the guards would watch and laugh and do nothing.

How many times had they tried? Twenty-some-odd? He hadn't counted. He'd fought them off every time, sent more than a few of them to the infirmary, ended up in the infirmary himself. Over the years, they'd gotten bolder, more aggressive, more violent, and he'd known it was only a matter of time before they got the best of him and turned him inside out.

Far from using another man as his piece of ass, he'd fought hard not to become one.

Why you fightin', Hunter? Afraid it'll hurt? Afraid you'll like it?

Fists and feet. The flash of a shank. Searing pain. The guards' laughter. Blood and water mingling, disappearing down the drain.

Something twisted in Marc's gut, left him feeling short of breath, shaky, nauseated. He walked to the window, cracked it open, sucked in cold air, fighting to clear his mind.

He was out of that place. He was out. He was *free*.

But when the cops caught him . . . Christ, if they caught him . . .

Jesus!

He'd have to face that again.

But this time he'd be ass out, his life worth less than a pack of smokes. The guards would want him to pay for escaping and making them look like fools. They'd want revenge for what he'd done to Kramer. Hell, Kramer would be all over him. Not right away, of course. They'd throw him in solitary for a few months of meditation. Then, after he was out, they'd set him up, put a hit on him, and give him a one-way pass to the morgue.

SHAKEN, SOPHIE SAT on her bed, still in her robe, her gaze fixed on her locked bedroom door. All she had to do was grab her cell phone from its charger and dial 911. The police would arrive in a few minutes, guns drawn, and take Marc away. As a law-abiding citizen, it was her *duty* to turn him in. So why couldn't she bring herself to do it?

Megan and Emily.

If she turned Marc over to the police, there was no chance that he'd ever find his sister, and Megan would be on her own, left to face anyone who might be after her without her brother's help. And with a baby to care for, no money, and no place to live . . .

But even as her mind clutched at that excuse, Sophie knew it was bull. The last thing Megan needed was to be on the run with another escaped convict, especially if she was in danger. She'd be better off back in prison, where she wouldn't have to worry about food or shelter or safety, where she could get help with her addiction, where she could try once again to rebuild her life. As for Emily—there was no doubt she'd be safer in the arms of her Mennonite foster parents than on the streets, cold and hungry.

And still Sophie couldn't bring herself to reach for her phone.

Truth was she didn't want to call the cops. She didn't want to stop Hunt from finding his sister. She didn't want to cause a confrontation that might end in his killing someone or being killed himself, especially if there was any chance that Julian would be involved. She didn't want to be the one responsible for sending Hunt back to prison.

You think I spent the past six years fucking men? The truth is I spent the past six years protecting my own ass!

She'd never seen anyone get that angry that fast. Except that it hadn't been anger she'd seen in his eyes. It had been . . . desolation, anguish, torment.

Sophie wasn't naïve. She'd been covering prisons for four years. She knew what happened inside those walls. Most of the time it was consensual—two inmates turning to one another for sexual release and perhaps even comfort. But there were men—and women—who thrived on hurting other people. They ganged up on other inmates to beat, maim, rape.

She had known when she'd seen his scars that he'd been in at least a few prison fights. Officer Green had told her as much the day she'd gone to interview him. As a former DEA agent, Marc would certainly have been a target for violence, especially at the hand of inmates he'd helped put behind bars. But she hadn't imagined that anyone would try to *rape* him.

Had they succeeded? Marc was big and physically powerful,

but he wasn't invulnerable. If he'd been outnumbered, injured, or taken by surprise . . .

She couldn't stand to think about it.

She got to her feet, let her bathrobe slide to the floor, caught her reflection in the mirror that hung on her closet door. Her lips were still swollen from his kisses, the skin of her chest flushed pink, her hair a tangled mess. She looked like a woman who'd just had great sex—except for the worry in her eyes.

She raised her fingers to her lips, felt the lingering heat of his kiss. What kind of power did he hold over her body and emotions to make her respond the way she had? She'd almost had sex with him, for God's sake!

When I wasn't looking over my shoulder, I was thinking about you!

She hadn't spent *every* day of the past twelve years thinking of him—just a lot of them. But she *had* measured every man she'd dated against him and found them lacking. And every so often, she'd dreamed about him.

The two of them were caught up in memories. That had to explain it. That night twelve years ago had been special for both of them, and their reaction to each other was nothing more than a messy collision of past and present. It was that simple.

It wasn't simple at all.

That's why you're hiding in your bedroom, Alton. You're afraid of him.

Yes, she was afraid of him—but not because she thought he might hurt her. Even his outburst a few minutes ago hadn't truly frightened her. It had taken her by surprise, but she hadn't thought for a moment that he would actually harm her.

No, she was afraid of him because of how he made her feel.

Angry with herself, she jerked open her closet door and yanked out a pair of jeans and an old navy blue sweatshirt. She dressed quickly, then brushed her hair and braided it.

She was done hiding. She was done acting like some kind of passive victim. She was done letting him call the shots. As of this moment, she was in control of her life again, not Marc Hunter. She would ask her questions, listen to whatever he had to say, and then . . .

And then she would have to make a decision.

CHAPTER 11

SOPHIE SAT ACROSS from Marc at her kitchen table, doing her best to act like drinking coffee in the middle of the night with an armed murderer, who also happened to be killer-sexy and a former lover, was nothing new. Telling herself this was just another interview—deep background, off the record—she took notes while Marc told her what he'd done so far in his quest to find Megan and Emily.

He seemed to dominate the small room, his shoulders broader than the back of the chair, his long legs filling the space beneath the table, his height obvious even when he was sitting. His face was emotionless, the look in his eyes inscrutable, both contradicted by the tension that rolled off him in thick, dark waves. Although he was sitting a good four feet away from her, she could still smell him—that mix of man and spice that seemed to emanate from his skin. Or maybe his scent had rubbed off on her.

"I questioned her old friends, checked the women's shelters and soup kitchens, cased the shooting galleries off East Colfax, even tracked down the pusher who got her pregnant, but no one—"

"You know who Emily's father is? There's no name on the birth certificate. I thought even Megan wasn't sure."

"Of course Megan knows. She wasn't that strung out. She probably just didn't feel like sharing that information with your readers. The guy is a dealer, an addict." He pinned her with his gaze. "A loser."

She ignored his attempt to throw her own words in her face. "What's his name?"

He shook his head. "Oh, no. If she'd wanted you to know, she'd have told you. Besides, you'll probably try to track him down, and I don't want you near him. He's dangerous. Even if you did find him, he's not going to tell you anything he didn't tell me. My methods of interrogation are more . . . persuasive than anything you can dish out."

Sophie glanced up, almost afraid to know more. "You didn't hurt him."

"Not as much as I wanted to."

"You're awfully comfortable with violence, aren't you?"

"You'd be surprised what a man can get used to." He spoke the words casually, but there was nothing casual about them.

The truth is I spent the past six years protecting my own ass!

Sophie took a nervous sip of coffee, set her cup down, glanced at the clock.

Five minutes to midnight.

"The bottom line is that I'm out of leads and out of time. If I can't find her, I need to find out who's after her—and that's where I need your help."

She cleared her throat, spoke slowly, articulating each syllable. "Anything I do to help Megan will be done legally."

"I wouldn't ask you to break the law, Sophie."

"Your being here is asking me to break the law."

"I broke in. You're blameless."

"I should have called the police—"

"Why didn't you?" His gaze seemed to pierce her.

Realizing she'd once again revealed too much, she ignored his question. "What exactly do you want me to do?"

"DOC did an internal investigation at Denver Juvenile after Megan reported Cross. It turns out that she wasn't the only girl he and his buddy brutalized. I need that report. I need to know the identity of Cross's accomplice, as well as the names of the other victims. It's possible that she's hiding with one of them."

Sophie didn't tell him that she'd already requested documentation on all such reports. She didn't want him to get the wrong idea. The fact that she was already investigating his claims didn't mean that she would share information with him.

She stood, walked to the counter, and emptied the dregs of her French press into her cup. "DOC will redact the girls' names because they were juveniles at the time. At best you're going to get the name of this alleged accomplice. What are you going to do with that information once you have it?"

"I'll track him down and make damned good and sure he doesn't pose a threat to my sister or any other woman."

That's exactly what worried her. "Will you kill him?"

He answered without hesitation. "If that's the only way to protect Megan, yes."

She walked back to her chair and sat. "In case you've forgotten, it's against the law to end someone's life because you think he raped your sister."

"And if I *know* he raped my sister?"

"Rape isn't a capital offense. Besides, that's what judges and juries are—"

He leaned forward, his face inches from hers. "I know all about judges and juries. Don't preach to me about trusting the system. If the system worked, my sister wouldn't be out there on the streets with her baby running for her life!"

Sophie held his gaze, refusing to be intimidated. "I won't give you information that will enable you to commit murder."

He sat back, rolled his eyes, as if she were being ridiculous. "How do you think I should handle it? Have a beer with him and ask him to leave my sister alone?"

"Let me expose him in the paper. If this accomplice really exists and he truly did what you say he did, Megan and the other alleged witnesses can help me bring him to justice. I'm not sure what the statute of limitations is on sexual assault on a minor, but I—"

"In case you've forgotten, Megan is missing, and even if we managed to find her, she couldn't handle that."

"Megan is stronger than you realize, and she trusts me."

"She didn't trust you enough to tell you she'd been raped at Denver Juvenile or to tell you who Emily's father was, did she? Besides, she's more fragile than you know." He reached over, covered her hand with his, stroked the back of her wrist with his thumb. "Even if she were tough as nails, I wouldn't want you to get caught up in this. I just need you to go under the radar and get me that report."

Sophie jerked her hand away, her skin tingling where he touched her. "I've been caught up in this since you held that gun to my head! Do you think I'd track down the report for you and just hand it over—no news coverage?"

She could see from the look on his face that that's exactly what he'd been thinking.

Then his frustrated frown curved into a smile. "Does that mean you're going to help?"

"Not so fast, Mr. Pistol Pants." She flipped to a blank page in her reporter's notebook. "I told you that you'd have to answer my questions, too. Remember? And no lies."

"Well, okay, then." He leaned back, crossed his arms over his chest, and grinned. "But when you say 'Pistol Pants' were you referring to my firearm—or my gun?"

MARC WAS IMPRESSED. For forty-five minutes Sophie had grilled him about the shooting with the relentlessness of a DA. How long had he known Cross? Why had he called Cross that morning? Was it normal for him to wear his sidearm when off duty and at home? Had he ever used his position to acquire and sell drugs? Who would want to plant drugs on him and why?

He'd read her articles while in prison, following her career from a distance, and he'd known she was good. Even so, he couldn't help but be amazed. If she ever got sick of journalism—not likely—she'd make one hell of a detective. He answered her questions carefully, more than a little distracted by the miracle of just being near her.

He'd known Cross for a little more than a year—since his first day on the job with DEA. He'd called Cross that morning and asked him to return a set of socket wrenches he'd borrowed. Yes, it was standard for him to keep his firearm loaded and on his person even when off duty; he had a permit for concealed carry. Hell, no, he'd never bought or sold drugs. *Ever.* The coke had been planted on him because some asshole wanted to avenge Cross by discrediting him, creating a motive for murder, and making sure he went down for good.

She wrote down his answers, then pored over her notes, tapping her pen against the fullest part of her lower lip—the part of her lip that he'd nibbled just a few hours ago. "When did you find out that Cross had raped Megan?"

And all at once Marc saw the trap she'd laid at his feet. She'd asked him the other questions before asking him this one, giving him all the rope he needed to hang himself.

Hadn't he known she was good?

"We're still off the record, right?"

She nodded. "Yes."

"I'm trusting you with Megan's life, Sophie."

She seemed to bristle. "I keep secrets all the time. It's part of being a journalist."

"Okay, then." He drew a deep breath, steeling himself. He'd never told anyone what he was about to tell her, not even his attorney. "I didn't know until Cross was standing in my living room. Megan had come over for supper. She and I had been reunited for about six months, and she'd been clean for about sixteen weeks—her first attempt to break free of her addiction. Cross stopped by to drop off the socket wrenches. Megan saw him from the kitchen and collapsed in hysterics."

No! No! Make him go away! Please, don't let them hurt me!

Sophie watched him through eyes soft with concern. "What did she tell you?"

"She told me that Cross had been a guard at Denver Juvenile, had raped her almost daily during the time she spent there and had gotten away with it. But it didn't come out in one coherent piece. I had to put it together bit by bit with Cross standing right there."

"What makes you think Cross had an accomplice?"

Please, don't let them hurt me! Make him go!

Marc rubbed his face with his hands, the wrenching sound of Megan's sobs echoing in his mind, making his gut churn.

"Several times, she said 'them.' Not 'him,' but 'them.' God, if you'd have seen her—she was so broken up. Jesus!"

Marc had never felt more helpless than he had that afternoon. Once again, he'd let Megan down—and this time it had destroyed both of their lives.

For a moment, Sophie said nothing, leaving him to rot in memories he wished to God weren't his. Then she set her pen down and looked at him through eyes that held . . .

Jesus—was that *pity*?

"So you and Cross got into an argument, and you pulled your gun and shot him in a blind rage, just like you told the police?"

Marc squeezed his eyes shut, gritted his teeth, unable to stop the scene from replaying itself in his mind.

Come on, Hunter! I had no idea she was your sister. Hell, I didn't even know you! Besides, you know how chick inmates are—bored and horny, dreaming of dick. Every time you walk by their cells, you know they're hoping you'll give it to them.

Bam! Bam! Bam!

Marc drew a steadying breath, opened his eyes, found Sophie watching him. "He admitted it, Sophie. He admitted that he'd raped her—and he laughed about it."

She swallowed, and he could see she was upset. "I'm so sorry."

"I'm not sorry he's dead, but if I had *planned* to kill him, would I have shot him in my home with my own weapon and then turned myself in? Cross and I were federal drug agents, for God's sake! All it would have taken was a bit of time and patience, and I would've been able to arrange for him to die a hero's death on the job."

She seemed to think this through. "There's no mention in the police report that Megan was there."

Was there any detail she hadn't noticed?

He hesitated. "I sent her home. I shoved her out the back door and told her to run home. She was so fucked up, so afraid. I wasn't even sure she'd be able to find her way home, but she ran. She started using again that night."

"She never told me, never said a word. I knew her time at

Denver Juvenile had been rough. She never wanted to talk about it. But I never would have imagined anything like this." Sophie closed her eyes for a moment, her sweet face an image of distress. Then she looked straight at him. "There's just one thing I don't understand."

"What's that?"

"Why did you keep this to yourself? You never once mentioned what Cross had done to Megan—not to the police, not during your trial, not even at your sentencing. You know the prosecutor never would have been able to get murder one from a jury under such mitigating circumstances, and you wouldn't have drawn a life sentence."

Marc felt the noose he'd made for himself tighten. "I didn't want to drag her into it. She would have had to talk to the police, testify, endure cross examination, and I didn't think she could take it. I wanted her to be able to get her life together."

She glared at him. "So you threw your *own* life away."

Was she *angry* with him?

"I knew I was going to prison, but I had no idea they'd plant drugs on me or send me away for life. I thought I'd get second degree—twenty years tops, out in six. If I had known . . . She's my sister, Sophie. She's the only family I have. I would do anything to protect her."

"And now you think this unknown accomplice is out to kill Megan."

"I'm sure of it."

"Why?"

"After the shooting, we were alone together just once. She warned me that 'they' would come after her. I don't think she understood that Cross was dead and gone. She told me that one day she'd disappear, and I would find her dead in a ditch. At the time, I thought it was nothing more than drug-induced paranoia. Then she was in and out of prison, and I had other things to worry about—her addiction and later the baby."

"But then she disappeared."

He nodded. "And left behind a stash of smack that couldn't possibly have been hers. A half ounce? What addict would leave that kind of gold mine behind? And where did she get the money to buy it with no job?"

Sophie sat slowly upright, her eyes growing wide. "You think that whoever planted the coke on you six years ago planted the heroin on Megan. You think he's the accomplice."

"You got it." Again Marc was impressed. "Megan must have seen him, must have known he'd found her and was coming after her. She took Emily and ran."

Sophie wrapped her arms around herself as if to ward off a chill, and he thought he saw goose bumps on her arms. "You should tell the police—call anonymously if you have to."

"No fucking way! My gut tells me that Cross's accomplice is still in law enforcement—someone with access to the halfway house. The last thing I want to do is tip him off." He met her gaze, held it. "Besides, do you really think they'd believe me?"

She seemed to consider it, then shook her head. "Not without some kind of proof, and for proof you need Megan."

"Megan stays out of this."

"But she—"

"No, Sophie!" The words came out harsher than he'd intended—but then he needed Sophie to listen. "*She stays out of this.* Do you understand?"

He could see from her eyes that she didn't.

She looked away. "You need to go."

Marc stood. "Are you going to help me get that report?"

"I filed an open-records request with DOC today. Don't worry. I didn't mention Megan. I should have an answer in three days if DOC brass cooperate."

Amazed, he couldn't help but smile. "Damn, you're good."

She lifted her chin, a hint of pride on her face. "It's Journalism 101, actually, but go ahead and be impressed if it makes you happy. If I do decide to share information with you—and I'm making no promises—how can I reach you?"

"I'm staying at—"

"No! No." She shook her head, her voice adamant. "I don't want to know where you are. I am not going to conceal your whereabouts, and I'm not going to have unlawful contact with a fugitive—not after tonight."

Somehow, he didn't think she was worried only about the legal consequences. What he'd said earlier was true—she still cared about him.

"E-mail then." He took her pen—the same pen that had touched her lips so many times—and wrote down his e-mail address: marked&hunted@gmail.com.

She glanced down, then gave him a wry look. "Clever."

"I thought so."

Strangely reluctant to leave, but knowing it was time for him to go, he willed his feet to carry him toward the front door.

"Uh-uh." She shook her head and pointed toward her sliding glass door. "I think it's only right that you leave the way you came in."

"You're kidding."

She put her hands on her hips and glared at him.

Okay, so she wasn't kidding.

"All right. Fine by me." He crossed the room, wishing he could find an excuse to stay, every fiber in his body wanting to be near her.

What if they catch you and you never see her again?

The thought dropped like lead from his brain into his gut.

He unlocked the sliding glass door, then turned back to face her. "I'm sorry I frightened you tonight, but I'm not sorry I kissed you."

Her face flushed pink. "Don't ever break into my home again."

He nodded. "Sure, if that's how you want it."

Then unable to stop himself, he slid his hand into her hair, ducked down, and kissed her, deep and slow. She gave a little gasp of surprise, but didn't fight him, her lips parting to give him access, her tongue swirling with his, her body soft and pliant.

Too soon it was over.

He touched a finger to her nose. "Goodnight, sprite."

She stepped back, hugged her arms around herself. "Please, Hunt—be careful."

"You can count on it." He slid the door open, stepped out onto her balcony, and shut the door behind him.

She locked it and dropped the dowel back into place, watching him through the glass, the sad expression on her face telling him she didn't expect to see him again.

Oh, but she would. If he had anything to say about it, she certainly would.

SOPHIE WATCHED HUNT lift first one leg over her balcony railing and then the other. He glanced at her, grinned, then adjusted his grip so that he was holding the vertical iron bars. Then in one smooth motion, his hands slid down the bars, and he dropped out of sight. A moment later, he reappeared striding through the snow toward the street, a shadow in the darkness.

Only after he'd disappeared from view did she realize she was crying.

She dropped the curtain back into place, then settled on the couch, drawing the blanket around her, giving in to her tears. She'd listened to a lot of horrific stories in her years as a reporter, but this one had been harder to hear than most, probably because she cared so much for Megan. The thought of what Megan had endured sickened her—a troubled teen raped repeatedly by men who were entrusted with her rehabilitation.

How afraid and alone Megan must have felt, how desperate, how betrayed!

Sophie had known Megan's drug use started sometime after she'd gotten out of Denver Juvenile—and now she knew why. The poor kid had paid for theft with rape. She'd been horribly traumatized and had started shooting up to make it all go away. Like many injection drug users, she'd been self-medicating.

But then she'd gotten clean, had her baby, done her time. She'd been on the threshold of a new life, and it had been taken from her, stolen by whomever had helped Cross. What kind of monster would do that to a young woman, to a new mother?

I'm not sorry Cross is dead.

Hunt had said it, and Sophie had no doubt he meant it.

And truth be told, she couldn't blame him for feeling that way. She couldn't condone what he'd done, but she could at least understand it. He had killed Cross in a desperate moment, and he was paying for it. Unless Megan was found and came forward, he would pay for it with the rest of his life.

Oh, Hunt!

Yes, he was a killer, but he wasn't a cold-blooded killer. He had taken a man's life, but he hadn't done it out of malice. That might be a small distinction from some peoples' points of view, but to Sophie it meant everything.

Yes, she would help him, but discreetly and on her own terms. She had promised to keep everything he'd told her tonight in confidence, but that didn't mean she couldn't dig deeper and start piecing it together. Hunt and Megan deserved justice, and maybe one day Sophie would be able to help them get it.

KRISTY HADN'T RECOGNIZED him till she'd gotten in his car, and by then it had been too late. It had been years since she'd seen him—if you didn't count her nightmares. She might have told him to fuck himself and jumped out of the car if he hadn't offered to pay so much. Usually she got no more than fifteen or twenty for a blow job, so fifty bucks was like a reverse twofer—do one, get paid for two. She'd liked that idea. That meant one less cock she had to suck or fuck tonight. And she had to admit that there was something perversely satisfying about making the rat bastard pay for something he'd stolen so many times before. When he'd offered her a few grams of heroin on top of the fifty, she'd called it a deal.

She'd sucked him off with her eyes closed, trying to block out the sound of his voice, then pocketed both the fifty and the drugs.

"Where does a cop get heroin?" she'd asked.

"Where do you think? We bust people, take their shit, and use it or sell it."

That didn't seem fair, but she hadn't said so. All she'd wanted at that moment was to get as far away from him as possible. She'd stepped out of his car, watched him drive away, then puked in the snow. Then she'd started back toward the cheap-ass apartment Rodney made her share with two other girls, looking over her shoulder the entire way.

Finally home, she let herself in and locked the door behind her, glad to find herself alone. She threw down her purse, took the baggie out of her pocket, took a small amount of heroin and put it in the bottom of the torn beer can she used as a cooker. Then she added a little water from the tap, held her lighter to the aluminum, and waited.

It had to be complete chance that she'd run into him tonight. He'd seemed just as surprised to see her as she was to see him. Well, she hoped she never saw him again. That fucker and his friends had taken whatever innocence she'd had left and shredded it. She'd have to hide if she saw him coming. No matter how much he paid her, she wouldn't do him again.

She watched the small chunk of heroin bubble down to liquid, tossed the lighter aside, and drew the precious fluid into an old syringe. Then she tied off her right calf with the leather belt she used as a tourniquet. The veins in her arms were getting worn out, and guys didn't want to buy sex from a whore who had big bruises on her arms. But no one ever looked at her feet, and the veins there were easy to find and still strong.

She wiggled her toes, slapped the top of her foot, picked her spot. Then she slid the needle into the vein, drew back on the plunger till she got blood, and injected salvation straight into her bloodstream. Tossing the syringe onto her bed, she pulled off the tourniquet and sank down onto her pillow, warmth shooting up her leg like liquid happiness.

It took her a few seconds to realize something was wrong, but by then she didn't care.

CHAPTER 12

SOPHIE DRAGGED HERSELF out of bed and toward the shower, feeling worn to the bone. She'd been too upset, too tense, too worried to asleep. She'd stared at the ceiling for what seemed forever, mulling over every word Hunt had said, trying to align what he'd told her with the facts of the case until her tired brain was tied in knots. Then, when she had finally managed to drift off, her thoughts had taken a disturbing X-rated turn.

She'd dreamed that she and Hunt were having sex—slow, sultry, mind-blowing sex. She'd felt every kiss, every touch. She'd even felt him moving inside her, silky smooth thrusts that had driven her to the edge. She'd jerked awake more than once to find herself alone, her body on the brink of an orgasm.

She felt like she hadn't slept at all.

She stepped under the spray and began to wash her hair, wishing her shampoo had caffeine that could sink directly into her brain. She'd began to wonder whether such a thing were chemically possible, when she realized that she was drifting into dreamland again.

Caffeinated shampoo?

Wake up, Alton.

She rinsed the lather from her hair, worked conditioner through to the ends, then began to shave her legs, the hot water slowly bringing her to life again, her mind sorting through the facts.

Cross had come by Hunt's house, where Megan had seen him and become hysterical. Hunt had pieced together what she was saying and had confronted Cross. Cross had admitted he'd raped Megan and laughed about it. Enraged, Hunt had pulled his gun and shot Cross in the chest—three bullets through the heart and lungs. Hoping to spare Megan the ordeal of being questioned, he'd sent her out the back door, not knowing that by doing so he was setting himself up for a life sentence. Then he'd taken responsibility for what he'd done and surrendered himself to police.

Though Sophie knew she was far from objective, she believed Hunt had told her the truth. It wasn't just the fact that nothing he'd said contradicted the facts of the case. It was the way he'd said it.

She'd seen the anguish on his face as he'd recounted Megan's ordeal. She'd noticed how his fists had clenched when he'd spoken of Cross. She'd seen the way he'd shut his eyes when he'd described the shooting—as if closing them could make the images in his mind go away. Underpinning it all, she'd sensed the deep love he felt for his sister. No wonder Megan viewed him as a hero. He had avenged her, protected her, looked after her.

She's my sister. She's the only family I have. I would do anything to protect her.

If anyone understood what he felt, it was Sophie.

What if someone threatened David? How far would she go to protect him?

Would she kill?

God forbid she was ever in a position to find out.

She finished her shower and toweled off, then dried her hair and put on her makeup, trying to hide the circles under her eyes. She leaned closer to the bathroom mirror and began to trace her lips with lip liner, her gaze falling on her own mouth. Her motions stilled, lip liner forgotten, sensation flooding her memory.

I'm sorry I frightened you tonight, Sophie, but I'm not sorry I kissed you.

Sophie regretted the kiss—but only because she'd enjoyed it. A couple minutes of lip-lock, and she'd been trying to get into his pants. And she'd thought he was a good kisser in high school.

Just because he's a good kisser doesn't mean you have to go into heat.

Except that he wasn't a *good* kisser. He was an *amazing* kisser. She'd had sex with men who gave off less heat with their entire bodies than Hunt generated with his lips and tongue—and not just when he was kissing her mouth.

Her gaze dropped to her bare nipples, which instantly began to tighten.

She remembered how wonderful it had felt to have his mouth—

Oh, no! You're not going there, Alton.

The last thing she needed was to get physical with an escaped felon. Contact with him was a good way to end her career and land her own butt behind bars.

Sophie hurried through the rest of her morning routine, dressing in her silk-lined gray woolen suit, more for warmth than style. Eager to get to work, she skipped breakfast and headed through rush-hour traffic to the newspaper, stopping for a cup of spiced chai along the way.

It was still cold outside, but the sun shone brightly in a blinding blue sky, the sight of the snowcapped peaks to the west lifting her spirits. By the time she reached her desk, she had her day planned out and was feeling more like herself than she had since all of this began.

She sorted through her e-mails and press releases, then listened to her voice mail. There was another message from Ken Harburg, calling once again to check up on her.

"I'd like to see you again—when you're ready, of course. I know this can't have been easy for you."

She wrote down his phone number, feeling a little guilty that she hadn't returned yesterday's message. It wasn't his fault seaweed had gotten caught between his teeth. That sort of thing happened to everyone eventually.

But do you really want to go out with him?

A few days ago she might have been able to muster some enthusiasm for the idea, but now it held absolutely no appeal. And it wasn't hard to figure out why.

Get your mind off Marc Hunter, Alton. Low probability of

having a meaningful, long-term relationship, high probability of going to prison.

She was busy getting her mind off him and organizing her notes for the I-Team meeting when her cell phone rang.

It was Tessa. "Hi, Sophie. How are you holding up?"

"Better. How are you and your little body buddy?"

"The baby's had hiccups all morning. It's driving me nuts. Every few seconds my whole belly jumps. It's almost as annoying as having them myself."

"Hiccups? I didn't know unborn babies got hiccups."

"Neither did I till my midwife told me. Julian thinks it's funny. He sat there with his hand on my tummy during breakfast, a big grin on his face."

Sophie couldn't help but smile at Tessa's happiness. No matter how annoyed Tessa sounded, Sophie knew her friend was deeply in love with a man who loved her right back. And now they were expecting their first baby. Life didn't get better than that.

"He won't find it so funny when he's pregnant with the next one."

"Exactly." Then Tessa's voice grew serious. "I know you've got an I-Team meeting in a few minutes, but I wanted to let you know that Julian got the preliminary report on DOC's internal investigation yesterday afternoon. This is really going to tick you off. They're blaming you for part of it."

"What?"

"The report claims that if you had notified DOC about the anonymous call, they would have realized Hunter was planning something and would have been able to stop him."

"That's ridiculous!" Sophie laughed. "So it's *my* fault I was taken hostage?"

"Do you want me to read this to you?"

"Sure."

" 'It is the determination of this panel that the victim bears some responsibility herself for being so eager for a news story that she ignored standard protocol and failed to report the circumstances of her interview with Hunter. Although there is no evidence that the victim colluded with Hunter in the escape—surveillance videos, in fact, show her attempts to fight back—her willingness to conceal certain facts from DOC officials enabled Hunter to accomplish his goal of escaping DOC custody.' "

Sophie found herself on her feet, her face burning. "That is a load of crap! I didn't violate any 'protocol.' I'm not required to report contact from inmates. They're trying to undermine my credibility!"

"I'm sorry to have upset you, Sophie. I know you've had enough to deal with." Tessa sounded upset herself. "Julian was so angry I thought he was going to hit something. He says they're just trying to cover their butts. He thinks they're hoping to take some of the momentum out of Reece's legislative investigation by decreasing public sympathy for you."

"All they have to do is make the accusation, and someone will believe it. People love to think the worst of reporters." Sophie turned to find the rest of the I-Team watching her. "When are they making the report public?"

"I'm not sure. I'll fax you a copy. But remember—you didn't get it from us."

"Thanks, Tess. I suppose I should tell Tom."

"Good idea." Tessa's voice went sweet as sugar. "He'll rip their little heads off."

HER TEMPER ON low boil, Sophie sat quietly through the I-Team meeting, while Tom checked in with each reporter. Matt was writing a follow-up to yesterday's article about the city councilman who'd tried to bribe his way out of a drug arrest. Kat needed ten inches for a piece about the natural gas boom and how the explosion of wells was impacting air quality along the Front Range. Natalie had a small story about a drug overdose in Federal Heights.

"It looks like she died after injecting fefe—fentanyl-laced heroin. Her roommates came home and found her dead on her bed, a small amount of the drug in a sandwich bag beside her. Police are worried that we're about to see an explosion of fefe-related deaths. The last time a batch of this drug hit Chicago, more than a hundred people died in a single week."

Tom raised an eyebrow—an unusual display of surprise. "Any chance you can find out how this shit gets into the state, where it comes from?"

Natalie nodded. "I'd also like to head out on the streets with the needle-exchange folks and see what the response is out there."

Matt looked over at Sophie. "Isn't that the same drug that killed that inmate?"

Sophie nodded. "I hope we're not on the brink of an overdose epidemic."

Tom turned to Sophie. "What's eating you this morning, Alton?"

TOM WAS JUST as furious as Tessa had predicted he'd be. He stomped out of the I-Team meeting, his copy of the report in hand, then he'd dialed the head of DOC and interviewed him as only Tom could. He started out with small talk, then moved on to the prison break, toying with DOC's director like a cat toying with a mouse, not letting the poor guy know he had a leaked copy of the report until the director had admitted Sophie had done nothing that violated DOC procedures. Then he laid into him, throwing the contents of the report in his face and letting him know that the paper would hold DOC accountable for every word.

"I know you'd like to believe reporters owe you the inside angle on every story involving your department, but the truth is we don't have to tell you anything! The bottom line is this: one of my reporters came to your facility, which is supposed to contain and control bad guys, and ended up being taken hostage at gunpoint! *Why* she was there is irrelevant to your investigation. What happened once she *got* there is what matters!"

Watching Tom work, Sophie remembered why she respected him. He might be a jerk now and then—okay, most of the time—but there wasn't a fiercer protector of the First Amendment on Earth or any other planet. He was hard on his reporters, but when the shit hit the fan, he stood by them.

She came to appreciate this even more two hours later when Glynnis, dressed in a bright pink column dress, called her into Tom's office and started questioning her. "You must have realized something was out of order."

In disbelief, Sophie looked to Tom, saw that he was surprised, too. "I knew Hunter had to be connected to make it happen, but it seemed to me to offer this newspaper an advantage. I had no idea what he had planned."

"Didn't it occur to you that DOC officials should have known about this?"

It was everything Sophie could do to keep the rage out of her voice. "I don't work for the DOC. I wasn't about to give them information that might impede my ability to gather information. If I'd have told them, I never would have gotten the interview."

Glynnis opened her mouth to speak, but Tom interrupted.

"Where, exactly, are you headed with this, Glynnis?"

"One of your reporters found herself in a life-threatening situation. I'm trying to determine whether her own actions contributed to—"

"Alton followed the book. She acted exactly as I'd expect one of my reporters to act. She was taken hostage not because she failed to disclose privileged information to DOC, but because one of their guards put this asshole in cuffs instead of full restraints."

Glynnis's mouth went flat. "There's no reason for coarse language."

"And there's no reason to waste Alton's time with this bullshit. You can go, Alton."

Sophie stood and hurried out of Tom's office, shutting the door behind her just as Tom and Glynnis started shouting.

IT TOOK MARC two minutes to shut down the alarm system and break into his new home. He moved in without fanfare, dropping his backpack on the master bed. Then, Glock in hand, he gave himself a tour of the place.

Master bedroom, master bath. Guest room, guest bath. Third bathroom. Another bedroom. Home office. Sitting room with the praying hands. Family room with a plasma TV and a fully stocked bar. Living room with a fireplace. Big-ass kitchen. Walk-in pantry with a freezer full of rib eyes, lobster tails, and chicken breasts. Formal dining room. Laundry room. Fourth bathroom. Sunroom with a patio that opened to a . . . deck with a hot tub.

Well, it wasn't the presidential suite, but he supposed he could get used to it. While Mr. Rawlings's pants were too big around the waist and his shirts and jackets were too tight around the chest and shoulders, his supply of scotch and steak fit Marc just fine.

He found the attic with its sea of trunks and boxes, checked out the finished basement with its home gym, ridiculous fifth bathroom, and storage rooms, then made his way to the garage. He opened the door, flicked on the light, and felt some of the dark mood that had been eating at him all day lift.

Wheels.

They'd taken the Lexus, but they'd left a fancy black Jaguar XK. It was probably the vehicle Mr. Rawlings had bought for himself when his dick had stopped working— which, given the cold bitch he'd married, might have been his wedding night.

Marc grabbed the set of spare keys hanging from a hook just inside the garage door and in a matter of seconds was sitting in the driver's seat, grasping the leather-bound steering wheel with both hands. It wasn't his old Chevy, but it would do. No more trudging for miles through the snow. No more risking hidden cameras on the buses. No more wasting cash on cabs.

Mr. and Mrs. Rawlings had hooked him up—no doubt about it. He had everything he needed—food, shelter, transportation, satellite TV, Internet, and solid cover. No one would ever think of looking for him in this neighborhood. He'd be able to search for Megan over a wider area, and when he wasn't on the streets he'd be here, digging through boxes.

Somewhere in this house he hoped to find records of Megan's childhood, clues to the life she had lived, perhaps diaries or photo albums that might lead him to friends that her adoptive parents didn't know about or had forgotten. If he was lucky, he'd also find that report.

He knew he needed to go back inside and start searching, but he couldn't seem to get out of the car. Before he could admit to himself what he was doing, he found himself backing out of the garage, down the driveway, and into the street. And then he drove.

He drove with no idea where he was going or even why he was doing this, window down, cold air blasting his face, his heart pounding in his chest. The streets rolled by, a blur of neon and halogen. Maybe he stopped at the red lights; maybe he didn't. And then there were no red lights, only open highway. He poured on the gas, the glitter of Denver disappearing behind him.

What the fuck is wrong with you?

He asked the question, but it only made him drive faster, the answer chasing him like an avenging demon. He pushed on the gas pedal, felt the Jaguar surge, speed an anesthetic. Only when he'd left the interstate four hours later did he realize where he was.

Just north of Colorado Monument.

He followed the winding road, knowing even before he got there where it would lead him. And then he saw it—the place he'd parked his Chevy on that night twelve years ago. He pulled over to the side of the road, stopped the car, stepped out into the cold night.

Compelled by something he didn't understand, he stepped over the guardrail and walked to the place where he'd spread the blanket on the ground. It was here. No, *here*. It had been late spring and warm. Sophie had laid back on that blanket and let him do everything he'd wanted to do to her sweet, virgin body. The world had seemed changed from that moment—so full of possibility. *He* had seemed changed.

He looked around, took the place in—the dark shadows of looming cliffs, the deeper black of the canyons, the glinting stars, the immense silence. His life had changed irrevocably since then, but the place itself hadn't changed at all.

For a moment he stood there, wondering what the fuck he was doing here. Then, all at once, the memories his conversation with Sophie had dredged up last night, memories he'd tried to ignore all day, memories he'd tried to outrun, caught up with him. He sank to the ground, staggered by the weight of his own regret, images colliding in his mind.

Leave her alone! She's my baby sister!

Your sister's gone to a better home. She's with people who will raise her right.

You know how chick inmates are—bored and horny, dreaming of dick. Every time you walk by their cells, you know they're hoping you'll give it to them.

Bam! Bam! Bam!

It is the hope of this court, Mr. Hunter, that you will die behind bars.

Why you fightin', Hunter? Afraid it'll hurt? Afraid you'll like it?

Please don't! I helped your sister!

Whatever I feel it's for the boy you were in high school, not the man you are now.

He squeezed his eyes shut, tried to silence his mind, his breath coming in ragged gasps, his fingers digging into the cold sand.

God, he'd fucked up. He'd taken the life he'd been given— far from perfect, to be sure—and he'd destroyed it. If only he could go back in time to this one night, the one night when everything had been perfect, and talk to the cocky young man he'd been.

And what would you say to yourself, Hunter?

Find Megan sooner and get her into therapy? Don't trust Cross? Don't keep your weapon loaded in the house? Run for the border?

Then staring into the darkness, he knew.

Don't let go of her, Hunt. Don't let go of Sophie. Don't let her out of your life.

If only he'd done that one thing . . .

He sat there in the silence, feeling as empty as the darkness that stretched out before him, remorse as much a part of him as the air he breathed. Then slowly the sun rose behind him, splashing the rock walls of the canyon in pink, stretching golden fingers across the sky.

It was too late for him, too late to right the wrongs he'd done, too late to correct his mistakes, too late to claim the life—and the woman—he'd let slip away.

But it wasn't too late for Megan, and it wasn't too late for Emily.

He stood, walked back to the car, and started the long drive back to Denver.

CHAPTER 13

"I'VE ALREADY TOLD you, Ms. Alton. We don't have any records matching that description."

Of all the PR flacks Sophie had worked with in her career, DOC's Allyson Harris irritated her the most. She always had a tone to her voice that managed to be not only snippy but condescending, as if Sophie were somehow both rude and stupid to be asking questions. Today it was worse than usual, and Sophie knew why.

The report on Hunt's escape had given Allyson the mistaken impression that Sophie was no longer worth taking seriously. Though Tom's scathing editorial had cut DOC off at the knees, the local papers had made a big deal out of the report anyway, and one local radio talk show host had spent the better part of an hour excoriating Sophie for putting all of society at risk by enabling a killer to escape. She'd found herself fielding calls from reporters and getting angry e-mails from readers. Though Sophie knew she should let it roll off her back, the past couple of days had been both infuriating and humiliating.

Even so, she wasn't about to let Allyson's attitude intimidate her. "That's impossible. I know the report exists. I spoke with someone who once saw a copy."

That wasn't strictly true, of course, but it was true enough. Hunt said the report existed, and so it must exist. Sophie couldn't say why she felt so sure of that, but she did.

How well do you really know him, Alton?

She'd once thought she knew all she needed to know about him, and she'd been wrong. Was she wrong now?

"Are you suggesting that I'm lying?" Allyson always pulled the "I'm insulted" routine.

"Don't be absurd. I know you don't go through the archives yourself. You only report back to me with whatever they tell you to say."

Allyson gave an indignant gasp, but Sophie steamrolled over her.

"What I'm saying is that, unless someone has destroyed the report in violation of state law, it's there. It might be buried, but it's there."

"No one here at DOC would do any such thing, Ms Alton. You're making wild accusations."

Sophie took a deep breath, bit back the words she really wanted to say. "You're creating conflict where there is none, Ms. Harris. I'm just trying to find this report, and state law says DOC has to help me."

Allyson's voice went arctic. "Perhaps if you'd tell us exactly what you're looking for instead of fishing with a net we'd be better able to accommodate your request."

But Sophie wasn't about to fall for that. "That's a great suggestion—except that we'd be starting all over, and DOC would get another three-day response period. I think I'll take this up with the newspaper's counsel."

"You do that, Ms. Alton. I'm sure the paper's attorney will tell you that we're not required to produce a document that doesn't exist."

"He'll also tell you that it's a crime to conceal one that does." Sophie hung up the phone, her mood having gone from bad to worse. "God, I hate that woman!"

"Was that your good friend Allyson Harris?" Natalie cast Sophie a sympathetic glance. "She's a piece of work."

"Yes, she is. I think DOC needs a broadside from legal—not that it will necessarily help. If they continue to claim the document doesn't exist, I'm not sure how I'll get a hold of it."

Kat walked past Sophie's desk, heading for the water-cooler, bottle in hand. "The Colorado Open Records Act is only the front door. You need to find the back door."

The back door.

Ken Harburg.

As Megan's parole officer, he'd have grounds to access to her entire record. He'd be able to search DOC files for anything that pertained to her. And he might be willing to hand Sophie the report under the table.

She searched through the sticky notes littering her desk and found the one she needed. Then, hoping he hadn't lost interest, she dialed Ken's number.

MARC WATCHED SOPHIE hurry to her car, then followed at a discreet distance as she drove from the paper to a downtown parking garage. He parked the Jag in the space beside her rental car, gave her a head start, then followed her up the stairs and down the busy street. She looked like the professional she was—long hair in some kind of classy braid, dark gray woolen coat, black pinstripe pants peeking out from beneath, black pumps on her feet, black leather purse.

Sleek. Sophisticated. Sexy.

She stopped in front of a sushi joint, glanced at her wristwatch, then turned back to look down the sidewalk. She was waiting for someone.

Marc ducked his head, pulled a quarter out of his pocket, and bought a newspaper—her newspaper, as it turned out. Unless she saw his face, he doubted she'd be able to recognize him. She'd never seen him dressed in a business suit.

He unfolded the paper and pretended to read, keeping a casual eye on her. She seemed nervous, impatient. Then she looked down the street past him and smiled.

A man Marc didn't recognize smiled back and hurried toward her—dark hair, five-ten, one-eighty, in his early forties. He wore an ugly, dark suit and sported a thick mustache that might have looked good on Tom Selleck in 1981 but looked stupid now. From the way his jacket draped over his right hip Marc knew he was strapped.

A detective?

Shit.

Marc watched the two of them disappear inside, not liking

it one bit when the man opened the door for Sophie and ushered her inside, his hand resting on the small of her back as if he knew her well. Giving them a few minutes to be seated— how well *did* she know this jerk?—Marc stood, tucked the paper under his arm, and went inside.

"How many today?" The hostess, a young Asian woman whose name tag read Leiha, drew a menu from the stack, a warm smile on her face, her blouse low-cut enough to reveal a tattoo of a dagger on the swell of her left breast.

"Just one." Marc looked through the restaurant, saw where Sophie was sitting, and picked his spot. He kept his voice quiet. "I'd like the small table in the back."

"This way, please." Leiha smiled at him with bright red lips.

He sat on the far end of the table, facing Mr. Mustache's back, able to see both Sophie and the restaurant's front door.

A young Asian woman with long dark hair walked up with a glass of water with lemon and a hot, wet washcloth on a little tray. "My name is Su, and I'll be your server today."

Su told him about the specials, her gaze traveling over him as if *he* were lunch, then left him to decide. He washed his hands, glanced down at the rectangular paper menu, and found himself staring at the page.

Tuna. Salmon. Yellowtail. Snapper. Shrimp.

How long had it been since he'd eaten sushi? Hell, he'd forgotten it existed.

And then he went insane.

Only after he'd finished filling out the menu did he realize he'd ordered enough sushi and sashimi to feed a shark. Painstakingly he scratched out most of what he'd checked. He'd get the sashimi lunch platter now and an order of sushi to go. Then he heard Sophie laugh and remembered that he hadn't come here to stuff his face.

Today was Day Three. Today DOC was required by law to respond to her open-records request about the report from Denver Juvenile. He was here to make sure Sophie gave him a copy of that report whether she felt like sharing information or not.

He watched as another server brought Sophie and Mr. Mustache two bowls of miso and a pot of tea. Sophie smiled, said something that made the guy laugh. Then she reached out and touched his arm.

She was flirting with him.

The realization hit Marc like a brick between the eyes.

The bastard was almost old enough to be her father! Half of the hair on his head was likely made in China. He probably needed Viagra to beat off and had a sperm count of two.

You're jealous, Hunter.

Hell, yes, he was jealous!

She's better off with him than she'd be with you, dumbshit, and she knows it.

That thought snapped him out of it—but only for a moment.

Then Sophie smiled, tilted her head to the side, exposed the delicious column of her throat—and Marc felt his teeth grind.

It was fortunate for all of them that Mr. Mustache chose that moment to take a leak. He excused himself, stood, and walked toward the restrooms in the back, leaving Sophie alone.

Marc fixed her with his gaze, leaned back in his chair, and waited.

The smile that had been on her face disappeared the moment the guy left the table, and she looked more irritated than excited or flirtatious. She glanced off to the side, her eyes focused on nothing in particular, as if she were thinking. Then slowly, her gaze traveled back across the room—and collided with his.

Astonished, Sophie could do no more than stare.

Hunt!

He sat no more than ten feet away from her dressed to kill in a single-breasted black suit and gray silk tie, his face clean shaven, his gaze laser-sharp. He looked so unbelievably . . . *hot.*

But that didn't stop her from wanting to bite his head off. His being here couldn't be a coincidence. He had followed her!

"What are you doing here?" she mouthed.

"Having lunch," he mouthed back. "Who's he?"

Was he jealous? Good!

"My date." She smiled, lifted her chin.

He gave a snort, shook his head.

"He's a parole officer and a nice man, and he's armed." Furious, she spoke in a loud whisper. "You shouldn't be here!"

"A nice parole officer? Well, that explains the ugly suit."

One of the servers approached his table and set his miso and salad on the table with a pair of chopsticks. "I'll be back with your sashimi."

Hunt gave the server a slow, sexy smile. "Thank you, Su."

Was he trying to make Sophie feel jealous, too?

As if!

Sophie waited for the blushing server to skedaddle then leaned forward to make certain he could hear her. "You should go! Now! All I have to do—"

"You won't do it, and we both know that. Did you get the report?"

So that's what this was about. He'd followed her, not because he wanted to see her, but because he wanted to get the report. Feeling strangely hurt, Sophie was about to tell him exactly what he could do with that report, when he suddenly glanced out the window.

Ken reappeared beside her and took his seat. "So what were you saying about DOC?"

Sophie forced herself to focus on Ken, doing her best to ignore the man who sat not far behind him. "Hmm? Oh. Not only are they trying to blame me in part for the escape, they're giving me the runaround on an open-records request that I filed with Denver Juvenile on Monday."

He picked up his chopsticks and attacked his California rolls. "What are you trying to lay your pretty hands on? I might already have it in my files."

"I was hoping you'd say that." She gave him a bright smile, weighing her words carefully. "I have reason to believe a series of sex assaults occurred there some years back. I've asked for a copy of a report that was made as part of the investigation into those allegations."

Ken frowned. "Does this have to do with Megan?"

Behind Ken, Hunt was sipping his tea and eating his miso, his gaze never wandering far from her. She leaned to her left, using Ken's head to block her view.

"I'm sorry, but I can't answer that one way or another. Source confidentiality."

"I understand." Ken nodded, then his face sank into a boyish pout. "And here I was hoping you'd asked me to lunch because you found me irresistible and wanted to see me again. You don't have to go out with me to ask for my help, Sophie."

Behind him, Hunt scooted back into her range of vision, just as the server appeared with a plate of sashimi. He gave the server another sexy smile, unwrapped his chopsticks, and picked up a piece of what looked like yellowtail.

Sophie felt a stab of guilt for hurting Ken's feelings. "Well, of course I wanted to see—"

Hunt lifted the sushi to his lips, curled the tip of his tongue around it, drew it slowly into his mouth, then chewed, his gaze riveted on her.

Heat unfurled in Sophie's belly, and her pulse tripped, every coherent thought in her brain vanishing. "—you."

For a moment she could do nothing but gape at him.

Then she jerked her gaze away from Hunt and was relieved to see that Ken was focused on his lunch. "It was sweet of you to worry about me."

"Of course I was worried about you. The entire state was worried about you."

Ken was telling her how he'd felt when he'd learned she'd been taken hostage, but Sophie barely heard him, her gaze drawn back to Hunt—who lifted a pale piece of tuna with his chopsticks, licked its juices with the tip of his tongue, and dropped it into his mouth, a look of bliss on his face.

Her breath caught in her throat, the heat in her belly spreading, moisture building between her thighs. Realizing that Ken had stopped talking and was watching her, she jerked her gaze away from Hunt.

"I'm sorry," he said. "It must be hard for you to talk about this. I just thought maybe he'd given you some idea where Megan might be."

Sophie realized Ken was talking about Hunt and felt an absurd impulse to laugh.

He's sitting right behind you!

"Yes," she said instead. "I mean no! No, he didn't say anything, but, yes, I guess it is still hard to talk about it."

Ignore him, Alton!

But she couldn't ignore him.

As if under a spell, she found herself compelled to watch as Hunt picked up a rosy piece of salmon, dipped it in soy sauce, then raised it to his lips. He flicked the pink fold of flesh with this tongue, licked off its juices, then sucked it into his mouth. This time he closed his eyes, and she swore she heard him moan.

Her inner muscles clenched—hard.

Instinctively, she crossed her legs, squeezing her thighs together to ease the inner ache, her gaze fixed on his face. But the pressure only made it worse, and she couldn't help but squirm in her chair.

"Do you know this report really exists?"

Snap out of it, Alton!

Sophie jerked her gaze off Hunt, found Ken watching her. "Well, I . . . Yes, I do."

"I asked you *how* you know it exists. Are you okay? You seem really nervous." Ken's eyebrows drew together in a concerned frown. He reached out, took her hand in his, gave her fingers a gentle squeeze.

Behind him, Hunt shot out of his chair, fists clenched.

For one terrible moment, she thought he was about to pick a jealous fight and get himself arrested or shot. Then he dropped some money on his table and strode stiffly away, his server running behind him with a takeout box.

Sophie took a deep breath, resisted the urge to jerk her hand from Ken's grasp. "I just have a lot on my mind. I'm sorry, Ken. I'm not very good company, am I? But back to the report. I almost hesitate to ask, but do you think you can help me get a copy?"

SOPHIE HURRIED THROUGH the freezing wind back to her car, fuming.

It was bad enough that Hunt had followed her, but he'd tried to embarrass her, too, licking and sucking his sashimi as if he were licking and sucking some part of her. Did he really think she'd found that sexy? Okay, so maybe it had been erotic in a crude sort of way, and maybe some part of her had responded. But that didn't mean she'd enjoyed it.

Did he understand how much trouble he'd have been in had Ken recognized him? Did he think he was invincible? Did he realize he'd made it harder for her to get a hold of the very thing he wanted—that bloody report?

Idiot! Jerk! Bastard!

She turned into the parking garage and started down the stairwell, grateful to be out of the biting wind and off the street. She needed to get back to work and talk to legal. Though Ken had promised to do his best to get the report, she wanted to have a plan in place in case they stonewalled him, too.

"I'll do what I can, but I don't have the ability to just walk in and take stuff out of their files. I have a process I have to go through, just like you," he'd explained. "If someone is trying to conceal this report, they'll probably do their best to make sure I don't get it either."

And not for the first time in her career, Sophie found herself wishing she could make herself invisible. She'd be able to walk in, search the files, and take whatever she needed without anyone knowing. Imagine the stories she could break!

She reached her floor, exited the stairwell, and walked to her car. A shiny, black Jaguar had pulled in beside her, its sleek paint job reflecting the overhead lights, its tinted windows reminding her of a limousine. She fished out her keys, half afraid to open her car door for fear of dinging the sleek sports car.

It's probably worth more than you make in a year, Alton.

She had just stuck her key in the lock and was imaging how many credits of vet school an expensive vehicle like that would cover when the driver's side door of the Jaguar opened.

"Get in."

Hunt!

CHAPTER 14

MARC SAW THE astonished look on Sophie's face and knew what she was going to say before she opened her pretty mouth.

"You stole this!"

"Actually, I borrowed it—from a very distant relative."

It was the truth. Sort of.

Her eyes narrowed. "You 'borrowed' it?"

"We need to talk. Get in."

"And if I refuse? Will you hold a gun to my head?"

He checked his temper, got out, and walked around to the passenger side of the car where she stood, leaning so close to her that he could smell her shampoo. "Please get in?"

"Fine." Sophie ducked into the Jag. "But we stay here. I'm not going anywhere with you in this fancy G-ride. You need to steal something less conspicuous."

"I told you—I didn't steal it." He shut the passenger door behind her and a moment later slipped into the driver's seat beside her. "I borrowed it."

She looked adorable in her outrage, her gaze fixed straight ahead, her arms crossed over her chest, those kissable lips bent in a frown. He couldn't blame her for being pissed. He'd pretty much trashed her lunch date.

"You ought to thank me, you know. That guy you were with—"

"Was Megan's parole officer." She glared at him. "I was trying to get a copy of the report from him."

Megan's parole officer?

Now do you feel like an idiot, Hunter?

Actually, he felt relieved. The thought of Sophie being romantically involved with that middle-aged loser had almost made him hurl. "Why were you trying to get the report from him? I thought DOC had three days—"

"DOC is stalling. They say no such records exist."

"That's bullshit."

"I know, but I can't prove them wrong unless I have the document in my hand, and if they refuse to give it to me . . . well, you can see how this goes nowhere fast."

"So you were trying to charm Megan's parole officer—hideous mustache, by the way—into getting it for you?"

She was staring straight ahead again. "Yes—if that's how you want to put it."

"You were *flirting* with him."

"Only a little, and he saw through it." A troubled look crossed her face. "I think I hurt his feelings."

Marc tried not to feel satisfied. "Is he going to help?"

"He says he'll do what he can."

And to think Marc had come close to taking the guy's head off. He'd seen him take hold of Sophie's hand, and he'd come out of his seat. Only when he'd realized he was acting like a lunatic had he found the presence of mind to pay the bill and get the hell out of there before he got himself arrested.

"I guess I owe you an apology."

"For what? For almost getting me killed? For putting me in a position where I have to keep secrets from my friends? For arranging your escape so that I would end up taking some of the blame? For breaking into my apartment? For following me like some crazed stalker? For embarrassing me during my lunch meeting?"

He listened to the inventory of his crimes, wishing it weren't as bad as it sounded. "Wait a minute—who's blaming you?"

"Haven't you been watching the news?"

"No, I've spent most of my time on the streets."

She took a deep breath. "DOC's internal investigation holds me in part responsible for the fact that you got away. They say I broke protocol by not telling them about the anonymous call asking me to interview you."

"That's just DOC covering its own ass. Don't let it get to you. It's bullshit, and everyone knows it."

"You need to listen to talk radio if that's what you think. Even my publisher believes I did something wrong. For the first time in my career, people doubt me. I've worked so hard to get where I am, and I won't let you ruin it!"

Her words were harsh, but it was despair he heard in her voice, not anger. A look of distress on her sweet face, she stared down at her hands, which were now clasped tightly in her lap. And for a moment he saw not the woman, but the teenage girl who'd once sat, crying and afraid, in the front seat of his old '55 Chevy.

Something twisted in his chest. He reached over, brushed a stray lock of hair off her cheek, the split second of contact igniting a need for more. "I'm sorry, Sophie."

She gave an almost inaudible gasp when he touched her, but she didn't push his hand away. "You'd better be. And that stunt you pulled in the restaurant?"

"Which stunt?" Under some kind of spell, he leaned closer, pressed a kiss to her temple.

Her eyes drifted shut and she slanted toward him almost imperceptibly, apparently as caught up in the spell as he was. "The one where you ate your sashimi . . ."

He traced his lips over her cheek, caught the whorl of her ear with this tongue. She tasted so damned good. "As if I were eating you?"

She shivered. "It wasn't sexy."

He nibbled her earlobe. "Not at all?"

"Mmm." She tilted her head to the side, gave him access to her throat. "N-no."

He chuckled at her blatant lie, ran the tip of his tongue along the sensitive skin beneath her ear. "Then I'll have to practice—on the real thing."

Her lashes lifted to reveal dilated pupils. "Y-you can't do that in a sports car!"

"Want to make a bet?" He kissed the corner of her mouth, his cock growing hard at the very idea of going down on her.

"I-I won't be able to relax. We're in public!"

"The windows are tinted. And, honey, you won't have to relax." He turned in his seat, intending to reach across her and recline her seat back, but his elbow hit the horn.

She gasped—and just like that the spell was broken.

She drew away from him as if he were toxic. "I-I need to get back to the office."

Some part of him knew she'd be better off if she got into her own car and ditched his ass as fast as she could. The rest of him couldn't think beyond how much it hurt to stop touching her. He caught her hand, held it, stroked her soft skin with his thumb. "You can't run away from this, Sophie."

She glared at him. "I'm not running away from anything."

"Yes, you are. There's still something between us— something strong. You want me as much as I want you. Getting out of this car won't change that. It will just waste time, and time is something I don't have."

"I'll e-mail you if I learn anything." She jerked her hand free, opened the door, and stepped out of the car. "In the meantime, stay away from me, Marc Hunter."

THERE'S STILL SOMETHING between us—something strong. You want me as much as I want you. Getting out of this car won't change that.

Sophie tossed a package of instant oatmeal into her shopping cart, then moved down the aisle, unable to get Hunt's words out of her mind. It might not have been so difficult if it weren't for the sinking feeling that what he'd said was true.

You know it's true.

Okay, so she knew it was true. But that didn't have to mean anything. She might be attracted to him, but she didn't have to *act* on that attraction. Just as she'd done this afternoon, she could walk away from it, turn her back, stay focused on what was important—her career, her brother, her friends. There was no room for trouble in her life.

And Hunt was trouble—living, breathing, sexy trouble.

Trouble with a capital *T*—for tongue.

With a few flicks of that skilled body part, he'd turned

eating sashimi into foreplay, firing her libido, making every nerve ending in her body wish he were licking and sucking her. She'd actually gotten wet watching him play with his food! And when he'd unleashed that killer mouth on *her*, she'd been a heartbeat away from begging him to go down on her in his "borrowed" Jag.

Thank God he'd bumped the horn!

She turned into the next aisle, stopped in front of the peanut butter, and reached for a jar of the store brand, trying not to notice the more expensive gourmet organic brands sitting a foot away. After David graduated, she'd eat all the organic peanut butter she wanted, but for now this was good enough. She put the jar in her cart and looked at her list to see what she had left.

Bread. Eggs. Milk. Yogurt. Detergent.

She turned her cart around and headed to the far corner, yielding for some poor mother with a very unhappy toddler.

"Tookie! Tookie!" Fat tears rolled down the little girl's rosy cheeks.

"Hush, Maddy, you've already had your free cookie!"

Sophie couldn't help but smile—sometimes a girl just needed another cookie—until she found herself wondering what her children would look like if Hunt were their father. The thought came out of nowhere, taking her by surprise, and she might have worried about her sanity if she hadn't remembered Holly's rule. She could fantasize about anything—as long as she didn't truly want it.

She certainly didn't want Hunt to father her children. What woman would? He might be drop-dead sexy, ripped, and phenomenal in bed, but he wasn't father material. He was an escaped convict, a lifer. Tomorrow or next week or next month the cops would catch up with him and send him back to prison, and that would be the end of everything. The next time he left the state pen, he'd be in a casket.

Time is something I don't have.

The full meaning of his words hit her, and suddenly it seemed so bitterly tragic—Hunt's entire life and everything he might have been forfeit because of one terrible, impulsive act. He'd shot Cross in a moment of wild rage and had given up his only defense in order to spare his sister the special humiliation society reserved for rape victims. He'd given up his future out of love for a sister who'd turned his sacrifice into nothing by giving in to addiction.

It was so brutally unfair.

If only there were some way to reopen the case. If only Megan would step forward and tell the court what Cross had done to her. If only there were enough evidence to force the court into giving Hunt a new trial.

And that's why you need to get a hold of that report.

Megan wouldn't be safe until the man who was after her had been exposed, and Hunt wouldn't be able to reclaim any part of his life until Megan felt safe enough to speak out. In the meantime, both Hunt and Megan—and little Emily—lived every day on the edge.

Sophie pulled up into the checkout lane, feeling a renewed sense of urgency. She would call Allyson tomorrow, threaten DOC with a lawsuit. Maybe she'd just show up at the office and demand to search—

"Paper or plastic?"

"Hmm? I have my own bags." Sophie grabbed the bundle of used plastic bags out of the cart and handed them to the sacker. At five cents per bag, it didn't save much, but every dime counted when David's tuition came due.

She paid her grocery bill, pushed the cart out to her rental car, and loaded her groceries into the trunk. Then she crawled into the front seat, started the engine, and headed home, trying to think up other ways she might be able to get the information in the DOC report. She had just turned out of the parking lot and onto East Ninth Street, when the overheads of a police cruiser flashed red and blue in her rearview mirror.

She pulled over so that the squad car could pass—only to find it drawing to a stop behind her. Had she been so deep in thought that she'd run the stop sign? Had she been speeding? Was one of the car's taillights out?

She fished her driver's license out of her purse, then leaned over to get her insurance card and rental car agreement out of the glove compartment, the glare of the squad car's takedown light eliminating any need to turn on her interior lights.

An officer appeared at the front passenger window, flashlight in hand.

Sophie rolled down the window and offered him the required documents. "Good evening, officer. Did I run the stop sign? I hope not!"

Without a word, the officer took the papers and her license and examined them under his flashlight. "Stay in the car, ma'am."

He turned and walked back to his vehicle to run her license.

"Great." Sophie sat, doing her best to be patient and wondering what she'd done and how much it would cost her. She hadn't had a speeding ticket for two years, so maybe he'd let her off with a warning. She couldn't afford to spend seventy-five dollars on nothing.

Another squad car approached and pulled to the curb in front of her, overheads flashing. Then another. An officer stepped out of each of the new arrivals and converged near the hood of her car, talking quietly to each other and huddling in their jackets.

Three squad cars for a routine traffic stop? Weren't there any criminals to chase?

After what felt like forever, the officer who'd taken her license reappeared, this time at the driver's window. "Ma'am, I'm going to have to ask you to step out of the car."

And suddenly this routine traffic stop no longer seemed so routine.

Her pulse picking up, Sophie unbuckled her seat belt and did as the officer asked. "Is something wrong?"

But he didn't answer her. "We'd like your permission to search your vehicle."

She shivered in her coat. "Search it? Sure, okay. It's a rental car, but it's fine with me if you search it. I have groceries in the trunk. Watch out for the eggs."

One of the other officers guided her to the side of the road and stood beside her. "We'll need you to stand over here, ma'am."

Feeling strangely uneasy, Sophie watched as two officers wearing nitrile gloves opened every hatch and door on the vehicle and then stood back to make way for an officer guiding a German shepherd.

A K-9 unit?

They were searching her car for drugs.

The realization was somehow reassuring. If they'd been looking for overdue library books or past-due parking tickets, she might have been nervous. But she'd never done drugs.

Maybe the last person to rent the car had used it to run dope. Maybe that's why they had pulled her over. The last driver had done something illegal, and the license plate number was on some kind of list. Maybe the cop had pulled her over because she'd done a sloppy job of stopping, and then the plate number had popped when he'd called it in.

She had almost convinced herself this had to be the case when the dog barked and lunged into the front passenger seat. The handler pulled the dog back, and one of the officers wearing gloves ducked headfirst into the car. When he emerged, he was holding a baggie with something white in it. The officers bent their heads together, examining the contents.

"That's not mine." Sophie didn't realize she'd spoken until she heard the surprised sound of her own voice. She spoke louder and started toward them. "Whatever that is, it doesn't belong to me."

But before she could take a single step, the officer who'd been standing beside her stopped her, blocking her path. "Stay where you are, ma'am."

She looked up, met his reproving gaze. "But I have to tell them it's not mine."

"You'll have plenty of time for that downtown."

Downtown?

"What? You can't mean . . ."

But she saw on his face that he did.

Blood surged to her brain. "Oh, my God!"

They were going to arrest her!

Heart thudding against her breastbone, she reached into her pocket, drew out her cell phone, and dialed Tessa's number.

Please answer! Please answer! Please answer!

Sophie gave a sigh of relief when Tessa picked up.

"Hey, girl. Julian and I were just talking about you. We were wondering—"

But Sophie didn't have time for that. "Tess, listen! I'm about to be arrested. I don't know what's going on. I got pulled over, and the cop asked to search the car, and I said okay, and their dog found something—cocaine or heroin, I think. They're about to arrest me, but the drugs aren't mine!"

"Take a deep breath, Sophie."

Sophie tried, but panic seemed to fill all the space inside her lungs. She heard Tessa say something to Julian, and then Julian's voice came on the line.

"Sophie, are you still there?"

"Yes." But she wouldn't be for long. The cops were looking at her now, and one of them was walking toward her. He was carrying handcuffs.

"Don't resist. Don't argue. Don't admit to anything. Got it?"

"Y-yes."

"Good girl. I'm on my way."

Sophie hung up just in time to have her phone taken away.

"Ms. Alton, you're under arrest for possession of a schedule I controlled substance. Step over to the vehicle, and put your hands on your head."

It was only after she'd been patted down, cuffed, and shut in the backseat of a squad car that she understood, the truth hitting her with the force of a bullet.

Seven years ago someone had planted drugs on Hunt. Two weeks ago someone had planted drugs on Megan. Now, only days after she'd requested information that might expose the truth about Cross's murder, someone had planted drugs on her, too. The man who had helped Cross rape Megan—the man who'd made sure Hunt went to prison for life—knew Sophie was looking for him. And he was trying to stop her.

CHAPTER 15

"THE SMACK WAS sitting on the passenger seat beneath your briefcase, Ms. Alton. Do you really expect anyone to believe you didn't know it was there? How could you miss it?"

Sophie looked into the detective's bloodshot eyes, feeling every bit as exhausted as he looked, her emotions worn to a single fraying thread. "It's not mine."

"Maybe it wasn't yours." The detective leaned forward so that she could smell the coffee on his breath, his wooden chair creaking. "Maybe you were holding it for someone else. Maybe your job was to transport it."

She shook her head, feeling anger toward him that he didn't deserve. He was just doing his job. "No! I don't use drugs, I don't sell drugs, and I wouldn't help anyone else sell them, either."

This was turning into the longest night of her life. She'd spent an hour in booking being ogled by drunks before they'd fingerprinted her, photographed her, and locked her in a chilly holding cell. There, she'd had time to think about too many things—the week's worth of groceries she'd just bought that would likely spoil, the bill she was going to get from the rental car company when they learned their vehicle had been impounded, the court battle that would follow if this mess didn't straighten itself out.

She'd tried telling herself that she was innocent and had nothing to fear. But then she'd thought of Hunt and how no one had believed him when he'd told police the coke they'd found in his house wasn't his.

Even you didn't believe him at first, Alton.

Would anyone believe her?

And where was Julian?

"Look, I know you've been through a rough time lately." The detective sat back, crossed his arms over his hopelessly rumpled shirt and tie, the silvery two-way mirror behind him reflecting the back of his gray-haired head. "I know all about how that bastard took you hostage at the state pen and got rough with you up in the mountains. I can't blame you for turning to drugs to forget about it. It must have been pretty terrible. It would be a lot easier on both of us if you would just tell me who sold you—"

Fighting tears, she pushed up her sleeves. "Do you see needle tracks? The drugs aren't mine! I didn't buy it, and I didn't use it! Someone planted it on me!"

He glanced at her arms, frowned, gray brows meeting above his nose. "Why would anyone want to plant drugs on you, Ms. Alton?"

"I think it has to do with an investigation I'm working on. I think someone—"

There came a knock, and the door opened.

Chief Irving stepped inside, acknowledging Sophie with a nod. "Ms. Alton. I can't say how sorry I am to see you here. Not only does it mean bad times for you, it means I'm about to get a call from your asshole boss."

Sophie might have laughed—if the mention of Tom hadn't made her think of her job and the repercussions she would face at work. How was she going to explain this?

Then Chief Irving motioned the detective out with a jerk of his head. "Let's talk."

The detective gave Sophie one last weary look, then stood and followed Chief Irving out into the hallway, shutting the door behind him and leaving Sophie alone with her fears.

They'd been gone only a minute or two, when the door opened again.

"Julian!"

He walked in, shut the door behind him, and then pulled Sophie into a warm embrace. "How are you holding up?"

"Oh, God, Julian! They think I was trying to sell heroin!"

"I know." He gave her a reassuring squeeze, then released her. "Have a seat while Old Man Irving buys us some time. We need to talk."

It was then she noticed the bag of carryout he'd set on the table.

"Is that food?" Her stomach growled.

"We're not allowed to bring inmates food. I bought this for myself, but I guess since I've already eaten supper I'm not very hungry. Think you can polish it off before Irving gets back?"

Suddenly ravenous, Sophie tore into the containers, her mouth watering at the spicy scent of what could only be chicken pad thai. "Thank you so much!"

"You're welcome." He turned a chair backward, straddled it, then sat.

She took a bite, moaned. It tasted both sweet and spicy, the heat of the red peppers making her mouth burn. "God, this is good! I was hoping to get out in time to grab something at the late-night Wendy's drive-through, but this is so much better."

Julian frowned. "That's one of the things I wanted to tell you. You're going to be here at least overnight, Sophie."

Overnight? In jail?

"Wh-what?" Sophie forgot about food. "Can't I get out on a PR bond?"

"They found thirty grams of fentanyl-laced heroin in your rental car. The DA's looking at possession of a schedule I controlled substance with intent to distribute—a serious felony. They won't let you out on personal recognizance. They'll want the judge to set bail."

Which meant she would be locked up at least until her first court appearance.

If she was lucky—very lucky—she'd be out tomorrow afternoon.

"Oh, God!" She squeezed her eyes shut to hold back tears. "This can't be happening! Please tell me this isn't happening!"

Julian took one of her hands, held it. "I'm sorry, Sophie. I know this is hard. I'm doing everything I can, but some things I just can't change. You're strong. You'll get through this."

"Pardon me if I don't feel so strong at the moment."

"We don't have a lot of time, so you eat while I tell you what's going to happen."

She picked up the fork she had dropped, not wanting the food Julian had smuggled in for her to go to waste, but what he told her left her feeling queasy.

"Because you're a felony arrest, you'll be strip-searched. A female CO will have you take off all of your clothes and tell you to bend over. Then they'll have you squat naked on the floor and ask you to cough while they watch your posterior." He grimaced, as if describing this was painful for him. "Jesus! I can't believe you have to go through this."

She couldn't believe it either.

He drew a deep breath and continued. "After searching you, they'll give you your jail uniform, let you dress, then take you back to the unit. It's late so the women are already locked down for the night. I've arranged for you to have your own cell—not an easy thing, given how overcrowded this place is. Do you understand all of that, or am I going too fast?"

Sophie cleared her throat, tried to find her voice. "I understand. Thank you."

"Do your best to sleep tonight, okay? I know it won't be easy, but try. Tomorrow morning John Kirschner, your attorney—"

"I don't have an attorney." She didn't even have money for an attorney.

"Yes, you do, and he's the toughest criminal defense attorney in the state. Kirschner would fight like hell to spring Jack the Ripper, and he'd probably succeed. He's the suit cops and prosecutors hate to see in a courtroom."

"But—"

"Tessa and I have taken care of it, Sophie. That's all you need to know."

Fresh tears stung her eyes. "Th-thank you."

"You're welcome. Now, I know it's not polite to talk with your mouth full, but can you tell me what in the hell is going on? You told Charlie you thought this was tied to one of your investigations. Does it have anything to do with that bastard Marc Hunter?"

Sophie almost choked. "Why would you say that?"

Julian raised a dark eyebrow. "Former DEA agent turned drug dealer and murderer takes you hostage at gunpoint. Now, a couple weeks later, someone plants drugs in your car. I don't know—call it gut instinct."

She took another bite, trying to decide how much she could tell him, the sense of guilt she'd battled these past two weeks pressing in on her. Once again her friends had come to save the day—and once again she was keeping secrets.

She dabbed her lips with the paper napkin. "I filed an open-records request on Monday asking for all documents pertaining to an internal investigation DOC did about eight years ago in response to allegations that a couple of guards were routinely raping girls at Denver Juvenile. I think whoever put the drugs in my car wants to destroy my credibility and bully me into dropping the request. I have reason to believe he left DOC but stayed in law enforcement. Get a copy of the request, Julian. Better yet, get that report."

She'd told him the truth. It just wasn't the whole truth. And every omitted fact scraped over Sophie's conscience like broken glass.

Julian seemed to consider what she'd told him. "Who tipped you off? Oh, wait—let me guess. You can't tell me. Reporter–source confidentiality, right?"

"Right."

"You know you can trust me, don't you, Sophie?"

"It's not that I don't trust you, Julian. It's just . . ."

What could she say? No matter now much she adored and trusted Julian, she couldn't tell him that Hunt had tipped her off. Or that he was dining on sushi and driving a Jaguar. Or that she was helping him find Megan. If Julian knew Hunt was here, he would turn Denver inside out to find him, and that would inevitably lead to some kind of confrontation. She wouldn't be able to bear it if either of them got hurt.

"This *is* about Hunter, isn't it? You had this same torn look on your face in the hospital. The bastard's got you mixed up in something." Julian leaned closer. "Look at me, Sophie. Does the heroin belong to him?"

She met Julian's gaze straight on. "No, absolutely not. I don't know who put it there. Someone—probably a cop—planted it on me to get me to back off. For eight years, he's gotten away with raping those girls, and he doesn't want me to find out who he is."

He studied her. "Well, shitty luck for him. Now he has someone else on his ass."

There came another knock at the door, and Chief Irving stuck his crew-cut head inside. "You done breaking the rules, Darcangelo?"

Julian glanced at the takeout containers. "Almost. Give me another ten minutes to finish my dinner, old man."

Chief Irving looked over at Sophie, who sat, frozen, fork in hand, and raised a bushy white eyebrow. "Make it five." He shut the door and was gone.

Five minutes.

And then she was going to be strip-searched and locked in a jail cell.

She couldn't have eaten another bite if she'd wanted to. "Oh, God!"

"It's going to be okay, Sophie." Julian reached out and took her hand. "I know you're scared. I know you're going to feel like you're alone in the world when they take you back there, but you aren't. You're all we're thinking about tonight. Remember that. I'm going to get home to find the entire I-Team, past and present, camped in my living room."

She tried to smile. "I guess I'll try to view this as research for some future article."

Julian grinned. "I'll pass that along to the guards. It'll scare the shit out of them."

MARC PARKED THE Jag down the street from Sophie's place and sat, watching the apartment, a sense of helpless rage making his gut churn.

This was his fault. It was *his* fault.

He'd known that getting her involved would put her at risk, and he'd done it anyway. To be fair, she'd filed the open-records request before he'd asked her to help, but she never would have done it if he hadn't told her about Megan. He'd left a trail of bread crumbs that no journalist could have ignored.

And if that trail leads her to prison, asshole?

No fucking way was he going to let that happen.

He stepped out of the Jag, activated the alarm, and walked down the dark street, backpack slung over his shoulder. He'd been following her, just keeping an eye on her, when he saw them pull her over. The moment the K-9 unit had pulled up, he'd known what they'd find. Wishing desperately that he could help her, he'd had to drive away so that he could beat the cops here.

The bastard who'd sent him away for life, the bastard who'd helped Cross brutalize Megan, had now set his sights on Sophie. Only this time it wasn't going to work. Marc knew his MO and had come here to fuck up his carefully laid plans.

Marc cased out her building, then walked up the stairs to her apartment, opting to break in through the front door this time. He pulled out a lock-picking kit—the sort of thing that would have cost him both balls on the inside—and quickly worked the lock. Then, weapon drawn, he let himself in, cleared the apartment, and got down to business.

She didn't have an attic or crawl space, so he started in the bathroom. Wearing cheap latex gloves, he turned on the lights and started searching. It had been years since he'd executed a warrant, but the rhythm came back to him, the ability to divide each room into a grid and meticulously work through it.

He checked the toilet tank, looked behind the toilet, probed the shower drain. He took everything out of the cabinet beneath her sink, checking for loose floorboards. He removed the covers on her light switches and electric outlets and checked inside them. He removed the light fixture and checked inside it. After an hour, the only incriminating evidence he'd found was a purple and green packet of Plan B—the morning-after pill—an unwelcome reminder that she'd probably had sex with other men.

You're the one who let her go, Hunter.

Not something he wanted to think about just now.

He repeated the same process in her living room, in her coat closet, in her kitchen, looking in every conceivable nook and cranny, turning over her couch, checking the back of her picture frames, pulling the books off her bookshelves—even probing her flour and sugar with a long wooden spoon.

Nothing.

But it was here, somewhere. It had to be.

He moved to her bedroom—and knew he was getting warmer. On the floor between her bed and her nightstand sat a used cooker and couple of syringes still wrapped in plastic— just the sort of evidence that would convince a jury. He carefully picked the paraphernalia up and dropped it into a plastic bag, then checked under her bed, beneath her mattress, behind her headboard.

He found her vibrator in the top drawer of her nightstand. Bubblegum pink, it was shaped like a dick—a thick, veiny, enormous dick. Except that no dick he'd ever seen was packed with tiny pearls. Or came with switches. Or quite so many ridges.

Feeling both humbled and curious, he picked it up, turned it on—and damned near dropped it when it started to twist, the pearls rolling over one another as the head rotated.

Geee-zus!

Marc's mind filled with images of Sophie rubbing the buzzing head over her clit, sliding the rotating shaft inside her, her muscles contracting around it as she came. Blood surged into his cock, which, lacking pearls or a motor, did nothing but press uncomfortably against his jeans. He turned the vibrator off and put it in his backpack.

No way was he leaving it here for the cops to find.

Fighting to get his mind off his crotch and back on the job, he opened the next drawer—and hit pay dirt. There, beside a stack of women's magazines, was a baggie holding what looked like seven or eight grams of heroin. Carefully, he picked it up and examined it through the plastic. Little green flecks told him it was probably laced with fentanyl.

Just like the shit they'd planted on Megan.

Marc had no way of knowing for certain, but he'd bet his

ass the stuff they'd found in Sophie's car was laced with fentanyl, too. It probably came from the same batch—all of it. It
had probably been stolen from the evidence room or straight
from the dealer.

He dropped the drugs into the plastic bag and put the plastic
bag inside his backpack, planning to dispose of both drugs and
paraphernalia once he got home. Trying to eliminate any lingering traces, he sprayed the drawer and the area beside the bed
with Lysol, knowing full well it wouldn't fool a well-trained
drug dog. But he'd thought of that and had the perfect solution.
He pulled the box of doggy biscuits out of his backpack,
opened it, and shut it in the drawer, spilling a few on the floor.

The dog would react—but no one would ever be sure why.

An hour later, after searching the rest of her bedroom just
to be certain there wasn't more, Marc let himself out and
walked back to the Jag, backpack on his shoulder.

The night sky was clear and cold, Orion sailing high in the
sky. Before too long, the police would show up with their
search warrant. They'd tear Sophie's apartment apart, but they
wouldn't find anything. It wasn't nearly enough to make up
for what she was going through tonight—Christ, he hated to
think of her in that place!—but it was all he could do for her.

He slipped behind the wheel and had just stuck the key into
the ignition when three squad cars, one of them a K-9 unit,
turned onto her street. "Sorry, boys. I beat you to it."

But, *damn*, talk about a close call.

SOPHIE ROLLED OVER to face the wall, the two-inch plastic
pad that served as a mattress doing nothing to lessen the dis-
comfort of lying on a bed of cold steel. Her tiny cell was dark
and chilly—steel bunk, steel toilet, steel sink with no faucet.
Though she couldn't see another living soul, she could hear
them, women whispering, laughing, crying in the dark.

This had to be the most humiliating night of her life.

*Spread your feet apart and bend over. Now squat and
cough.*

They'd taken everything she had on her and had handed

her a stack of folded clothing—two pairs of white cotton panties that bore faint menstrual stains from a previous wearer, a bra with bad elastic fatigue, a pair of socks, a lame pair of sneakers, a T-shirt, and a blue jumpsuit. They'd also handed her a rule book, a towel, a toothbrush, and a small comb that might work on a man's short hair but looked like it would lose teeth the first time she hit a tangle.

What they hadn't given her was pajamas. Or anything to wash her face with. Or aspirin for her headache. Or truly warm blankets.

She pulled the thin cotton blanket up to her chin and stared into the darkness, butterflies swirling in her stomach. How strange it was to think that this experience was reality for most of the people she'd written about as a journalist. She'd listened to their stories over the years, had done her best to sort real injustice from whining, and she'd known that incarceration was hard. What she hadn't known was how humiliating it was to lose your freedom or how terrifying it was to hear that thick steel door clang shut—and not know when it would open again.

And then it hit her.

Hunt had lived this way for more than six years.

More than six years.

He'd gone to prison, knowing he was innocent of drug dealing and premeditated murder. Had he felt then the way she felt now—hopeful that the courts would see the truth?

How betrayed he must have felt in the end—and how completely alone.

At least she had her friends.

You're all we're thinking about tonight. Remember that.

Sophie tried to concentrate on the simple act of breathing, letting oxygen fill her lungs, willing herself to relax. It was going to be all right. Tomorrow morning the attorney Tessa and Julian had retained for her—how could she repay them?—would get her out of this place. She'd explain things to Tom and do whatever she had to do to prove she wasn't involved with drugs—take a lie detector test, submit to a blood test, swear on a stack of dictionaries.

Yes, it would be all right.

She must have fallen asleep because the next thing she knew, a key was sliding into the lock on her cell door. She came awake with a surge of adrenaline and sat bolt upright, barely able to breathe. Outside the narrow Plexiglas window, a shadow moved in the darkness.

Then there came a burst of radio static and a garble of words. ". . . Looking for you. Where in the world are you? We need you down in psych. Over."

"Fuck!" A man swore under his breath, then spoke in a normal voice, apparently answering. "I'm taking a leak. That okay with you? I'll be right out. Over."

Taking a leak?

Whoever was outside her door was lying. Whoever was outside her door didn't want anyone to know he was there. Whoever was outside her door . . .

Chills skittered down Sophie's spine.

Maybe the man Hunt was looking for wasn't a cop.

Maybe he was a CO at the Denver County Jail.

Heart slamming, she waited.

She heard the key withdraw from the lock, followed by the sound of a man's receding footsteps. She shuddered with relief, afraid to think of what might have happened. Then belatedly realizing her opportunity, she leapt off her bunk, ran two steps to the door, and pressed her face to the window, hoping to catch a glimpse of the bastard's face.

But it was too late. He was gone.

And if he comes back, Alton? What will you do then?

Dread slithered through her belly. She backed away from the door and sat on the bunk with her back against the cinder block wall, watching, waiting.

CHAPTER 16

MARC AWOKE TO find himself staring at familiar gray concrete. He knew every bump, every indentation, every crevice and crack. A strangled gasp in this throat, he lurched upright, jumped to his feet, banged his shin against the steel rim of the toilet.

He was back. In his cell. In the pen.

Blood rushed out of his head, left him dizzy.

What the hell?

He'd gotten out. He'd escaped. He'd gotten away.

How could he possibly be back here again?

Maybe you've lost your fucking mind.

He squeezed his eyes shut, opened them again.

He was in prison.

Christ Jesus!

Had it all been a dream?

No, it hadn't.

He'd seen Sophie, held her, kissed her, and she'd been real.

It was then he heard her scream. He leapt to the cell door, pressed his face against the slab of Plexiglas and saw her.

The shower hawks had her, and they were dragging her away.

"What's the matter, Hunter? Afraid she'll like it? Afraid we'll hurt her?"

"God, no, Sophie!" He banged on his door, tried to get Kramer's attention. "Help her!"

But the bastard either didn't hear him or didn't care.

"Kramer, you son of a bitch! Help her! Kramer!" Marc

banged and shouted until he grew hoarse, Sophie's terrified cries making him desperate.

But still Kramer didn't seem to hear him.

Marc shouted like a madman, clawing at the door, trying to tear six inches of solid steel apart. Only when he saw blood on the door—his own blood—did he realize it was hopeless.

He couldn't help. Her couldn't save her. Just like he hadn't saved Megan.

"Sophie! Oh, Christ, Sophie!" He leaned against the door, sank to the floor.

Marc's eyes jerked open.

He found himself staring into the dark, drenched in sweat, cotton sheets tangled around his bare thighs, his heart pounding like a jackhammer in his chest.

A nightmare.

It was just a nightmare.

He sucked air into his lungs, kicked off the sheets, and walked naked to the family room, where he'd seen that bottle of William Lawson's. He grabbed it, screwed off the top, and drank from the bottle, feeling it burn its way to his stomach.

Holy fucking shit.

He hadn't had a nightmare like that since his early years in prison. But this nightmare hadn't been about him—not really. It had been about Sophie.

She was in trouble, and not only because she'd been arrested. Someone was after her, someone who wanted her out of the way. Someone who probably wouldn't hesitate to kill her if given the chance.

Happy now, Hunter? You dragged her into this.

What a fucking mess! Marc was no closer to finding Megan and Emily, and now Sophie's life was being torn apart, too. Not what he'd planned.

Whether Sophie liked it or not, she needed him. He was better suited to protect her than anyone else. He knew more about what she was up against than the cops, and he could do whatever it took to keep her safe without worrying about breaking rules or laws because he was already fucked. But more than that, no man alive cared for her the way he did.

He put the bottle to his lips and took another swallow of scotch, then set the bottle down. Outside, the sunrise had turned the eastern horizon pink. It was morning. For some reason, God had decided to grant the human race another day.

Knowing there was no chance in hell he'd be able to sleep now, Marc walked back to the bedroom, slipped into a T-shirt and gym shorts, and headed downstairs. He'd pump iron and run a few miles on the treadmill, work off some of this tension, sweat the nightmare out of his body and mind. Then he'd take a hot shower, get something in his gut besides whisky, and head downtown.

Sophie needed him, and he wasn't going to fail her.

"HOLD OUT YOUR wrists."

Sophie did as the guard asked, gasping as steel grew tight against her skin. It hadn't felt like this when Hunt had put her in cuffs. "They're really tight."

"They're supposed to be tight." The guard, a young man with short blond hair, connected the handcuffs to a chain that encircled her waist then shackled her ankles, while another guard stood off to the side, watching as if he thought she'd turn violent. "Come on."

Sandwiched between the two men, she shuffled down the hallway with awkward steps, feeling like she was living someone else's life. The last time she'd been wearing handcuffs, she'd been stuck in a blizzard with an escaped convict and afraid for her life. It had felt surreal then. It felt surreal now. Only this time *she* was the supposed criminal and the men she feared weren't convicts, but those sworn to uphold the law.

Last night, someone had come in secret to her cell and would have done God only knew what had he not been called away. But who was he?

He couldn't have been either of the men walking beside her. There'd been a change of shifts at seven, so whoever it was had probably gone home to bed. If she hadn't been such a damned chicken, if she hadn't hesitated, she might have gotten a glimpse of his face or even seen his name tag and been able to ID him. Instead, she'd been so afraid she hadn't thought to look until it was too late.

At least he hadn't come back.

Sophie had sat there in the darkness, unable to sleep, so afraid her stomach had hurt, the hours stretching into what had felt like eternity. Finally, at five the lights had come on when two female COs brought in the prior day's orders from the jail commissary—chocolate bars, tampons, potato chips, lotion, lip balm—and she'd finally fallen asleep.

Breakfast had arrived two hours later, and lockdown was over. Exhausted, she'd wanted to go on sleeping, but she'd known there wouldn't be another meal until noon, so she'd dragged herself out of her cell and into the dayroom, where about twenty other women sat eating runny scrambled eggs and limp white toast. Most of them had seemed to know who she was and why she was there, probably because they had nothing better to do than watch television all day. She'd found herself asking them questions about their lives until one of them had jokingly asked whether she was really in jail just to interview them.

God, how she wished that were true!

The guards led her through a checkpoint to one of the visitation rooms, where she found a middle-aged man with a shock of bright white hair and—

"Holly!"

Looking gorgeous in a gray Prada blazer and skirt, Holly hurried over to her on a pair of purple Miu Miu pumps and gave her a hug, her brown eyes filled with worry. "God, Sophie, what have they done to you? Look at the dark circles under your eyes!"

Before Sophie could answer, Holly reached into her own blouse, pulled a small Gucci makeup bag out of her cleavage, and set it on the table. "It set the alarm off, but I told them it was the underwire in my bra. Sit down. We don't have much time. John is going to talk you through the lawyer stuff, while I see what I can do with your hair and face. I'm his paralegal for the day. It was the only way I could get in to see you."

Sophie sat, unable to keep from smiling. She was in jail

under arrest for a major felony, and Holly had lied to the jail staff in order to do her makeup? It sounded like the premise for a new reality TV show—*Prison Makeovers*.

"I love you, Holly."

"You're welcome."

While Holly conducted cosmetic CPR, combing the tangles from Sophie's hair, washing her face with a premoistened facial cloth, and putting moisturizer and makeup on her face, Sophie listened to John Kirschner talk about her bail hearing, his gaze veering every few seconds to Holly's round butt.

So that's how Holly charmed him in to letting her become his "paralegal."

"Sorry to meet you under these circumstances, Ms. Alton." He was dressed in a dark green suit that looked like it had cost several months' salary. "I've always admired your work."

Sophie said the first thing that came to her mind. "The heroin wasn't mine."

"Of course it wasn't." Kirschner sounded like he didn't care one way or the other. "The DA's probably going to push for a hundred grand, but there were no fingerprints on the evidence, and a search of your home yielded nothing—"

Sophie found her mouth hanging open. "They searched my apartment?"

"Of course. Thirty grams of heroin is more than enough to pull a warrant. As I was saying, given the totality of your circumstances—that you were recently held hostage by an escaped murderer and drug trafficker, that your profession makes you a target, and that you've got no priors, I'm going to ask for ten grand. We'll probably get fifty."

Sophie's stomach sank. "I don't have fifty thousand dollars."

"You'll only have to put up ten percent. Will you be able to manage that?"

"Yes." It would take every dime she'd set aside for David's tuition.

God, what would she tell him?

"Is there anything you think I should know before we head to court?"

There was one thing.

She quickly told him about the guard who'd come to her cell last night and explained how she thought he might be connected not only to the heroin, but also to her investigation of sexual assaults at Denver Juvenile. "I didn't file a complaint because I have no idea who he is or who his friends are. I thought it would be safer to tell someone on the outside."

Kirschner took down a couple of notes, his white eyebrows pinched together in a frown. "So you believe whoever sexually assaulted those girls is trying to keep you from uncovering his identity and that he not only planted heroin in your car, but also tried to assault you last night?"

"I'm not sure what he would have done, but we need to find out who he was."

Kirschner nodded. "Absolutely, we do."

"Don't talk for a minute." Holly outlined Sophie's lips, then brushed on gloss. "Now say 'mwah.' You know, this is exactly why I work in arts and entertainment. Rock stars and actors never come after you with guns."

Kirschner glanced at his Rolex. "Do you like dogs, Ms. Alton?"

The question seemed to come from nowhere. "Dogs?"

"When they searched your home, the drug dog alerted them to the nightstand in your bedroom. Instead of drugs, they found dog biscuits."

Sophie started to say that she didn't own a dog, much less dog biscuits, but something in Kirschner's expression stopped her. And then she understood.

Someone had planted illegal drugs in her apartment, and someone else had removed them and replaced them with dog biscuits, somehow knowing that a K-9 unit was on its way.

She wasn't sure what she felt more—shock and rage to think that the same bastard who'd planted heroin in her car had also broken into her home or relief that someone was watching out for her. If police had found drugs in her home . . .

Like Hunt, she would never have been able to convince a jury that the heroin didn't belong to her.

Hunt.

It had to have been him. He must have heard what had happened to her and had taken it on himself to make sure her apartment was clear. He'd risked being caught by the police in order to make sure she was safe.

"I love dogs," she said at last.

Kirschner smiled. "Doesn't everyone?"

Several strokes of mascara later and Holly pronounced Sophie ready for her court appearance. "You look gorgeous—well, except for the clothes and the shoes and the chains."

Sophie was surprised at how much better she felt just knowing that she was presentable. Last night, her dignity had systematically been stripped away, and Holly had helped to restore it. "Thanks, Holly. I owe you big time."

Holly dropped her cosmetics back into the bag and tucked the bag back into her bra. "You can do the same for me if I'm ever arrested."

Sophie stood and walked, Kirschner at her elbow and Holly behind her, out of the room and into the hallway, where her two guards were waiting together with Julian.

Julian watched Holly walk by, a bemused expression on his face, then looked at Sophie, one dark eyebrow raised.

But Sophie had other things she need to talk about besides Holly's unauthorized presence. "There's something important I need to tell you—in private."

One of the guards looked first at her then at Julian but said nothing.

Julian frowned. "Okay. Let's get bail set and get you out of here. But I'm warning you—this is going to be a media circus."

MARC SAT IN the back of the courtroom, watched them bring Sophie in, the sight of her in restraints like a fist to his gut. But apart from the shadows beneath her eyes, she looked fresh and beautiful, as if she'd just stepped out of the office and not a jail cell. No sooner had she stepped into the room than a dozen cameras clicked, flashes lighting the room like strobes.

Rather than turning away from the cameras or seeming flustered, she smiled and waved—or tried to wave—her chin held high. She was flanked by two uniformed COs and followed by a tall man in a black turtleneck and jeans whose long, dark hair was pulled back in a ponytail. The two COs looked young and green as grass—naïve, inexperienced, overconfident—but the one with the ponytail was a pro.

He moved like a man who'd spent his life in action, his gaze never resting. He seemed to be watching over Sophie more than guarding her. He rested a protective hand on her arm, ducked down, muttered something in her ear. She looked up at him, smiled, an expression of complete trust on her pretty face. But who was he?

As if he sensed Marc watching him, he turned his head and looked straight into Marc's eyes. Something unspoken passed between them—one killer instinctively recognizing another—before his gaze passed over Marc and through the crowded courtroom. Marc looked away, too, not wanting to give himself away by focusing on Sophie. When he looked back, she was seated off to the side with the other inmates, the man with the dark ponytail standing against the wall behind her.

Coming here was probably the most idiotic thing he'd done—and given what he'd been up to these past couple weeks that was saying something. Despite the risk, he hadn't been able to stop himself. With the nightmare trapped inside his skull, he'd needed to see her. He'd needed to know she was all right. So he'd put on his suit, had driven downtown, and had walked through the front door of the Denver jail, passing through security and making his way to the courtrooms, fairly certain the cops weren't looking for him in their own living room.

"All rise."

Marc stood while the judge took her seat at the bench, his thoughts drifting as she worked her way through her first few cases. He'd read in the papers this morning that police had searched Sophie's home and found nothing. He'd have given money to see the look on that bastard's face when he learned that the heroin he'd planted in her bedroom had been transformed into doggie treats. Of course, that was nothing compared to the shock the fucker would feel staring down the barrel of Marc's Glock the moment before Marc pulled the trigger.

"The people versus Sophie Alton."

Sophie stood and went to join her attorney, a man with a head of wild white hair.

The prosecutor rose and asked for one hundred thousand, pointing to the severity of the allegations against Sophie.

Then her attorney stood and addressed the bench. "Your Honor, my client is innocent of this crime and is, in fact, the victim of a series of incidents related to her work as a journalist—the latest of which occurred last night in this very jail."

What the hell?

Marc found himself on the edge of his seat, his gaze on Sophie.

What the hell had happened last night?

Her attorney didn't bother to explain. "Ms. Alton has no priors and is an upstanding member of our community with a record of public service, integrity, and honesty. Keeping her in jail is a gross injustice and only serves the interests of those who are trying to intimidate her. I ask that bail not exceed ten thousand dollars."

The judge seemed to consider the arguments, reading through what was probably Sophie's arrest report. "The court is extremely concerned about any allegations of intimidation against the press, particularly those involving law enforcement. I hope you encourage your client to report whatever occurred last night to the proper authorities. The court further recognizes that Ms. Alton has no criminal record and acknowledges both her contributions to our community and the extreme and violent hardship she has recently endured. However, thirty grams of heroin was found in her possession. Until that issue is resolved, this remains a criminal matter. The court sets bail at twenty-five thousand."

With the bang of a gavel it was over.

Sophie stood and was engulfed in the excited embrace of

her attorney's platinum blond sex kitten of an assistant. Then she turned to a group of women behind her, one of whom was heavily pregnant, and accepted their hugs, her wrists still in restraints.

He knew the moment she saw him. Her eyes went wide for a second, then she looked hastily away, as if trying not to betray his presence, her attention focused once more on her friends. But someone had noticed.

Behind her, the man with the ponytail was watching him.

It was time to get the hell out of Dodge before the man truly recognized him.

Marc slipped into his trench coat and strode casually out of the courtroom. It would be at least a couple of hours before Sophie's bail was processed and she was free to go. But when she got out, he would be waiting.

CHAPTER 17

"As I'm sure you know, credibility is a newspaper's most valuable asset." Glynnis sat in Tom's office, her hands, with their fake nails and French polish, clasped in her lap. "The *Independent* simply cannot afford to let this go without a suitable public response. Pending the outcome of your case, you're suspended with pay."

"Wh-what?" Sophie gaped at Glynnis, unable to believe what she was hearing. "*Suspended?* But that could take weeks!"

"Months," Tom added.

"It doesn't matter how long it takes." Glynnis adjusted the jacket of today's red pantsuit. "The paper cannot keep you on staff as long as your character is in question."

"But the heroin wasn't mine! I'm being set up!" The doubt she saw in Glynnis's cold eyes cut like a blade. "Tom, you know I'm telling the truth, don't you?"

"Of course. There's no question of your innocence, Alton. This is clearly an act of retribution against you as a journalist." He spoke matter-of-factly, but she could see that he was furious. "Unfortunately, the paper is more concerned about its image than standing by you, even though this incident is a direct result of your doing your job."

Sophie could have bought him a beer, hugged him, kissed him on the cheek.

Glynnis looked like she wanted to kill him. "This is about what's best for the newspaper. Might I remind you that this is the second incident in which Ms. Alton's character has been called into question?"

Tom rolled his eyes, shook his head.

Glynnis went on. "Think of it as a paid vacation. I'm sure a lot of people would love—"

"I don't want a vacation! I'm a journalist!"

Glynnis ignored her. "If you're acquitted, your job will be waiting for you. If not, your employment will, of course, be terminated. In the meantime, please take anything you need from your desk. Security will come to take your *Denver Indy* ID and your key card and escort you from the building shortly."

Take her ID and her key card? Escort her from the building?

They were treating her as if she'd already been fired.

The breath left her lungs in a single, slow exhale, leaving her empty.

Tom stood, his size dwarfing the publisher. "That won't be necessary, Glynnis."

Glynnis rose to her feet, too. "It's standard operating procedure—"

"It's bullshit!" Tom's shout made Sophie jump. "Alton's been a valuable member of my staff for four years, and you are *not* going to treat her like a fucking criminal!"

Glynnis stood there, glowering, her lips pressed tightly together, nostrils flared. When she spoke, her voice was as smooth and cold as ice. "Report to my office in ten minutes."

And then she was gone, her heels clicking down the hallway.

Feeling as if she were made of wood, Sophie willed herself to stand. She took her ID and key card, which hung on a chain around her neck, lifted them over her head, and set them down on Tom's desk. "Thank you, Tom."

"I'm sorry, Alton." He reached out, put a hand on her shoulder. "If it were up to me, you'd be at your desk working on deadline."

Sophie nodded, fought back the tears that pricked her eyes. "I know."

She turned and walked to the newsroom, aware that Kat,

Natalie, Matt, and Joaquin were watching her and waiting to find out what the shouting had been about. She managed to get three words out before her throat grew too tight to speak. "Glynnis suspended me."

"Oh, honey!" Natalie looked as shocked as Sophie felt. "I can't believe it!"

Sophie picked up her briefcase, set it on her desk, and opened it, reaching for files and setting them down again, strangely confused, her mind muddled.

Think, Alton! Think!

She'd need her files on Hunt and Megan. And a copy of the CORA request. And her card file and probably her . . .

She felt a hand on her arm and looked to find Kat standing beside her. Then Kat did something she'd never done before. She put her arms around Sophie and hugged her tight. "This isn't right."

Touched beyond words, Sophie blinked back tears, returned the embrace.

"This is so fucked!" Matt was on his feet. "I'm going to tell that stupid hag exactly what I think about this."

"I'll go with you," Natalie offered. "I have a few things I'd like to say."

"Count me in." Joaquin set his camera down.

"Harker, Benoit, Ramirez, sit down!" Tom's voice filled the room. "It's my honor to deal with our esteemed publisher, and I don't feel like sharing the fun. Instead, why don't you do something useful like figure out who's going to handle Alton's beat while she's away. And, Alton, as far as I'm concerned, this story is still yours. Whatever you need to get the job done, you've got. I expect to hear from you every day."

Tom disappeared down the hallway in angry strides.

"Oh, to be a fly on that wall." Natalie stared after him.

Joaquin nodded. "Clash of the Titans."

Sophie finished packing her things together, trying to think of anything she might have forgotten. Then she stepped back and looked at her desk.

She'd worked hard to earn the right to sit in this seat—four years of J-school, two grueling internships, long months of busting her butt at the *News*. All-nighters. Early mornings. Missed meals. Hate mail. Threats.

If they fired her . . .

God, what would she do?

If they fire you, it means you have bigger problems—like a prison sentence.

"Do you need a ride home?" Kat interrupted her thoughts.

But Sophie couldn't go home.

Julian had made that clear this morning after they'd left the jail. "You can stay at our place until we catch this bastard. If this son of a bitch is desperate enough to plant drugs in your car and good enough not to leave a trace, there's nothing to keep him from breaking into your apartment and strangling you in your sleep."

That had been a reassuring thought.

Of course, whoever the jerk was, he'd already broken into her apartment. In fact, her home had been break-in central lately. But Sophie didn't share that information. Much to her relief, Julian hadn't yet asked her about the dog biscuits, and she didn't want to do anything to prompt him in that direction.

"Julian was going to pick me up after work, but I'll just catch a cab. Thanks for the offer, Kat." She turned to face her coworkers. "Thanks for everything. You're the best."

Before she could dissolve into tears, she turned and hurried out of the building.

She had every intention of doing exactly what she'd said she was going to do—hailing a cab and taking it to Julian and Tessa's house. But when she reached the street, a gleaming black Jaguar slid up to the curb in front of her, its window rolled down to reveal the one person in the entire world who might truly understand how she felt.

Without thinking, without hesitation, Sophie opened the door and climbed inside.

MARC SAW THE bleak look on Sophie's face—a numb mix of shock and grief and fear—and felt an answering tug in his chest. He'd brought this down on her. Her life had been moving along fine until he'd used her to escape. Whatever she was going through right now was as much *his* fault as that of the bastard who'd set her up.

She sat in silence, clearly having had all she could take, her briefcase held awkwardly in her lap, her gaze focused on nothing. He took her briefcase, tucked it behind her seat, then reached over and buckled her seat belt. Without a word, he merged into the flow of traffic and headed west toward Speer.

She said nothing as he threaded his way across town to Cherry Creek. She didn't even ask him where he was taking her. Only when he pulled into the Rawlingses' driveway did she look over at him, confusion on her face.

He stopped the engine, closed the garage door behind them, and answered her unasked question. "I'm house-sitting."

She said nothing, her silence worrying him more than if she'd grabbed her cell phone and called the cops on him for breaking and entering. Something was very wrong. Whatever had happened to her in the past twenty-four hours, it had shaken her to the core.

He got out, walked around, and opened her door, then took her hand. "Come on, sprite."

He led her indoors, took her coat, and settled her in the kitchen, his stomach knotting at the stricken look on her face. Not sure what to do, he poured her a double scotch and pushed it into her hands. "Drink."

She took a sip, grimaced, coughed, then looked at the tumbler as if she'd been expecting lemonade.

He drew up a chair, sat down in front of her. "Tell me what happened. Take your time. I'm not going anywhere."

For a moment, she stared at the floor. Then she looked up at him, her blue eyes expressionless, her voice strangely monotone. "I saw you at the jail."

He brushed a stray strand of hair from her cheek. "I needed to know you were all right."

Her eyebrows drew together in a frown. "Julian saw you, too. I was afraid he would recognize you."

Julian? So that was the guy's name. "Is he a friend?"

She nodded. "Julian Darcangelo is my best friend's husband. He's a cop and former special agent. If he'd have recognized you . . ."

"I was careful." Friend's husband was good. Cop and former special agent was not so good. *Shit*. "Drink."

She took another sip, shuddered. "You broke into my apartment. You left dog biscuits."

So she'd figured that out. "Yeah."

"Thank you."

"It was the least I could do." *It was the only damned thing I could do.* "Now tell me, Sophie, sweetheart. What happened?"

Slowly, she recounted the experience of being pulled over, arrested, and booked. By the time she got to the part about being strip-searched, she seemed to be coming back to herself, emotion returning to her voice, shock giving way to the distress he knew she must be feeling.

"I've known for years that inmates are strip-searched, but I had no idea how degrading and dehumanizing it feels. They made me . . ." Her voice trailed off, her free hand reaching for one of his and clasping it tightly.

It was a simple gesture of trust, of need, and it made warmth blossom in his chest. He caressed the back of her hand with this thumb. "I know the routine."

He knew it only too well.

"They took me to my cell. Everyone was already locked down. I tried to sleep, but I was so scared. I felt like I was trapped in someone else's life."

"I bet." He'd felt that same sense of unreality many times since watching Cross fall dead on his living room floor. "You keep thinking the nightmare will end, but it doesn't."

She met his gaze, her eyes soft and filled with empathy. "I tried to tell myself that everything would be okay, but then I thought of you and how no one had believed you when you'd told them the cocaine wasn't yours."

"The dead body might have had something to do with that."

For a minute or two she said nothing. "Last night, a man tried to get into my cell."

Marc's pulse picked up. This was what he'd been waiting for. He kept his voice calm. "One of the guards?"

She nodded. "It scared me because it was still dark, and no one else was around. Something about it seemed wrong. I woke up when he stuck his key in the lock. Then I heard a burst of radio static—someone asking him where he was. He told them he was on a bathroom break and that he'd be right back. Then he stomped off, swearing."

Marc took in the information, did his best to rein in his anger, to stay focused on Sophie. She needed him. The guard could wait—for now. "Did you get his name?"

She shook her head. "I didn't think to look until it was too late."

"Did he come back?"

"No, but I was so afraid he would! I was so scared, Hunt!" The lingering panic in her eyes and the grip she had on his fingers told him just how afraid she'd been. "God, I was such an idiot! If only I'd gone to look through the window, I might have seen his face. Then we'd know who he is. I feel so stupid!"

He tucked a finger beneath her chin, forced her to meet his gaze. "Listen to me, Sophie. You're anything but stupid. It's *good* that you didn't get a look at him. It might have driven him to do something desperate."

He could see on her face that she hadn't thought of that.

Then tears filled her eyes. "Worst of all . . . the publisher suspended me!"

He took her drink, set it on the table, and did what he'd wanted to do since she'd slipped into the car. He pulled her against him and held her, offering her what little comfort he could, as she sobbed out the pain and fear of the past twenty-four hours.

It felt right to be close to her like this, to feel her, soft and sweet, in his arms. He pressed his lips against her hair, closed his eyes, inhaled her scent, dumbstruck by the bone-deep bliss of just holding her. If it hadn't been for the fact that she was miserable, he would have wanted the moment to last forever.

Her body trembled as she wept, her face pressed against

his chest, her tears seeping warm and wet through his shirt. Then she lifted her head and looked up at him, her eyes glittering with tears, her cheeks wet, her lips slightly parted. She ran her fingers lightly over his lips, her gaze dropping to his mouth. "Please, Hunt—kiss me."

Knowing how upset she was, he hesitated, not wanting to do anything she'd regret later. But she didn't seem to appreciate his half-assed attempt at chivalry. With an impatient little whimper, she slid her fingers into his hair and drew his head down, taking his mouth with hers.

Heat slammed into him at the first soft brush of her lips, but still he held back, letting her have control, allowing her to shape the kiss, yielding to her rhythm. She tasted of salty tears, whisky, and woman, her lips soft and warm. But then she slipped her tongue inside his mouth, gave his tongue a tentative flick—and he no longer gave a damn about chivalry.

Sophie felt Hunt's control snap. He groaned, fisted a hand in her hair, and pulled her onto his lap, returning the caress of her tongue with a full-scale invasion of his own, taking over with a forcefulness that left her breathless.

God, yes!

No man had ever kissed her the way Hunt kissed her—this intensity, this heat, this perfect balance between rough and tender. Other men didn't seem to care whether she really enjoyed their kisses, a bit of lip action nothing but a means to an end, one step toward the goal of getting laid. But Hunt kissed her as if it were his reason for living, sharing each breath, each shiver, demanding everything, giving everything, bringing her to the edge with just lips and teeth and tongue, his body hard against hers.

How could she have gone so long without this, without him?

Well, that didn't matter because he was with her now, his mouth working magic, the slick glide of his tongue making her ache to have him inside her in other ways, liquid heat pooling between her thighs. He hadn't even touched her, but her breasts already felt heavy, her nipples tight against the lace of her bra.

She knew she shouldn't do this, but she didn't care. Her world had turned upside down, and only Hunt could make it right again. She wanted him more than she wanted to breathe.

She pressed herself into him—God, he was already hard—and slid her hands over his chest, searching for buttons, her fingers fumbling in her desperation to get to skin. She wanted to feel him, needed to feel him, *had* to feel him.

He dragged his mouth from hers, stilled her hands, his heart beating hard against her palms, his darkened gaze searching hers. "Are you sure?"

She nodded. "I want you inside me."

With a groan, he reclaimed her mouth, sloughing off his suit jacket, yanking off his shirt and tie, baring planes of heavy muscle and soft skin to her touch. She ran her hands hungrily over his chest, his scars, his tattoos, drinking in the hard, male feel of him, unable to get enough. It had been so long since she'd burned for a man like this.

He drew her to down to the carpet, rolling with her in a tangle of limbs, breaking the kiss to yank off their remaining clothing. And then he was above her, his thighs forcing hers wide apart, the thick head of his cock nudging her slick entrance. He seemed to hesitate, his breathing rapid, his gaze raking over her. Then he slid into her with single, slow thrust.

It felt like a homecoming.

Their moans mingled as he buried himself to the hilt, huge and rock hard, stretching her, filling her completely. And then he began to move, driving himself in and out of her with strong, silky strokes, the slippery fiction so intensely wonderful that she wanted to scream.

"Sweet Jesus!" Marc felt his balls draw tight and knew he was in trouble. He willed his body to relax and pumped into her, burying himself, savoring every snug, slick inch of her vagina. Twelve years of wanting her. Six years of fantasizing about her, of imagining himself taking her in every way a man could take a woman, of fucking his own fist just thinking of her. But no fantasy could compare to the mind-blowing sensation of being inside her.

It was like falling dick first into paradise.

Sophie. His Sophie.

Her eyes were closed, her lips parted, sexy little moans rolling from her throat with each thrust. Her breasts rose and fell with every ragged breath, jiggling each time he drove into her, their rosy tips puckered with arousal, begging to be touched and sucked. And her scent—that musky sweet scent he'd tried to remember for six long years. *Christ!* It made him want to swallow her whole.

Then she wrapped her long, silky legs around his waist, opening herself fully to him, and he damned near lost it. Fighting back that first hint of orgasm, he thrust himself deep inside her, then held himself still, and ground the root of his cock over her swollen clit, hoping to slow himself down and give her the time she needed.

She whimpered, her inner muscles tensing around him, her nails biting into his biceps. "Oh! Oh, Hunt! God, yes!"

He ducked down, sucked one velvety nipple into his mouth, tugging it with his lips, flicking the tip with his tongue, grazing it with his teeth. She liked that. She liked it a lot, if the frantic sound of her moans was any indication. He liked it, too, loved the taste of her, loved the way each flick of his tongue made her arch and twist beneath him, his hips keeping up their rhythm, grinding against her.

Her fingers slid up to his head, fisting in his hair, holding him against her breast, her breath coming in shudders, her legs drawing tighter around him. Then he felt the tension inside her peak, felt her body stiffen, and knew she was flying.

She cried out and arched beneath him, a look of rapture on her sweet face as she came around his cock, her inner muscles clenching him, caressing him, drawing him deeper inside her.

And that was it.

With a groan, he pounded himself into her, his hips a piston, his control gone. He couldn't think, couldn't stop, his body driving desperately toward release. She was too much, too much—all soft curves, musk, slippery heat.

God, yes!

This is what it felt like. So good . . . so good . . . so god-damned good. Slick. Hot. Her muscles gripping him, holding him, stroking him. Heat in his belly. Burning . . . needing. It had been too long . . . too damned long. And she was so wet, so tight, so completely . . . perfect.

"Help me, Sophie! God, help me!" He had no idea what the hell he was saying or what he meant, except that he was dying. Stroke by stroke, he was dying. He was going to burn up and die inside her.

Somehow she understood. Somehow she knew what he needed, her arms holding him close, her lips whispering kisses over his flaming skin. And then he exploded, orgasm blazing through him in a white-hot surge, tearing a cry from his throat, searing him to his soul, his cock jerking in great spasms as he spilled himself inside her.

CHAPTER 18

MARC LAY WITH his face nuzzled against Sophie's neck, his mind blissfully empty, warmth permeating every inch of skin and muscle and bone. He had no idea when he'd last felt this way, no idea how long he lay there on top of her. His awareness returned bit by bit, and it was the little things he noticed first. The scent of her skin. The slow in and out of their mingled breathing. The steady rhythm of her pulse against his cheek. The softness of her breasts against his chest. The languid slide of her silky calves down the back of his thighs till her ankles rested in the bend of his knees.

And then it dawned on him that he was lying like a deadweight on top of her—a good two hundred pounds on her slender one-twenty. He raised his head, looked down at her sweet face, and felt his breath hitch in his chest.

She was so damned beautiful—the sun and the moon and the stars rolled into one. Red gold hair loosed from its braid. Dark lashes resting on her tear-stained cheeks. Creamy skin flushed pink with the afterglow of sex. Lips rosy and swollen from kissing him.

If it weren't for her slight smile—and the lazy little circles she was tracing on his biceps where her nails had left marks—he'd have thought she was sleeping.

His brain reconnected with his mouth. "Am I too heavy?"

"Hmm-mmm." Her voice soft and sexy, she opened her eyes and smiled a sexy smile that made his heart trip. "Stay where you are."

Where he was, exactly, was on top of her, between her thighs, his cock already growing hard again despite what had been the most explosive orgasm of his life. By all rights, it ought to have blown his balls off, maybe even killed him, but he seemed to be intact.

And functioning.

He flexed his hips, nudged himself inside her, seeking home.

Her lips parted on a shuddering inhale, her inner muscles clenching reflexively around him. He chuckled, pressed a kiss to her forehead, then flexed his hips again, his cock now rock hard. She was wet, so silky wet, his cum mingled with her cream.

Shit.

He hadn't planned on this, hadn't even thought about protection. Not that he wasn't safe. After almost seven years of celibacy and mandatory yearly blood tests, he was as safe as a man could get—except that he was a man. She had enough to deal with right now without him planting a baby inside her. He'd have to pick up condoms—pronto.

"How long had it been?" She asked the question out of the blue, her voice still sexy soft.

He knew what she was asking, but he wanted to think about her and what he was going to do to her next, not his past, not prison. He withdrew, then slowly entered her again. "Almost seven years."

She sighed, a sound of pure pleasure. "Were the two of you close?"

"Who?" He withdrew again, then slid himself inch by inch into her.

Her eyes drifted shut, and she gave a little moan. "You and the last woman you were with . . . before your arrest."

All the blood from his brain must have drained into his dick—that was the only explanation for the admission that poured out of his mouth. "You're the only one I thought about . . . Six years, Sophie. Every night . . . you . . ."

He ended with a hard, deep thrust.

Her eyes fluttered open on a gasp, her gaze soft, sympathetic. *"Hunt . . ."*

Then she kissed him and lifted her hips, meeting his next thrust, sheathing him deeply, scrambling his brain.

He managed a few words, some vague thought of carpet burn in his mind. "Not here, sprite. The bed."

Sophie moaned in protest, too impatient to let go of him for the short time it would take to walk to the bedroom, wanting him, wanting to please him, wanting to make up for those six long, lonely years. She wrapped both her arms and legs tightly around him, holding him fast, her mouth finding its way to the sensitive skin beneath his ear.

He groaned, slipped one arm beneath her, and used the other to push her up with him, the muscles of his shoulders and chest shifting as he raised them both into a sitting position and drew her on top his hard thighs, his erection still sheathed inside her.

She moaned, arched into him, and played cowgirl, her head falling back as sweet pleasure swept through her, one sensation spilling over the next. The rasp of his chest hair against her nipples. The hard feel of his man's body. The erotic slide of his cock.

"Jesus!" He nipped and kissed her exposed throat, sending shivers over her skin. Then he caught one arm around her waist.

She felt the two of them sway, as he lurched upward, rocked back on his heels, and struggled to his feet. She gasped, clasped her arms around his neck and her legs around his waist, sure they were both about to crash to the floor. "Wh-what . . . ?"

"I've got you." He took a few unsteady steps, and she understood.

He was carrying her to the bedroom.

And he was still inside her.

A bolt of heat shot through her, some primal, feminine part of her thrilled by his male strength, his raw physical power, the potent feel of his body as he moved. With a moan, she nipped the fullness of his lower lip, then slid her tongue inside his mouth, seeking, tasting, stroking, her hips moving with a rhythm of their own, curling against him.

He chuckled, groaned, staggered. "Mmm, Sophie, honey, I need to see where—"

They bumped into something and ricocheted into a wall, still kissing. Then he pivoted, and they were moving again.

Something crashed to the floor. Glass shattered.

"Christ! Honey, I can't see—mmmm."

She couldn't quit kissing him, couldn't get enough of him. Another turn, the squeak of hinges, enfolding darkness.

A few more steps—and they were falling.

Sophie landed on top of him on a wide bed, their bodies still joined, her gaze colliding with his. He was the most beautiful man she'd ever seen, his mouth full and wet, his lashes long, the shadowy hollows of his cheeks emphasizing his square jaw and high cheekbones. Sweat beaded on his forehead, trickled down his temples, the scent of him like salt and man and sex. But it was the heat in his eyes that caught her, driving the breath from her lungs in a rush.

No man had ever looked at her like this—raw, sexual need mixed with some emotion she recognized but wasn't sure she wanted to name.

He ran his knuckles over her cheek, thrusting slowly from beneath. "I never thought I'd see you again. I never thought . . ."

"Me neither." Sophie felt her throat grow tight, his words pressing against some sore spot inside her. "God, Hunt, what are we going to do?"

He cupped her cheek, his gaze burning into her. "Savor the moment. That's all we have. There's no 'happily ever after' for us, sprite. There's now. Only now."

An aching sadness swelled behind her breastbone, tears pricking her eyes. But if now was all she had, she would take it.

She slid her hands over the sweat-slick perfection of his chest, his dark curls damp against her palms, her fingers tracing the outline of his flat nipples, his muscles, his scar. Ten minutes ago, this beautiful, strong man had come apart in her arms, his body shaking with the force of a release that was far more than physical, the vulnerability and desperation in his voice making her heart ache.

Help me, Sophie! God, help me!

He'd needed her. He still needed her. And, God, she needed him!

She found just the right angle and began to move in slow circles, her hands coming to rest on his shoulders. He held himself still beneath her, letting her set the pace, surrendering his body to her, as she slowly built the rhythm, pleasure flowing through her like molten gold.

"Oh, Hunt, it . . . feels . . . *so* . . . good!"

Breath hissed from between his clenched teeth, his brow furrowed, his heart leaping beneath her palm—telltale signs that he was burning, too. But still his hips didn't move. He was holding back for her sake, his hands cupping her breasts, his fingers teasing her throbbing nipples, plucking, stroking, pinching, the sensations shooting straight to her belly.

She moaned, unable to catch her breath, the heat inside her already a tight, incandescent ache. "Hunt . . . Hunt . . . *Hunt!*"

As if in answer, he reached between their bodies and drew circles over her sensitive clitoris with his thumb—a new form of blissful torture. In a heartbeat, her body hovered on a razor's edge, somewhere between pleasure and pain, wanting . . . needing . . . craving . . .

And then it hit her, orgasm surging through her in a tide of quicksilver, white-hot and shining, the sweet shock of it forcing a keening cry from her throat, delight seeming to stretch on forever in unending, rippling waves.

"*Sophie* . . ." Hunt whispered her name, a note akin to awe in his voice.

Then, in a single fluid motion, he rose up and took her beneath him, pinning her arms above her head, raining kisses on her face, her throat, her breasts.

"*Sophie.*"

And then he was driving himself into her, thrusting deep, his mouth taking hers, his smooth strokes plunging her into another shattering climax moments before he groaned and claimed his own release inside her.

Floating, her body replete, Sophie was only vaguely aware of it when he rolled onto his back, drew her into his arms, and settled her head against his chest. When at last he pulled the covers over her, she was fast asleep.

MARC LAY IN the darkness, holding Sophie in his arms, lost in the miracle of being beside her. He watched her sleep, the sight of her stirring emotions inside him that he was almost afraid to feel. Her face was relaxed, her lips slightly parted, her breathing deep and even. Her hair lay in red gold strands across his chest. She looked defenseless, completely vulnerable, adrift in the healing forgetfulness of sleep.

He ought to sleep, too, but he didn't want to close his eyes, unwilling to surrender a single moment of being with her, not when his future held an eternity of endless nights without her. As content as he felt right now, he knew this wouldn't last. There were only three ways for him to get out of this fucked-up mess—a fugitive's life south of the border, a lifetime in prison, or death. None of those scenarios included Sophie.

He found himself trying to memorize every detail of her face. The spray of tiny freckles on her little nose. The absurd length of her lashes. The slight slant of her eyes. The fullness of her lower lip. The translucence of her skin. The delicate line of her eyebrows. The high, delicate curves of her cheeks.

Sprite.

He didn't deserve this. He didn't deserve her. She sure as hell didn't deserve him. The last thing she needed was to get tangled up with a man whose life would probably end in a hail of bullets. And yet here they were, about as tangled as two people could get, her scent on his skin, his ejaculate deep inside her, both of them spent from making love.

They were tangled in other ways, too. He'd gone to her for help, stupidly thinking that a simple request for records would fly under the radar and get him what he needed without endangering her. Instead, the fucking worst had happened.

But whoever this guard was, he'd made a fatal mistake.

He'd all but given himself away. Under pressure from her at-torney, the jail captain would hunt him down. And when they identified him, Marc would take him out. It was strange to think that the bastard had turned out to be a guard at Denver County. Marc had always been sure he was a cop.

Sophie stirred in her sleep, snuggled tight against him.

If he weren't such a selfish bastard, Marc would tie her up and leave her someplace where her cop friend, Julian, would find her, together with explicit instructions not to let her out of his sight. But Marc needed her help finding Megan and little Emily. And he needed *her*—her passion, her feminine sweet-ness, her quick mind and big heart.

No woman had ever gotten to him the way Sophie had, sliding beneath his skin until there was simply no getting away from her. He'd tried twelve years ago. He'd left her standing in tears on the street and had spent every day since then regretting it.

And that's why he would take every stolen moment he could get, hoarding them in his soul against the day when she was once again beyond his reach.

It was only a matter of time.

Man, he was *fucked*. He was so completely fucked.

It was only a matter of days—maybe hours—until some-one caught up with him. If the cops found him first, he might go to prison. If the boss found him, he'd wind up dead.

He stuffed everything he could grab into an old suitcase—clothes, his passport, cash, his old wedding band, ammo—then forced the zipper. The damned thing weighed a ton, enough to make his bad back ache when he picked it up. But if he didn't move fast, he'd have more painful problems than a herniated disk. He needed to get the hell out of Denver, out of Colorado, and hole up until this bullshit with the journalist and that whore Megan Rawlings had blown over.

He'd fucked up. No one had to tell him that. He knew it. The moment he'd been called away to help with that crazy bastard in the psych unit, he'd known going to her cell had been a mistake. But how was he supposed to know he'd get called away? All he'd needed was a few minutes, and he'd have had that bitch bent over. He'd have hurt her in ways no one could see and left her too afraid to tell anyone. Yeah, he'd have taken the fight right out of her and solved all their problems.

Instead, he'd been called away and hadn't had a chance to get back to her before the shift change. And now he was fucked.

He hurried down the dark hallway, lugging the suitcase, one hand on his service weapon. He had more ammo in the garage and a nice stash of cash in an empty paint can in the rafters. He'd stash his shit in the trunk, grab the money, then come back for his H&K nine millimeter—a hot little semi that could stop a truck. In five minutes— ten tops—he'd be gone.

Not wanting to make himself a target, he'd left the lights off, but sneaking through his own house in the dark gave him the creeps. He entered the kitchen, opened the door that led into the garage, and stepped into chilly pitch-black, nearly falling down the steps.

"Goddamn it!" Then he froze.

Above the odors of motor oil and gasoline, he smelled it. Cigarette smoke.

He dropped the suitcase, stumbled back up the stairs, one hand reaching for the light, the other clutching for his weapon. "That you, boss?"

The only answer was the racking of a slide—cold steel gliding on steel.

Then he heard a familiar voice. "Leave your weapon in the holster and get your hands over your head."

He raised his hands slowly, his heart slamming in his chest, his mouth bone dry.

Then the light came on, and he nearly shrieked.

Standing just beside him by the light switch was one of Denver's more notorious drug dealers, Juan Diego Garza, a grin on his scarred face.

And he knew he was dead.

He swallowed hard, pried his tongue from the roof of his mouth. "Y-you're going to kill me."

The boss shook his head. "No, I'm not going to kill you. You're my friend. Why would I do that? It would only make the cops and papers dig more, and I don't want them digging. Besides, you and I go way back. No, I'm not going to kill you. You're going to kill you."

He felt dizzy, sick. "Wh-what?"

Garza pointed a .45 at his head and motioned him forward. "Get into the car."

He shook his head. "If you think I'm swallowing a balloon of heroin—"

"Nothing like that. Just get in the car. That's where you were headed, wasn't it?"

That's when he noticed that both men were wearing gloves.

The pieces slid together in his mind with a final click.

The car. Carbon monoxide poisoning. *Suicide.*

The boss wanted him to die, and he wanted it to look like a suicide, just like they'd done with those two druggie bitches.

He shook his head, took a step backward, his heart about to blow. "I-I know I fucked up, boss. I was going to get her to shut up. I just didn't get the chance to finish it."

"She's a journalist. They don't shut up. We had her taken care of before you tried to get to her. It won't take them long to figure out it was you. And when they do, they're going to work you hard. They'll put together whatever they get from you with whatever that bitch reporter has told them, and that might lead them to me. I'm not willing to take that chance, not even for our friendship. But I am willing to spare you pain, so get in the car. Or should I let Garza here pull out his knife and do what he does best?"

He turned to run, panic surging through him like ice.

But Garza was faster and stronger, probably wired on meth.

In a heartbeat, he found himself shoved headfirst into his own car, the door shut behind him, his escape blocked on both sides.

"Just let me drive away. I'll even give you my money. Just let me go!" He knew he was bitching up, knew he was whining like a baby, but he didn't want to die.

The boss leaned down, shouted through the driver's side window. "Take out your keys and start it. We've got the hose from your wet vac rigged through the trunk. It won't take long. And don't try to pop it into gear. You won't get anywhere."

His bowels turned to liquid, his hands shaking almost uncontrollably as he fished the keys out of his pocket and worked them into the ignition. Then for some reason, his hand dropped from the keys and sought out his weapon. If he could convince them he'd rather die that way, maybe he could use the gun on—

"There are two of us and one of you. It won't work, buddy. Start the car."

He didn't want to die, hadn't planned to die. Not like this. Not for a long time. But they weren't going to let him out of here alive. "W-will you get them for me? Megan and that bitch journalist?"

The boss nodded, pulling out a gas mask. "You bet we will."

Sobbing, he pushed on the brake, reached up, and turned the key.

CHAPTER 19

SOPHIE AWOKE THE next morning feeling languid and content, Hunt's hard body spooning hers, his arm around her waist, his thighs pressed against her bottom. She smiled and stretched, still warm from last night's incredible, unbelievable, earth-shaking sex. She turned until she was facing him, almost unable to believe it had been real.

He grinned down at her. "Sleep well, sprite?"

"Mmm-hmm." She buried her face in his chest, ignoring the shadows that pressed in from the edges of her mind. She didn't want to deal with reality just yet. "How about you?"

"I probably would have, but I couldn't quit watching you." He said the words lightly, but she could tell he was serious.

She tilted her head back, looked up at him, noticed the fatigue on his face. "Why in the world were you watching me?"

His hand traced lazy designs over the bare skin of her back. "What do you remember about that night up at the Monument?"

She remembered everything. "I remember thinking I was the luckiest girl in Grand Junction because Hunt What's-His-Name—"

"You really didn't know my name?"

She shook her head. "—because Hunt What's-His-Name—"

"It's Marc." He nuzzled her hair. "Say it. Say my name."

"Because *Marc Hunter*, the hottest guy in school, was willing to take my virginity."

He laughed—or coughed. "*Willing?* You make it sound like

a sacrifice. Yeah, I was willing, all right. Damned noble of me, wasn't it?"

"I wasn't pretty and popular like Dawn Harper or Kendra Willis. I figured a guy like you wouldn't want—"

Now he did laugh, the fatigue disappearing from his face, the sound warming her like sunshine. "I haven't thought of Dawn or Kendra since I drove you away from that damned party. But I sure as hell have thought of you. And what do you mean you're not pretty? Hell, woman, compared to you Dawn and Kendra were just average. You had looks *and* brains."

She pushed him onto his back, wriggling upward until her breasts rested on his chest. "Did you sleep with them?"

"With Dawn and Kendra? Um . . ."

She felt an absurd spark of jealousy. "You did, didn't you?"

He slid his fingers into her hair and shook his head, grinning. "Nope. I did have one or two heavy makeout sessions with Dawn under the bleachers, but that's it. As I recall, she had really big—"

Sophie narrowed her eyes, glared at him.

"Feet! I was going to say feet!"

"So who *did* you sleep with? After I went to college and started dating, it didn't take me long to figure out that you were better in bed at eighteen than most men ever hope to be."

He frowned. "I don't think I want to hear about *how* you reached that conclusion."

She smiled, some part of her thrilled to see that, he, too, could be provoked to jealousy. "Answer the question. Who?"

His lips curved in a slow smile that made her belly flutter. "Ms. Meadows."

Stunned, Sophie gaped at him. "The *English* teacher?"

He nodded. "She offered to help me bring up my grades, and I took her up on it."

Sophie tried to conjure an image of her former teacher, but remembered only that she'd been tall with long, dark hair. "She was *old*."

"I was fifteen when she popped my cherry, and she was thirty and newly divorced. She gave me the kind of education every high school boy dreams about."

But Sophie didn't find it funny. She wouldn't turn thirty for another two years, and the thought of having sex with a fifteen-year-old boy was revolting. "That's statutory rape."

He chuckled. "Don't expect me to press charges anytime soon."

"It was still wrong of her."

For a moment, neither of them spoke.

Then Sophie asked the question she'd wanted to ask all night. "How did you do it? How did you get through six years of prison without losing your mind? I was in jail for one night, and it was terrible. I can't imagine what it would be like to endure that every day, year after year, for the rest of your life."

Marc watched the changing emotions on Sophie's face, running his fingers through the silk of her hair, touched that she cared so much. "You get used to it. After a while, it becomes your world. It's all you know, all you remember. It's all you want to remember because remembering anything else, remembering the world outside, only makes it harder. There are good days, and there are bad days, and then there are days where you think you might go fucking insane because you think of all the things you'll never see and do again. Even worse, you think of all the things you never took the time to do that you'll never get the chance to do."

Shut up, Hunter. You sound pathetic.

But sex must have short-circuited his brain because he kept talking.

"Then one day you realize that whatever life you'd been given you've pissed away, that *this* is your life—everyday the same shit, the same four walls. You wonder if you'd be happier on death row, waiting for that big shot to send you over. And that's when you get the joke—a life sentence isn't about life. It's about death—*slow* death, the kind that starts inside and eats through you. But you hang on because you have no choice."

She watched him, her blue eyes brimming with tears. "What did you miss most? What did you wish you'd done that you haven't done?"

Regret cut into his gut, lacerating him, and he found himself struggling to form words, his voice breaking, his throat tight.

"Well . . . I always wanted a cabin in the mountains. A wife . . . and kids. I always wanted . . . to be a father . . . to have a family."

Because he'd never had one. He'd never really had a family. He'd never known his father. His mother had done her best, but she'd lost her battle with addiction and landed in prison. His sister had grown up a stranger, raised in a different family, while he'd endured one foster family after the next. No, he'd never had a family.

And you never will.

Sophie nodded, and he knew she understood at least some of what he felt.

The conversation lapsed into silence, Marc trying to stop the slow bleed inside him, fighting to tie off his emotions to staunch the flow.

Then she smiled. "Did you really think about me?"

He ran his knuckles over her cheek. "Every damned night. I never should have left you that morning. Did you hate me for it?"

She looked confused, then shook her head, absently threading her fingers through his chest hair, her breasts soft against him. "You had to leave for the army. You didn't have a choice. I knew that."

"Of course, I had a choice. I should have driven you to your grandmother's house, confessed to deflowering you, and let her force me into a shotgun wedding."

Sophie laughed, the sound as sweet as honey. "She'd have gone for her shotgun, all right, but there'd have been a funeral instead of a wedding. Besides, I might not have appreciated it very much at the time. I had big career plans. I wanted to—"

She gasped and her eyes flew wide. "Oh, God! Tessa and Julian!"

In an obvious panic, she wriggled across the bed and grabbed for the phone on the nightstand.

"Don't!" Marc lunged for her, jerked the receiver out of her hand, and slammed it down. "If you call from this phone, they'll be able to find us. Wait until—"

But she wasn't hearing him. She hopped out of bed, started toward the door. "Where's my briefcase? My cell phone?"

Marc leapt to his feet, caught her around the waist, and held her fast. "Breathe, Sophie. Breathe. Your briefcase is in the hallway by the door. I turned off your cell and took the battery. Now tell me what's wrong."

She took a deep breath. "I was supposed to catch a cab and go to Tessa and Julian's house last night. I'm supposed to be staying with them until this is over. Oh, God, they must be so worried! Julian has probably called the marines! I need to call them and let them know I'm all right!"

"Fine, but you need to think through what you're going to say before you call, and you need to get dressed because you're going to have to call them from a pay phone. They'll be able to use GPS to trace your cell."

She nodded, drew away from him, and ran a hand through her long, tangled hair, still gloriously naked. "I'll tell them I went home instead and that I fell asleep and that I'll be over this afternoon."

Marc shook his head, trying to focus on the problem and not the firm mounds of her breasts or the soft curve of her belly or extremely fine ass. "If he's any good at all, Julian will already have put your apartment under surveillance, and he's probably not the only one. You're staying with me until this is over, for your sake and theirs."

She stopped short. "What are you saying?"

"I'm the only one who has any real idea what you're facing, Sophie. If you stay with your friends, you'll bring this down on them. Do you think that whoever set you up is going to stay away from you because you're living with a cop? Hell, he'll probably use his connections to find out when this Julian guy is out of the house and make his move then."

"But I can't stay here! I don't even know where 'here' is!"

"This is the home of Megan's adoptive parents. They're in Florida till April. They mistook me for a cop and asked me to watch over the place when they found out Megan's killer brother had broken out of prison to look for his sister."

She gaped at him, then glanced around her. "Oh, my God! I'm a criminal! Aiding and abetting a known fugitive. Breaking and entering. Illegal use of someone else's bedroom."

"You did break a vase, I think, but I did all the entering."
When she didn't laugh at his stupid joke—and it really *was*
stupid—he drew her back into his arms, kissed her hair. "This
is the safest place for you. No one would ever look for either
of us here. I can protect you, and we can work together to find
Megan. And if the cops do catch up with us, I'll convince
them that I needed nookie and took you hostage again."

She glared up at him. "What about my court dates? I can't
skip bail. You might think it's fun to have your picture up in
the post office, but I wouldn't like it one bit. Besides, I need
that money back for David's tuition."

She just didn't get it, did she?

Marc tried to explain. "You can't go. Everyone will be
waiting for you there. And if the bad guys don't get their
hands on you, Darcangelo certainly will. He won't let you out
of his sight again. Then the bad guys will know exactly where
to find you, and when they find you, they find your friends."

She lifted her chin. "I won't miss that hearing!"

Marc dropped it, not wanting to upset her anymore than he
already had. There was no point in arguing about it anyway. Until they found Megan, she wasn't going anywhere without him,
and if that meant holding her against her will, then so be it.

He pretended to relent. "We have until Thursday then."

Less than a week.

The fight seemed to drain from her. She sat on the edge of
the bed. "Dear God, what am I going to do?"

He sat beside her, drew a blanket around her shoulders.
"Let's just take it one day at a time. Call your friends and tell
them that you decided to stay in a nameless little hotel until
this is over because you don't want to endanger them and that
you fell asleep the moment you walked into the room."

She buried her face in her hands. "They're going to be really angry."

AN HOUR LATER, Sophie walked into a drugstore in Aurora,
a shopping list clutched in one cold hand, a knot of dread in
her chest. She felt like Bonnie—as in Bonnie and Clyde.

Which was ridiculous because she hadn't come here to rob the place. No, she'd come here to do something worse. She'd come here to lie to a friend.

Hunt, certain the place was equipped with electronic surveillance both inside and out, had parked a good block down the street to wait for her. "If this Julian guy is any good, he'll trace the pay phone number and view the surveillance tape to make certain you weren't being coerced. He'll move fast, so after you make that call, get out."

Sophie had thought that sounded extreme, even for Julian. "Would he really go that far?"

"I would." Hunt had grinned at her from beneath his sunglasses, his lips curving in a killer smile. Lips that had kissed her senseless. Lips that had been all over her. Lips that had driven her out of her mind.

She'd found herself staring at his mouth, something fluttering in her abdomen besides the swarm of butterflies that had made it impossible for her to eat breakfast.

"He looked right at me in the courtroom," Hunt had explained. "I don't think he recognized me, but if he sees me with you, or if he makes the license plate on the Jag . . ."

He hadn't needed to say more.

Sophie picked up a red plastic shopping basket on the way through the door, glanced over the list, and set off in search of toothpaste.

It would be so much easier—not to mention cheaper—if she could just go to her apartment and pack an overnight bag. Everything she needed was there—her toothbrush, her makeup bag, her shampoo. She was still wearing the clothes she'd had on when they'd arrested her, and she desperately wanted to change. But Hunt wouldn't let her go near the place, certain it was under surveillance.

She made her way through the aisles in search of the needed items, her gaze inadvertently drawn to the ruby globes of the not-so-hidden cameras. They bulged out of the ceiling like big, red eyeballs, watching her, recording every move she made. It was more than a little unnerving to think that Julian and the DPD might be watching this in the next couple of days. Is this what it felt like to be a criminal—the adrenaline, the edginess, the uneasy feeling of being naked?

Toothpaste. Toothbrush. Dental floss. Mouthwash. She reached for one of each and dropped them into her shopping basket, mentally crossing them off her list before moving down the aisle toward the antiperspirant.

It was strange to think that three weeks ago her biggest worry had been saving enough money to pay David's spring tuition. Now she was on the brink of losing everything she'd worked for—her income, her seat on the I-Team, the respect of her peers. She was facing felony charges, spending tuition money on bail, hiding from both the good guys and the bad guys, having soul-shattering sex with a known fugitive, coming perilously close to falling in love with said fugitive, and lying to her friends—not to mention wigging out in a drugstore.

Her life was an out-of-control mess. What had happened?

Deodorant. Disposable razors. Shaving cream.

Of course, she knew what had happened, or rather *who*. He sat a block down the street in a *borrowed* black Jaguar looking criminally sexy in a pair of faded jeans, a denim jacket, and a black turtleneck, a loaded weapon in his pocket. Marc Hunter had forced his way into her life at gunpoint, bringing chaos and catastrophe with him, turning her world upside down, making her feel things for him she shouldn't feel.

Damn you, Hunt! Damn you!

She didn't mean it, not really. She couldn't blame Hunt for her situation. Not entirely. He'd known someone was after his sister, had known no one would believe him, and he'd done what he had to do to protect Megan and her baby. It was desperation that had led him to put a gun to Sophie's head and drag her into this nightmare, not a perverse desire to destroy her life. Now he seemed to think it was his job to protect her.

Of course, it wasn't as if she herself were blameless. She could've gone back on her word and told Julian everything she knew about Hunt and Megan three weeks ago. She could've turned Hunt over to the police any number of times—when he'd broken into her apartment, when he'd followed her to the restaurant, when he'd showed up in the courtroom. He hadn't been holding a gun to her head any of those times. No, she'd made her own decisions.

Hand lotion. Facial cleanser. Moisturizer.

Yes, she'd made her own decisions. Last night, she'd impulsively gotten in the car with him instead of going to Tessa and Julian's house. Hunt hadn't forced her to come. He hadn't forced her to kiss him, and he certainly hadn't forced her to make love with him. In fact, she had initiated that part of it on her own. She'd been so upset, so afraid, and he'd been there for her, listening to her, doing his best to comfort her, holding her, his body so hard and strong and warm, his embrace a refuge. And suddenly she'd wanted him so badly, needed him so badly, that nothing else had mattered.

It had been a mistake, a terrible mistake, but she couldn't bring herself to regret it, probably because it hadn't *felt* like a mistake. It had felt . . . so right. Astonishing. Perfect. Just as he'd done twelve years ago, Hunt had given her everything she'd needed and more, taking her to a place no other man had taken her.

You're in love with him, Alton!

No! Oh, no! No, no, she wasn't! Falling in love with him would be the stupidest thing she could possibly do. It didn't matter that he had a body like a Greek statue and made love like a god. It didn't matter that he was a strong and decent man who'd served his country, protected his sister, and turned himself in when he'd killed the man who'd raped her. It didn't matter that the drugs had been a setup and that his sentence exceeded his crime. In the eyes of the law, he was a cold-blooded murderer, drug dealer, and an escaped fugitive.

And unless he was very lucky, the law would catch up with him.

Fighting back a wave of queasiness, Sophie glanced down at her list, suddenly unable to remember what she'd been looking for. *Shampoo.* Hair stuff.

She couldn't stand the thought of Hunt being locked away in prison for the rest of his life. Other than answering her questions this morning, he hadn't told her a thing about it, and yet she knew he carried more with him than just physical scars. He'd come unglued when she'd suggested that he'd had sex with men, all but admitting that he'd been assaulted. And this morning there'd been an edge to his voice, his pain so palpable that Sophie had hurt, too.

There are good days, and there are bad days, and then there are days where you think you might go fucking insane because you think of all the things you'll never see and do again.

He'd done a terrible thing, yes, but what Cross had done had been even more terrible. And although Cross's crimes didn't justify Hunt's violent response, what brother wouldn't lose control or be tempted to pull the trigger under those circumstances?

Either he would get away to Mexico with Megan and Emily, or Sophie would do everything in her power to see that he got a new trial. It wouldn't be easy for Megan to sit on the stand and tell the world what Cross and his accomplice had done to her, but it couldn't be any worse than the life sentence her brother would endure otherwise. Surely Megan cared about what happened to Marc. That's how brothers and sisters were.

When Sophie had called David from the courthouse, he'd told her to do whatever she needed to do with the money she'd saved and not to worry about him. Then he'd offered to get on the next flight. But he'd already given up a week of his semester taking care of her, and she didn't want her problems to impact him. She had insisted he stay in California and focus on horses. Each of them had been thinking of the other.

Certainly Marc had done all he could for Megan and then some. It was time for Megan to step up to do her part.

Shampoo. Conditioner. A brush and comb. Elastic bands. A barrette.

She glanced down at the list, then threaded her way back to the pharmacy counter, only one thing left on her list. "A packet of Plan B, please."

She took the box from the pharmacist, grabbed a box of

condoms, then carried the heavy basket to a checkout lane up front, the knot of dread in her chest growing tighter.

She didn't want to do this. She didn't want to lie to Tessa. She'd tried to make herself feel better reminding herself that Tessa had once lied to her, denying flat-out her plans to head into Aurora to question gang members despite the price on her head. If not for Julian, Tessa would have died that day, shot down in the streets. Sophie had shouted at her for a full five minutes when Tessa had finally checked in, shaken but unhurt.

But still the memory did nothing to assuage Sophie's sense of guilt.

She watched the cashier ring up her order, then handed over her credit card.

"That'll be one-ten-twenty-eight on your Visa." The cashier ran the card, then handed Sophie the slip to sign.

Sophie scrawled her signature. And then it was time.

She carried her three plastic shopping bags toward the exit to the pay phones, then fished three quarters out of her coat pocket. She picked up the receiver, dropped the quarters in the slot, and dialed Tessa's number, feeling almost sick.

The phone rang twice before Tessa answered.

"Hi, Tess. It's Sophie."

"Sophie? Oh, thank God! Where are you? Are you all right?"

"I'm fine. I'm so sorry I never showed up yesterday. I decided to check into a hotel, and I fell asleep the moment I got into the room." Why did it sound so convincing when Hunt said it, but so ridiculous when she said it?

"My God, Sophie! Do you know how worried we've been?" Tessa's voice broke, and Sophie knew she must be close to tears. "After everything that's happened I was afraid you were facedown in a ditch somewhere! Julian has the whole force looking for you!"

Sophie cringed at the anger in Tessa's voice, knowing it was the result of hours of unnecessary worry. "I'm so sorry! The moment I woke up I realized what I'd done. I was just so upset when I left the paper. The new publisher suspended me, and I hadn't slept at all in jail . . . I don't even know what to say. I'm really sorry."

Some of the anger left Tessa's voice. "As long as you're safe, that's the important thing. God, I'm so relieved! Where are you? I'll come pick you up so I can yell at you some more."

"N-no, Tessa. I can't stay with you. I don't want you or the baby or Julian to get hurt."

"Don't be silly! Julian wouldn't let anything happen to any of us. You know that." Tessa paused. "If you're at a hotel, why does my caller ID say 'pay phone'? Where's your cell? Sophie, what's going on?"

It sucked trying to lie and keep secrets when your friends were investigative reporters.

"My cell battery ran out, and I just popped into the drugstore to buy a few things. I'm afraid to go home and just need to be someplace where no one can find me. It's the only way any of us will be safe. I'll check in when I can. I'm so sorry, Tessa. Tell Julian how sorry I am. I didn't mean to cause you any trouble. I have to go now."

"Sophie, wait! What—"

Tears pricking her eyes, Sophie hung up the phone, guilt making her empty stomach churn. It was for the best, she told herself. This way, Tessa and her baby wouldn't be in danger, and she and Hunt would be able to work together to find Megan and Emily. Yes, it was best for everyone this way.

Then why do you feel like the world's worst traitor, Alton?

Her vision blurred by tears, Sophie turned away from the phone, picked up her shopping bags, and hurried out into the cold wind.

MARC COULD SEE she was crying even before she reached the car. He didn't have to ask why. Twelve years ago, she'd been unwilling to lie to her grandmother about where she'd spent the night. Today, she'd had to lie to her best friend about the same thing—but for much different reasons. It wasn't lost on Marc that both times revolved around him.

Bringing happiness to the people he cared most about—that's what he did.

Yeah, you're a ray of goddamned sunshine, Hunter.

He got out of the car, opened her door, and took the bags from her hands, dropping a kiss on her forehead. "It's cold. Get in."

He stuck the bags in the back, then got behind the wheel, started the engine, and pulled an illegal U-turn to keep the Jag off the drugstore's outdoor surveillance cameras. Beside him, Sophie sat in silence, huddled in her coat, tears glistening on her cheeks.

He cranked the heater. "How'd it go?"

She shook her head, sniffed, wiped the tears from her face. "Tessa was really upset. I don't think she believed me. She started asking questions, and . . . *I hung up on her.*"

Her voice dropped to a distressed whisper at the end, her unhappiness an indictment.

He let go of the gearshift, took her cold hand in his, gave it a squeeze. "You've got good friends. At least you know that she and her baby are safe."

"Yeah."

"That Julian is one determined cop." Determined was only half of it. The man obviously had the instincts of a wolf and didn't hesitate to follow them. "Look."

From around the corner came two squad cars, running silent, lights flashing. They were headed straight for the drugstore.

Sophie's eyes went wide with surprise as the cars tore past them. Then she looked over at Marc, a stunned look on her sweet face. She was having trouble keeping up with the situation, he knew. She wasn't used to this, wasn't used to living on the other side of the law. If she wasn't careful, she was going to make a mistake that would cost both of them.

It was time to get down to business.

Marc downshifted and pulled to a stop at a red light. "I know your head must be spinning, Sophie, but we need to talk."

CHAPTER 20

SOPHIE COMBED THE tangles from her towel-dried hair. It felt weird to use some stranger's bathroom like this—what was with all the blue plastic fish on the wall?—but she was grateful finally to have had a hot shower, even a stolen one. She'd still been able to smell jail on her skin, even after a night of sleeping in Hunt's arms. It was heaven to be clean again—and to have time to think things through.

Hunt had taken time on the drive back from the drugstore to bring her up to date on reality, dragging the shadows she'd held at the periphery of her thoughts to center stage. She couldn't leave the house alone for any reason. She couldn't open the curtains or play loud music. She couldn't use her cell phone or the landline. All communication with her attorney, her friends, and the newspaper would have to take place via the Internet relay Hunt had set up. She couldn't use her credit card. In short, she couldn't do anything that would lead anyone to her—or to this address.

"I've looked for Megan everywhere, and I haven't found her. Somewhere in this house, there must be information about Megan's childhood, something that might tell us where she's hiding. You can help me find it. We'll search room by room, tear this place apart if we have to."

"What if we find nothing?"

He'd ignored her question. "In the meantime, we stay out of sight except to follow solid leads or bring home supplies. This is the real thing, Sophie. If the good guys find us, I go back to prison and Megan ends up dead. If the bad guys find us, we're all dead. Think of this as protective custody."

Protective custody.

She knew Hunt wanted her with him so he could keep her safe. She knew, too, that she needed protection. If the heroin in her car hadn't driven that point home, then the midnight visit in jail certainly had. But staying with Hunt meant she was breaking the law—several laws, actually. Of course, Hunt's solution for that problem was as irritating as it was simple. If the cops caught up with them, she'd become his hostage again. Sophie didn't like that plan one bit, despite Hunt's insistence that the cops couldn't do anything to him they hadn't already done.

"They can shoot you," she'd pointed out. "They can kill you."

Julian already suspected Hunt was at the heart of this. He probably believed that Hunt was coercing her in some way. And that meant he believed Hunt was in Denver *and* that he would have men on the streets looking for him. Not a good thing. If the two of them ever faced each other . . .

God, she couldn't even think about that.

She couldn't stop thinking about that.

Hunt wouldn't pull the trigger unless he felt he had no choice, but that wasn't going to matter. Julian had a hard-earned grudge against criminals who hurt women. Knowing Hunt was armed, Julian wouldn't hesitate to shoot if given cause—like the sight of Hunt holding a gun to her head—and that meant things were likely to get deadly fast.

She couldn't let that happen.

It was time she got focused again. The only way she could help Hunt or Megan or herself was to find the man who'd helped Cross brutalize Megan—and expose him. She couldn't do that if she was feeling sorry for herself or obsessing about things that might never happen. She was an investigative journalist, and it was time she went back to treating this like she would any other investigation.

She would sit down this afternoon, go through her notes, and talk through them with Hunt, getting his impressions and ideas. Then she'd e-mail Tom and find out whether DOC had responded to her request for the report. She was willing to bet they hadn't. The moment they'd heard of her arrest, they'd probably tossed her CORA request in the trash. If so, that was their mistake.

Making a to-do list in her head, she finished combing her hair, put on her makeup, and slipped into the blue cotton T-shirt and gray boxer briefs Hunt had given her to wear until her clothes made it through the washer and dryer. Then she took the packet of Plan B out of the bag and opened it, reading quickly through the directions.

She'd never had to use it before because she'd always been ultracareful—no mistakes, no lapses, no slipups. But last night had taken her completely by surprise in so many ways— how badly she'd needed him, how intense the sex had been, how connected she'd felt to him from the first kiss until she'd fallen asleep with his arms wrapped around her. She hadn't thought about protection until this morning.

Which is probably why they call it the morning-after pill.

She read the directions, then walked out to the kitchen to get a glass of water, pill pack in hand, the grinding beat of Nine Inch Nails drifting up from the basement where Hunt was lifting weights. She searched the cupboards till she found a drinking glass, filled it with water, and popped the first pill from the packet into her hand. The drug wasn't foolproof, but it was her only option now that . . .

I always wanted . . . to be a father . . . to have a family.

She brought the pill to her lips, then hesitated, Hunt's words coming back to her. Once the police caught him—and it could happen at any moment—it would be over. He would never have another chance to do what they'd done last night. He would never again have the chance to make love, to lose himself inside a woman, to make her pregnant. He would never have another chance to be father, and she would never have another chance to . . .

Have Hunt's baby?

God, she could *not* be thinking what she was thinking!

The pounding of her pulse, the little wave of dizziness told her that she was.

But she couldn't have a baby now. Her entire life was a

mess. Bad guys, good guys, heroin, prison, guns—all that stuff. If she lost her job, if she lost her career, she wouldn't even have the means to support a child. And if she was exonerated and got her job back, how would she handle working at the paper with a newborn? If she went to prison . . .

She stared at the pill where it lay, bright white, in her palm.

What if right now egg and little spermy were on a collision course? What if they were about to merge? What if she was only hours away from becoming pregnant?

This pill could stop it all.

That's what she wanted, wasn't it? Of course, it was!

No *way* had she gone to college to wind up being some man's babymama, even if that man were Hunt. Hadn't she thought through this the other night at the grocery store? Yes, she had—although pregnancy had been part of a little fantasy then, not a real possibility.

Sophie put her hand on her belly, imagined it getting big and round like Tessa's, Hunt's baby growing inside her. Her womb clenched, signaling its approval, a shiver of something like desire pulsing through her pelvis. Obviously, her biological self was into the idea.

But what about the baby? He or she would grow up without a father, either because daddy was living in Mexico or rotting in prison . . . or worse. Sophie had witnessed firsthand the shame that children of inmates carried with them—the stigma, the anger, the isolation. It wouldn't be fair to bring a baby into this mess.

There's no "happily ever after" for us, sprite. There's now. Only now.

She raised her hand to her mouth, dropped the pill onto her tongue, took a mouthful of water . . . and spat it in the sink.

The pill slid into the garbage disposal and was irretrievably gone.

Quickly, as if afraid she might change her mind, Sophie popped the second pill from the packet and dropped it into the sink, too. Then she turned on the faucet.

Heart pounding, she shut off the water, turned away from

the sink, and leaned back against the counter, trying to catch her breath and wondering if she was crazy.

God, what had she just done?

COVERED WITH SWEAT, still feeling the burn in his muscles, Marc headed upstairs to the kitchen and found Sophie in journalist mode, arranging manila folders, newspaper clippings, and documents on the dining room table, a determined look on her face. His old T-shirt was baggy on her, but she was wearing the *hell* out of his boxers, the curves of her ass putting a stretch on that cotton that knocked the breath from his lungs. *Jesus!*

He walked over to the sink, filled a glass with cold water, and guzzled, trying to get his mind back where he needed it to be. He'd have thought that making love with her last night would have taken some of the edge off his raging libido. Instead, it seemed to have made that edge sharper, his senses fine-tuned to her—her scent, her mood, every move she made. He was more sexually revved than he'd ever been, as if finally tasting sex after six years had sent his balls into testosterone overload.

Bullshit, Hunter. This is about Sophie. You're in love with her.

Okay, he could knock *that* shit off right now. Even if it were true, Sophie would never feel the same thing for him—a convict with a life sentence. She wasn't stupid. The last thing she needed was some *loser* hanging on her. And no matter what he felt for her, he hadn't broken out of prison to find romance. He was supposed to be finding Megan and Emily.

Get your priorities straight.

That's obviously what Sophie was doing. She looked up from her work and gave him a little smile. "Hey."

"Hey." Marc filled his glass again, his gaze drawn to her ass, heat skimming through his belly. "Looks like you're getting organized."

She nodded. "I'm trying, anyway. I'm just hoping I brought

everything with me. I was so upset when I left the paper that I couldn't think straight."

Marc leaned back against the counter and drank, listening as she worried out loud about the files she wished she'd downloaded from her computer. When he sat the glass down, his hand brushed over something. He glanced down and saw a torn purple and green packet.

It looked vaguely familiar, so he picked it up, turning it over in his fingers, reading the label: *Plan B Levonorgestrel Emergency Contraceptive.*

She must have brought it from home. Except that she hadn't been home.

Shit.

He held it up, cut off whatever she was saying. "Please tell me you didn't buy this at the drugstore this morning."

She glanced over, then her eyes went wide. She looked toward the sink, then away. "Of course, I did. It was my only option—"

"God, I wish you'd asked me first!"

Her gaze snapped back to his. "*Asked* you? I hardly think I need your permission."

She didn't get it. She didn't understand.

Marc took a deep breath. "That's not what I mean. God knows, I wouldn't blame you for doing everything possible to prevent yourself from having a baby by me. In fact, I owe you an apology. I should have used a condom last night, and I'm sorry I failed you, Sophie."

She hugged her arms across her chest, as if to soothe herself. "You're not the only one to blame. I should have—"

"No, condoms are the man's responsibility."

She blinked, turned pinker. "Well, I, um . . . I bought some of those, too."

He groaned, wishing to God he'd thought to warn her. He walked over to her, put his hands on her shoulders. "Do you realize that your friend Julian now knows you're with a man?"

Her eyes went wide again, and she paled. "What?"

"The surveillance tapes. The pharmacist." Marc watched understanding dawn on her face. "If Julian viewed the tapes or had his men question the staff, and I'm certain he did, he knows what you bought. He knows you're with a man, and I'll bet my ass he suspects it's me."

She dropped her forehead against his sweaty chest. "God, I'm an idiot!"

He stroked her hair, kissed it, the feminine scent of her shampoo sending another pulse of heat through him. "No, you're not. This is just different than anything you've done before. All you had to do was ask, and I'd have gone out last night or early this morning to get whatever you needed. This isn't about me controlling you; it's about staying safe. If they find us together, I've got no choice now but to play out the hostage scenario. I won't let them punish you for this."

"And I won't hide behind you."

"I knew you were going to say something stupid like that. But, sweetheart, here's the thing about hostages: they don't get a choice."

"I THINK THAT'S everything." Sophie studied the time line she and Hunt had put together on a sheet of poster board she'd found in the basement. "Chronology is our friend."

Hunt sat at the dining table beside her, wearing nothing but a pair of faded, low-slung jeans and aftershave, his hair tousled from his shower. He read through the time line, a thoughtful frown on his clean-shaven face, while she tried hard not to ogle him. "What's next?"

"Now we go through each event, listing questions, observations, and ideas and see if anything connects. After that, we ought to know which leads we want to follow first."

"Okay." He nodded, an almost amused look on his face. As a former agent, he was indulging her, she knew. He was letting her show him how she handled an investigation.

Sophie fought to keep her mind on their work. "The first thing that pops for me is the whole cocaine-in-the-crawl-space thing. The police searched your home the day you killed Cross, didn't they?"

He leaned back and stretched one powerful arm across the

chair to his right, exposing his army crest tattoo and revealing his chest and six-pack in their full, heart-stopping glory. Did he know what he was doing to her, or was he as oblivious as he seemed? "Yes, they searched it. The first time they found nothing, but they didn't enter the crawl space, and they didn't use dogs. That's how they managed to convince the jury it had been there all along."

Sophie stood, walked into the kitchen as much to make herself another cup of tea as to escape the shimmering cloud of sexual heat that seemed to surround him. "So someone planted it there after the shooting and then orchestrated a second search with dogs—maybe called in a tip or pretended to have new evidence against you."

"That's what I've always assumed."

She filled the tea kettle, put it on the stove, then turned to face him, leaning back against the counter, waiting for the water to boil. "Two kilos of coke is a *lot* of coke. That has to be worth—"

"About five hundred grand on the streets. The shit was uncut."

"Wow! Geez!" She couldn't even imagine that much cash. Okay, so maybe she could *imagine* it. "So someone stole it from the evidence room and planted it on you to make it seem you had a motive and a reason to premeditate murder."

Hunt nodded. "Something like that."

"That seems like a lot of work and a lot of risk. Why not just kill you?"

"That's easy. Think about it. If I'm caught with drugs, Cross's death makes sense. I shot him because he discovered I was crooked, and I go to prison. Crime solved. But if I'm found with a bullet in my head—"

She understood. "Then the cops have another crime to solve and lots of loose ends."

He grinned. "Exactly. The cops start digging, asking questions about Cross, about me. They find Megan. The whole thing blows up in this guy's face. By making sure I went down, this bastard covered his own ass. He made sure the buck stopped with me."

"So the man we're looking for had to have access to the evidence room. That means he had to be DEA or a police officer back then, right?"

He shook his head. "Not necessarily. The stuff they found on me was an exact chemical match for some shit Cross and I had brought in a couple of weeks prior to the shooting— eighteen bricks of uncut Colombian. That's why it was so incriminating. I'm guessing Cross lifted some of it himself when he and I drove it to the incinerator."

Sophie mulled over this information, got nowhere, moved on to something else. "Here's something I don't understand. Whoever planted the heroin on Megan had to have access to New Horizons. Would a guard from Denver County Jail be able to come and go from a halfway house at will?"

Hunt seemed to consider this. "Only if he were transporting someone that day. Otherwise, probably not."

"Would New Horizons have video surveillance?"

"They might, though not in residents' rooms. Still, we might be able to see who entered her room if they have cameras in the halls. If it happens to be a guard from Denver County, we'll know we have him."

"The place was swarming with cops that morning. There were five squad cars there." Sophie remembered how stunned she'd been to realize the police were there because of Megan. "I'm sure lots of people entered her room."

"You know, that's the thing." He leaned forward, rested his arms on his knees. "I've always figured Cross's accomplice for a cop. Whoever he is, he was able to stash the drugs like a pro and arrange for a second search of my house."

"Who's to say he isn't? Maybe the guard thing was totally random—" And then it hit her. "Or maybe Cross had more than one accomplice. You told me that Megan said 'they' would come after her, right? Maybe she wasn't as drugged out as she seemed. Maybe she wasn't referring to Cross. Maybe she really meant 'they.' "

Hunt stared at her. Then he squeezed his eyes shut and buried his face in his hands, and she knew he was thinking of his sister. "God! Gang raped? *Gang raped*, Sophie?"

It was a horrifying, sickening thought.

Then he looked up at her, his gaze seeming to measure her. "You'd make a good agent."

Behind her, the kettle whistled.

"Obviously not, or I wouldn't have screwed up today at the drugstore." Sophie turned back to the stove, filled her mug with steaming hot water, then set the kettle aside.

It all seemed so obvious in hindsight. Women who were hiding alone in hotels didn't need pills or condoms, therefore she shouldn't have been seen buying any. Why hadn't she realized that herself?

"Hey, I told you—this is new for you." He walked up behind her, slid one arm around her waist, nuzzled the side of her throat, planting little kisses that made her insides melt and her knees go wobbly. "Quit beating yourself up."

"It's not a small mistake, Hunt. I endangered both of us." She took her tea, pushed past him, and walked back to the table. "So, is there anything that stands out for you?"

He opened the fridge, grabbed a Murphy's, popped the top. "The smack I found in your apartment looked like it was laced with fentanyl."

"So did the stuff they found in my rental car."

"And wouldn't you know it, the stuff they found in Megan's room tested positive for fentanyl, too. I think you ought to ask the paper or your attorney to demand the lab results on all of it. If we can find out where it came from, we might be able to find our perp."

"I guess fentanyl is the hot thing these days." She took a sip of her tea. "There've been two overdoses in the past couple weeks—one involving a young prostitute and the other a female inmate at the Denver County . . . *Jail*."

She heard her own words, looked up at Hunt, chills skittering down her spine.

He crossed the room until he stood over her, the look on his face dead serious. "*Two* ODs? Both young women and both involving fentanyl? That's damned strange."

"The one at Denver County was found dead in her cell, a ruptured balloon in her stomach. I covered it." And she'd been so distracted by Hunt that she'd barely paid attention to the details of the article. She couldn't even remember the victim's name.

"Jesus!" He set his beer on the table. "I want to know everything there is to know about both victims."

"Couldn't it just be coincidence?"

"If drop dead were on the streets, there wouldn't be *two* ODs. There would be fifty or a hundred. Injection drug users would be dropping like flies all over Denver, and the ERs would be packed with addicts on respirators."

"So you're saying the drug *isn't* on the streets. How would they get it?"

"Maybe it *is* just coincidence, but we know that Cross and company brutalized other girls besides Megan." Hunt sat down, met her gaze, his face hard. "What better way to get rid of someone you want to silence, particularly someone with a history of addiction, than to give her a deadly drug she can't resist?"

CHAPTER 21

SOPHIE LOGGED OFF the Internet, wishing there were more she could do tonight. She'd sent e-mails to her attorney and to Tom, asking for the information she needed and telling them as much as she safely could about her situation. She'd asked Hunt to read the e-mails before she sent them, just to make certain she didn't inadvertently screw up again.

"I'm Marc Hunter, and I approved this message," he'd joked, kissing her cheek.

Not surprisingly, Tom had written back almost immediately. The man lived at his desk and was never far from his e-mail. He'd told her he'd already planned to follow up with DOC on her open-records request on Monday morning and assured her the paper would not let it drop. He'd also promised to get a hold of the test results on all of the heroin and to order CBI background checks on both overdose victims. Then he'd warned her to keep her head down.

"Your desk is waiting for you," he'd written.

Since when did an e-mail from Tom leave her feeling choked up?

Since your life went to hell, Alton.

Oh, yeah. Well, okay. As long as there was a reason.

John Kirschner had replied in short, staccato sentences, letting her know that he'd already filed a formal complaint with the jail and would be more than happy to subpoena New Horizons's surveillance tapes—if any such tapes existed. Then he'd reminded her not to miss her arraignment on Thursday morning and asked her to schedule an appointment sometime in the next couple of weeks to go over her case in detail.

Sophie shut down Hunt's laptop and walked out of the bedroom to the laundry room, where she retrieved her clothes from the dryer and changed into them. Then she followed her nose toward the incredible smells that seemed to be coming from the kitchen. Had Hunt made dinner? God, she hoped so, because she was suddenly starving. The last time she'd eaten a real meal had been lunch. And that had been yesterday.

She turned the corner but found the kitchen empty, pots on the stove and dishes piled in the sink. Then she heard the unmistakable *pop* of a champagne cork coming from the living room. She walked down the hallway, stepped through the doorway, and froze.

Two white candles sat in silver candleholders in the middle of a coffee table, their golden flames reflected in the dark, polished wood. The coffee table sat in the center of the room between two plush sofas and across from the fireplace, where a cozy fire crackled. Two places had been set with linen, silver, and crystal. Nearby on the floor sat a silver champagne chiller filled with crushed ice. The sultry sound of jazz drifted in the background.

Hunt poured out the champagne. "How'd it go?"

"Wow." For a moment, that's all she could say.

"Are you hungry?" He bent down, stuck the bottle in the chiller, then stood and walked toward her. He was still wearing his jeans, but he'd put on a sleek black shirt and had rolled up the sleeves. He looked casual, sexy . . . delicious.

"This is amazing."

When was the last time a man had done something romantic like this for her?

Never. That's when.

"I hope you like salmon." He slid his arm around her waist, ducked down, and brushed a kiss over her lips.

"I love salmon. What are we celebrating?"

He pressed his forehead to hers, looked straight into her eyes. *"Now*, Sophie—we are celebrating *now."*

She felt her breath catch, something bittersweet rushing through her, part hope, part despair. And suddenly she didn't know whether to laugh or cry.

"Go make yourself comfortable." He released her and strode down the hallway toward the kitchen.

She walked over to the coffee table, sat on the thickly carpeted floor, and stared into the fire, its warmth seeping into the cold places inside her.

There's no "happily ever after" for us, sprite. There's now. Only now.

Could it be that simple?

Could it be any more simple?

Neither of them had any idea what was going to happen tomorrow or even five minutes from now, but rather than worrying about it, Hunt was savoring every moment, trying to experience as many of the pleasures of life as he could before they were taken from him forever.

Tears pricked Sophie's eyes, but she fought them back, determined not to spoil the mood Hunt had obviously worked so hard to create. She needed to put her fears aside and take hold of this little taste of heaven he was offering—if not for her own sake then most certainly for his. This was as close to a normal life as he was going to get.

There's now. Only now.

Well, happy endings were overrated anyway.

Hunt walked back through the doorway and set two dinner plates on the coffee table. Sophie's mouth watered. On each sat a grilled salmon filet covered with a relish of tomatoes and black olives next to buttery baby potatoes and steamed asparagus.

"I didn't know you could cook."

"I can't—but I can read a recipe as well as the next guy." He sat, a lopsided grin on his handsome face. Then he picked up his champagne glass and fixed her with his piercing gaze. "To now."

She raised her glass, smiled. "To now."

Champagne tickled its way down her throat straight into her empty stomach. She set her glass down and tucked her napkin in her lap.

He picked up his napkin. "So what did they say?"

It took her a moment to realize what he was asking. "Tom

said he'll follow up on the request for the report and do the background checks. My attorney said he'll subpoena the halfway house's surveillance records if they have any."

"How long do you think it will take?"

"I can't be sure, but I'm guessing we'll have the information from the background checks by midday Monday. That usually takes only a couple of hours."

"Perfect. That means we can spend the weekend searching this place for information about Megan's life." He picked up his fork. "Bon appétit."

The food was delicious, the salmon soft and flaky, the relish adding tang and saltiness, the asparagus cooked to a perfect crispness. The champagne was cold and dry with a long mineral finish that went straight to Sophie's head. The tension of the past week began to melt away, the shadows chased away by good food and drink, the warmth of the fire, and the heat of his gaze. She found herself telling him about her parents' restaurant—how she'd all but grown up in the kitchen, being coddled, fed, and fussed over by a staff of finicky French chefs and a sommelier who took her wine education seriously, even when she was six.

"That sounds like a wonderful way to grow up."

"I probably would have become the manager or maybe the wine buyer if . . ."

If her parents hadn't been killed.

Marc saw the grief in Sophie's eyes and knew where her thoughts had taken her.

She cleared her throat. "Sorry. I'm babbling."

"No, you're not." He reached over, took her hand, gave it reassuring squeeze. "It must have been the most horrible thing in the world to lose your mom and dad."

She nodded, took a deep breath—and then changed the subject. "So tell me about the army. Did you grow up wanting to be a soldier?"

He couldn't help but laugh. "Hell, no! I grew up wanting my mother to stop drinking and using and start acting like other kids' moms. I didn't spend a single moment thinking about the future. By the time I was a senior, it was clear that the army was my only chance to avoid mowing lawns and changing oil for the rest of my life."

As they finished the meal, he told her about boot camp and how the meanest master sergeant on the face of the earth—a bastard by the name of Stracher—had kicked his ass into gear. He told her how he'd discovered he had skill with target shooting. He told her how he'd been transferred into Special Forces after 9/11 and deployed to Afghanistan as a sniper, where he'd spent a winter high in the frigid mountains near Tora Bora.

"It must have been very hard." Her cheeks were flushed, her body relaxed, her gaze focused on him, a dreamy look in her big blue eyes. She was obviously feeling the champagne. "I'm so glad you made it home in one piece."

"You know what kept me warm at night?" He leaned in closer, brushed a strand of hair from the satin of her cheek. "I kept thinking about this beautiful girl from my hometown. I only spent one night with her—just one night—but it was the sweetest night of my life. She gave me her virginity and told me to shoot for the stars. I tried, Sophie. I tried to shoot for the stars."

He must have been feeling the alcohol, too, or he never would have said anything like that. Or maybe it wasn't the champagne. Maybe it was just being near her like this. He seemed to be running at the mouth a lot lately.

She turned her head, nuzzled her cheek against his palm, her skin unbelievably soft, her eyes drifting shut. "Did you really think of me these past six years?"

He ran the pad of his thumb over her lower lip. "Oh, yes. I thought about you. Dreamed about you. Fantasized—"

Her eyes flew open, her pupils wide and dark. "About me?"

"Yeah." *Slow down, Hunter. Do you really think a woman wants to know that sort of thing?* "Does that bother you?"

She shook her head, the flush on her cheeks going deeper, her lips parting on a breathy whisper. "I was just thinking we could . . . you know . . . try out a few of those, um, fantasies. While we have the chance."

And that *right there* blew away any fantasy.

He tried to say something, but all the blood in his body had rushed to his crotch.

"So, Marc Hunter, where do you want me?"

Geez-us!

Where did he want her? God, he wanted her everywhere. Against the wall. Spread-eagle on the bed. On her hands and knees. In the hot tub. On the dining room table. In the Jag. Hell, *on* the Jag.

But one fantasy stood out above the rest. "It's not so much *where* I want you, Sophie, as it is *how*. Nothing tastes quite like a woman, and no woman tastes like you."

She gave an almost inaudible gasp. "Then you want . . ."

"I want dessert." He stood, reached for her, drew her onto the couch beneath him.

He kissed her out of her blouse, suckling her through her bra until she was whimpering and writhing, her nipples straining against the wet lace. Then he moved on to her pants, drawing the fabric down her long legs, tasting his way down her silky skin, over her sensitive calves to the tips of her little toes. But as scrumptious as her skin was, this wasn't the taste he hungered for most.

He worked his way back up her legs, nudging her thighs apart with his hands, inhaling the wild, musky scent of her arousal, filling his lungs with her. Yes, *this* was it, the scent he'd wanted inside his head for so, so long. But now he wanted a taste.

He licked her inner thighs along the edge of her panties, heard her gasp, her fingers sliding into his hair, rough lace and soft skin both sweet against his tongue. Then he drew back and licked his way up the lace where it covered her cleft, the soft folds of her labia beneath. When his tongue felt the tiny bud of her clit, he held himself still, flicking it through the thin cloth, feeling it swell.

She whimpered, lifted her hips eagerly toward his mouth. "Please, Hunt!"

He chuckled. "Sorry, but this is my fantasy, and I'm going to take my sweet time."

She gave a pained moan. "Is this your 'torture Sophie' fantasy?"

"No, it's my 'Sophie lets me do whatever I want to do' fantasy. I'm going lick you everywhere, until your scent is imprinted on my brain, until I can taste you in my dreams, until you saturate my skin. So settle in because this is probably going to take awhile."

He saw her belly contract, felt her shiver, and knew what he'd said excited her.

"But . . . what about you?"

"Sweetheart, this *is* for me."

Sophie couldn't believe what she was feeling, the arousal so fierce as Hunt tormented her with his lips and teeth and tongue, licking, nipping, and sucking her most tender places, bringing her to the edge again and again, only to trail scorching kisses across her belly or the inside of her knees or her throat, letting the inferno inside her cool before finding his way back to the place she burned hottest. And she *was* burning, her skin now so sensitive that no matter where he touched her, his mouth felt like fire, a river of hot cream flowing between her legs. Her senses were overloaded, her lungs straining for breath, her nails cutting into his shoulders, into the fabric of the sofa, into her own palms as she tried to hold on.

And he hadn't even taken off her panties yet.

When he did, slipping his hands beneath her to pull the soaking cloth down her legs, the anticipation was almost more than she could take. She opened her eyes, felt her heart trip as he settled his head between her thighs and parted her gently with his fingers, his gaze fixed on the most private part of her, an expression of blatant male hunger on his face.

"Hunt, I—oh!"

He cut her off with one long swipe of his tongue, whatever she'd wanted to say lost in a rush of pleasure. "Give yourself to me, Sophie."

And then Sophie was lost, his tongue stroking her, flicking her, thrusting deeply into her, his lips tugging on her aching clitoris, suckling her, drawing her into the heat of his mouth, one of his arms thrown across her hips to keep her from bucking. Again and again he drove her to the brink, only to back off and leave her hanging in midair, desperate, panting, begging him to fill the throbbing emptiness inside her and finish this.

Then at last he slid up the length of her body and kissed her long and hard on the mouth, his skin drenched with her own wild taste and scent. She reached for his zipper, frantic to free the bone-hard ridge of his cock and feel it inside her. But he caught her hands.

"*No!* Not yet." He stood, scooped her into his arms, and carried her across the room until he stood in front of the fireplace. Then he sank to the floor, laid down on his back, and drew her up his body, grasping her hips and guiding her until she straddled his face, her weight resting on her shins, her core hovering just above his mouth.

"Oh, God!" She was breathless, trembling, more aroused than she'd ever been.

"God, what a view!" He steadied her above him, then reached up to unclasp her bra, catching the weight of her breasts in his hands, his fingers teasing her nipples with strokes she felt deep in her belly. And then he unleashed his mouth on her again, and all she could do was surrender.

Marc was in heaven, surrounded by Sophie, his senses full of her. He palmed her breasts, teased the rosy velvet of her nipples, drinking in the flood of warm honey that was her body's response. He could have kissed her like this forever. It didn't matter to him that his cock felt like it had rigor mortis or that his balls had probably gone from blue to black or that the Glock he'd tucked into his jeans—and subsequently forgotten—was jabbing him in the small of the back. He wanted to give her every bit of pleasure she could take.

He'd gone slowly with her, searching out what she liked most, gauging her reactions, learning to read her body's sexual rhythm, and now he was putting that knowledge to good use, drawing out her pleasure, making her wait, giving both of them time to savor it. Then he knew it was time to let her go. He closed his mouth over her clit and suckled her.

She whimpered, her back arching, her breasts pressing

more deeply into his hands, her fingers fisting in his hair. "Hunt . . . oh, God . . . oh, Hunt!"

He wasn't sure he'd ever known a woman as sensual and responsive as Sophie. Even when she'd been a virgin and sixteen, she'd been unafraid to give herself over to sexual pleasure. She'd blown him away that night. And she sure wasn't holding back now, the sounds coming from her throat uninhibited, raw, blatantly sexual.

He drew a hand down, probed her slick entrance with one finger, then two, teasing her.

Her reaction was immediate. "Oh, *yes* . . . please . . . please!"

He thrust inside her, stroking her, feeling her inner muscles tighten around his fingers. He suckled her harder, keeping his rhythm steady both inside and out, her cries more frantic, every muscle in her body tense.

Her breath caught and held, her body going stiff as the first tremors washed through her. She exhaled in a shuddering cry, coming against his mouth in a gush of hot nectar, her body shaking with pleasure. He stayed with her, letting her ride it out, the moisture of her orgasm wet on his fingers and lips and tongue. God, he loved her.

Yes, he loved her. He loved everything about her.

Too damn bad for both of them, really, but that's how it was.

"Hunt." She looked down at him, breathless, the longing in her eyes seeming to mirror the hunger inside him. Then she stretched out next to him and lowered her mouth to his in a slow, deep kiss, her fingers fumbling with the buttons of his shirt.

And suddenly he couldn't get out of his clothes and into her fast enough. He helped her take off his shirt, then pulled a condom out of his pocket, working it onto his erection, while she pulled off his jeans and briefs. Then he eased her beneath him and settled himself between her thighs, his gaze colliding with hers as he slid into her with a single slow thrust.

"Oh, Sophie, honey, I . . ." *Love you. I love you.*

He bit back the words, forced himself to focus only on the

physical act of loving her, grinding his pubic bone against her with each hard thrust, the slippery friction driving them both insane. God—*Christ!*—she felt so good. He was hanging on the edge . . . hanging . . . holding back, wanting it to be good for her, wanting her, wanting all of her, until with a cry, she gave herself to him, her eyes squeezed shut as the crest of another climax surged through her, carrying him over the edge, his orgasm hot and fast and strong.

And as the pleasure peaked, he saw it all—the man he might have been, the life he might have lived. It was there in her perfect eyes, looking up at him.

CHAPTER 22

SOPHIE OPENED A box labeled "Misc." and found herself digging through a strange assortment of electronics junk—old computer power cords, cell phone chargers, circuit breakers, switch plates, and antenna wires. Did Mr. and Mrs. Rawlings keep everything?

She packed the wires and cords back into the box, closed it, and carried it to the far basement wall where Hunt was stacking boxes that had already been checked. "More junk."

He glanced down at her, nodded. "Go ahead and put it down there."

She'd awoken to find him still asleep, all six feet four inches of him stretched out naked beside her, a sheet dragged over one hip. For a while, she'd watched him, her gaze drifting over him—the ridges and valleys of his muscles, the soft curls of his chest hair, that *mouth*.

That mouth had given her the single most explosive climax of her life. Never had she felt so deliciously out of control, so sexually needy, so completely at a man's mercy. He'd taken her to the brink not once, but twice, the first with his lips and tongue, then with his body, driving into her hard and fast, his gaze seeming to pierce her soul. Then afterwards he'd held her, kissing her until the fire died down and she got chilly and it was time for bed. She'd felt blissfully exhausted, replete— and so deeply in love with him that it had hurt.

Despite all her dire warnings to herself, she'd fallen in love with Marc Hunter.

Or maybe she'd loved him all along.

As she'd watched him sleep, she'd felt a strange surge of

protectiveness. Despite the muscles and tattoos, he'd seemed somehow vulnerable. Maybe it was his long eyelashes. Or the lines of fatigue on his face. Or the way he nudged toward her in his sleep, as if he needed to be closer to her. Or maybe it was knowing what he would face if he were caught—a life of isolation, loneliness, deprivation.

Just the thought of it had left her feeling sick.

She'd found herself needing to touch him and had explored his body, savoring the feel of him, watching his body's response. He'd awoken with a moan, the surprise on his face turning to bliss when she'd taken him into her mouth. He'd watched her give him head, holding her hair back from her face, his breath hissing from between his clenched teeth.

"God, Sophie, you are *too good* at this."

She'd teased him with her tongue, worked her hand and mouth in tandem up and down his length, loving the hard feel of him, taking her time, enjoying her sense of control. Just as he'd done for her, she'd tried her best to drive him crazy and had felt a thrill when he'd begun to unravel, saying her name over and over again, one big hand fisting in her hair, the other clenched in the sheets. At the last second, he'd lifted her mouth off him and had come in her hand, his head falling back on a groan, his back arching off the bed, ribbons of hot white semen shooting from deep inside him.

They'd lain there for awhile in silence, then he'd made long, slow love to her, every touch so tender and intimate that Sophie had come close to tears. Even though he hadn't said it, she'd known what he was thinking, had seen it in his eyes.

There's now. Only now.

Afterward, she'd made omelets, hash browns, and coffee for breakfast, while he'd taken a shower and dressed in jeans and a dark green T-shirt. He'd devoured every bite with such enthusiasm that she'd wished she'd made more. Then it had been her turn for a shower. By the time she'd dried off and dressed in a pair of borrowed jeans and a sweatshirt—she and Mrs. Rawlings were thankfully close in size—he was down here in the basement hard at work.

They'd already gone through almost half of the boxes in

this room, searching for anything that might tell them where to look for Megan next—a diary that mentioned childhood friends, videos or photographs of friends or relatives who might have taken her in, favorite places she liked to visit. Instead they'd found old hymnals, mimeographed Sunday school lessons, old clothes and shoes, extra clothes hangers, broken kitchen gadgets, and cheesy Christmas decorations.

Sophie could tell from the occasional frown on his face that he was worried about his sister and niece and more than a little frustrated by their lack of progress, and she couldn't blame him. The idea that the two overdose victims might somehow be related to Megan's disappearance was terrifying.

Sophie pushed a heavy box aside, leaving it for Hunt, and found several smaller, dusty boxes tucked behind it. They were taped shut, the tape yellowed with age. She reached down, grabbed the bottom box to pull them out—and shrieked and stumbled backward as something large and black and probably eight-legged darted out from behind the box.

Strong arms caught her. "You okay?"

She pointed. "A really big spider—"

"I see it. Looks like a black widow."

"Oh, God! I almost grabbed it!" A cold, greasy feeling slid through her stomach.

Hunt set her upright and walked past her toward the boxes she'd been moving, and she could tell from his voice that he was smiling. "I didn't know you were arachnophobic."

"I'm not. The word *phobia* implies there's something abnormal about my reaction to spiders—horrid little monsters! They deserve to be hated!"

He chuckled, then knelt down. "Oh, she's a big one, all right. Look at that fat belly."

Sophie moaned, her stomach turning.

He glanced over at her, a grin on his face. "She's a lot more frightened of you than you are of her."

Sophie shook her head. "I don't know about that."

But Hunt kept on. "Think about it. This is the end of the line for her, and some part of her tiny spider brain knows it. See how she's trying to hide?"

Sophie looked away, her skin crawling. "Oh, stop!"

She heard a *thunk*, then Hunt walked by her, holding something—an old boot?—in his hands. A moment later she heard the toilet flush and water running in the sink. Then Hunt reappeared and drew her into his arms.

"It's okay, sprite. You're safe now. I saved you from the big, bad spider." He pulled her against him, ducked down, kissed her hard on the mouth. Then he walked back to the boxes she'd been moving and nudged them with his foot. "Let me just check behind here and see whether . . ."

Sophie stiffened. "Are there more?"

He shook his head, bent down, and turned the boxes to face her.

And there on the side, scrawled in black marker, was the word *Megan*.

MARC SET THE little plaster plate on the table, lay his open hand on top of the tiny handprint in its center, and felt something sharp twist in his chest. The indentations formed by Megan's fingers barely spanned his palm. He looked at the date etched into the plaster—May 14, 1988. Only a few months after she'd been taken away.

"Isn't this cute?" Across from him, Sophie held up a Christmas ornament that consisted of a tiny picture frame suspended from a red ribbon. In the center was Megan, giving the camera a shy smile. She was missing a tooth. "How old do you figure she was here? Six? Seven?"

"I don't know." His words came out cold, indifferent.

He set the plaster plate down, reached into the box, pulled out a stack of drawings—a very fat goldfish, three bright blue butterflies, the outline of a child's hand turned into a turkey, a menagerie that must have been Noah's ark—each one signed by the artist in a child's simple scrawl: M-E-G-A-N.

"This is hard for you, isn't it?" Sophie watched him, her gaze soft.

"Yeah." He'd known it would feel strange to sift through the debris of Megan's childhood. He just hadn't expected the experience to dredge up so many memories, so many old feelings, so much shit. He felt like shouting at someone, breaking something, his skin too tight, his fuse short.

"She loves you."

Marc didn't know what to say, so he said nothing.

"I read through my notes before coming to interview you. She mentioned you every time I spoke with her—how you helped her get into a good rehab program, how you put money in her commissary account, how you encouraged her when she was going through withdrawal."

"Yeah, I'm a fucking hero."

"Megan thinks so."

"Well, we both know that Megan has issues, don't we?" Marc set the drawings aside, stood, and walked into the kitchen, pretending to need a drink of water when what he really needed was space—or a chance to live his entire life over again.

Ain't gonna happen, dumbass.

He turned on the faucet, filled his glass, drank.

"You know what I think is so wonderful about the two of you? Even though you were separated as children and didn't see each other for almost fifteen years, you still care so much about each other. Megan was only four. It's amazing that she even remembered you after—"

Marc slammed his glass down. "Stop! Just stop!"

He turned to face Sophie and immediately felt like a dick. She stared at him, a surprised look on her face, the stack of Megan's drawings in her hands. *Shit.* "I'm sorry, Sophie. You didn't deserve that."

"Do you want to tell me what it's about?"

Not really. He walked over to the table, pulled out the chair next to her, and sat. Then he took a deep breath, rubbing his face in his hands. "Has Megan ever told you about the night Social Services came to take her away?"

Sophie shook her head. "I only know it was after her mother—*your* mother—was arrested for her second DUI."

Marc remembered that day only too well. "I came home from school to find Mom hurting for booze and Megan sitting in front of the television, still in her pajamas. Mom grabbed whatever cash we had and headed off to the liquor store, leaving the two of us at home like she sometimes did.

"A lot of time passed. Megan got hungry, started crying. I made a box of macaroni and cheese and jelly sandwiches—my specialty at the time. It got late. I tried to put Megan to bed, because she was a little kid and Mom had left me in charge, but Megan wanted to watch cartoons. I got bossy. She got mad and threw a little tantrum. Then the doorbell rang."

He couldn't believe he was telling Sophie this. He had never talked about it with anyone, not even the stupid shrink the courts assigned to evaluate him for war-related posttraumatic stress. But now that he had started he couldn't seem to stop. The memories had been playing in his head like a bad movie ever since he'd opened that first box.

"I should have known better than to answer the door, but when I saw two cops standing out there . . ."

"You trusted them."

He nodded. "They had a social worker with them, an older woman. She explained that Mom had done something wrong and was in jail and that we needed to go with the nice police officers. But I was afraid Mom would get out of jail and not know where to find us. I told them we would have to wait till she came home. God, I was an idiot!"

"No, you were a *child*." Sophie's voice was soft, sympathetic.

"The social worker explained that it would be a long time before our mom was allowed to come home and that they had come to take care of us. Then one of the officers picked Megan up and started to carry her out of the house. She was afraid and started crying and calling for me. I tried to get her away from him . . ."

Let her go! Leave her alone! She's my baby sister!

He could hear his own pathetic shouts and Megan's frightened crying.

"But they cuffed me—"

"They *cuffed* you? A ten-year-old boy? Oh, Hunt!"

"I was a hellion. I hit the officer who had her, kicked him, bit him. They put me in the back of one squad car, and Megan in the other, still in her pajamas. That night was the last I saw of my sister until after I left the army."

Sophie watched as Hunt struggled with his emotions. She'd sensed that something was eating at him. From the moment they'd started looking through Megan's things, he'd lapsed into a thick, dark silence. His face was expressionless as he spoke, but she could feel the emotion beneath—the rage, the sense of loss, the guilt. Images filled her mind, images of a neglected young boy fighting to defend his little sister against those sent to help them. How afraid he must have been, so much responsibility dumped on his ten-year-old shoulders. How helpless he must have felt when they put Megan in that car and drove her away. And the grief of losing his sister, of never seeing her again, of having been the only family nearby when they'd taken her . . .

Her throat tight, she fought to speak. "That must have been terrifying for both of you."

"Yeah. Like ice in the gut. I threw up in the squad car." He stood, took a few steps, faced the drawn curtains as if he were looking out the window, his back to her, both fists clenched. "It turns out my mom had been so hard up for a drink that she'd downed a bottle of peppermint schnapps in the parking lot of the liquor store and had run over some guy on her way back home. She damned near killed him."

Sophie stood, walked over to him, wrapped her arm around him, resting her head between his shoulders, wanting somehow to comfort him, to reach the boy inside him. "So Megan was brought here—to Mr. and Mrs. Rawlings."

"Yeah." His voice sounded flat, empty. "Within a year, the courts had terminated my mother's parental rights where Megan was concerned. She became Megan Rawlings instead of Megan Hunter. I went from one foster home to the next, too old and too angry and too much trouble to interest adoptive parents."

"You acted out because you wanted to stay with your mother."

He turned his head, glanced down at her, a suspicious look on his handsome face. "Yeah. Are you psychic?"

"No. You told me twelve years ago. Remember?" It was obvious from his confused expression that he didn't. "You said something like, 'If I'd have been a good kid, they'd have found a home for me and taken me from my mom. No matter what she's done, she doesn't deserve that.' But you didn't tell me about Megan."

Now that she knew about his sister, Hunt's teenage years made even more sense. Always in trouble, always at the center of mayhem. He'd lost his little sister, seen her taken from their home and . . .

And then Sophie understood. "That's what this is all about, isn't it? Tracking her down after the army. Killing Cross. Going out of your way to help Megan from your cell. Breaking out of prison to look for her. Risking your life to find her. You blame yourself. You blame yourself for what happened that night, and you keep trying to make up for it."

His body tensed. "That has nothing to do with this."

Sophie stepped to stand in front of him, lifting her palms to his cheeks. "It has everything to do with this. You couldn't save Megan that night, and you've beaten yourself up for it ever since."

He glared at her. "I'm her older brother. I'm supposed to take care of her!"

"Is that what your mother said? Did she try to shift the blame from herself onto you? I know you loved her, Hunt, but what she did was wrong."

A muscle clenched in his jaw, and Sophie knew her words had hit home. For a moment she thought she'd pushed him too far. But then he closed his eyes and drew a long, shaky breath. "Megan was so little and so afraid. I should've—"

"You were ten years old! There was nothing you could have done! You needed protection as much as she did. Don't you see that? It wasn't your job to save her."

He opened his eyes, gave her a sad, lopsided grin. "Is it your job to try and save me? It's sweet of you, but it won't work, Sophie."

She ignored him. "What made you decide to find Megan after you left the army?"

He wrapped his arms around her, kissed the top of her head. "My mother died while I was stationed overseas. Losing Megan destroyed her. She quit drinking, but she started shooting up and just couldn't stop. It killed her in the end—hepatitis C and liver cancer."

"So Megan was your only family."

"Yeah. After Afghanistan I felt like I'd straightened myself out enough to be a decent brother to her. But when I found her . . . God! It was like looking at a younger version of my mother."

Sophie held him tighter. "I'm so sorry, Hunt! I'm so sorry!"

She knew the rest of the story. Hunt had gotten his sister into rehab and was helping her to turn her life around, when Cross had come over and Hunt had learned the truth about his DEA buddy—and had killed him. It was terrible beyond words.

But at the same time . . .

"You know, if we could win you a new trial and present all of this to a jury, prove the drugs weren't yours—"

"No!" He set her away from him, looked straight into her eyes. "No new trial. No jury. I told you already. I won't put Megan on the stand. She's been through too much already."

"She's not a helpless little girl anymore, Hunt. She has the right to make that decision for herself! Do you think it will do her any good to watch you rot in prison, knowing that she could have helped you and didn't?"

"It won't accomplish anything! Even if my conviction is overturned, I'll still end up in prison for a long damned time, and Megan will feel like she's been raped all over again. Think about it. On top of Cross's murder, I would also be facing charges of assault on an officer, theft, felony menacing, kidnapping, breaking and entering. What do I stand to gain, Sophie?"

"Justice!" She shouted the word, tears pricking her eyes. "Even if they sentence you to life, at least you'll have a chance for parole. I won't watch you throw your life away, not if there's the slightest chance for us—"

"For us to be together? Are you going to wait for me until I'm sixty?" He shook his head, gave a little laugh, drew her back into his arms. "Remember what I told you? No happy endings. Don't try to make these few stolen days more than they are, Sophie. You'll only end up getting hurt."

But Sophie knew it was already too late for that.

CHAPTER 23

By NOON, THEY'D found three more boxes in the basement, each of them holding mementos of Megan's childhood. None of it would help them find her, but every piece of it felt like a prize to Marc—crafts projects, two blue ribbons from track-and-field day, a little book of poems she'd written. He looked at each one, held them, then passed them on to Sophie for repacking. Somehow, telling her had made this easier, as if some of the weight he'd carried for so long had been lifted from his shoulders.

It was Sophie who found it, scrawled in black marker on the foot of an old brown teddy bear. She held up the stuffed animal's foot for him to see, her eyes glittering with tears, a sad smile on her sweet face. "Look what she named him."

Mark.

Megan had spelled it wrong, but there it was—his name.

Sophie ran her thumb over the awkwardly spelled letters. "So Megan snuggled with a teddy bear named 'Mark.' I'd say she missed you and that thinking of you made her feel safe. How wrong it was to tear two siblings apart like that! My relatives talked about splitting David and me up, but my grandma, bless her heart, wouldn't hear of it. I don't think I fully appreciated what she did for us until just now."

Marc took the bear and looked at his misspelled name, feeling like his chest might burst. The stuffed creature was lumpy and worn, a few of its seams threadbare, one of its eyes sewn back on with a different color thread than the other. It looked as if it had been hugged a lot before it ended up in this dusty box.

And just like that Marc knew what he wanted to do. "Let's pack this stuff up and go."

"Go where?"

"Mr. and Mrs. Rawlings disowned Megan. They tossed her out of the house on her eighteenth birthday. This stuff no longer belongs to them. I'm taking it someplace safe."

"And where's that?"

"Boulder."

The drive up US-36 took only thirty-five minutes. It could have gone a lot faster, but Marc decided it was best to stick to the speed limit. Besides, with Sophie beside him and classic rock on the radio, he was right where he wanted to be. The day was sunny and warm, one of those strange Colorado winter days that seemed like spring. Ahead of them, the Rockies stretched as far as the eye could see to the north and south and far into the west, a horizon of jagged white.

"I understand why you're doing this, and I can't say I blame you." Sophie looked over at him from beneath her sunglasses, her expression neutral. "But technically this is theft."

Marc grinned. "Details."

And then they came to his favorite part of the drive, where the highway came to the top of McCaslin Mesa and the entire Boulder Valley opened up in front of them, plains colliding with mountains and reaching a compromise with the foothills.

"God, I've always loved this view—Bear Peak, Green Mountain, the Flatirons."

She nodded, smiled. "Me, too."

He glanced at the digital clock on the dash. It was almost two. "You hungry?"

He drove her to University Hill—or The Hill as it was known to locals—and stopped for a couple of sub sandwiches.

"Are you sure this is a good idea?" Sophie said under her breath as they walked into the sub shop. "Aren't we supposed to be staying out of sight? What if someone recognizes you? What if there are cameras?"

He slipped his arm around her shoulder, kissed her temple. "Would you relax? I haven't seen a single camera, and no one is paying attention to us. They're not looking for us here."

His mouth watering, he perused the menu for ten minutes before deciding to go with the pastrami. They ate outdoors on the patio, taking in the tie-dyed, dreadlocked, pierced-lip street scene, soaking up the sunshine, talking about everything and nothing in particular, the ordinariness of the moment seeming so extraordinary to Marc. He did his best to absorb the feeling, that crazy indulgent feeling of being with her, of being able to reach over and touch her hand or lick mustard off her lower lip, of watching her face and hearing her voice as she spoke, of simply having *time* with her.

After lunch, they strolled back to the car, Marc dragging Sophie into an ice cream shop where she got a single scoop of strawberry and he got a bowl piled high with four scoops—cookie dough, mint chocolate chip, double fudge chocolate, and peanut butter—which he immediately devoured.

"Damn this was good." He licked his spoon. "I should've gotten the rocky road, too."

Sophie watched Marc polish off the last of his ice cream, both amused by his enthusiasm for such simple pleasures and saddened by it. It made her happy to see him enjoying himself, but it also reminded her of everything he would lose when he was caught. She wished she could give him everything—a lifetime's worth of taste and touch and smell and sound to carry him through any darker days that might lay ahead. And not for the first time she found herself praying that he and Megan would reach Mexico and find a way to build a life there.

She hadn't told him about the pills yet—the pills she *hadn't* taken. She wasn't sure how he'd feel about it. She didn't want him to worry, and she didn't want to get his hopes up. The night they'd had sex had been twelve days into her cycle—she'd counted on the calendar last night—so there was a good chance she'd been fertile. Instead of feeling horrified by that thought as she ought to have been, she'd found herself hoping she *was* pregnant. At least she'd have a part of him to hold onto.

Thursday would be here far too soon, and after that . . .

She didn't want to think about it.

"You're going to have to slow down on the eats if you want

to keep your trim figure," she teased, poking him in his 3-percent-body-fat, hard-as-steel abdomen.

He looked at her over the top of his sunglasses and grinned. "You'll have to help me work it off later."

And Sophie felt herself blush.

THEY WALKED BACK to the car, fingers twined, then headed north on Broadway.

"So are you going to tell me where we're going?"

"I have a storage locker. I rented it when I was still out on bond, paid for it in cash, put it under my mother's name. The cops and the feds didn't manage to take all my assets—I had some savings from the army they couldn't touch and all my personal belongings. I brought it all here—cash, clothes, gear. I set it aside in case I needed to leave town fast. For awhile, I thought of taking Megan and making a run for it, but I didn't want her getting caught up in all of it. I think some stupid part of me still thought I'd get a sentence I could live with—twenty years with parole in ten or some shit."

"Well, you were wrong about that."

The storage facility was on the north edge of town not far from the strip club and the homeless shelter. Hunt drove through the open front gate and wound his way through rows of what looked like garages, all painted bright sherbet orange. He turned into the last row, drove three doors down, and parked.

"You need to see this," he said.

Sophie got out of the car and followed him, watching as he bent down and turned the numbers on the door's combination lock—6-9-1-9-9-6. For a moment, she didn't think anything of it. And then it clicked.

June 9, 1996.

"That's . . . !" The night of the graduation party. The night they'd first been together. "You remembered."

"Of course." He pulled the lock free. "Most important night of my life."

The door rolled up, just like a garage door. Inside was a cold, dark space about the size of a single-car garage that was piled high with boxes. While Hunt carried Megan's stuff in from the car, Sophie walked inside and glanced around. A mountain bike stood propped up against boxes. A kayak lay on its side against the far wall next to some skis. There was a dusty bookshelf and an old VCR. And there, on the floor to one side was a familiar-looking backpack. Beside it was a sleeping bag in a stuff sack.

"You came here. After you left me at the cabin, you came here."

"Yeah. I crashed for a few hours, then changed clothes and headed into Denver."

"And to think I was worried."

He set the last two boxes down and glanced over at her. "You worried about me?"

"I was afraid you'd frozen to death." She poked around, looked in some of the boxes and found clothes, shoes, books, CDs, videos, photo albums.

Sophie picked up one of the photo albums, brushed off the dust, opened it. Whatever she'd been expecting, it wasn't this—a portrait of Hunt in an army dress uniform in front of an American flag. He looked handsome enough to make her knees weak, happy, and confident, his face free of the worries he carried now.

So that's how he was before all of this happened.

She turned the pages. Hunt wearing only briefs and dog tags, hanging with his buddies in the barracks. Hunt sitting in full combat gear in a helicopter, mountains visible outside the chopper's door, his jaw set. Hunt standing on a desolate patch of dirt road, stubble on his face, body armor over winter camo, holding a mean-looking rifle and standing in front of what could only be a land mine.

"Afghanistan." He came up behind her, wrapped his arm around her waist. "Damn mines were everywhere."

"What happened to your army buddies?" She was almost afraid to ask.

"Some of them left the service. Most stayed in, went to Iraq. A few were killed there."

"I'm sorry." She turned the pages, fascinated by the

photographs, each one a window on a part of him that she knew nothing about. Hunt outside a mud hut. Hunt next to a Humvee parked beside the rubble of a bombed village. Hunt in a T-shirt and khakis playing soccer with a group of Afghan boys. "Do your army buddies know?"

"About my situation? Yeah. They stood by me at first. The cocaine in the crawl space was too much for them. I don't blame them."

"What's this?" She pointed to a photo of him standing, cleaned up and in dress uniform, shaking the hand of someone who, judging from the ribbons on his chest, must have been a high-ranking officer.

"I'm getting my Bronze Star."

Astonished, she looked up at him. "You earned a Bronze Star?"

He nodded. "Doesn't matter now, does it?"

"It matters to me." She closed the album, slid it back into the box—but not before sliding a few of the photographs out and tucking them in her purse.

"Come here." He took her hand, led her to a box full of kitchen stuff, and pulled out a coffee can. He opened it, reached in, and pulled out a stack of hundred dollar bills. "After today, there will be only about five grand left in here. I never told Megan about it, because I knew she'd spend it on drugs. But I want you to know. That's one of the reasons I brought you here. If anything happens to me, everything in here goes to you. Do whatever you want with it, but please watch over Megan and especially Emily."

Sophie had to turn away to keep from bursting into tears.

MARC DROVE SOUTH on 28th Street, which would eventually turn into US-36. Sophie sat beside him in silence, and he knew he'd upset her. There hadn't been any way around that, as far as he could see. The situation was what it was, and he couldn't change it. He'd wanted her to know about his stash, and now she knew. If he were killed or landed back in the pen, his stuff would end up going to someone who cared about him instead of landing in the trash. And if she ever needed cash in a hurry, she knew where to find it.

He pulled up at a red light, glanced to his left. "Wow! Look at that."

"They tore down the old mall a few years ago and built this. Pretty upscale, huh?"

"Yeah." He popped on the turn signal, slid into the turn lane.

"What are you doing?"

"Taking you shopping."

She turned in her seat and gaped at him. "What? Are you nuts?"

"You haven't figured that out already?"

"You're taking too many risks, Hunt! You can't do this!" She was still protesting as he parked in the underground garage. "You can't go in there! They've got tons of cameras. I won't do it, Hunt. I won't go in there with you. I won't do anything that will put you in danger!"

"You're right—I can't go in there. But you can." He reached into his pocket and pulled out a stack of hundreds. "I hate seeing you in Mrs. Rawlings's ugly shit. Go buy yourself a few nice things. I'll wait right here."

"I won't take your money, Hunt. You're going to need that."

He raised an eyebrow. "Am I?"

She glared at him. "You scare me when you say things like that. I hate it!"

He caught her chin, forced her to meet his gaze. "We both know where I'm likely to end up. If I want to spend my money on you, let me."

Her eyes filled with tears. Then she nodded and took the money from his hand.

"And, Sophie," he said as she stepped out of the car, "don't hold back on the lingerie. Feel free to surprise me."

He watched her walk away and settled in for the wait.

SOPHIE WALKED OUTSIDE, most of her new wardrobe in bags, the rest on her body. She couldn't believe she was doing this. But Hunt had said she should feel free to surprise him, and she had taken him seriously. With the help of three or four sales staff who'd sprung forward to help her when they'd seen the cash she was carrying—and a very helpful makeup artist at the Lancôme counter—she'd didn't look anything like the woman who'd entered the store forty-five minutes ago wearing jeans and no makeup.

Her hair was now shaped in a French twist, her face carefully made up, her body sheathed in a short silk dress as black as sin. Black patent leather heels, black silk stockings, black lace garters, and a matching black lace bra completed the ensemble. No panties.

If only she had Holly's sexual courage—and her skill at walking in spiked heels.

Doing her best to step gracefully, Sophie made her way down the stairs into the parking garage, spied the gleaming black Jaguar, and, pulse racing, walked right past it. She stopped at the end of the row and stood there, waiting. Hunt was a smart man; he would figure it out.

And she hoped he figured it out fast. She was freezing her bare butt off.

She heard the Jag's engine roar to life and took a deep breath, a giggle welling up inside her. She subdued it, fought to keep a straight face, hardly able to breathe. She couldn't blow this. She just couldn't.

The Jag rolling slowly, Hunt circled the row of parked cars like a predator circling its prey. When he finally drew along side her, she was on the driver's side. The car slowed to a stop, and the window slid down with a buzz. He raked her with his gaze, down and up and down again. "Do you need a ride?"

She lowered her voice, let the words come out slow and sultry, looking at him from beneath her eyelashes. "Only if you can take me where I need to go."

"Oh, babe, I know I can." He smiled, a slow, sexy smile. "But what's in it for me?"

Sophie walked closer, switched her shopping bags into one hand, and lifted the front of the dress just enough to show him what was—and wasn't—beneath it.

Air rushed from his lungs as if he'd been hit. "Get in."

Sophie dropped her dress back in place, took a step back-ward. "You're my first . . . customer. How do I know you won't hurt me?"

He looked at her through dark eyes. "You don't."

A tremor of excitement rushed through her. She walked around to the passenger door, which opened for her, and let Hunt take her bags. Then she slid into the seat, the heat of his gaze all over her, a look of blatant male hunger on his face.

As the car began to move, she reached over, unbuttoned his jeans, and slid her hand inside, her blood going hot when she found him already hard as granite. "You're so big!"

But he didn't answer, his eyes on the exit, his jaw clenched.

She freed him from his jeans and stroked his entire length, working him slowly, paying special attention to the engorged head. "Does that feel good?"

"Hell, yeah."

Sunlight flooded the car as it left the garage for the street. As the car turned onto the highway, she bent down and took him into her mouth.

Marc gripped the steering wheel with both hands, his mind completely blown. When he'd told her to surprise him, he'd been thinking of a white lace teddy and maybe a thong or two, not a full-blown sex game and road head. Oh, but here he was, driving on the highway, going fifty-five, and getting the best blow job of his life, his cock in her hot, wet mouth.

And, Jesus, what was she doing with her tongue?

Merging traffic. Slow down.

"You're pretty good, babe." The words came out ragged and gruff. "God, yeah, really good."

She moaned, tightened her grip, took him into her throat.

Throbbing heat filled his pelvis, made his balls ache.

Speed limit fifty-five. Speed up. Whoa! Slow down.

He reached down, sank his fingers in her hair, holding the steering wheel with one hand, his hips lifting of their own ac-cord, urging her to go faster. "God, yes! Fuck me with your mouth!"

Faster. Faster. Yes!

The Louisville exit passed in a blur.

Slow down!

Then she reached down, forced her hand between his thighs, and cupped his balls, keeping up the rhythm with her mouth, her tongue swirling over the aching head of his cock, swirling, flicking, stroking.

Orgasm shot through him in great, wracking spasms, the pleasure sharp and hot, Sophie taking all of it. How he managed to keep the car on the road, he didn't know. All he knew was that when he could think again, they were still on the highway, and no one was dead.

She sat up, ran kisses along his throat, his jaw. "Did you like that?"

Two could play at this game.

"I'm not finished with you yet, babe. I intend to get my money's worth."

She shivered. "What do you want from me?"

"Lean your seat back, spread your legs and rest your knees on the dash. Then lift your dress above your waist."

"But—"

"Do it!"

She did as he asked, exposing her soft inner thighs and the red gold curls of her muff, opening for him like an exotic tropical flower, rosy and sweet. One eye on the road and one on her, he indulged himself and played with her, feeling the softest part of her, teasing her swollen clit, sliding his finger inside her. Soon she was lifting her hips, whimpering, pleading with him. By the time he'd pulled into the garage, she had already come once, and he was hard again, his libido sent into overdrive by her erotic game.

He jerked the car to a stop, turned off the engine, and closed the garage door behind them. Then he walked around to the passenger side, opened her door, and hauled her into his arms for a long, hard kiss. But he wanted more. He pulled her around to the front of the car, turned her to face away from him, and bent her over the hood of the Jag, lifting her dress, exposing her delicious bare ass.

"I'm going to fuck you now just the way I want to—hard

and fast." He reached into his pocket, pulled out a condom, opened it, and rolled it down the length of his erection. Then, gripping her hips, he drove into her.

She closed around him like a fist, the fit so perfect that it seemed a miracle, every thrust better than the one before. He wanted to make it last, wanted to make sure she enjoyed it, too. But the sight of her bent over the hood of the Jag in her sexy black dress, her bare ass exposed, his cock pounding into her, brought him hurtling toward the edge.

Faster . . . God, yes! Harder . . .

She felt so damned good.

Slick . . . tight . . . like heaven.

He felt the tension inside her peak and shatter. Her breath broke, became a cry, her back arching as she came. And then he was thrusting into her mindlessly, lost in the hot rush of release.

"JUST A LITTLE more. Over. Over. There! Got it!" Triumph sounded in Hunt's voice as the snowflake settled on Sophie's nipple and instantly melted. He ducked his head around and licked the tiny droplet of water up with this tongue. "Mmmm."

Sophie laughed, closed her eyes, her body floating in the steaming water, her head resting against Hunt's shoulder, his arm around her waist. They'd been catching snowflakes like this for a while now, and she could have stayed in the hot tub forever, skin to skin with him, the night sky overhead, snow falling in lazy, fat flakes around them. It was a perfect moment, and she didn't want it to end.

He nuzzled her ear. "You're turning into a prune, sprite."

She didn't care.

After having crazy sex on the Jag, the two of them had taken a nap. Then she'd made dinner—salmon again—while Hunt had moved his search into the attic. After dinner, she'd modeled her new clothes for him, focusing especially on the lingerie. Naturally, this had resulted in more crazed sex—this time straddling his lap in front of the mirror so that she could watch him enter her body—and then he'd brought her out to the hot tub for champagne under the stars.

"Come on. It's time to go inside." Ignoring her moan of protest, he stood, lifted her to her feet and climbed out of the tub, his bare butt a sight to behold. He pulled two towels out of the towel warmer. "Here."

"Thanks." She stepped into the towel's toasty warmth, her body so heated that the night air didn't bother her—for a couple of seconds. "God, it's cold!"

They hurried inside through ankle-deep snow, hand in hand.

"You can have the first shower. I'm going to poke around on the Internet."

Sophie pressed a kiss to his bare chest, then walked off to the bathroom to rinse off. She dropped the towel, turned on the water, and stepped under the spray, suddenly very drowsy. By the time she was dried and wearing her new silk bathrobe, she could hardly keep her eyes open. Must have been all that hot water.

And all that hot sex.

She brushed her teeth, then shuffled from the bathroom, making a line for the bed.

That's where she found Hunt. He'd slipped into a pair of jeans and was leaning back against the headboard, looking at the screen of his laptop, a frown on his face.

He glanced over at her. "When did you last check your e-mail?"

"This morning."

"Well, you might want to check it now. There's breaking news. A man was found dead in an apparent suicide this weekend. According to your paper's website, he worked as a guard at Denver County Jail."

CHAPTER 24

MARC PASSED THE semi, dirty slush spraying over the Jag's windshield from the truck's massive tires. He sprayed wiper fluid over the glass and turned on the wipers. "I'm not buying it. It's too simple, too tidy. Corrupt guard screws up and sparks an internal investigation. He knows he'll get caught, so he panics—and kills himself? Kind of drastic."

"I see what you're saying." Beside him, Sophie was glancing at the CBI reports she'd gotten from Tom this morning. "But maybe he realized this internal investigation would expose his earlier crimes—multiple counts of first-degree rape, prisoner abuse—so he freaked out and killed himself. We need to see it from his point of view—disgrace, humiliation, prison."

Marc shook his head. "I can't say why, but it still doesn't feel right. I really need to read through the police and autopsy reports, look at the facts myself."

She looked up at him. "You think he was murdered."

"I think it's a possibility."

"The coroner's office ought to make the report public in the next couple of days. The police report is probably already waiting in my e-mail."

"But here's the thing, Sophie. Even if this Joseph Addison was the same guard who tried to get into your cell—and we don't know that for sure yet—it doesn't necessarily mean—"

"That he was one of the men who assaulted Megan and the other girls. Yeah, I know."

"Maybe he had his own gig going on at the jail. Or maybe

he developed a fascination with you after all the news coverage. Maybe he just wanted an autograph to sell on eBay."

In journalist mode, she ignored his joke. "So as I see it, here are the possibilities: either he was working with Cross, or he wasn't working with Cross. Either he committed suicide, or he was murdered. If he did commit suicide, that tells us nothing. If he was murdered *and* he was working with Cross, then we know there's someone else out there."

Someone willing to do anything to hide the past.

"Sounds right." Marc glanced over at Sophie, feeling a sense of pride in her investigative abilities. She really would make one hell of an agent. "Of course, the difficult part is gathering enough evidence to decide which of those scenarios is true."

"Endicott." She pointed to the exit sign. "Then turn left."

They drove in silence for a time, Marc mulling over the guard's alleged suicide, while Sophie went over her interview questions. They'd gotten the CBI reports on both overdose victims this morning, and what they'd learned had convinced Marc that they were on the right track. According to the CBI, both girls were Megan's age, and both had sealed juvenile records and a history of drug abuse. On the surface, it might seem like coincidence. But the fact that they'd overdosed on fefe within a week of each other—the two of them, and *no one else*—hinted at a very different story.

"I'm starting to think driving the Jaguar wasn't such a good idea."

"Yeah. Me, too." Marc glanced around at lovely downtown Endicott, Colorado.

Signs of poverty and deprivation were everywhere. Endicott looked like a squatter's village, with dilapidated homes, lean-tos, and trailers making up the bulk of the houses in town. Old, rusted-out cars and pickups sat on cinder blocks in people's front yards or on the streets. Snow lay in muddy drifts beside bins overflowing with garbage.

The Jag stuck out like a black stallion in a barnyard of goats. And Sophie, with her gleaming hair and classy new suit, would stand out, too. It made Marc uncomfortable not because he was afraid someone would steal the car or try to hurt Sophie with him nearby, but because they would be noticed—and remembered.

"A tornado came through here about five years ago and leveled the place," Sophie told him. "Most of the people were poor and lived in trailers and weren't eligible for federal aid. We did a big story on it. I guess they've rebuilt as best they could."

"Looks like it."

Marc and Sophie had used the CBI reports to track down the family of one of the victims, and they'd come here to interview the parents and to see whether they could confirm any connection to Megan. If Marc's hunch paid off and there *was* a connection, then there was a chance the parents might have the DOC report or might remember details like the guards' names. It was even possible that they might have some idea where Megan was hiding. It was a long shot, but their only alternative was to sit around until Sophie got test results back on the heroin. Neither of them felt like waiting.

And yet as much as Marc wanted to get to the bottom of things, there was a part of him that hoped this was a dead end. It enraged him to think that these young women might have been murdered and that the same man or men might still be after his sister. Even more, he hated the fear that prowled the back of his mind—his growing fear that Megan was already dead.

After Sophie had gone to sleep last night, he'd surfed the Internet for reports about unidentified bodies, abandoned babies, and fefe, but hadn't found anything that could have been Megan. The body of a black or Hispanic woman on a Miami beach. An abandoned newborn in Detroit. A dead teenage boy in the bus station in East St. Louis. The bones of what appeared to be a woman in Alaska. But that didn't mean Megan was still alive.

Hiding a corpse wasn't that difficult—if you knew how.

"That should be it just ahead—423 First Street." Sophie double-checked the address she'd printed out from her computer. "Yep, that's it."

The house was little more than a clapboard shanty, gray wood showing through the worn white paint. A chain-link fence surrounded part of the front yard but was missing entirely from the east side. The screen door was missing its screen.

She took a pen and her reporter's notebook from her brief-case and made sure her digital recorder was in her purse. "I don't know how long this will take. Their daughter died only a few days ago. They might not be ready to talk yet."

Hunt pulled to a stop in front of the house and parked. "I know you'll do your best."

She got out of the car and made her way up the front walk, smiling at two young boys who had stopped playing in the yard next door to stare at the car. She walked up the front porch—really just wooden planks hammered crookedly together—and knocked on the door.

A woman answered, eyeing Sophie suspiciously, her gaze traveling to the Jaguar. "You lost or somethin'?"

The woman was probably in her fifties with long hair that was now more gray than blond, gray eyes that held a lifetime of hardship, and a flat mouth that expressed her mistrust. She was dressed in some kind of work uniform, navy blue poly-ester pants and matching shirt.

"Lisa Brody? I'm Sophie Alton from the *Denver Independent*. I'm really sorry to just show up on your doorstep like this, but I wondered if you might be able to answer a few questions about your daughter, Kristina Brody. I've been covering—"

A deep voice came from the back. "Who is it?"

Mrs. Brody's voice was gritty, the voice of a lifelong smoker. "Some girl from the paper come to talk about Kristy."

A tall man with a prodigious beer gut and short dark hair appeared from what must have been the kitchen. Dressed in a stained tank top and jeans, dark bristles on his chin, he in-stantly put Sophie on edge. His gaze slid over her, and he smiled. "Well, let her in."

"Thank you." Sophie stepped inside and was led to an old sofa that was covered by a tattered quilt. She sat and pulled out her digital recorder. "First, let me say how sorry I am about your daughter's death. I can't imagine what you must be going through right now."

"That's one fancy car you drive." The man held out his hand, not looking bereaved in the slightest. "The name's Ed. Ed Brody."

"Sophie Alton." Sophie took his hand, shook it, and instantly wished she hadn't because he wouldn't let go, a look of blatant lust in his eyes.

Beside him, Mrs. Brody seemed to shrink into her chair.

Sophie dragged her hand from his grasp. "So you're Kristy's father."

"As far as I know." He smiled again, giving her the creeps. "Kristy was always in trouble for one thing or another. I guess it ain't no surprise how she died."

"I've been investigating a series of drug overdoses in Denver that seem to be connected. I was hoping you might be able to help me put some pieces together by answering a few questions about Kristy's background. I understand she served time in the juvenile offender system. Do you remember where she was incarcerated and what year that was?"

"Hell, I don't remember. From the time she sprouted tits, she was trouble. I tried my best to straighten her out, but she never gave a goddamn what her daddy had to say."

Sophie felt an overwhelming sense of sadness slide through her. This man's daughter had died, and all he could do was ridicule the girl.

He leaned forward, touched her knee. "Want something to drink, Miss Alton?"

"No, thank you. I'm fine." Sophie shifted out of reach and turned to Mrs. Brody, who had sat in silence all this time. "Mrs. Brody, do you remember where your daughter was sent or what year it was?"

Mrs. Brody nodded. "She was sent to that fancy new place in Denver for about eleven months when she was sixteen. Her boyfriend shot someone up, and she was with him. They punished her same as him."

The "new place" could only be Denver Juvenile.

And the date—Sophie did quick mental math—was a dead match.

Kristina Brody had been incarcerated in the same place at the same time as Megan. And now she was dead. Somehow killed by what was starting to seem like a not-so-accidental overdose.

Murdered.

The hair rose on the back of Sophie's neck, chills sliding down her spine.

"Lisa, go fetch Miss Alton something to drink. Make a nice pot of tea."

Shaken, Sophie pulled her thoughts together. "No, thanks, I'm—"

"Go make our guest some tea. *Now.*" It was an order, the words spoken with an authority that allowed no defiance.

Mrs. Brody hurried to the kitchen.

If Sophie hadn't been so rattled, she might have seen it coming. But when Mr. Brody sat next to her and put his meaty hand high on her thigh, it took her by complete surprise.

His gaze dropped to her breasts. "I had a special relationship with Kristy. I know more about her than her mother did. I knew my daughter's nature, and—"

"Get . . . your . . . hand . . . *off* me!" It was all Sophie could do not to smack him.

He gave her a little caress, his fingers dangerously near her crotch, then withdrew his hand. "Just being friendly."

"I came here looking for answers. I'm not interested in anything else." For Megan's sake, Sophie let it pass, biting back what she truly wanted to say, afraid she'd lose the chance to learn more otherwise. Now that she knew what was at stake, she needed to do everything she could to get whatever information might be in this odious man's head.

Thank God Hunt was outside in the car!

"What kind of answers do you need, sweetheart?"

"Did Kristy report being raped when she was in Denver Juvenile?"

Mr. Brody shrugged "You know how girls are. They're always showing off how sweet and firm they are, wanting attention. And then when they get it, they're ashamed of themselves and blame it on the man."

Spoken like a true abuser.

Sophie refused to let him see how much his words upset her. "Actually, false reports of rape are no more prevalent than false reports of other serious crimes, Mr. Brody. Did Kristy report being raped while in Denver Juvenile?"

"What are you—one of them uppity feminists who turns up her nose at a man?" He shook his head as if in disgust, a mocking smile on his face. "Yeah, she and some other girls said the guards were using them. Turns out, they were using the guards, trading pussy for favors. Kristy showed her choice of profession early, I guess."

His words, so cold, so putrid, turned Sophie's stomach. She swallowed—hard. "Did you keep the report that the state issued after the investigation?"

"No, I didn't keep it. Why the hell would I? The girl shamed us."

"Do you remember the names of the other girls or the guards who abused them?" Sophie knew she was grilling him now, all pretense of politeness gone.

"Abused 'em?" He laughed. "Didn't you hear what I said? The girls took advantage of the guards. And, no, I can't remember no names."

She pushed harder. "John Cross? Joseph Addison? Or maybe Megan Rawlings? Charlotte Martin?"

He leaned closer. "If I had a little more time, I might remember, but—"

"Thanks for your help, Mr. Brody. I'll show myself out." She gathered her things, stood, and took a step toward the front door. She had the information she needed and couldn't stand being in his presence another second.

He shot to his feet, blocking her path, crowding her, his arm managing to brush against her breast. "You're a cold one, aren't you? Here we are, alone. We could be having a nice little conversation, being friendly, and you want to rush off."

Sophie was so angry she was shaking. "You see that car out there? My boyfriend is sitting in it. He's a former army Special

Forces sniper. Earned a Bronze Star in Afghanistan taking out the Taliban. Carries a forty-five. Touch me again, and I'll make *sure* he knows about it. *Get out of my way!*"

"I don't believe you." He glared at her, the lust in his eyes colored around the edges with contempt, and she found herself wondering if Hunt would be able to hear her scream. Then Mr. Brody stepped aside. "It's bad manners to reject a person's hospitality."

Sophie walked past him and opened the door, then paused and looked back at him. "It's even worse manners to try to grope your guest. And you're right. I'm an uppity feminist, but I don't turn my nose up at real men. Just at pigs masquerading as men."

She walked outside, tears of rage filling her eyes, profanity following her down the walk. Ahead of her, the Jaguar waited, its engine already running. She opened her door and slipped inside, her body trembling.

"What's wrong? Sophie, what happened?"

"Kristina Brody knew Megan."

MARC DROPPED ANOTHER box on the attic floor and jerked it open.

Sweaters.

Goddamn it!

He shut the box, shoved it aside, and turned to grab another.

You're going to lose her, Hunter. You're going to lose Megan again—and Emily with her.

Like *hell* he was.

He would find his sister if he had to tear the world apart to do it.

The basement had turned up some of Megan's personal belongings, but nothing that told him where to look for her. He damned well better find something up here—and fast. His sister's life depended on it. Today's little adventure in Endicott had driven that point home with painful clarity.

God, Marc *hated* being right.

And what if she's already dead?

The thought carried the force of a fist every time it struck him, driving the breath from his lungs, leaving a terrible helpless rage in its wake.

Leave her alone! She's my little sister!

He'd listened to what Sophie had learned on the drive back to Denver, his anger growing. Then she'd finally told him what had happened in that shack in Endicott, and he'd exploded, wanting to ram Ed Brody's balls down his throat.

"This is exactly why I didn't tell you," she'd said, using the voice women reserved for misbehaving men. "You'd have charged in there, and God knows what would have happened. Drop it, Hunt."

But he hadn't dropped it. And when he'd heard how she'd gotten away from the son of a bitch—by threatening to sic her former army sniper boyfriend on him—he'd laid into her for giving away his identity, conveniently overlooking the fact that his beating the shit of the man would have done the same and worse.

"If your buddy, Julian, starts piecing this together and visits Endicott himself, you'll have given him everything he needs to know for certain that you're with me and that you're not being held captive. Did you think about that?"

She'd fled the room in tears, leaving Marc with only his anger.

He opened another box. And another. And another.

Winter clothes. Keepsakes. Tax records.

Nada.

And a pattern emerged—important things in the attic, junk in the basement. And Megan's things had been relegated to the basement.

"I'm sorry."

He jerked his head around, saw Sophie standing at the top of the stairs, wearing the gray angora sweater and black leggings she'd bought at Macy's, her arms hugged around herself. He could tell she'd been crying, her eyes red and puffy. And just like that his anger vanished.

He walked over to her, drew her against his chest, held her

tight, her body soft beneath the silky angora. "No, Sophie, *I'm* sorry. I'm sorry I dragged you into this. I'm sorry that bastard Brody manhandled you. And I'm really sorry I acted like an ass."

She melted into him, held onto him, and he realized how deeply shaken she still was. "I keep thinking of those two women and wondering if they knew they were going to die. Were they forced to take the drugs? Did they take them by choice? Did they—"

"Don't, Sophie. Don't let your mind go there." He rocked her in his arms, kissed her hair. "You've got enough to think about."

"I'm scared, Hunt. I'm scared about my arraignment Thursday. I'm scared of seeing my friends again and seeing on their faces how I've lied to them. I'm scared for Megan and Emily. I'm terrified for you."

"I know." He wished he could tell her that everything was going to be all right, except he didn't believe that himself.

She looked up at him, fresh tears on her cheeks, then stood on her tiptoes and pressed a kiss against his lips. "Make me forget. Just for a minute. Please!"

She didn't need to ask twice.

He ducked down, brushed his lips over hers, then kissed her, a slow, soft kiss that smoldered, growing deeper and hotter by degrees, sexual need fueled by raw emotion.

Sophie. His Sophie.

She was worried, afraid, overwhelmed, and she needed to escape into him as badly as he needed to escape into her. A caress. A shiver. Soft lips against lips. Tongues and teeth. Lust in the blood like adrenaline. Frantic hands searching, shoving aside clothing, sliding over soft skin, offering pleasure, comfort, oblivion.

She reached inside his zipper and freed his aching erection.

And then he remembered. "Damn it! I need to get a—"

She held a finger to his lips. "No more condoms! I want you. All of you!"

Marc shook his head, but the thought of being inside *her*

again . . . of truly feeling *her* around him . . . of coming inside *her* . . .

Christ

Heat sheared through his gut, his brain buzzing with hunger. He pushed her up against the wood panel wall, jerked her pants down, and lifted her off her feet, his fingers digging into her bare ass. Her legs clamped around his waist like a vise, and then—*Jesus God!*—he was inside her, driving home. She felt so good, so impossibly good, her slick heat gripping him as he pounded into her again and again and again, her soft cries driving him crazy. She came hard and fast, her head falling back on a groan, her contractions milking him until he spilled his soul inside her in a rush of wrenching bliss.

For a moment, it was all he could do to breathe, his mind empty and dazed, his heart still slamming in his chest, Sophie limp in his arms. It was a good while before reality hit, but when it did . . .

Shit.

"We shouldn't have done that. If we're not careful, I'll get you—"

"Pregnant. I hope so." She spoke in a dreamy voice, bliss still on her face. "I didn't take those pills, just so you know. I spit the Plan B down the sink."

He was so stunned by what she'd just said that it took him a moment to realize why it felt like the earth was moving beneath his feet.

The wall behind her had come open.

CHAPTER 25

HER BODY STILL feeling warm and liquid, Sophie watched as Hunt looked inside the hidden closet. Barely more than a cupboard, it was kept shut by a latch that opened under pressure. Well, leave it to the two of them to discover it the way they had.

Hunt reached in and turned on a light. "Why didn't you tell me upfront? It's not like I would've forced you to take the pills. That's your decision to make, not mine."

Though he was trying not to show it, she could tell that he was angry. She couldn't blame him. "It shocked me, too. I guess I didn't say anything because I didn't know how to explain it."

"Do you want to give it a shot now?" He bent down and started opening boxes.

"Well . . . I kept thinking about what you'd said about always wanting to be a father and how that was your biggest regret. And then I realized that this might be it—your only chance to be a father—and I spit the pills in the sink."

"So you heard me say I wanted to be a father, and you decided to put your uterus at my disposal. Is that it?" He glanced over his shoulder at her, his gaze cool. "That's awfully selfless of you, Sophie."

When he put it like that, it sounded so stupid and . . . demeaning.

"Well, you said—"

"I said I wanted a *family*." His voice was hard now. "My knocking you up doesn't make us a family. It just creates another struggling single mother and another kid growing up without a dad. That was pretty stupid, Sophie. It's the only truly stupid thing I've ever known you to do."

His rejection felt like a slap in the face. "You've done your part, too."

"Yeah, I certainly have, and I'm not proud of myself."

"Besides, there's more to it than that." She needed him to understand.

"I hope so, because I can't see a woman with your brains offering her womb to any man out of pity." He shoved a box out the door behind him, then another.

"It's hard to tell you something this personal when you won't even look at me."

He stopped what he was doing, turned to face her, and leaned against the door frame, arms crossed over his chest, a telltale muscle clenching in his jaw. "I'm listening."

"I didn't do it just for you, and I didn't do it out of pity. I wanted"—she drew a deep breath, tears blurring her vision, the words catching in her throat—"to keep some part of you . . . with me."

There. She'd said it. And he could think whatever he wanted.

He stared at her, a strange expression on his face. "What?"

"I-I wanted to keep a piece of you with me. I still do. At least there would be something left of you . . . of *us* . . . no matter what."

For a moment he stood there, looking at her. Then he took one step and another, until he stood right in front of her, his gaze searching her face. He brushed a knuckle over her cheek, then drew her into his arms. "God, Sophie . . . If there were any chance that we could be together . . . If there were any woman I'd want to be the mother of my . . . *Shit*, this is so hard."

"No, Hunt, it's simple. If right now is all we have, if this is all we get, then I'll grab it with both hands and take all I can." Sophie looked up at him, desperate to reach him. "I've never felt about any man the way I feel about you. Let me have a baby for us."

Marc felt her words wash through him, pushing up against that deep, aching loneliness in his gut. It was more than he'd ever hoped for, more than he'd dreamed she'd ever say. A part of him wanted to drop onto his knees, to tell her how much he loved her, to give her any part of himself she wanted, any part of him she would take.

What she was offering him, what she was willing to do . . . He'd be a damned liar if he said some selfish asshole part of him wasn't hoping that he'd already done the deed, that she was already pregnant. She wanted his baby? Well, he'd be more than happy to drain his balls dry to make it happen. But he wasn't worthy of her, and he never had been. Not twelve years ago, and certainly not now. Besides, they had more than themselves to think about.

"I know what it's like to grow up without a dad, Sophie, and I know what it's like to grow up with a parent in prison. I wouldn't wish it on anyone." He slid his hand to her nape, massaged her neck, kissed her temple. "I don't want any child to feel ashamed because of me."

"You grew up alone, Hunt. Your mother might have loved you, but she wasn't there for you. I'm not like her. I have a job and good friends and my brother—"

"And how will you explain it to them? What will you put on the birth certificate where it says 'father'—no name or a name that could land you in prison? How will you handle a career and a baby?"

"I don't know! I don't know!" She buried her face in his chest, fear and grief rolling off her in waves. "All I know is that I feel sick when I think about you being locked in a cage forever or . . ."

She didn't finish, but they both knew what she was thinking.

He stroked her hair. "Having a baby together won't make any of that easier, Sophie, just more complicated."

Then it hit him that he might not live long enough to know whether she was or wasn't. But he didn't say that. "What's done is done, but I won't take that risk again."

Even as he said it, a part of him wondered if he'd be able to stick to his guns on that score. A few minutes ago he certainly hadn't.

"No happy endings?"

"For you, I hope one day. Not for us. Not for me." It was a damned awful thing to have to say. "You'll meet someone, a man who can be what you need him to be, and then—"

She drew away, changed the subject, obviously too upset by the topic to continue. "So have we discovered Blackbeard's lost treasure?"

Her desperate attempt at humor humbled him. She was everything a man could hope for—strong, smart, beautiful, funny, compassionate. And soon, she would be out of his life forever one way or another.

Accept it, Hunter, and move on.

He walked back to the boxes he'd set aside and pulled out a VHS tape. "Put some popcorn in the microwave. It's home movie night."

THEY WORKED THEIR way through the box of videos, going chronologically according to the dates on the labels.

"Happy birthday, dear Megan, happy birthday to you!"

On the TV screen, Megan was blowing out twelve candles on a white cake dripping with pink frosting roses. She was wearing a pretty blue party dress, and her hair was pulled back in a braid and tied off with a matching blue ribbon. Freckles on her nose, a smile on her face, she looked young and innocent and bright, her friends gathered around her, a stack of brightly wrapped gifts on the picnic table. It looked like an idyllic childhood—at first glance, anyway.

The reality was something very different, as the videos also showed. Rarely a minute passed without Mrs. Rawlings criticizing her daughter in some fashion, doing her best to impose her rigid ideas of femininity and control on her outgoing, cheerful child.

"That's not ladylike, Megan."

"Good little girls sit quietly."

"Now you've scuffed your shoes! Honestly, Megan, you are a trial!"

"Quit making silly faces."

"Look at how quiet and ladylike Jennifer is, Megan. She would never get mud on her dress like you have."

Sophie snuggled deeper into Hunt's chest, felt his arm tighten around her. She couldn't imagine what he was feeling, watching his sister's life roll by, years that he had missed. She'd felt the tension in him almost from the beginning and knew there wasn't anything she could do to make this experience easier for him beyond just being with him.

Not that watching these videos had no effect on Sophie. She'd come to care deeply for Megan during the months she'd covered Megan's story, and it hurt to watch while Megan's parents slowly squeezed the spontaneity and joy out of her, their disapproval subtle but constant. It was just as painful to see the sweet child Megan had been and to know the horror that lay ahead of her—imprisonment, rape, addiction.

Sophie knew that Hunt hoped to use information from these tapes to find his sister, but apart from the name of the church her parents attended and the first names of a few of her friends, the videos had offered very few clues.

On the television, the scene now switched to summertime in the mountains. Megan stood in a white blouse and blue skirt with other preteen girls singing a song about the women of the Bible, a sweep of ponderosa pines behind them. Each girl had a solo, Megan's shy soprano sending thin but clear notes skyward. The song was pretty, even if the lyrics rubbed Sophie's feminist sensibilities the wrong way—like the part about Eve being made from Adam's rib.

"I am *not* your rib," she said, giving Hunt a nudge.

He chuckled and hugged her tighter against his side. "I don't know about that. You seem to fit really well right here."

When the song ended, the choir of young girls beamed as their parents applauded, Megan looking hopefully toward the camera.

Mrs. Rawlings's voice came from somewhere nearby. *"I don't know why they gave Megan a solo. She never could sing."*

Megan's face fell, her expression of hope shattering like glass.

"God, I *hate* that woman!" Sophie felt her face burn.

Hunt said nothing, his anger dark and palpable.

While the other girls ran to their parents, Megan wandered off to the side and up to an older man—a preacher from the way he was dressed.

"Did you have a good time at camp?" The man wrapped his arm around Megan's shoulders and hugged her.

"The best time ever." Megan hugged him right back.

"Where is this?" Hunt reached for another cookie.

In addition to popcorn, Sophie had shared the family secret and made him chipless chocolate chip cookies. She'd eaten three. He'd eaten at least a dozen.

"I think there's a glimpse of the sign off to the left when the girls are singing."

Hunt pointed the remote at the television, hit rewind, scrolling backward through images until he came to the beginning of this segment.

Sophie sat up, leaned forward, and waited. "See there? Pine River Christian . . . I can't see the last word."

"I think it said 'Girls Camp.'" He scrolled back once more, then hit play again.

"Yep, that's it."

"I think we should find this place, see if we can track down that old preacher. She seems like she really trusted the old guy."

"I hope he's still alive."

ON THE NEXT video, it became clear exactly why the tapes had been kept in that little closet. Although the first twenty minutes of each of the remaining videos had footage of Megan, the rest had been taped over with something entirely different.

It was just another insult, another way of proving how little Megan had been loved, and it made Marc want to hit something. Mr. and Mrs. Rawlings had wanted the perfect daughter, and instead they'd gotten a little girl who'd been loved but also neglected and traumatized. Rather than helping her heal, they'd heaped their expectations and disappointment on her, shredding what little self-esteem she'd had.

"So Mr. Rawlings has a thing for hard-core porn. I wonder what his uptight holier-than-thou wife would have to say about that. I think she ought to know, don't you?"

"Absolutely."

On the screen an extremely hung man was fucking the lipstick off some starlet's mouth, while another young woman buried an enormous dildo in the starlet's vagina.

Marc turned off the TV, popped out the tape, and switched it with one of Mrs. Rawlings's cooking videos. "This ought to do it."

But Sophie was still staring at the TV screen, looking perplexed. "Was that anatomically advisable? I mean, that thing was . . . really *huge*."

And then Marc remembered. *Oh, shit.* "You know, I took something from your apartment when I was there. I found it in your bedside table when I was searching for the drugs and . . . well, I figured you might not want Julian or the other cops to find it."

She looked up at him, confused, then her eyes went wide and her face turned bright red. "*Oh, my God!* You have my—"

"I don't know what it is, but it's pink and looks like a dick and buzzes and has little pearls and rotates."

She buried her face in her hands. "I'm going to die now."

"Instead of being embarrassed, show me how it works and let me use it on you."

She looked at him, her cheeks still pink. "I don't know if I can—"

"Sure you can." He ducked down and nuzzled her ear, willing himself to set Megan and her troubles out of his mind for just another hour or two. "Think of how it will feel when

I slide it in and out of you while I go down on you. Imagine how it will be when I hold that buzzing head against your clit and pound my cock into you. Or maybe while you're on your hands and knees, I can slide it into you from behind and—"

"Is this one of your fantasies?" She was breathing harder, her pupils dilated.

"Damn straight it is." He'd made himself hard just talking about it.

She stood, reached for his hand. "In that case, I'm willing to give it a try."

He scooped her up in his arms. "You are so selfless."

TWO HOURS LATER, Sophie collapsed, boneless and breathless, against Hunt's sweaty chest. "You . . . are . . . *incredible*."

He traced a lazy line up her spine with his fingers. "Are you talking to me or your battery-operated lover over here?"

She couldn't help but laugh. "Don't tell me you're jealous of my vibrator."

"I don't think I've ever heard you *scream* like that before."

It *had* been a-*ma*-zing. "That wasn't the vibrator. That was *you*."

"But I don't have pearls, and I don't buzz."

She propped herself up on his hard chest, kissed a wine red nipple, whispered, "No, but you have fingers and killer lips and the most amazing tongue—and you rotate just fine. Besides, I love it when you come. Your muscles get so hard and tense, and then you shake apart, and your head goes back and you say my name like it's a prayer. *'Sophie!'* No vibrator does that. I'd take you over rotating pearls any day, Marc Hunter."

He chuckled, and then she realized he'd been joking. He turned onto his side, drawing her with him. "As long as I'm your favorite sex toy, I'm satisfied."

"Then rest easy. You're the best."

She started to drift, her mind edging toward dreams, then she realized that he was still wide awake, his hand still caressing her back. She opened her eyes, glanced up, saw him staring off into the darkness, lines of worry on his face. She didn't have to ask why.

"We'll find her, Hunt. We'll find her."

"I hope so."

SOPHIE WOKE EARLY the next morning, took a shower, and then made breakfast. This time she made eggs Benedict. She was trying to make something new every day, giving him a chance to enjoy as many different things as she could. And her efforts were rewarded every time by stunned surprise— "*French toast?*"—followed by his devouring every bite as if it were his last meal. And, of course, there was always the terrible possibility that it would be.

But the kitchen was running low on supplies. They'd made good use of the wealth of steak and salmon the Rawlingses kept on hand. But someone needed to make a run to the store, particularly given that Sophie wanted to make a Thanksgiving-style dinner tonight, complete with turkey and all the trimmings. Who cared if it was February? They only had until Thursday—just two days away. Somehow they had to live their entire lives in those two short days. And then . . .

She heard a toilet flush, and a few minute later Hunt shuffled down the hallway, looking sleepy and sexy, wearing nothing but stubble and black briefs. She pressed a kiss against his whiskery jaw. "Good morning."

"That's what I like—to wake up and find my woman barefoot in the kitchen." He grinned, wrapped his arms around her, rubbed his whiskers on her face. "What you making?"

"Eggs Benedict. I'm just finishing the hollandaise now."

"Eggs Benedict? Oh, man!"

Sophie ate her meal slowly, entertained by the way Hunt breathed his, groaning over every bite as if he were in the midst of a culinary orgy. "Someone needs to go to the grocery store today. Maybe we can do it like we did at the pharmacy and at Macy's, where you park down the street and I go in and shop."

He met her gaze over his cup of coffee, a sexy grin on his

face. "Let's do it the way we did it outside Macy's. I liked that."

Sophie leaned forward, unable to suppress a smile. "I just bet you did."

While Hunt took a shower, Sophie logged into her e-mail account, deleted all offers to enlarge her penis, and started sorting through her messages. There was an e-mail from Ken Harburg expressing his concern and telling her that he knew in his heart she was innocent. There was also an e-mail from David and one from Kat, two from Tessa, and one from Julian. Dreading opening the ones from Tess and Julian, she opened David's message first.

Hey, sis. I'm told you went into hiding or something. I don't know if you'll get this e-mail, but I want you to know that I'm working hard to finish the semester early so I can come out there and be with you during your trial—that's if these bull-shit charges aren't dropped by then. I love you and miss you. Please let me know you're all right.

She wrote a quick response, asking him to put vet school first and telling him not to worry, that she was fine but being very careful. Then she read Kat's message.

I thought you should know that Tom and Glynnis have been at each other nonstop since you were suspended. Glynnis wants him to back off the CORA request you made to DOC until your case is sorted out. He thinks she's trying to make nice with their director, but we all think she's doing it to undermine you. Now she's accusing him of being insubordinate—which, of course, he is—and has asked the board to replace him. I know he won't tell you this, but I wanted you to know. I hope you're safe. Mitakuye Oyasin. Hágoónee', Kat.

Sophie had no idea what those last words meant—she assumed they were Navajo—but she knew what would happen if Tom lost his job. She'd find herself unemployed.

Was there any part of her life that was normal?

Poor Tom! How could Glynnis possibly persuade the board to get rid of the editor who'd single-handedly turned the *Denver Independent* into a competitive, hard-hitting newspaper? He had more national awards than any journalist she knew, including a Pulitzer. No, Glynnis would never get away with it.

Sophie took a deep breath, replied to Kat, thanking her for keeping her informed and asking her to pass on a hello to Tom and the rest of the I-Team. Then she took a deep breath—and opened the e-mails from Tessa. Both were apologies and pleas for her to call and to come stay with them.

I'm sorry I got so angry on the phone, Sophie. I just want you to be safe. Julian thinks you're caught up in something and that maybe this guy who held you hostage is using you or hurting you in some way. I don't know if you'll get this e-mail or if you'll be able to reply openly, but please let us help you! Please call my cell phone, night or day, and Julian will be on his way, armed to the teeth, to get you.

Unsure what to say, Sophie told Tessa not to worry, assured her that she had every right to be angry, and promised to call as soon as she could.

Last of all, she opened Julian's message. The screen seemed to freeze for a moment, and she thought her computer had crashed. She was about to reboot when the program started to work again.

I asked DOC to give me a copy of the report you requested. They say no such report exists and that no complaints were made against guards at Denver Juvenile during that period. Where in the hell are you, Sophie? Is he with you? I know something is wrong. Please trust me.

Sophie answered him.

I do trust you—with my life. Look up Charlotte Martin and Kristina Brody, both at Denver Juvenile at that time, both dead from overdosing on fefe. Check the heroin lab tests. I believe it will be the same as that found in my car. DOC is LYING to you. That report will save lives.

Starting with mine, she thought as she hit Send.

Maybe she shouldn't have given him that much information. She didn't want to send him out to Endicott. But at the same time, he had a greater chance of getting that report from the inside than she did from her bolt-hole here in Cherry Creek. What did it matter who caught the bad guys as long as the bad guys were caught?

A new message hit her inbox—this one from Tom. She opened it, read through it, her heart starting to pound. "Hunt was right. He was right!"

She jumped up and ran toward the bathroom, threw open the door, and stepped into the steam. "Hunt, I just got—*oh, God!*"

Hunt had turned on her, his face that of a stranger, the .45 in his hands—and pointed straight at her.

CHAPTER 26

HEART SLAMMING, MARC stared down the barrel of the Glock at . . . *"Sophie?"*

Oh, God! Jesus! Shit!

She stood frozen in place, her eyes wide, the blood drained from her face. "I-I'm so sorry! It's okay. I'll . . . just . . . go."

Then she walked backward out of the bathroom and closed the door.

He lowered the gun, feeling dizzy, his mind reeling, his stomach churning.

Shit! Jesus Christ!

What in the hell had happened? What the fuck had he just done?

Horrified, he dropped the gun onto the floor, sagged against the wet tile, his legs barely strong enough to hold him up, his heart a jackhammer, his breathing ragged.

He'd been rinsing soap off his skin . . . and he'd . . . he'd heard . . .

I'd fuck that ass. You boys wanna fuck that ass?

Why you fightin', Hunter? Afraid it'll hurt? Afraid you'll like it?

He'll like it. Get him! Hold him! Why the fuck can't you hold him?

He squeezed his eyes shut, tried to silence the voices, past all mixed up with present—mixed up, fucked up, confused.

God, he'd just gone postal on Sophie. He'd pointed a Glock at her head, his finger on the trigger, the chamber loaded with a hollow-point round. One easy tug on the trigger, just five pounds of pressure, and he would have . . .

Christ!

He would have blown her head *clean goddamned off*.

He leaned against the wall and sucked air into his lungs, water sluicing over his body for endless minute after endless minute, until the shower ran cold. Gradually, his heartbeat slowed and his breathing returned to normal, echoes of the past dying away. Feeling as if he were made of lead, muscles stiff from the cold, he reached down and turned off the water, then stepped out of the tub and dried off.

Jesus, what was he going to say to her? How was he going to explain this?

Wearing only a damp towel, he opened the bathroom door and found her sitting on the edge of the bed, waiting for him, her arms hugged around herself. Her gaze met his, her eyes filled with worry and wariness. She reached for him, held out one slender hand—a lifeline.

He took it, let her pull him in.

God, you're pathetic, Hunter.

"Your fingers are ice-cold!" She drew him to the bed beside her and pulled a blanket up around his shoulders. "You must be freezing."

Freezing? No, he felt numb.

How was he going to tell her?

Try words, dumbshit, starting with . . .

"I'm sorry, Sophie. Christ, I'm so sorry!"

Her voice was soft, her hand warm. "It's okay. You surprised me, that's all."

He felt an absurd impulse to laugh. She had no clue. "No, it's not okay. I pointed a loaded weapon at your head."

"Well"—she shrugged, obviously reaching—"you've pointed it at me before."

For a moment, he could do nothing but stare at her.

Leave it to Sophie to say something like that.

"That was different." It had been so very different. He'd been in control of himself during the prison break, not lost in his own head. "I wouldn't have hurt you then. This time I . . . I might have—"

She pressed her fingers to his lips. "But you didn't."

He drew a breath. No, he hadn't—but that wasn't the point.

"So, are you going to tell me what just happened, or are we going to pretend like nothing's wrong?" She stroked the back of his hand with her thumb. "I know something happened to you, Hunt. I know something's tearing you up inside. You try not to show it, but I know it's there. I've known it since the night you broke into my apartment, maybe even since the night at the cabin when I saw your scars."

But Marc had just shut the door on those ghosts and *no way in hell* did he want to open it again. "You're an expert on prisons, Sophie. You know the score. It's a violent place."

He stood, crossed the room, and grabbed a pair of briefs from the basket of clean laundry, her gaze boring into his back as he began to dress. Then he heard the bed creak, heard her soft footfalls, and felt her behind him.

"Yeah, I know what happens in prisons." She ran her hand over the scar on his bare back, her touch branding him. "But I don't know what happened to *you*. Tell me, Hunt. You don't have to hide it from me."

He hated the compassion in her voice, hated how broken it made him feel on the inside, hated that fact that some part of him *wanted* to tell her. He turned and glared down at her, letting anger close around him like a wall. "So you want the sordid details, is that it? Fodder for another award-winning exposé?"

That was out of line, dumbass.

She stiffened at the insult, but she didn't back down, her voice soft, her blue eyes warm with concern. "I care about you, Hunt. Whatever hurts you hurts me. Let me help you."

Didn't she get it? No, of course, she didn't.

"Sophie, I . . . Christ!" He squeezed his eyes shut, gritting his teeth to keep himself from shouting in her face. *"I don't think I can do this!"*

Sophie watched Hunt fight with himself, wishing there were some way to make it easier for him. She pressed her hand against his chest, felt the hammering of his heart beneath her palm. "I'm right here. With you. Help me understand what's going on inside you. Please."

He opened his eyes, looked away, a muscle clenching in his jaw. Then he walked past her and lay back on the bed, one arm thrown over his eyes. When at last he spoke, his voice was flat, emotionless. "I was a target. From the day I walked through the door, I was a target."

Sophie sat down on the edge of the bed beside him and waited for him to say more.

"The inmates had read the papers and knew I'd been a drug agent, and more than a few of them were doing time thanks to me. The first week I was there, five of them—gang members whose meth ring I'd busted up—decided it was payback time. They caught me outside the gym, tried to shove a shank into my jugular. If I hadn't been watching for it, they probably would've killed me. As it was, they managed to cut my chest pretty badly before I took them down."

His first week here, he put five guys in the infirmary.

Sophie glanced at the scar next to his right nipple, remembering what Officer Green had told her. Now she knew the whole story—and it sickened her. "Shouldn't you have been placed in protective isolation?"

That was standard operating procedure whenever someone from law enforcement landed behind bars—total separation from other inmates.

Hunt sat up, shrugged. "Somehow that part of my orders was never implemented."

"Didn't the guards try to stop them?"

"Shit, no." Hunt gave a snort, stood, took a few restless steps across the room, then stopped, staring out into the empty hallway. "From their point of view, I was a traitor, a cop-killer. They didn't give a goddamn what happened to me, as long as it was painful. Most of the time they made a half-assed effort to intervene, but sometimes they watched and laughed. It didn't take me long to realize that I'd been sentenced to execution by inmate."

Sophie could hear the anger in his voice, felt her temper spike. "That's not justice."

But he didn't seem to hear her. "I thought for awhile that breaking a few heads that first week would be enough to keep the bulldogs in check. If you bitch up, they break you. If you fight, they back off. For awhile it seemed to work. It gave me the respect I needed to start building some connections. But some people just don't know when to stop."

She listened, her stomach in knots, as Hunt described how twice more men he'd arrested had tried to kill him, once in the mess hall by striking him in the back of the skull with a sock weighted with rocks and once in the yard by trying to gut him after blinding him with a handful of sand. She couldn't imagine facing that kind of violence, couldn't imagine having to fight again and again just to stay alive. How could any human being live that way?

"Each time I gave worse than I got. I'd spend a few days in the infirmary, then get sent up to D-Seg—disciplinary segregation. Pretty soon I had the kind of reputation every prisoner wants. Stay clear of Hunter. He'll kick your ass if you fuck with him. Weaker prisoners—young guys, guys who'd already been ripped, new guys who didn't know how to fight—hovered around me, offered me everything you can imagine in exchange for protection. I could have had my cock sucked morning, noon, and night if I'd been into that. I watched out for them, but I didn't make them pay for it—at least not like that."

Sophie tried to comprehend what he'd just told her, the horrific world he described so foreign to her despite her years of reporting. "So the violent inmates left you alone?"

"Not all of them. Eventually, DOC brass transferred me to maximum security. There was a group of prisoners—all lifers—who got off on turning out other prisoners. Gang rape. They decided it was time someone took me down a notch. They started watching me, talking shit, calling me a pretty boy and a punk. I told them to fuck themselves."

Marc barely recognized his own voice as he spoke, the words seeming to come from someone else, the story part of someone else's life. Not his life. Not his. "The first time it happened, they caught me by surprise. I saw three of them standing outside the showers, watching me, looking me over like I was a piece of meat. I turned my back on them. They seemed to like that even more. They cheered and whistled and talked about my ass. I ignored them, trying to get through my shower as fast as I could. But I wasn't fast enough."

Not fast enough by half, were you, Hunter?

"It wasn't your fault. There's no way you could have—"

"It's not what you think. They didn't succeed." Marc fought to say the word. "They didn't . . . rape me. Oh, they tried. They tried again and again. They must have tried at least a dozen times before I broke out. Stalking me became their hobby. A few times a year, they'd corner me, most often in the shower. That was their MO. The guys called them the shower hawks. I'd fight them off, inflict some damage, get cut up, then spend a few days in the infirmary before getting sent up to D-Seg again."

Marc closed his eyes, a cold feeling settling in his stomach. "Over time it got worse, more violent, until . . ."

I'd fuck that ass. You boys wanna fuck that ass?

"Last summer, they orchestrated some kind of distraction for the guards while I was in the shower and came after me hard—three of them. They had weapons, and they wanted blood." Marc felt his body start to shake. Nauseated, he stepped backward until his back touched the wall, then he slid down to the floor. "I fought hard . . . broke one bastard's nose . . . split another one's lip. I tried not to slip on the wet floor, maneuvering my way around them toward the hallway. I didn't know the fourth guy was waiting just beyond the door—not until I felt the shank sink into my back."

He could feel it as if it were yesterday—searing pain, the unbearable pressure in his chest of a collapsed lung, the cold horror of knowing he'd finally lost.

"My lung collapsed. There was blood . . . everywhere. I tried to stand, tried to fight, but . . ." He closed his eyes, let his head fall back against the wall. "They slammed me down onto the tile. I couldn't breathe. I tried to twist away, got out a few kicks, but . . ."

Why you fightin', Hunter? Afraid it'll hurt? Afraid you'll like it?

He'll like it. Get him! Hold him! Why the fuck can't you hold him?

"One of the guards, a decent man who sometimes did favors

for me, heard the ruckus and stopped it. If he hadn't . . . *Jesus!*" Marc felt his gorge rise, swallowed hard. "The last thing I remember . . . is lying facedown on the tile and watching my own blood wash down the drain. I thought it was over."

He heard Sophie's breath catch and realized she was crying. He opened his eyes, watched her leave the bed and walk toward him, tears streaming down her pretty face. Without a word, she knelt beside him and cradled his head against her breast, offering him comfort, her fingers sliding through his hair, her lips hot against his forehead.

What had he done to deserve her? He didn't know. He didn't care. He wrapped an arm around her waist and let himself go, sinking into her, taking everything she offered—softness, solace, salvation.

Sophie held Hunt, kissed him, feeling sick with rage and grief for him, trying to take in the nightmare he'd just described. She'd known from his scars that he'd been in at least a few fights, but she hadn't imagined anything so brutal or constant. She could only guess at the loneliness he'd felt, the anger, the despair, the fear, always keeping his guard up, always watching his back, having no way out, no escape, no choice but to fight.

She kissed him again, wanting somehow to erase those six terrible years, wanting to drive away the brutality, fear, and pain. Her lips traced a line down his temple across his clean-shaven jaw to his mouth. He responded, kissing her back, his lips soft and warm, his arm drawing tighter around her waist. Soon, they lay stretched out on the bed, Sophie kissing his scars while Hunt slowly peeled off her clothes, his hands seeking her most sensitive places, making them both burn. And when at last he settled himself between her thighs and nudged himself inside her, there was no more anguish, no more pain, no more cruelty. There was only the two of them—Hunt and Sophie.

THEY LAY ON the bed, holding one another, legs tangled, bodies replete, neither of them feeling like moving as morning stretched toward noon.

Marc ran his fingertips down the column of her spine. "I can't go back there, Sophie."

Her voice was soft and tinged with sadness. "I know."

SOPHIE WATCHED AS Hunt read through the scanned reports she'd gotten via e-mail—the reports she'd been trying to tell him about when he'd been in the shower. Tom had acquired the chemical tests on the four separate samples of heroin—how he didn't say, but then Tom had secret sources everywhere—and they were all identical.

"They're dead-on. Same batch. No doubt." He looked up from the page, dropped the papers on the table next to the chronology Sophie had made a few days ago. "So let's go over this again."

"Megan grabs Emily and sneaks out of New Horizons because she realizes she's in danger. The cops find a half ounce of this shit in her room." Hunt tapped his finger on the drug tests. "Did Cross's buddies plant it on her after she bolted? Did they give it to her? Did she buy it or trade sex for it and then decide not to touch it? Unless or until we find Megan or get access to surveillance footage from New Horizons we won't know."

Sophie nodded. "Then only a few days later, Charlotte Martin, who is the same age as Megan and has a sealed juvenile record, swallows a balloon of the same batch of heroin while staying at the Denver County Jail. She dies in her cell when the balloon ruptures."

"*If* it ruptured." He bit his lower lip, frowned. "I'm betting someone made certain it would rupture—poked holes in it, nicked it with a razor blade or something. Of course, there's no way to know that either."

Sophie glanced back at her notes. "A few days after that, Kristina Brody shoots up in her room—same batch of fefe—and ODs on her bed. Was she forced to take the drug? No way to know. All we know for certain is that she was in Denver Juvenile at the same time as Megan."

"Then the next evening, a few days after filing an open-records request that would have exposed Cross and his cronies, you're pulled over and thirty grams of the same shit is found in your car and your apartment. That same night, a guard at Denver County Jail tries to enter your cell and lies about his whereabouts to a coworker. A few days later, a guard from the jail—we're not yet sure it was the same man—is found dead of an apparent suicide."

Sophie weighed the facts in her mind, tried to see anything she might be missing. "Charlotte and Kristina were sentenced to Denver Juvenile at the same time as Megan. I don't see any other possibility—they must have been Cross's other victims. Whoever went after Megan decided to go after them as well."

Hunt lifted his gaze, looked into her eyes, his expression grave. "And when you started digging, searching for the truth, they went after you."

Sophie wrapped her arms around herself, warding off a shiver. "That's what we know. What don't we know?"

Hunt stood, came up behind her, began to massage her shoulders, his hands working magic on muscles she hadn't realized were tense. "We don't know whether the guard on the slab at the morgue is the same one who came to your cell. We don't know whether he really killed himself. We don't know whether he was one of Cross's accomplices. We don't know how many accomplices Cross had, for that matter. We don't know where the heroin came from exactly. And we don't know where my sister is—or whether she and Emily are still alive."

Sophie could hear the worry in his voice. "We'll find her."

"Yeah." He didn't sound convinced.

"So how can we get the answers we need?"

"We could answer almost all of these questions if we had that report from Denver Juvenile's investigation, of course. In the meantime, we won't know about the guard until the county jail completes its internal investigation, which could take weeks. And we won't know if he was one of Cross's accomplices until we talk with an eyewitness—Megan."

"So our focus now ought to be getting that report and finding

Megan. Since I can't think of any way we can get the report short of breaking in and stealing it, that means we need to focus on finding Megan, tracking down anyone we can find who was on those videos—the family's minister, her childhood friends, the preacher from the Bible camp she liked so much."

He bent down, kissed her cheek, then walked into the kitchen. "I say we start with the Bible camp and go from there."

But Sophie's gaze was back on the fact sheet. "You know what I find strange. Charlotte, Kristina, the guard—they all died apparently self-inflicted deaths."

She turned to look at Hunt, who was pouring himself a glass of orange juice.

"I noticed that, too." He lifted the glass, drank. "Is it coincidence or triple murder?"

CHAPTER

27

I<small>T WAS LATE</small> afternoon by the time Hunt dropped Sophie off down the street from Lakeview Christian Church. The sky was overcast, the scent of snow in the cold air. Hugging her coat tightly around her, Sophie glanced back at the Jaguar where Hunt waited, then hurried down the sidewalk toward the church, careful to sidestep patches of ice. She'd dressed to look professional—pinstriped pants, blazer, tailored blouse—and that meant heels.

Lakeside was one of those mall-sized mega-churches, its sprawling brick building surrounded by an enormous parking lot, now mostly empty. It had its own traffic light and its own bus stop. Out front a marquee advertised the theme of this coming Sunday's sermon: "Are you too busy for God?"

Sophie and Hunt had spent the past two hours tracking down the Bible camp where Megan had seemed so happy only to learn that Pine River, located outside Jamestown, had closed two years ago when the minister who'd owned it had retired and sold off the land. It had been their most promising lead, and it had turned into a dead end. Sophie had wanted to cry.

Because none of the girls in the videos with Megan were mentioned by last name, Lakeview's pastor was their last hope. If he didn't remember Megan or her friends, if he'd forgotten them, Hunt would have no other option but to start looking on the streets again, placing himself in greater danger of being caught—or killed.

The very idea filled Sophie with dread. She'd heard of people who'd committed suicide by cop, pointing a weapon at police in a reckless attempt to end their own lives and dying in a hail of bullets. Was Hunt desperate enough to do something like that? Until today, she'd have answered with an unequivocal no. But after this morning, she was no longer certain. She'd heard the hell he'd lived through, seen the brutality of it on his face, felt the viciousness of it when she'd held his shaking body.

I can't go back there, Sophie.

No, he couldn't. And she would do everything in her power to make sure he didn't.

She hurried up the neatly shoveled walk to what she thought must be the main entrance—four sets of glass double doors. Inside was a wide lobby, its walls covered with children's art work. An arrow labeled Offices pointed her down a hallway off to the right.

She found the minister's office about halfway down, its door wide open, an older man seated at the desk, reading something through his bifocals. She recognized him from the videos and the church's website. "Pastor Paul?"

He glanced up, stood, and smiled. "That's me."

She held out her press card. "I'm Sophie Alton from the *Denver Independent*. I wondered if I might be able to speak with you about one of your former congregants, a young woman named Megan Rawlings."

He gestured her through the door, a thoughtful frown on his face. "Megan Rawlings? Would that be Frank and Emma Rawlings's daughter?"

He remembered her!

Thank God!

"Yes—their adopted daughter and only child." Sophie sat in the chair across from him, trying not to look too desperate. "She recently disappeared with her baby girl, and I'm trying to find her. I was hoping you might remember who her friends were or be able to give me some idea where she might turn for help."

Then Pastor Paul looked at her as if noticing her for the first time. "You're that reporter who was taken hostage, aren't you? I recognize you now."

"Yes, sir. I was trying to find information about Megan then, too." Sophie hoped that was all he knew about her.

The troubled look on his face told her it wasn't. "They arrested you. Drugs, wasn't it?"

"Yes, sir, but the drugs weren't mine. Someone planted them in my car to keep me out of the way so that I couldn't help Megan."

His thick gray eyebrows rose, and Sophie couldn't tell from his expression whether he believed her or not. Then he frowned. "My memory isn't what it once was. Besides, Frank and Emma have always been active in our congregation, volunteering, tithing, attending regularly. I feel uncomfortable talking about their daughter without their consent."

"They've disowned Megan, sir. And Megan is an adult. Besides, this is for background only. I'm not going to publish anything you tell me. I'm just trying to find Megan." And then Sophie's professional façade crumbled. "Please help me bring her and her baby safely back. She's in danger out there alone. You're my last lead. You must know something."

He seemed taken aback. "Your last . . . ? Well, I'm sorry but . . . Why don't you tell me where you've looked so far?"

She told him what she could, bending the truth when she needed to. She told him how she'd searched for Megan on the streets, how she'd tracked down Emily's father, and how she'd even tried to find the summer Bible camp Megan had liked so much only to discover it had long since closed.

He shifted uncomfortably in his chair, his body language telling Sophie that he felt uneasy talking with her. He obviously took the privacy of his congregants seriously—a quality Sophie would have appreciated under most circumstances. "Have you tried talking with Pastor John Stevens? He ran the camp."

"I was told he'd sold the land and retired two years ago."

"Yes, that's right. He did." The pastor's gaze moved from Sophie to the phone and back. "But he's still here. He still lives in his old house, in fact. He sold the land around the house, but kept a few acres for himself and his wife. He said he couldn't stand the idea of moving down to the city."

Sophie's pulse picked up a notch. "He's still . . . up there?

"Oh, yes, he and his wife, Connie, are still there." Pastor Paul glanced at the phone again. "They come down from Jamestown to join us for services now and again, but it's getting harder and harder for Connie to get about with her rheumatoid arthritis. Can you excuse me for a moment? I need to run to the restroom. I'll be right back."

"Of course."

He stood, hurried toward the door, glancing back at her as he stepped into the hallway, a troubled look on his face.

Sophie chalked his uneasiness up to the fact that he was talking with her behind Mr. and Mrs. Rawlings's backs, her mind focused more on what he'd just told her. The pastor who'd run the camp, who'd hugged Megan in the videos, who'd cared about her *was still living in the mountains*. He was still living where Megan had last seen him.

Finally, *finally*, it felt like they were getting somewhere. If she'd had her cell phone, she'd have sent Hunt a quick text message to share the news. Instead, she sat . . . and waited.

A few minutes had passed when she thought she heard the pastor's voice coming from the room next door. Suddenly uneasy, she stepped into the hallway and walked quietly toward the sound, stopping at a door that stood slightly ajar.

"—already called the girl's parents in Florida. They don't want me talking to her at all. You'd asked me to call you if she came around, so that's what I'm doing. I'm not sure what kind of trouble she's in, officer, but she doesn't *seem* dangerous. She acts like she really wants to help the Rawlings girl. Yes, she's sitting in my office right now."

Oh, God! Oh, God! Oh, God!

Sophie backed away from the door, her heart tripping, panic scattering her thoughts.

She had to get to Hunt. She had to warn him.

Her wits returning with a surge of adrenaline, she ducked into Pastor Paul's office, grabbed her coat and purse, then slipped off her shoes and tiptoed back into the hallway, walking as quickly and quietly as she could, hoping he wouldn't suddenly open the door and catch her.

When she reached the lobby, she ran.

MARC SAW SOPHIE running hell-bent down the sidewalk in his rearview mirror, her shoes clutched in her hand, her hair swinging wildly behind her. "Shit."

What kind of trouble could she have gotten into at a church, for God's sake?

He shifted into first, his foot on the clutch, then threw open her door.

She jumped in and shut the door, a look of panic on her face. "Drive!"

He eased the Jag into traffic, leaving the church behind them. "You want to tell me what just happened?"

Out of breath, she nodded. "The pastor . . . called the cops. Someone had told him . . . to call if I came to see him."

"Your friend Julian?"

She shook her head. "Whoever it was . . . made the pastor believe I was dangerous."

Marc turned onto a side street, pulled over, and slammed on the brakes. "That means it had to have been one of Cross's accomplices."

She nodded. "Exactly."

"I knew one of them had to be a cop!" He slammed his fist against the steering wheel. "So why am I driving away? This is the son of a bitch I've been looking for!"

He put the car into gear.

"No, Hunt! Whoever he is, he's a cop! You can't just lie in wait and shoot him when he steps out of his car. That's murder!"

"That's what he deserves!"

"Maybe so, but it's not what *you* deserve. You're not a cold-blooded killer. You can't do this! Besides, I have a lead on Megan, and if the pastor gave me the information about the camp, he'll probably share it with the guy on the other end of the phone."

Stunned, Marc listened as Sophie recounted her brief conversation with the pastor from the moment she'd introduced herself until she'd overheard him talking about her. After all this time, to finally have a true lead on Megan, to think he might actually find someone who'd cared about his sister, someone who might be able to help him find her, someone who might even have been willing to shelter her . . .

Did you have a good time at camp?

The best time ever.

God, what if Megan was there? The chances had to be next to nil. There were so many other places she could be—hiding out in some pimp's stable, hunkered down in some filthy alley, hiding under an alias at a battered women's shelter.

Yes, but what if she *was* there? What if she'd been there all along?

Then it might well turn into a race to see who found her first—him or the son of a bitch this pastor had just tipped off.

Marc hit the gas, part of him listening to Sophie, part of him planning his next step.

"For a moment, I panicked. But I knew I had to get to you, so I grabbed my stuff from his office, snuck down the hallway, and then ran."

"That may have drawn more attention to you than just staying put, but given the circumstances it was probably your only choice."

She let out a gust of breath. "I didn't want the bad guys to show up and then have you do something stupid and noble like come inside to save me."

He couldn't help but laugh. "You'd rather have me leave you to them? Not a chance!"

"There's nothing they could do to me in a church." She paused. "Shouldn't we be headed into the mountains?"

"We need to stop by the house first and get our stuff."

She stared at him, eyes wide, the excitement vanishing from her voice. "You're not coming back, are you?"

"If by some miracle Megan is there, I want to have my gear so that she and I can hit the highway. With a little luck, by this time tomorrow, she and I can be home free. If she's not there, you and I will just come back and take up where we left off."

He didn't want to think about leaving Sophie, saying good-bye, turning his back on the only woman he'd ever truly loved. Instead, he tried to think about how it would be to see his sister again, to hold Emily for the first time, to cross the border with the two of them and know that the long nightmare was finally over.

Except that for Sophie it wouldn't be over. Someone was still after her. She was still facing drug charges. She might still lose her job. To top that off, there was a chance that he'd gotten her pregnant.

When you trash someone's life, Hunter, you're thorough.

But no way in hell would he trade her freedom or her life for his.

He'd given a lot of thought over the past few days to how he was going to get her out of this mess. She wasn't going to like his plan, but he didn't give a damn. He needed to keep her safe, and he needed to keep her out of prison. That's what mattered.

They drove in silence to the house, then gathered their things, Sophie taking a few minutes to switch into more suitable clothes and shoes before helping Marc pack the car. While Sophie waited in the Jag, Marc made a systematic sweep of the house to make certain they hadn't forgotten anything. Only after the house had disappeared from his rearview mirror did he realize that the happiest hours of his life had been lived within its walls.

IT FELT LIKE déjà vu—the darkness, the snow, driving west on US-6. Only this time, instead of being terrified of the man sitting beside her, she was terribly afraid of losing him. If Megan was hiding at Pastor Stevens's house—and Sophie hoped against hope that she was—Hunt would be leaving her life in a matter of hours and making his way to Mexico, where he and Megan and Emily could live free of the horrors of the past.

How strange to hope so desperately for the something that would break her heart.

And yet living without Hunt and knowing he was free would be much easier than living without him and knowing he was suffering behind bars.

No happy endings.

They neared the mouth of Clear Creek Canyon, where Hunt had defied the police blockade, jumped the curb, and shaken the helicopter off their tail. The memory was vivid, but it seemed as if it had happened a thousand years ago. So much had changed since then.

Hunt glanced over at the canyon as they passed, and Sophie knew he was remembering, too. "I want you to know that if there'd been any other way, I never would have put you through that. I was desperate, and you were the only answer. I'm sorry, Sophie."

Sophie swallowed the lump in her throat. "You don't owe me any more apologies."

"The hell I don't! God, Sophie, I—"

"You did what you had to do for Megan's sake and Emily's. I'm happy I helped you get out of that hellhole. More than anything, I want you and Megan to be safe someplace where none of this can touch you. I just hope . . ."

"What?"

"I hope you can find a way to let me know you made it, that you're alive and safe."

"I will." He glanced over at her, his expression grave. "You can count on it."

"I'll be living for that moment, Hunt."

Without saying a word, he reached over and took her hand.

BY THE TIME they neared Jamestown, fat flakes were falling, and the snow had begun to stick to the road. The Jag had good tires—not as good as Sophie's studded tires—but Marc was still forced to drive more slowly than he wanted.

"Here it is—County Road 35." Sophie pointed to a small paved road off to the right.

Standing at the end of the road was a mailbox clearly labeled Stevens.

Marc braked, then slowly turned the corner. "How much farther?"

"It's two miles down and on the right."

He turned the fog lights on, giving them a clear view of the snowy road. "No tire tracks. We're the first ones to drive here since the storm started."

"Well, that's a relief. It means we beat that rat bastard here, doesn't it?"

"Unless he can fly."

But the situation was far from perfect. The road was narrow with few driveways or turnouts. If someone else were to come along, they'd have one hell of a time hiding. With no way to know where the road emptied out—it might be a dead end—there was a chance that they could find themselves trapped.

"So here's the plan. When we get closer, I'm going to cut the lights and park the car out of sight of the Stevens's house. Then I'll move in—you stay behind me—and make sure no one beat us there. If the coast is clear, I'll motion you forward. Then you go in and talk to them and see what they can tell you. But be quick. I don't want us to get blocked in here."

"And what if Megan is there?"

"Then I'll come in, get her and the baby, and we'll figure it out from there." Marc felt her gaze on him and knew she was trying to decide whether he truly didn't have a plan or whether he was being deliberately vague. But the less she knew the better.

Then he saw the sign—Pine River Christian Girls Camp. "We're here."

He cut the headlights and turned off onto a small gravel road that must have been a service road for the cabins. Grateful for the muffling properties of the snow, he nudged the car forward until it was hidden between two cabins and invisible from the highway. Not that someone following them wouldn't see his tire tracks, but they'd have to be looking to find them.

He killed the engine, unbuckled his safety belt, and pulled the second Glock out of the glove box. The other was tucked tightly in the waistband of his jeans. "You stay a good twenty feet behind me and out of sight."

She nodded. "The main house is on the north end."

They got out of the car and shut the doors silently. The air was crisp and cold, the scents of pine and snow mingling with smoke from a wood fire. Above them the sky was dark, storm clouds lying over the mountain peaks like a heavy blanket.

Marc moved to the first cabin, checking the parking lot meticulously for tire tracks or any sign that anyone had made it here before them to stake the place out. He saw nothing. No tire tracks. No footprints. No ski tracks.

Motioning to Sophie to follow, he worked his way around the perimeter, using the cabins for cover until the Stevens's house stood just ahead of them, golden light spilling from its frost-covered windows. Four inches of snow lay on the steps and the front porch, not a single footprint anywhere. "Go head and knock on the door. If anyone's there who shouldn't be, I'll have you covered."

Sophie nodded, a look of determination on her face.

But before she could take a step, he reached for her, caught the back of her neck with his free hand, and drew her into a slow, lingering kiss. Then he looked into her eyes, wanting her to know, wanting her to understand. "You're the smartest, bravest, most wonderful, most beautiful, most precious woman I've ever known, Sophie Alton. When I'm gone, remember that."

Their mingled breath rose around them, a cloud of crystalline white.

"You mean everything to me, Marc Hunter." Snowflakes on her lashes, she pressed her fingertips to his lips. "Wherever you go, remember that."

Then she turned and walked quickly over to the house, up the steps and to the front door, her knock startling the silence. After a few seconds, a tall thin man with glasses and short gray hair opened the door. Marc recognized him instantly—Pastor John Stevens.

Behind him, baby in arms, stood Megan.

CHAPTER 28

SOPHIE STARED, ALMOST unable to believe what she was seeing. *"Megan!"*

Megan stood in the middle of the kitchen holding little Emily in her arms, an astonished look on her face. "Sophie Alton?"

"Come inside where it's warm." Pastor John gestured Sophie indoors. "Tonight's no night to be out and about."

But no one seemed to hear him.

Just then, Megan looked past Sophie, and her eyes flew wide, her lips forming a silent *O*. Hunt stood at the base of the stairs, arms at his side, gun still in hand and pointed at the ground, his gaze fixed on his sister.

With a cry, Megan pushed past the pastor and ran out the door, baby still in her arms, meeting Hunt at the top of the stairs, sobbing her joy against his chest.

Gun now in his coat pocket, he crushed them both against him, enfolding his sister and niece in his embrace, his cheek resting against the top of Megan's head, his eyes squeezed shut, his voice a ragged whisper. "Thank God!"

Tears blurred Sophie's vision, blurred her sense of time, blurred everything except for the warm surge of relief that washed through her—and the bittersweet ache in her chest.

Megan and Emily were safe. They were *safe*. They'd been safe all along.

And now that Hunt had found them, he would be leaving.

Sophie couldn't remember another moment when she'd felt happier and so completely desolate at the same time.

You knew this moment would come, Alton. This is what

you've been hoping for. This is the best possible thing that could have happened.

Yes, it was. But that didn't make it any easier.

Then little Emily, perhaps upset by her mother's tears, started to cry, her tiny face an image of distress. She'd grown so much since the last time Sophie had seen her, the dark hair on her head thicker, her cheeks chubby and pink, her fuzzy yellow pajamas making Sophie think of a little duckling.

Hunt drew back, looked down at his niece, a wide grin on his face. "She's beautiful, Megan. Truly, she's beautiful. She has your eyes, and she's so . . . *little.*"

Sophie couldn't help but smile, tears still streaming down her face.

Megan laughed. "She's grown so much. She's almost eight months old now."

"She's probably cold." A woman who must have been Connie Stevens, the pastor's wife, poked her head through the doorway, the silver front legs of her walker visible behind her husband. A heavyset woman with tight, white curls, she gave them all a no-nonsense look. "Come inside, for goodness sake! You're letting all the heat out."

They found themselves herded into a large, homey kitchen, the snowy night shut out behind them. Dishes sat in sudsy water in the sink, the delicious scents of dinner lingering in the air. A plate of cookies sat on the counter next to the oven. A country-style kitchen table dominated the room, a high chair at one end, salt and pepper shakers and a sugar bowl pushed toward its center.

"We've got some leftover pot roast if you're hungry—mashed potatoes, green beans, biscuits." Connie shuffled back to the table and sat in a wood chair cushioned by a pillow. "Take your coats off and make yourselves at home."

And suddenly it all seemed so bizarre. Two strangers show up on the Stevens's doorstep in the dark of the night, one of them a man carrying a gun, and the first thing the pastor and his wife do is invite them in and offer to feed them?

That's probably not what Sophie would have done.

Not knowing what to say, she fell back on professional habit and introduced herself, offering her hand first to Connie, then to the pastor. "I'm Sophie Alton."

Pastor John looked down at her through his bifocals, took her hand, shook it. Big and rangy, his jaw fiercely square, he'd obviously been a strong man in his day. "Welcome, Sophie. I think I've heard Megan mention you. And you must be Marc, her brother."

But Hunt and Megan were caught up in each other—and the baby.

Megan bounced Emily, crooning to her, calming her. "This is your Uncle Marc. Can you say, 'Hi, Uncle Marc'?"

Hunt ran his big man's hand gently over the baby's head, then ducked down and kissed her. "Hey, little girl. Don't cry. It's going to be all right."

And through a fresh rush of tears, Sophie hoped with all her heart it would be.

MARC LOOKED INTO Emily's big blue eyes and knew he was a goner. No longer crying, she yawned, then gave him a sleepy smile that put dimples in her cheeks and showed off four itsy-bitsy teeth. She leaned toward him, reaching for him with one pudgy little hand.

"She wants you to hold her." Without warning, Megan shifted the baby into his arms.

Shit!

"Um, I don't think . . ." He froze, doing his best not to drop Emily, sure there must be a thousand ways he could hurt her.

He'd expected the baby to start crying again. He was a stranger, after all, a man who didn't know a damned thing about babies except how they were made. But instead of crying, she rested her little head against his chest, popped a tiny thumb into her mouth, and began to suck, her eyes drifting shut, delicate lashes resting against her rosy cheeks.

He pressed his lips to the downy hair on her head, his heart seeming to swell inside his chest until it hurt. She was so precious—small, helpless, utterly innocent. Somehow he loved her already, loved her down to his DNA. Was this what it felt like to be a father?

He would never know. Unless . . .

Without meaning to, he looked over at Sophie and found her watching him, a smile on her pretty face, tears gliding down her cheeks, her hand resting low against her belly in a gesture that told him she was thinking exactly the same thing.

And just like that the regret he'd been trying so damned hard to ignore sank into his chest like a knife, pain flaring sudden and sharp behind his breastbone. He didn't want to leave her, couldn't leave her, *had no goddamned choice* but to leave her.

In fact, he ought to be on the road already. There wasn't time for this. Someone might be close on their heels, someone who wanted both Megan and Sophie dead. The thought jolted him back to reality.

The old man was saying something about guest rooms. "We'd hate for anyone to be out in this storm. The roads can be dangerous."

"I'll never be able to thank you enough for all you've done for Megan, Pastor Stevens." Marc kissed Emily's soft head and handed her carefully back to Megan. Then he reached out and shook the pastor's hand. "I'm eternally grateful."

"It's been a blessing to have her with us." Pastor John smiled. "She's been a big help to Connie and a pleasure to have in the house."

"Unfortunately, we can't stay. Megan, get your stuff. We need to go. And hurry. We don't want to bring unwanted company down on these good people."

Megan's eyes went wide, then narrowed. She glanced back and forth between Marc and Sophie. "How did you find me? Why are you two together? How did you get out?"

"Long story. I'll explain when we're back on the highway."

But Pastor John shook his head. "You can't run forever, son. Sooner or later, this is going to catch up with you."

Marc wondered how much this man knew about him. "Megan's told you about me?"

"Connie and I know everything."

Everything?

Something in the way Pastor John looked at him set off a peal of warning in Marc's brain. "Megan, get your things. *Now*."

Megan looked over at the pastor as if seeking guidance, then met Marc's gaze. "No. He's right. We can't keep running. I need to face this. Somehow I need to—"

"Charlotte Martin and Kristina Brody are dead, Megan, and whoever killed them is probably on his way here right now. And he's not just after you. He wants Sophie, too."

Sophie watched the blood drain from Megan's face and wished Hunt had found a less terrifying way to break the news. Sadly, it was the truth. "He's right, Megan. We need to go."

Connie worked her way to her feet, her gaze on the phone that hung on the wall nearby. "It sounds to me like we ought to call the police."

"And what if this guy *is* the police?" Hunt walked over to the kitchen window and peeked outside. "Besides, no way in hell am I going to let my sister go back to prison. Megan, get your stuff and the baby's. Hurry!"

Sophie stepped forward. "I'll help. Where are your things? Upstairs?"

"Don't, Megan." Pastor John's voice took on a stern edge. "Run now, and you'll be running forever. Debts are meant to be paid."

Holding her drowsy baby close, Megan nodded, her gaze downcast.

"And what about your debts?" Hunt took a step toward the pastor, a hard look on his face, the tension inside him palpable. "Do you realize they'll probably arrest the two of you, too? You've let Megan hide under your roof. That's a class three felony. Do you know what it's like on the inside, old man?"

"If Connie and I face charges for sheltering Megan, that's a price we're willing to pay." Pastor John didn't sound the least bit intimidated. "But I doubt they'll arrest us. Ministers have a certain leeway when it comes to keeping confidences and offering sanctuary."

"And what about Megan? If we turn ourselves over to the police and survive, she'll go back to prison, and she might lose Emily forever."

"Sooner or later she'll have to face what she's done, and we'll support her every step of the way. But if she keeps running, she'll never really be free of her past." Pastor John's eyes narrowed, and he seemed to measure Hunt. "Why don't we talk about you for a moment? You've sacrificed so much for Megan already. How much more of your own life are you willing to give up for your sister, son?"

In the next instant, Hunt crossed the room and stood nose to nose with Pastor John, a muscle clenching in his jaw. His voice was quiet, menacing. "I will do whatever is necessary to make sure *no one* hurts my sister again."

When he stepped back, the gun was in his hand.

Megan gasped. "Marc, no!"

Sophie stared in shock at the weapon. Surely, he wouldn't—

"I'm done talking. Mrs. Stevens, stay away from the phone. Megan, move!"

"Put your gun away." Pastor John dismissed the threat with a wave of his hand. "It doesn't frighten us. We know you're an honorable man. We know you didn't kill John Cross. Megan did."

It took a moment for the pastor's words to penetrate Sophie's brain.

You didn't kill John Cross. Megan did.

And the pieces slid into place with a terrible, deafening *click.*

Hunt hadn't told police that Megan was at his house the afternoon Cross had been murdered because *Megan was the killer.*

MARC TOOK A step toward the pastor, his first impulse to force the words back down the man's throat, but the stunned look on Sophie's face stopped him.

She stared at him as if she'd never seen him before, her voice almost a whisper. "You're innocent. You were innocent all along. You took the blame, went to prison, went through hell to protect Megan. *And she let you.*"

"Sophie, I—"

"You *lied* to me." The hurt in her eyes was unmistakable.

"If I'd told you the truth, would you have kept it to yourself, or would you have spilled it to your cop friend? Would you even have believed me? I don't think so." He saw from her face that she didn't understand. "If you'd been there that afternoon, if you'd seen her . . . Christ, Sophie! She was so broken up, hysterical . . . I wasn't even sure she realized what she'd done. The system hadn't protected her before, and I couldn't let her be hurt again."

"I put myself on the line for you!" She lifted her chin and shot a hurt glance at Megan, who looked guiltily at the floor. "I want the truth, the whole truth, and nothing but the truth, so help you God, Marc Hunter!"

The sound of an engine caught Marc's ear. He held up a hand for quiet, took a step backward, and glanced out from behind the curtains in time to see an SUV making its way slowly up the road. "Any of your neighbors drive a black SUV?"

The pastor seemed to think for a moment, then nodded. "The Fosters up the way."

Marc dropped the curtain and turned to look at Sophie. "You want the truth? Fine. Cross came over. Megan saw him, became hysterical, grabbed my gun, and shot him."

Sophie shook her head. "No! I want the whole truth. And, Megan, that starts with you."

And just like that the entire night turned into a goatfuck. Despite Marc's repeated warnings that they didn't have time for this, he found himself in the living room, listening to Megan describe her ordeal. Everyone but him sat around the fireplace, Megan and Sophie side by side on the couch, Connie in a rocking chair giving the baby a bottle, and Pastor John in a recliner. Marc had opted to stand by the window, where he could keep an eye on the road.

"Char and I shared a room. Kristy was next door by herself. There weren't many girls—only seven or eight—and they left the younger ones alone. Char said you had to be fifteen or sixteen for them to notice you, and she'd been there longer than me."

A log settled in the fireplace, sending up a shower of sparks.

Megan stared at her hands, which were clasped in her lap so tightly that her knuckles were white. "My first night there, the guard just unlocked the door, shut it behind him, and walked over to Char. He told her to take off her pants, then he climbed on top of her and did his thing. On his way out he asked me if I'd seen how it was done because I was next. I started crying and asked Char what he meant, because I was really scared. She got mad at me and slapped me and told me to quit being a baby. 'That's how it is here,' she said."

Not for the first time Marc wished he *had* been the one to kill Cross. The man deserved every moment of his time in hell. How could any man do that to a teenage girl? He'd have to be absolute scum, an animal.

"The next night, he came for me—came in and told me to undress. I told him to leave me alone, told him he couldn't do that. Then he . . ." Megan's voice broke, and she took a long shuddering breath.

Marc's guts knotted to see his sister so upset. He wasn't sure she could handle this. Hell, he wasn't sure *he* could handle it. "You don't have to do this, Megan. You don't have to go there."

He might as well have been talking to the fricking wall.

Ignoring him, Sophie took Megan's hand and spoke to her in a soothing voice. "You're safe now, Megan. They can't hurt you here."

That wasn't true, of course. They could drive up and shoot everyone. But Marc had already tried to make that point—and had failed.

Megan went on, her face now impossibly pale. "H-he hit me and grabbed my hair and told me that he was the law and if I didn't do what he said I'd be in jail forever. I was so, so scared! So I did, and h-he . . ."

"He raped you." Sophie finished for her.

Marc wanted to hit something, anything. He wanted to piss on Cross's grave, to dig up his body just so he could spit on the bastard's corpse. He wanted to find the guards who'd helped Cross and drill them through the skull with a forty-five—after feeding their dicks to a Doberman. He wanted to hurt them, make them pay for stealing the joy from his sister's life.

Megan nodded, tears rolling down her cheeks, her voice quavering. "I-I was a virgin, and it hurt. Then he gave me a chocolate bar and told me to stop crying. After that it became a regular thing, sometimes every night depending on who was working. There were four of them, and they took turns on us, using their radios to keep track of the other guards."

It seemed to Marc that the floor tilted beneath his feet.

Four of them?

Christ! Jesus Christ!

He felt sick, bile rising in the back of his throat.

Every one of those bastards deserved to die.

"And none of you ever got pregnant?"

Megan shook her head. "They wore condoms. 'No babies, no DNA evidence,' they said. *I hated them!*"

Marc swore under his breath. "Goddamn fucking bastards!"

And from inside his own mind came the unwelcome echoes of another night, another time he hadn't been able to help his sister.

Let her go! Leave her alone! She's my baby sister!

He broke into a sweat, guilt sliding thick and greasy through his gut. And yet even through the heat of his rage and regret, he was struck by how much stronger and calmer Megan seemed tonight than she'd been seven years ago. Though he'd heard some of this story before, Megan had been hysterical then, beyond his reach, and he'd had to piece it together. But tonight, Megan was telling the whole thing, from start to finish, and although she was visibly upset, she was clearheaded and coherent.

His little sister was finally beginning to heal.

Sophie fought back her tears, trying to grasp the horror of what had happened. Megan had been repeatedly raped by four guards while in Denver Juvenile, later killing Cross in a state of hysteria. To protect her, Hunt had taken the fall, enduring six years of hell on earth.

Why didn't you tell me, Hunt? You should have told me.

She could feel Hunt's desperation and rage building from across the room, and she couldn't blame him. What had happened to his sister was unfathomable, unspeakable, unforgivable. But it was more than anger tearing him up, she knew.

Some part of him blamed himself.

She focused her attention on Megan, gave the young woman's clammy fingers a reassuring squeeze. "What happened wasn't your fault, Megan. Those men did something terrible. They had no right to touch you or hurt you, even if you were an inmate. They deserve to spend the rest of their lives in prison. We're doing everything we can to make sure they don't hurt anyone again."

God, her words sounded so lame! But what could she possibly say that could offer Megan any comfort? Nothing.

"That's right." Connie spoke softly, still rocking the baby. "Those guards were supposed to watch over you. They betrayed that trust and abused you instead."

"What they did was violent and shameful. A man is not a man who hurts women and children." Pastor John rose, walked to the fireplace, and added another log to the flames. "It wasn't your fault. You bear none of the shame."

Megan seemed to hang on their words, looking from face to face, until her gaze came to rest on Sophie. "I got sick. A fever. Pain. They sent me to the infirmary. The doctor said I had a pelvic infection. I trusted the doctor, so I told him what was happening—a mistake."

Sophie listened as Megan told her how the administration launched an internal investigation but refused to suspend the guards, only transferring them to the boys' unit.

"I thought the guards would be punished, but the investigators twisted everything. They acted like we'd done something wrong. They said that we'd had sex with the guards so that we could get special favors." Megan paused, still clinging tightly to Sophie's hand. "Cross came to my room just before I was released. He told Char and me that if we ever mentioned this again, they'd kill us. And so I never said a word."

"Until the afternoon you saw Cross again," Sophie added.

Megan nodded, then buried her face in her hands and began to sob, her entire body shaking. "I-I didn't mean to k-kill him. I-I didn't think . . . I didn't . . ."

Sophie reached to wrap her arm around Megan's shoulder, but Hunt was there. He knelt before his sister, drawing her into his arms, murmuring words of comfort, the gentleness of his voice at odds with the violent expression on his face. While Megan wept, her face buried in her brother's shoulder, he finished the story.

"Cross had come over to return my tool set, just like I told the police. Megan saw him, became hysterical, told me bits and pieces of what had happened, too incoherent to make much sense. But I understood enough. I confronted the bastard, ready to take him apart, only to have him laugh about it. I didn't know she had my gun until she fired. By then it was too late."

Sophie knew the rest. "Then you sent her away and took the blame. Was it the adult man who made that decision, or the terrified ten-year-old who still feels it's his job to carry the world on his shoulders?"

He shot her a sharp glance, but didn't answer her question, still stroking his sister's brown hair. "I wiped her prints off the gun and sent her home. I thought that with my military record and no adult priors I'd get a lighter sentence than she would with her long history of drug arrests. I didn't want her to have to testify. I didn't want her to land back in prison. I didn't think she could handle it, but I was sure I could. I had no idea how it would turn out."

Megan lifted her head, a pleading look in her tear-filled eyes. "I-I'm so sorry, Marc! I-I let you take the blame, and

I hate myself for it! The drugs made me forget for a while. I'd shoot up and forget what they'd done to me. I'd forget what I'd done. Sometimes I'd even forget you . . . forget that you were in prison, forget what I let you do for me. I'm so sorry! I d-don't know why you even care about me!"

"You're my sister, Megan."

For awhile there was no sound except for Megan's weeping. But there were still so many unanswered questions, so many things Sophie needed to know.

"Why did you take Emily and run, Megan?"

Megan sniffed, looked at Sophie. "I-I never should have let you interview me. They saw the articles and were afraid of what I'd told you. When I got out, one of them was waiting for me. He offered me heroin, tried to make me have sex with him, but I couldn't. I just couldn't! I told him that if he didn't leave me alone, I'd tell you everything, and he said he'd kill us both. I should have warned you, but I was so afraid. I took Emily and . . ."

More quiet sobs.

Sophie hated to push Megan, but needed to know. "Was John Addison one of them?"

Megan's body went stiff, then she nodded, whispered, *"Yes."*

Sophie shuddered, realizing how close she had come. The bastard had tried to get into her cell! "Addison is dead. He's gone, Megan. Who are the others?"

Megan didn't seem to hear her.

Hunt met Sophie's gaze, then looked down at his sister. "I'm taking you away from this, Megan. I'm taking you where they'll never be able to find you or hurt you again. But Sophie needs to know who the other two are so she can protect herself."

Megan sniffed. "Officer King."

"Officer *Gary* King?" Sophie couldn't believe it. He'd been with Julian when they'd rescued her from the cabin. He'd questioned her in the hospital. "Who else?"

"The Boss." Megan shuddered. "That's what they called him. But his last name is . . . Harburg. He was the worst. He offered me heroin and tried to make me have sex with him the first time I reported to his office. But I wouldn't do it. He said he'd revoke my parole if I refused and kill me if I told you. So I took Emily and ran."

Ken Harburg?

Sophie felt dizzy.

Hunt raised an eyebrow, his green eyes hard as jade. "The 'nice' parole officer?"

Her mind reeling, she tried to recall her last conversation with him. "At the restaurant, he asked if you'd told me where Megan was, and I said you hadn't. Then I asked him to help me find that report."

"And that night, knowing that you knew about them, they planted drugs in your car and your apartment."

Sophie shivered. "I need to call Julian. I need to give him their names. He'll find them, bring them in for questioning."

"So now you trust me?"

Sophie's head jerked around at the sound of the familiar, deep voice, the breath leaving her lungs in a rush. *"Julian!"*

CHAPTER 29

"YOU SHOULD HAVE come to me with this, Sophie." Julian stood in the doorway dressed entirely in black—black leather jacket, black turtleneck stretched over Kevlar, black jeans, black boots, black scowl on his face. His gaze passed over her and settled on Hunt, who was already on his feet, weapon pointed straight at Julian's chest.

"No!" Heart pounding, Sophie jumped up and put herself in the line of fire between them. "Please, don't do this! Please don't!"

"Sophie, move!" the two men barked in unison.

"N-no! I won't let you shoot each other!"

Somewhere nearby, Megan whimpered, the baby cried, and Connie muttered a prayer.

Julian looked past her. "He's not going to shoot me."

"You willing to bet your life on that, cop?" Hunt's voice was ice-cold.

"I already have."

And then Sophie saw.

Julian wasn't holding a gun.

"H-he's unarmed, Hunt. You can't—"

"Like hell he is! He's got a piece in a shoulder holster, and I bet he's lethal on the draw."

"If you wanted me dead, Hunter, I'd be dead." Julian stepped sideways, making himself a target again. "You're one hell of a shot. Set a new record for your sniper unit, didn't you? Eighty-five confirmed kills."

"Eighty-six." Hunt held the gun steady, his gaze unwavering.

"Yeah, that's right—eighty-six. Including that Taliban leader you took out from a hillside three quarters of a mile away. God knows how you were able to adjust for wind speed and bullet drop at that distance. That was one in a million. You're deadly, Hunter—stone-cold. But you're not a murderer—not yet, anyway."

Sophie gaped at Julian in astonishment. He knew things about Hunt that she didn't. And somehow he knew that Hunt was innocent. "You overheard—"

Julian cut her off, his gaze fixed on Hunt. "I've made it my business to learn everything about you, Hunter. I know how you stood by your mother, bouncing from foster home to foster home. I know you graduated from Grand Junction High School—two years ahead of Sophie. Is he the one you told Tessa about, Sophie? The school bad boy? Your first? The one who left to join the army the day after he took your virginity?"

Stunned, Sophie opened her mouth to speak, but Hunt beat her to it. "None of your goddamned business, cop."

Julian took a step toward him. "I know you got a *D* in geometry and an *A* in astronomy. I know about your juvie record—petty theft, vandalism, a couple of fistfights. I know you straightened up enough to get into the army, then paid Uncle Sam back by kicking ass in Afghanistan. You earned a Bronze Star. In fact, you left with a chest full of ribbons, didn't you? Not bad for a kid who grew up with an alcoholic, drug-addicted mother—and no father."

Barely able to breathe, Sophie saw a muscle clench in Hunt's jaw and wondered why Julian was doing this. Was he trying to provoke Hunt into firing?

Julian went on. "I know you came back to Denver to find Megan and signed up with the DEA, hoping to bring down dealers like the ones who helped destroy your mother. I know you found Megan, paid for her rehab, got her off the streets. I've memorized the court transcripts and your prison file. I know about the attacks in prison, about the inmates you protected, about the guard whose life you saved."

"You're a walking encyclo-fucking-pedia, Darcangelo."

"All of that, together with the handful of clues Sophie gave me—the open-records request, the tip about the heroin, the other victims' names—helped me to put most of it together. What I just overheard has filled in the blanks."

"Is there a point to this, or are you stalling, waiting for backup?"

"I admire you, Hunter. You've earned my respect. Not every man would try so hard to turn his life around or care enough about his sister to get her off the streets. Not every man would go to prison for life to protect her. Don't throw yourself away."

"Cut the shit. How'd you find us?"

Julian met Sophie's gaze, his eyes hard. "That was easy. The e-mail I sent Sophie this morning was embedded with a trace program. She opened it, and it downloaded to her hard drive, sending out a GPS signal over her wireless connection and monitoring her Internet activity. It's a test program designed to help us locate online child predators. I saw she'd downloaded a map for this address, and I followed her GPS signal here."

Sophie remembered how her computer had seemed to freeze when she'd opened that e-mail, and she felt like an idiot. "I-I didn't know . . ."

"It's all right, Sophie." Hunt's gaze stayed on Julian. "I don't blame you."

Then Pastor John seemed to remember this was his house. He stood, confusion and anxiety on his face, his gaze moving from Julian to Hunt and back again. "I don't want violence in my home. And you, sir, I don't know who you—"

"Easy, Hunter. I'm just getting my badge." Julian slid his hand slowly inside his jacket, pulled out what looked like a black billfold, and flipped it open for Pastor John to see. "I'm Detective Julian Darcangelo with the Denver Police Department. I've come to take Hunter and his sister into custody."

"Turn around and walk away, Darcangelo. Take Sophie with you, and guard her with your life. I'm leaving, and Megan and the baby are coming with me."

Julian shook his head. "Over my dead body."

Sophie's mouth went dry.

MARC FIGURED HE had three choices, and all of them sucked.

He could take out the cop—one clean shot between the eyes—except that Darcangelo was clearly one of the good guys. Besides, the man had a wife and a baby on the way, and he was a good friend to Sophie. Darcangelo had risked his life for her and would do all he could to protect her once Marc was gone. No, killing him wasn't an option.

Marc could try to overpower him with a few nonlethal moves, but Darcangelo was clearly a pro and probably had a few moves of his own. If they got into a full-blown fight in this confined space, someone else would probably end up getting hurt.

Or Marc could trust Darcangelo, turn himself over to the police, let them take Megan—and hope for the best.

No fucking way.

"Why can't you let them go, Julian?" Sophie's voice took on a pleading tone.

"I'm going to pretend you didn't ask me that, Sophie, or I might feel insulted. I'm not the judge or the jury. I'm just an officer of the law, and right now the law says that Marc Hunter is a convicted murderer, an escaped fugitive."

"But you know he's innocent!"

"He's not innocent!" The cop gave a snort. "He might not have killed that agent, but he tampered with a crime scene, perjured himself, assaulted a correctional officer, kidnapped you—or was the whole hostage scenario an act?"

Sophie's head snapped back as if Darcangelo had struck her. When she spoke, her voice was almost a whisper. "It wasn't an act. I thought he was going to kill me. I didn't recognize him until later that night."

Megan looked back and forth between Sophie and Marc. "Y-you took Sophie hostage?"

But Marc didn't have time to explain. He didn't like the direction the cop's thoughts had taken. "Sophie's not a part of this."

Darcangelo glared at him, undisguised rage in his eyes. "You made her a part of this, you son of a bitch!"

It was the truth, and Marc hated himself for it. "Take her, and go. She's why you're here. Get her out of here, and keep her safe."

Darcangelo crossed his arms over his chest and seemed to study him. "You're pretty tough, Hunter, but do you really think you can do it with a woman and a baby? Cross the border, I mean. The place is a no-man's-land. You got drug runners, coyotes, sex traffickers, border patrol—and they're all armed to the teeth. Do you think your sister is up for that? Look at her. She's been brutalized enough—her parents, those COs, drug dealers. Is life on the run what you really want for her?"

Hell, no, it wasn't what Marc wanted for Megan—or for Emily—but it wasn't like they had any other choice. "She'll be safe with me."

The pastor cleared his throat. "Why don't you ask Megan what she wants?"

Julian nodded. "Good idea. Megan?"

Megan stood, her gaze fixed on Emily. "I-I'm tired of being afraid. I want this to be over. I want you to be free, Marc. I want my baby to be safe."

Marc saw the anguish on Megan's face, heard the longing in her voice, and felt something twist in his chest. "Megan, honey, there's a chance they'll lock you up for the rest of your life. You might never hold Emily again."

Megan broke into desperate sobs. "I-I . . . d-don't know . . . what else . . . to do!"

"Turn yourself in to me, Hunter, and I will make it my life's mission to put away the bastards who hurt her. I'll make sure she gets the help she needs. I'll even testify on her behalf. And I'll make sure you're both kept in protective isolation in the city jail under DPD jurisdiction and not in DOC."

Marc stared at him, astonished. "Why? Why would you do that for us?"

The cop glanced over at Megan, and for a moment his gaze softened. "Your sister is the victim of a crime. She deserves justice. She deserves a life. Her baby deserves a mother. As for you, well, you might be a scum-sucking bastard, but you're not a murderer. You deserve justice, too.

"But more than that, Sophie is family to me, and she cares about you. She cares about you enough to put her entire future on the line to help you. That means I have to care about you— even if what I'd rather do is *kick your ass*. That good enough for you?"

Marc looked into the other man's eyes and weighed what he saw there. "Swear you'll look after Megan, Emily, and Sophie and keep them safe."

Darcangelo met his gaze straight on. "You have my word as a cop—and a man."

The room seemed to hold its breath.

And suddenly the gun felt so heavy in Marc's hands. He lowered it, opened his fingers, let Darcangelo pull it from his grasp.

From nearby he heard the pastor's wife let out a sigh. "Thank you, Jesus!"

"You're doing the right thing." Darcangelo tucked the gun inside his jacket, drew out his Nextel phone, then called someone named Irving and passed on the names of Megan's attackers. "I don't want to believe it either, but I'm willing to bet my badge it's true. Thanks, chief."

"You didn't tell him about us," Marc said after Darcangelo hung up.

"If it's all the same to you, I'd like to give your sister some privacy. We'll roll into the station, nice and quiet, and by the time the media hears about it, you'll already be inside." He drew out a pair of handcuffs. "But apart from that, we do this by the book, Hunter. You know what that means."

At the sight of the cuffs, Marc's lungs seemed to implode, blood rushing to his head, his heart thudding in his chest. Willing himself not to panic, he sucked in a breath and assumed the position, forcing his feet apart, clasping his hands on top of his head.

What the fuck have you done, Hunter? You're going back to prison.

"You have the right to remain—"

"Skip the sonata, Darcangelo. I know my rights."

And as the cop patted him down, confiscating the other Glock, his spare magazine, and the keys to the Jag, Marc found himself clinging to the hope he saw in Sophie's eyes.

SOPHIE SAW THE panic on Hunt's face and watched him subdue it, breath by slow, steady breath, his gaze locked with hers as if she were his lifeline. She took a step toward him, wanting to touch him, to comfort him.

He shook his head, his jaw tight.

"No contact, Sophie." Julian held up the handcuffs. "I know you've got a talent for breaking out of these, Hunter, but I'm going to ask you not to do that."

Sophie heard Hunt's quick intake of breath, saw his body jerk when the metal touched his skin. But he didn't resist as Julian locked his arms behind his back, then forced him to sit in a nearby chair.

And then it hit her.

This was good-bye.

Julian would take him to the station. Hunt would be booked, strip-searched, maybe even put through a body-cavity search. Then he'd be locked down. And the next time she'd be able to see him would be . . . when?

Maybe never.

"Pastor, I'll need you to follow me down to Denver in your car with Sophie and Emily. I have room only for two in my unit and no child seat. Why don't the two of you go get the baby's things and give Megan a moment to hold her?"

Pastor John helped his wife to stand, and Connie placed the distraught baby gently in Megan's arms. Then the two of them made their way upstairs.

A dazed look on her tear-stained face, Megan sat in the rocker, her gaze fixed on her daughter. And, as Sophie watched, Megan began to sing, her voice quavering with tears.

It was a song she'd obviously made up herself. "Baby Emily/You are so pretty/Mommy loves you with all her heart/She's loved her girl right from the start."

Tears blurred Sophie's vision, spilled down her cheeks. She looked over at Hunt, saw him watching his sister, an expression of torment on his face.

God, this was unbearable, and it was happening so fast!

Julian stood next to the rocking chair and put his hand on Megan's shoulder, his voice soothing. "I know it's hard, Megan, but it's for the best."

Hunt shifted his gaze from his sister to Julian, and if looks could have killed, Julian would have been dead that instant.

HIS INSIDES CHURNING, Marc trudged through the snow around to the back of the house where Darcangelo had hidden his unit. Megan walked beside him, Darcangelo's arm hooked through hers to keep her from slipping or falling down. He could tell from her irregular breathing that she was still crying, but he couldn't see her face.

Despite her tears, she'd handled being separated from Emily much better than he would ever have imagined, giving the baby one last kiss, then handing her over to Darcangelo with a wobbly smile and thanking him, as if he'd done her a big favor.

"Make sure she stays warm," she'd said.

Marc had wanted to slam his fist into Darcangelo's face.

Except that the bastard *was* being gentle with Megan.

No other officer would have given her time to hold her baby. Or skipped the pat down out of respect for her past trauma. Or cuffed her hands in front instead of behind her back.

Watching him work, Marc had realized that under different circumstances he and Darcangelo might have been friends.

The sound of a woman's voice drifted through the silence of the trees, bringing Marc's head around.

Sophie.

The house blocked her from his view, but he knew she was

carrying the baby out to the garage. The pastor had agreed to drive Sophie and Emily to the Denver police station, where Sophie would be questioned and Emily would be handed back over to the Mennonite family that had cared for her since birth. And they would all be back where they'd started.

Except that nothing was the same. Megan would be facing murder charges. Sophie's life was in a shambles. And what lay ahead of him was anyone's guess. Prison certainly, but for how long? Months? Years?

But something else had changed. He was no longer obsessed with Sophie in the way he'd been before his escape—he was madly and deeply in love with her. Saying good-bye to her was one of the hardest things he'd ever had to do. He'd realized he might never see her face-to-face again, that he might never have a chance to talk with her or touch her again. And for a moment, he'd thought his heart might actually break through his chest and land on the floor in bloody pieces.

"I love you, Hunt," she'd said.

Then, ignoring Julian's warning, she'd hurled herself against him, stood on her tiptoes, and kissed him, tears streaming down her cheeks. The kiss had been hot and desperate—and short, thanks to the cop.

Darcangelo had drawn her away. "No contact, Sophie. Do that again, and I'll put you in handcuffs, got it?"

"Stay safe, sprite," Hunt had managed to say.

There were so many things he'd needed to tell her, so many things he ought to have said, and now he might never get the chance. God only knew when he'd see her again. He hadn't even told her he loved her.

They reached the vehicle—an unmarked SUV. It stood, a hulking black shape, amid the shadows of trees.

Marc leaned up against it while Darcangelo helped Megan climb in. The snow had stopped falling, and the sky was beginning to clear. Orion was visible to the west, his belt of stars gleaming cold and white. Marc drew a deep breath, then another, trying to memorize the scent of snow-soaked pine, panic cresting inside him again.

He couldn't go back there.

Breathe, Hunter. Breathe.

Beside him, Julian had just secured Megan's seat belt and shut the door.

"Your turn, Hunter."

Just as Marc turned, something caught his eye.

The gray gleam of gunmetal in starlight.

"Megan, get down!" He slammed into Darcangelo, knocked him to the ground.

"What the—!"

Bam! Bam!

The first shots rang out, striking the side of the vehicle where the two of them had stood only seconds ago. Marc rolled, brought his cuffed wrists beneath his ankles and to the front of his body, then leapt to his feet and took cover behind a tree.

"Son of a bitch!" The cop rolled onto his back and returned a rapid spread of fire.

Bam! Bam! Bam! Bam!

Then he scrambled to his feet and ducked behind the tree beside Marc. "That sound like a Glock forty-five to you?"

"Yep. One shooter. I'm guessing eleven shots left—service magazine."

Two more shots rang out, hitting the vehicle with a metallic *ping ping*.

Inside, Megan screamed.

"Give me a fucking weapon!" Marc wanted blood.

"No can do, Hunter!" Darcangelo watched the trees. "Just stay out of sight!"

"And wait for that fucker to kill my sister? Fire at the flash!" Marc stepped out from behind the tree, saw a shifting shadow, then ducked back just as the shooter squeezed off two more rounds, a bullet whistling past his ear.

Darcangelo fired—and clearly didn't hit a goddamned thing. "What the fuck do you think you're doing?"

"I'm trying to keep you from wasting ammo." Marc kept his gaze focused on the trees. "I draw his fire, and you shoot toward the flash. Got it? And aim a bit to the right. He's circling that direction, trying to flank us."

Darcangelo got into position. "I *hate* backseat drivers!"

"Tough shit." Marc took a breath, stepped out.

Bam! Bam!

Double taps.

This time one of the rounds creased his left bicep.

But Darcangelo had been ready and was already returning fire.

Bam! Bam! Bam! Bam!

A grunt, followed by a groan indicated that at least one of those rounds had hit its mark.

And then night became day.

Marc looked over to find Megan sitting behind the wheel of the SUV, its headlights blaring. Never mind that they weren't pointing in the right direction. Their light was enough to show a man writhing in the snow, holding his thigh.

"Get down, Megan!" Marc called to his sister.

Quickly, Darcangelo moved in on the shooter. "Sergeant Gary King—you son of a bitch! And to think I've eaten lunch with you, you worthless piece of shit!"

Marc ran over to the driver's side door and opened it, forgetting until he hugged Megan that he'd been hit. *Shit!* "Are you all right?"

She clung to him, her body shaking. "I-I tried to help. Y-you needed lights, and I—"

"You did great, honey. He's down. It's okay."

She shook her head. "Wh-where is he? There's one more. The Boss."

Marc looked over his shoulder to where Darcangelo was rolling in the snow with King, who seemed to be trying to escape despite his wounded leg. "When you're done fucking around, ask him where Harburg—"

Then Marc heard a single shot and the baby's terrified wail.

Wrists still cuffed, he ran.

CHAPTER 30

LITTLE EMILY CLUTCHED in her arms, Sophie took a shaky step backward, her legs like water, her blood shards of ice. "Y-you *killed* him!"

Ken Harburg glanced down at his handiwork and shrugged. "Collateral damage."

Pastor John lay still, facedown in the snow, a bullet in his back. He'd heard the shots and had run toward the house to fetch his shotgun, shepherding her and the baby to safety, when Harburg had stepped out from behind the garage and fired.

"Collateral damage?" Sophie took another step, her heart flailing against her ribs, her mind racing for a way out, a way to protect the baby, a way to protect herself.

Time.

What she needed was time. If Hunt or Julian were still alive, they would come. They would help her. They would do all they could to save her and the baby.

And if they're dead, Alton? What then?

Oh, God!

The panic inside her shot to a higher pitch, made her stomach turn, fear for them coiling with fear for herself and little Emily.

Please please please let them be safe and alive!

"Yeah, *collateral damage*." Harburg's gaze flicked nervously toward the cabins. He was obviously wondering what had happened, too. "You know the term. It means I didn't come here to kill him—I came here to kill you. He just got in the way."

Sophie's mouth went dry. She took another step backward, pulling words out of the air, trying to keep him talking. "Y-you're supposed to be one of the good guys."

"I *am* one of the good guys." He glared at her as if she'd just said something idiotic.

Her fear flared to white-hot rage. "Good guys don't steal drugs from the evidence room! They don't rape! They don't commit murder!"

"Those girls got what they asked for! They flaunted themselves at us, tried to manipulate us, wanted extra privileges. But damned if they didn't learn their lesson. You play with fire, you get burned."

Sophie shook her head, unable to believe what she was hearing. "You had no right—"

"We had *every* right!" His shout echoed through the eerie, snowy silence. "They *owed* us. This whole damn city owes us! For fifteen fucking years I've earned shit pay working to keep the streets safe. I've watched scum work their way through a court system that gives crooks more rights than the rest of us. If I want to steal some pussy or earn some extra cash by selling drugs to a bunch of loser addicts, I can. The good I've done outweighs all the rest!"

Please—Hunt, Julian, hurry!

"Do you really think you're some kind of *hero*?" She laughed—a high-pitched, manic sound. "You just killed an elderly preacher who spent his life helping people. You killed Charlotte Martin and Kristina Brody. Did you kill John Addison, too?"

His head jerked as if in surprise, his reaction betraying him. "Addison's death was ruled a suicide, and the girls overdosed—"

"On fefe you and your buddies gave them! The same fefe you all put in my car and Megan's room at the halfway house! Did you hold them down and force it into them, or did you give it to them and just not warn them it was laced?"

"All we did was offer it to them. Well, I think Addison made sure the balloon had a hole in it, but the little whore swallowed it all on her own. King even managed to get a blow job out of it." He seemed to find this amusing, his indifference so cold that it turned Sophie's stomach. "Unfortunately, I'm going to have to kill you outright. Not that I regret it entirely. You might be a hot piece of ass, but like every other reporter you're a bleeding heart, wasting your time on trash like the Rawlings girl."

"She was fifteen!"

"She's a thief and a drug user!"

"She has the same right to respect and dignity as the rest of us!"

"Enough of this bullshit." Harburg's gaze twitched toward the cabins again, and he slowly raised the gun. "Think I can kill both of you with one shot?"

The breath left Sophie's lungs on a sob, her knees about to buckle, terror buzzing like white noise in her brain. "P-please, the baby! Y-you can't hurt the baby! She's innocent!"

"Just you, then." Harburg adjusted his aim. "Don't worry. A clean shot to the head, and you won't feel a thing."

And Sophie knew she was dead.

BAM!

She heard her own scream and the baby's terrified shriek—and saw Harburg spin to his left, grabbing at his side.

"Goddamn it!" He looked toward the house.

Stunned to be alive, it took Sophie a moment to realize what had happened.

Connie!

The preacher's wife stood in the shadows of the house beneath the iced-over eaves, holding a shotgun, struggling to reload.

"You should have used something bigger than bird shot, stupid bitch!" Harburg shifted his aim toward Connie, his free hand still pressed against his side.

"No!" Sophie's muscles tensed, some thought of kicking him and knocking him off balance half formed in her mind. If only she could—

"You fucking son of a bitch!"

Hunt!

He lunged out from behind the garage, charging out of the

darkness straight at Harburg, his wrists still cuffed, murderous fury on his face.

But his shout had given him away.

Harburg spun toward him, gun in hand, finger on the trigger.

"Hunt, watch out!"

Marc heard Sophie's shouted warning, but this was exactly what he'd wanted—to draw Harburg's attention away from the women to himself. And he was more than ready, seven years of pent-up hatred mixed with pure adrenaline. He jumped, pivoted, kicked—and felt the heel of his boot connect with Harburg's temple in a bone-jarring moment of satisfaction.

With a grunt, Harburg sprawled sideways in the snow, the gun falling from his grasp and disappearing into fresh powder.

Marc might have been able to finish him off right then, but the snow was slick and his hands were still cuffed. He landed off balance, slipped, and fell flat on his back.

Way to kick your own ass, dumbshit!

By the time he was on his feet again, Harburg was on his hands and knees, fingers closing around the handle of the pistol.

"You want it, don't you, asshole?" Marc leapt forward and drove his boot into Harburg's jaw. "Sorry. Can't have it."

Harburg gave a stifled shriek, his head snapping back, his jaw obviously broken. A kick to the gut, and he toppled over in the snow, dead or unconscious, weapon in his limp hand.

Marc took the gun, retrieved its twin from the shoulder holster inside Harburg's jacket and tucked the pair—a couple of Glock 37 .45 G.A.Ps—into the front of his jeans, his gaze seeking Sophie. "You all right?"

His heart still slamming, he did his best to keep his voice calm, though he'd never felt less calm in his life. He'd run as fast as he could, afraid he was already too late. He'd planned to sneak up behind Harburg, but then he'd seen that bastard pointing a gun at Sophie, heard the shot fire and—*Jesus Christ!*—his heart had nearly crashed through his chest. If it hadn't been for the old lady and her shotgun . . .

It had been so close—too goddamned close.

Sophie gave a wooden nod, rocked the crying baby almost absentmindedly in her arms, and he could tell she was in shock. "I-I thought you were dead."

"I'm fine—Darcangelo and Megan, too." He didn't want to take his eyes off her, needed more than anything to hold her, to comfort her, to feel her alive in his arms. But there were other priorities. He hurried over to the preacher. "Looks like he took a round in the back."

"Harburg came up behind us."

Marc knelt down beside Pastor John, pressed his fingers against the old man's carotid—and felt a thready pulse. "He's alive."

But he wouldn't be for long if they didn't get him to the hospital.

Knowing he needed to work quickly, Marc reached down to pull off the pastor's coat, then remembered he was still in handcuffs. *Goddamn it!* He'd need a crowbar to get the damned things off thanks to Darcangelo, who had double locked them. He glanced over his shoulder to Connie, who shuffled toward them, dragging the shotgun in the snow, her face pinched with grief and shock. "Your husband's alive, Connie. Can you help me?"

She nodded, sank to her knees in the snow beside them. "What do I need to do?"

"Help me get his coat off."

The round had penetrated just beneath the pastor's right scapula, leaving a bleeding wound that bubbled with each shallow breath. The bullet had clearly torn up his lung and God knew what else—but it hadn't left an exit wound.

Anti-personnel round. Hollow-point. Made for one purpose—to kill.

Marc wadded up the old man's scarf and pressed it hard against the wound, trying to seal it off. "He needs direct pressure."

"How do I do it?"

"Like this." Marc guided Connie's hands, showed her the kind of pressure that was needed, sure she would cope better if she were able to do something to help her husband. "We need to slow the bleeding and keep him from drawing more air in through the wound. You're doing great. Just keep that up."

She muttered the words of a prayer, her voice a whisper.

Marc got to his feet and glanced over to where Sophie stood, crooning to Emily, a dazed look on her face. He knew he ought to go see what was keeping Darcangelo, but he didn't want to leave the women alone. He stepped over the pastor, walked toward Sophie, unable to keep himself away from her one moment longer. "You should go inside. It's cold out here, and it will take a while before . . ."

Out of the corner of his eye, he saw movement.

He turned and found Harburg propped up on one elbow, slack-jawed and bleeding, another gun in his hand, its barrel pointed straight at him.

And he'd thought the fucker was out cold.

Marc's hands itched to pull one of the Glocks from his jeans, but he knew he'd only provoke Harburg into shooting. And since Harburg's weapon was already clear—where in the *hell* had that come from?—that meant Harburg would get his shot off first.

You should've done a better job patting him down, dumbass.

He met Harburg's gaze. "Shoot me if you want, but it won't do you a damned bit of good. The truth is out. Whether I'm dead or alive, they're going to throw your ass in a cage."

One side of Harburg's mustached mouth turned up in a twisted smile, then he shifted his aim, pointed the gun at Sophie, his gaze darting back to Marc, his unspoken message as clear as if he'd said it aloud.

I might go down tonight, but I'll hurt you by killing her first.

With no time to do anything but react, Marc threw himself into the line of fire, drew the gun from his jeans, and pulled the trigger.

Bam! Bam! Bam!

He saw a round hit its mark, felt something punch into his chest, driving the breath from his lungs and throwing him onto his back. He lay still for a moment, tried to breathe, but couldn't, blinding pain and pressure hitting him all at once. And he knew he'd been shot.

Shit!

But Harburg was down.

Sophie was safe. She was safe.

Better you than her, Hunter.

Yes, better him.

Time seemed to stop. Or maybe he blacked out.

The next thing he knew, Sophie was there beside him, tears streaming down her cheeks, her hands pressing something against the entry wound. "Please, Hunt, stay with me!"

He drew a labored breath, the pain and pressure excruciating, his heart pounding erratically in his chest. Unable to move his right arm, he tried to reach for her with his left, but his wrists were still cuffed. "Please . . . get them off . . . Get them . . . off."

He didn't want to die in chains.

He felt someone fiddling with his wrists, felt the steel slide away, and the cop's head swam into view. "Hang in there, Hunter. Flight for Life's on its way—ETA seven minutes."

But Marc didn't need a doctor to tell him that his chances of lasting till the chopper arrived were slim to none. He'd seen enough death to know what it looked like, how it felt. He reached for Sophie, wanting to feel her, needing to tell her what he ought to have told her twelve years ago. "Sophie . . . I . . ."

But he was drifting again.

"God, no!" Sophie watched Hunt's eyes close, fear twisting slick and dark in her belly, tears streaming down her cheeks. "I love you, Marc Hunter! I love you! Please wake up!"

"Let me." Julian knelt beside her, nudged her hands aside, pressed the blood-saturated cloth she'd torn from Hunt's T-shirt against the terrible wound in Hunt's chest. "Six minutes, thirty seconds."

Hunt's blood on her hands, Sophie scooted around a weeping Megan to Hunt's left side, looking to Julian for some sign that he believed Hunt would make it that long. Instead, she saw only worry.

"It wasn't supposed to be him." She took Hunt's cold

fingers in hers, tried to rub life into them. "It wasn't supposed to be him."

"He knew what he was doing, Sophie. He's a Special Forces veteran, a former federal agent. He made a choice. Don't blame yourself."

Julian was trying to comfort her, she knew, but it didn't work.

One minute she'd thought the ordeal was finally over. The next, Hunt had thrown himself in front of her, gun drawn and blazing. She hadn't seen the danger, hadn't known anything was wrong until that moment. And then it had been too late.

He'd taken a bullet for her, saved her life.

And if he didn't get help soon, he would die.

If they catch me, they'll probably bring me back in a body bag.

"Six minutes."

As Julian counted down the longest few minutes of Sophie's life, she held Hunt's hand, spoke to him, caressed his face. She could tell he was in pain even when he was unconscious, his forehead furrowed, cold sweat trickling down his temples, his jaw clenched. His respiration was uneven, the muscles of his bare chest straining with each labored breath, his body shivering.

"Shock," Julian said. "He's lost a lot of blood."

A couple of sheriff's deputies arrived, spoke with Julian, and went off to see to the others, calling for additional backup and a second chopper when they discovered that Harburg was still alive.

"Four minutes."

Then Hunt opened his eyes. When he spoke, his voice was barely a whisper. "Sophie?"

"I'm here." She leaned in so that he could see her, forced herself to smile.

He met her gaze, gave her fingers a squeeze, then spoke haltingly. "I'm sorry . . . Dragged you into this."

"Shhh!" She ran her knuckles over his cheek, trying not to cry and failing miserably. "You just rest now. Save your strength."

"Don't cry . . . No happy endings . . . not for us . . . not this time. But for you . . . you'll find happiness . . . the right man."

"Don't you even say that, Marc Hunter, damn it!"

"You helped me . . . find Megan. Thank you . . . is not enough." He looked to where his sister sat crying quietly, the baby clutched in her arms. "I love you, Megan . . . Promise me . . . no more drugs. Be . . . a good mom. Tell Emily . . . I love her, too."

"I-I promise." Her face contorted with grief, Megan gulped back a sob and held the baby out so that he could touch her, Emily's little fist closing around his finger.

"Cop . . ." Hunt's gaze shifted to Julian. "Watch over Sophie. Megan and Emily, too."

"You know I will." Julian met Sophie's gaze. "Three minutes, thirty seconds."

"Sprite?" Hunt took another shaky breath, his pale face a mask of pain, his gaze searching for her.

"I'm here, right here." She squeezed his hand, but this time he didn't squeeze back.

His seemed to relax when he saw her. "I . . . love you . . . Always have . . . Every day . . . you. My fairy sprite."

"I love you, too, do you hear me?" She sobbed the words.

His mouth curved in a weak grin. "I . . . hear you."

Their gazes locked, the love she saw in his eyes undimmed by pain. And for a moment it was just the two of them—just her and Hunt.

"You mean everything to me, Marc Hunter. *Everything*." She leaned down, pressed her lips to his, her palm pressed against the rapid thrum of his heart.

He answered her kiss, his lips like ice.

Then the distant beat of a helicopter drew her gaze to the sky.

By the time she looked down again, his eyes were closed.

HUNT'S BLOOD STILL on her hands, Sophie drifted through the drive back to Denver and the interrogation that followed— bright lights, faces swimming in and out of her vision, voices.

She was barely aware of the coffee the victim's advocate brought her or the questions Chief Irving asked her or the shouting match that Chief Irving and Julian had right in front of her, her thoughts scattered except when it came to Hunt.

Had they relieved his pain? Was he in surgery? Was he still alive?

God, please let him live!

"You've lost your objectivity on this one, Darcangelo. She's already got felony charges pending! I don't like it anymore than you do, but we need to detain her until we can get this clusterfuck of a case sorted out!"

"I'm telling you she can't handle that! Look at her! Jesus, Irving, not only are the felonies completely bogus, but she's just lived through fucking hell!"

"In your opinion does she require medical attention?"

"She's in shock! Can't you see that for yourself?"

But Sophie didn't care whether Irving threw her in a cell or threw her to the lions, her mind wrapped tightly around an unceasing prayer for Hunt.

Dear God, please let him live! Please let him live!

He hadn't opened his eyes again, not even when the chopper had landed, blinding everyone with its searchlights and sending up a blizzard of snow. The paramedics had put him on oxygen, strapped a blood pressure cuff to his arm, stuck electrodes on his chest, and started IVs in each arm. And what they'd said to one another had terrified her.

Can you get a pulse?

Hell, I don't know. The machine says it's 146.

He's trying to breathe. Open those fluids wide, and get another Lactated Ringers ready.

Have you ever started a jugular?

No.

Shit. Me neither.

BP is forty over nothin'. Fuck! He's crashing.

I'm going to intubate.

They'd traded an oxygen mask for a handheld ventilator, pumping air into his lungs, breathing for him. Then they'd packed and run, loading him into the chopper beside Pastor John and taking to the sky.

Sophie had watched the helicopter disappear, sending prayers to chase after them, then found herself huddled with Megan and Connie, a chilling fear settling inside her that made it impossible even to cry.

He has to live. Please let him live!

Julian knelt down in front of her, interrupting her thoughts. "We're taking you to the hospital now, okay, Sophie?"

"Okay." But Sophie didn't really care.

They transported her in an ambulance, then checked her in to the ER under guard. She did what the nurses told her to do or at least went through the motions, undressing, putting on a hospital gown, letting the doctor examine her. She barely felt the IV and broke down only once—when they made her wash her hands, Hunt's lifeblood sliding down the drain.

Please, God, keep him alive! Let him survive!

But when they tried to give her a sedative, she refused.

"I don't want to sleep! I can't!" she shouted at the nurse, knowing full well that she must sound crazy. "If I sleep I won't be able to pray for him or help him! I won't know what's happening with him! I need to know—"

"I'm sorry, but doctor's orders. If you struggle, we'll put you in restraints." The nurse gave her a sympathetic look—then injected the drug into her IV.

CHAPTER 31

SOPHIE STRUGGLED TO open her eyes, feeling strangely groggy and disoriented. Daylight streamed through a wide window to her left, the sky outside bright and blue. A little blue plastic pitcher sat on a bedside stand with her last name written on it. In the back of her left hand was an IV. Why was she in the hospital?

For a moment it made no sense.

No happy endings . . . not for us . . . not this time.

And in a heartbeat, the night's memories crashed in on her, riding a surge of panic.

"Hunt!" She sat bolt upright. "No!"

She hadn't meant to drift off, hadn't meant to fall asleep, but they'd sedated her, and now she had no idea—

"It's okay, Sophie." Tessa sat beside her, dark circles beneath her eyes, a book resting in her lap. "Rest easy. You're safe."

But Sophie hadn't been thinking of herself. Dread coiled in her stomach, she asked the question, afraid to hear the answer. "Hunt—Marc Hunter . . . Did he . . . Is he . . . alive?"

Tessa nodded. "He's in ICU. He made it through five hours of surgery. He's still on life support, but the doctor said he expects him to pull through."

Sophie closed her eyes and sank back into her pillow, relief rushing through her more potent than any drug, tears pricking her eyes.

Thank God! Thank God! Thank God!

Tessa took Sophie's hand, gave it a squeeze, her voice soft and reassuring, her Georgia accent soothing. "The old preacher made it, too. His wife is with him. Nice woman. I hear she saved your life."

Sophie nodded, tried to rein in her emotions. "I'm so glad! What about Harburg?"

"Alive and miserable. The round severed his spine, and his jaw had to be wired. He'll spend the rest of his life in a wheelchair going potty through tubes and bags."

That seemed a fitting, if woefully inadequate, punishment for rape and murder.

Tessa went on. "Gary King is fine. He lost a lot of blood, but they saved his leg. He told Chief Irving that he wants to make a deal with the DA."

So that's how it would play out. King would turn state's witness in exchange for a lighter sentence and send Harburg away for life, maybe even land him a spot on death row.

Sophie drew in a steadying breath, tears somehow still leaking from her eyes and running down her temples. "And Megan?"

"She's down the hall doing as well as can be expected, I'm told. Her baby's back with her Mennonite foster parents." Tessa handed Sophie a tissue. "You did it, Sophie. You found them. You helped save their lives."

And slowly it began to sink in.

They were alive. They were *all* alive. And it was over.

Sophie swallowed the lump in her throat. "Thanks, Tess."

"That's what are friends for."

There was a strained silence, and Sophie knew the moment had come.

She opened her eyes, met Tessa's gaze. "I'm sorry, Tess. I'm sorry I kept secrets, and I'm so, so sorry that I put Julian in harm's way."

Tessa looked away, her expression troubled. "I wasn't going to bring this up, but now that you mentioned it . . . Your friends stood by you, Sophie. We've been worried sick about you. My husband put his life and his reputation on the line for you. Some day I hope you can make me understand why you didn't trust us with the truth."

And so Sophie tried.

She started at the beginning and told Tessa everything from that magic night twelve years ago at the Monument to the terrible moment when the helicopter had lifted off and she'd realized she might never see Hunt again.

Tessa listened, her eyes filling with tears when she heard the full extent of Megan's ordeal and the truth behind Cross's murder. And when Sophie, still so raw from last night's horror, began to sob, Tessa took her hand, fingers clenched in friendship. "You go ahead and cry it out. God knows you've been through hell."

And Sophie did, crying like she hadn't cried since the night she'd found out her parents had been killed. "I-I love him, Tess. I love him so much!"

Tessa handed Sophie another tissue, took one for herself. "I can see that. You'll have to pardon me, though, if it takes me awhile to warm up to him. After what he did to you, taking you hostage, holding a gun to your head . . ."

"I'm sorry I didn't tell you all the whole truth. At first it seemed irrelevant, and then I was so afraid that Hunt would get thrown back in prison and have to face that horror again or that he and Julian would end up shooting one another. I wouldn't have been able to live with myself if one of them had hurt or killed the other."

Tessa gave a little laugh. "So you were trying to protect *them*."

Sophie nodded, then moaned and buried her face in her hands. "God, I bet Julian hates me now. He probably—"

A deep voice interrupted her. "Not a chance."

She looked over to see Julian standing in the doorway—and found herself fighting a fresh wave of tears. "I'm so sorry, Julian!"

He crossed the room, stood beside the bed, rested his hand on her shoulder. "It's okay, Sophie. I won't say I wasn't angry, because I was. But mostly I was worried about you. I'm just glad you're safe and this whole damned mess is wrapped up."

He released her, walked around the bed, and bent down to kiss Tessa's cheek.

Aware there was still a guard outside her room, Sophie

steeled herself and asked the question she hoped Julian could answer. "I'm going to jail today, aren't I?"

He grinned. "That's what I came here to tell you. King is singing like a canary. He's already bragged about planting coke on Hunter and putting heroin in your car. He also says he plotted with Harburg and Addison to kill you. Apparently, the heroin was meant to discredit you long enough for Harburg to arrange a hit. I expect the drug charges against you to be dropped by this afternoon. The DA might seek a warrant for criminal attempt— aiding and abetting a fugitive—but given the many layers to this case, that's going to take some time to unravel. We'll take you back to the station once you're discharged to finish questioning you, and I expect you'll be going home after that."

Sophie took in this news, both horrified to think just how close she'd come to being murdered and relieved to think she might at last be going home. She held out her hand for the friend who'd done so much for her. "Thanks, Julian, for everything— especially for not shooting Hunt."

Julian frowned. "I wanted to, believe me. For a time, I'd been looking forward to it."

"When can I see him?"

"You're both in police custody, and he's in ICU. Not for a while, Sophie. Not for a good, long time."

"Can we come in?" Kara poked her head through the door, Holly, Kat, and Natalie behind her.

Julian frowned. "Technically, she's not supposed to have visitors—not even you, *wife*."

Tessa looked indignant. "I'm not a visitor. I'm . . . well . . ."

Julian's eyes narrowed. "Right."

Taking Julian's lack of an outright "no" for a "yes," Kara and the others piled through the doorway, offering Sophie kisses and hugs and gathering around the bed.

"Are you up for telling us what happened?" Kara asked at last. "All I've seen is wild speculation on CNN."

"I don't even have all the details, and I'm covering it." Natalie pulled out a notebook.

But Kat looked at Sophie uncertainly. "I can see you're upset. We should let you rest."

"To heck with that!" Holly plopped herself down on the bed. "Tell us *everything*—especially any juicy details having to do with that sexy man who caught a bullet for you!"

MARC KNEW HE was alive because he hurt so goddamned much. He opened his eyes, looked up into a woman's face. Not Sophie.

Where was Sophie?

He tried to ask the question, but couldn't speak.

Something was in his mouth, blocking his throat.

"Don't try to talk." The woman pushed buttons on some kind of monitor. "You're in Intensive Care on a ventilator. If you remain stable, we'll start weaning you off life support to-morrow."

ICU? Life support?

That explained all the tubes and machines.

Shit!

"The surgeon removed the bullet from your chest and saved your lung, but it was pretty touch and go for a while. You had a few shattered ribs and lost a lot of blood. We gave you four units your first twenty-four hours here."

How long had he been here?

"I'm just programming your morphine pump. You should be feeling less pain in a moment. If you're not getting the re-lief you need, the call button is right here." She guided his hand to a gadget clamped to the bed rail.

With a smile, she turned and was gone.

He wanted to push the button, to get her back in here, to write his questions to her on paper so he could get some an-swers. But then something warm slid into his vein, and he was dreaming again.

THE NEXT TWO weeks of Sophie's life passed in a blur of in-terrogations, meetings with the district attorney, and court hearings. Because of King's confession, the drug charges against her were dropped, but the DA was pursuing felony criminal attempt, pushing her to testify against Hunt in exchange for some kind of plea bargain. John Kirschner, her attorney, told her to stand strong, assuring her that the DA would've filed charges by now if he believed he could actually win a case against her.

But because she was still under suspicion of wrongdoing, she couldn't return to work. Though Tom's board hearing had resulted in Glynnis being fired instead of him—a result that had led to heavy drinking in the newsroom—the board was watching the outcome of Sophie's case closely, and her job was still on the line. So instead of writing about the investigation that had nearly gotten her killed, Sophie was reduced to a background role, handing her research over to Natalie, whose reportage had gotten national exposure almost overnight.

"This is really your story, Sophie," Natalie told her. "I feel bad getting the glory."

"You've given me plenty of credit, Natalie. I'm just grateful to be alive, really. Besides, I have other things to think about right now."

Like the horde of reporters that always lurked outside her apartment and followed her everywhere. Like the nightmares that kept her awake, the shooting replaying itself over and over again in her mind. Like the exhaustion that made it almost impossible to get through the day without a nap. Like the charge of first-degree murder the DA had filed against Megan and the long list of felonies Hunt now had to face.

God, she missed him! She missed him so much it hurt. She hadn't seen him—not even a glimpse—since they'd loaded him into the helicopter. The judge had placed him in protective isolation and barred him from having contact with any of the witnesses in his case. Sophie found herself reliving the days they'd spent together, remembering his touch, remembering the sound of his voice, remembering what it felt like to fall asleep in his arms and wake up beside him.

It's not so much where I want you, Sophie, as it is how. Nothing tastes quite like a woman, and no woman tastes like you.

Sometimes it seemed they would never be able to be

together—if that was still what he wanted—and she'd spent more than a few nights crying herself to sleep.

"It's just posttraumatic stress," Kara told her.

"Of course he wants to be with you!" Tess said. "When a man takes bullets for you, it's true love. Take my word for it."

But by the third week, Sophie began to wonder if something else might be to blame—at least for the exhaustion. She wasn't able to buy a test herself, thanks to the ever-present paparazzi—when they followed people into the grocery store that's *exactly* what they were—so she made an appointment with her doctor, who ordered a blood test, then called her on the phone with the results.

"You're pregnant."

"I . . . I am?" Sophie had no reason to be surprised, but, even so, it took a moment for the news to sink in. *"Oh, God!"*

"Is this good news or bad news?"

Tears running down her cheeks, Sophie laughed. "It's the *best* news."

"Congratulations, then. Based on the date of your last period, your baby will be born sometime around November eighteenth. You should schedule a prenatal visit."

Elated, Sophie made the appointment, then hung up the phone—only to realize she was going to have to hide her pregnancy from almost everyone. If the tabloids found out, they'd have a field day. And who knew what kind of legal ramifications this might have for her and for Hunt?

She dialed Tessa's number, wondering if Tess would share her joy or chew her out. "Tess, I have the most wonderful news."

Marc shuffled into the interrogation room, cuffed by both wrist and ankle. He sat, waited. Why in the hell had he been brought here? He'd already told them everything he knew down to the most minute details. He'd thought the cops were done questioning him.

Darcangelo walked in, shut the door behind him—and gave Marc a dark look. "Sophie's pregnant."

The cop's words hit Marc square in the forehead. *"What?"*

"You deaf?"

Marc shook his head, still stunned. "Is she . . . is she all right?"

"Well, other than being *pregnant* and *unmarried* and *heartsick*, sure." Darcangelo shrugged. "I'm guessing you know when and how it happened."

"Yeah." He didn't bother trying to explain to Darcangelo that Sophie had deliberately tried to get pregnant. Regardless of the choices she'd made, Marc had been the one who'd failed to wear a condom—more than once. The responsibility lay with him. "I do."

Those precious days and nights seemed like a dream to him now—making love with Sophie, holding her in his arms, watching her sleep. He could still recall every detail of her face, the scent of her skin, the feel of her against him. The memories kept him sane.

Although the Boulder County Jail, where they'd placed him in protective isolation, was a hell of a lot nicer than the state pen, he was still in a cage. With more felonies than he could count filed against him, he was likely to be in a cage for a long time. And now Sophie was pregnant. Hadn't he warned her this might happen?

Then why do you feel so goddamned happy about it, Hunter?

He couldn't help but smile. "Can you tell her I love her?"

"Do I look like fucking Cupid?" Darcangelo glared at him. "Besides, why would I do that when what I really want to do is knock your teeth out?"

And still Marc couldn't wipe the idiot grin off his face.

August 25–Six months later

AN ENTIRE SWARM of butterflies in her stomach, Sophie walked up the steps of the Denver City and County Building, past the clicking cameras and the TV microphones. Reece walked slightly ahead of her, Kara beside her, holding her hand, both of them doing all they could to shield her.

"Is that Marc Hunter's baby you're carrying?"

"Did Hunter sexually assault you?"

"How do you respond to Ken Harburg's claims that you and he dated briefly and that he is the father of your baby? Will you consent to a paternity test?"

That last question took her completely by surprise, and her step faltered. It wasn't the first time Harburg had lashed out at her from his prison cell, and she knew it wouldn't be the last. Though prosecutors were seeking the death penalty, Harburg's case hadn't yet made it to trial. And even if he was convicted and sentenced to die, most death penalty cases took at least ten years to wind their way through the appeals system. As long as Harburg had access to the media, he would find ways to strike out at her.

Kara took her hand, gave it a squeeze, whispered in her ear. "It's okay, Sophie. We're almost inside."

But Sophie's nerves were already on edge, and she felt positively sick.

After what seemed an eternity, it all came down to today. Today, the judge would sentence Hunt to God only knew how long in prison, and Sophie would know whether she and Hunt had a chance for a future together—or whether they were doomed to a life apart.

Reece opened the door for her, guided her inside, his arm in the small of her back. "Why don't the two of you slip into one of the empty witness seclusion rooms for a while? We're a good fifteen minutes early. I'll save you both seats in the courtroom."

"Good idea," Kara said. "Save a seat for Tessa and Julian, too. Their babysitter canceled at the last minute so they're running late and bringing Maire Rose. And look for Holly and the gang. They're coming, too."

Reece raised an eyebrow. "So, save an entire row?"

Kara kissed his cheek. "You're pretty smart—for a man."

They entered the sparsely furnished little room, and Sophie sank into a chair and let the tears come.

"It will be all right, Sophie." Kara sat beside her, held her hand. "Remember how afraid you were for Megan? And that turned out better than anyone could have imagined, didn't it?"

Sophie nodded.

Megan had been tried for first-degree murder, but the jury, touched by her heartrending testimony, had accepted her defense team's assertion that she'd killed Cross out of fear for her own life and as the result of extreme mental duress—and had acquitted her. The judge, moved almost to tears, had sent Megan to live with Pastor John and Connie, rather than sending her back to the halfway house, arguing that the pastor and his wife had had more of a positive impact on Megan than the criminal justice system. He'd also mandated mental-health counseling and granted her visitation with Emily. To Sophie, it had seemed a miracle.

"You were afraid you'd go to prison, and they didn't even press charges against you," Kara reminded her.

Sophie laughed despite herself and pulled a tissue out of her purse. "Thanks to John Kirschner and Tom."

The district attorney had sat through a few meetings listening to Kirschner and Tom rant about Stockholm syndrome, freedom of the press, source confidentiality, and the need for reporters to gather the news and had decided he had bigger—and easier—fish to fry. Sophie had returned to work the next morning to find her desk buried in flowers, a giant Get Out of Jail Free card hanging overhead.

But if things had turned out well for her and Megan, they hadn't gone so well for Hunt. He'd been acquitted of murder—but convicted of almost everything else. And that's what terrified Sophie.

"Kirschner says Hunt could still get a good twenty years or even more."

"Yes, but he also said the judge might sentence him to ten and let him out in two to five on good behavior." Kara put her arm around Sophie's shoulder. "I know the convictions sound bad, but there are a lot of mitigating circumstances here. The judge won't ignore that. Now take a deep breath. This stress isn't good for you or your baby boy."

Sophie wiped her tears from her face, filled her lungs with air, but still the butterflies swirled, the baby kicking restlessly inside her, as if he could feel them, too. "Thanks, Kara."

"No problem. We've got a few more minutes, so take your time."

MARC ENTERED THE courtroom, scanning the crowd for Sophie as he always did. She was sitting in the front row directly behind his seat, surrounded by her friends. He could tell she'd been crying, and he wondered if it had anything to do with Harburg's latest attempt to harass her or whether she was just worried about him.

The sight of her was like sunshine in winter.

She saw him and smiled, her face lighting up. Then she stood and turned slightly to the side so that he could see her beautiful belly.

Marc smiled back, warmed to the core. It still blew his mind to think a baby—*his* baby, their *son*—was growing inside her. Darcangelo had leaked him the ultrasound results last week, along with a small black-and-white ultrasound snapshot that clearly showed a baby's face. Marc had been dumbstruck.

But it would be a long time before Marc would be able to spend time with Sophie or their baby. Today the judge would send him back to prison, and this time it was for crimes he *had* committed—perjury for lying about Cross's murder; tampering with a crime scene for sending Megan away; criminal attempt for concealing his sister's guilt; second-degree assault on a peace officer for his attack on Kramer; first-degree kidnapping for taking Sophie hostage; illegal possession of a firearm for stealing weapons; felony menacing for using said firearms when he'd escaped from prison; criminal impersonation for pretending to be a police officer; aggravated burglary for breaking into the Rawlingses's home and borrowing their car. There were a few other little things tacked on there, but those were the highlights.

Sucks to be you, Hunter.

Then again, it could be worse. A year ago he'd been stuck in the state pen serving life without the hope of ever getting out.

He took his seat, unable to keep himself from turning to face Sophie, the "no contact" order be damned.

She scooted closer, reached out to touch his arm, and whispered, her voice breaking, "I love you, Marc Hunter. No matter what happens today, I'll wait for you."

It was the first time she'd spoken to him since the night he'd been shot, and the sound of her voice flowed over him like honey. But he needed her to know. "I want you to be happy, Sophie. I want you to feel free—"

"All rise."

The judge entered, then took his seat, looking grim-faced. "Be seated."

His Honor spent the first few minutes boring them all with a recitation of Marc's convictions. "These are serious offenses. The defendant deliberately and quite effectively derailed the judicial process, delaying justice in the shooting death of John Cross for seven years. He then compounded those offenses by assaulting a guard, taking a hostage, and setting off the largest and most expensive manhunt in our state's history. He broke the law repeatedly, with complete disregard for the consequences."

You're going down, and going down hard, Hunter.

Hadn't he known better than to hope? He'd been through this before.

No happy endings.

"However," the judge droned on, "these crimes took place in the midst of mitigating circumstances the likes of which this court has not seen before, circumstances for which the criminal justice system is at least partly to blame. The defendant's sister, while still a minor, was subjected to almost ritual sexual abuse at the hands of men who'd been entrusted by the state with her safety. The terrible impact of that inexcusable violation cannot be underestimated."

Jesus, the man liked to talk! Couldn't he just get down to it?

"Furthermore, the defendant committed the majority of these crimes in the successful attempt to locate and protect his sister and others from those same men, believing, perhaps correctly, that the criminal justice system was uninterested in and incapable of protecting them. There is no doubt that he saved their lives, almost losing his in the process. In the course of his actions, the defendant demonstrated courage and loyalty. That he eventually surrendered himself and cooperated with police has also been taken into account during my deliberations.

"Will the defendant please rise?"

Here you go, Hunter.

Marc steeled himself, stood, met the judge's gaze.

"It is the judgment of this court that you be sentenced to time already served—"

There was an uproar in the courtroom, drowning out the judge's words.

Or maybe that was Marc's pulse thundering in his ears.

What the fuck?

The judge met Marc's gaze, smiled, gave Marc a little nod—then banged his gavel.

Time already served.

Was it over?

Marc heard cheers and shouts of congratulations, felt hands slapping him on the back—his attorney, Darcangelo, Sophie's senator friend Reece.

"Let's get those off." The bailiff stepped forward with a silver key.

Still reeling, Marc watched as the shackles that bound his ankles were unlocked and the chain that encircled his waist was removed.

"Hold out your wrists." The bailiff turned the key twice.

The steel fell away.

Marc was free—really, truly *free*.

And then Sophie was there—his beautiful, glowing, round Sophie. Tears streaming down her cheeks, she threw her arms around him, her body shaking as she wept.

Sophie. His Sophie.

Afraid she was dreaming, Sophie held Hunt tight, reluctant ever to let go. She felt his arms enfold her, felt his lips on her hair, her forehead, her cheeks, heard him whisper her name over and over again. It felt so good to touch him, so right to be close to him.

Then he released her—and slowly sank to his knees in front of her.

Carefully, as if he was afraid he'd hurt her, he pressed his palms against the hardness of her swollen womb, a look of wonder on his face. A lump caught in her throat, her heart so full she thought it might burst, she watched as he ran his hands over her, then leaned in and kissed her belly.

Then he looked up at her. "Marry me, Sophie. Today. *Right now*."

"I know a minister who'd be willing to do the job." That was Pastor John.

Was he here, too?

The courtroom filled with laughter—then drifted into expectant silence.

But there was never any doubt of Sophie's answer. She smiled, laughed. "Yes! Yes, Marc Hunter, I'll marry you!"

The room around them erupted with cheers.

Hunt stood, cupped her cheek. "Only happy endings for us from now on, sprite."

She nodded. "Only happy endings."

And when he kissed her, she knew that's exactly how it would be.

EPILOGUE

One year later

"DOES HE HAVE any idea?" Tessa nodded her head toward Hunt, her hands full with wriggling sixteen-month-old Maire Rose, who didn't want to have sunscreen put on her face.

With her daddy's dark hair and her mother's big blue eyes, little Maire, named after the Irish mother Julian had never known, was going to be a heartbreaker one day—if her very protective daddy let boys get anywhere near her.

Sophie shook her head, unable to hold back her smile, her sense of anticipation growing. "Not a clue."

Tessa laughed. "I can't wait to see his face!"

"Neither can I."

She'd worked hard for this day, waited a long time.

Hunt had waited far longer—even if he didn't know it yet.

Between Sophie's bare feet, Chase played contentedly in the sand, sinking his little fingers and toes into the fine grains with the focus of a scientist exploring the mysteries of astrophysics—and periodically trying to fit a handful into his mouth. Now nine months old, he seemed a miracle to Sophie. He had Hunt's green eyes, downy brown hair that curled sweetly at his nape and six tiny—and very sharp—teeth. And though he couldn't yet walk, not without holding onto furniture, he was a speedster when it came to crawling.

Chase Orion Hunter had been born a week before Thanksgiving on a clear winter's night in the house Sophie and Hunt had bought in Denver's Capitol Hill neighborhood. Having been with Kara when she'd given birth to Caitlyn and Brendan at home and having stayed at Tessa's side during Maire's home birth, Sophie had known she'd wanted to have her baby at home, too.

She hadn't regretted it. Hunt had been with her the whole time, holding her hand, giving her sips of tea, easing her from one position to another, rubbing her back, rocking her in his arms, his embrace holding her together. He'd told her he loved her a thousand times that night, his voice her anchor. And although it had been the most painful sixteen hours of her life, she'd never felt more cherished. When at long last, Chase had slid from her body in a rush of fiery pain, there'd been tears on Hunt's cheeks. As she'd watched him cradle their newborn son, she'd known that she would be willing to endure it all again in a heartbeat.

The man who'd thought he'd die alone in prison had become a father.

The sound of giggles drew her gaze to the swings, where Kara was pushing her two youngest—Caitlyn, now four, and Brendan, two and a half—in swings. Connor, who had recently turned nine and didn't want to play with little kids, dangled from the parallel bars like a monkey. In the shade of mature cottonwoods, Megan and Kat were setting out cake and ice cream for dessert, while Emily, a sunny little girl who was definitely in her terrible twos, painted one of the picnic benches with red popsicle juice, in which one of the adults— probably Holly because she was wearing white—would inevitably sit.

Beyond that, in the center of the park, the men played football. Hunt, Julian, and most of the SWAT guys formed one team, while Reece, David, and some of Julian's vice buddies formed the other. It was a hot August Saturday, and the guys had long since shed their shirts, drawing the attention not only of women passing by, but from Holly and Natalie, who sat on a blanket, ogling them openly.

Sophie couldn't blame them. She'd done her fair share of discreet drooling today, feasting on the sight of her husband, feeling the thrill of knowing that all of that man and muscle was hers. And she planned to make good use of it tonight.

She watched as the men gathered at the line of scrimmage, then surged into action at the snap of the ball. Julian dropped back and threw a pass that sailed above Hunt's hands, then bounced off a nearby tree trunk.

"How about next time you throw the ball to me instead of the damned tree?" Hunt shouted, tossing the football to Julian.

Julian caught it. "How about you get the lead out and move your ass?"

Sophie and Tessa shared a smile.

"If you'd told me that morning in the hospital that Marc was going to become Julian's closest friend, I'd have thought you were crazy." Tessa released a now thoroughly greased Maire back into the sandbox and stowed the sunscreen in her diaper bag. "Marc is like the brother Julian never had."

Sophie laughed. "You'd never get them to admit that."

They might deny it, but Hunt and Julian *were* as close as brothers. They antagonized each other incessantly, kicked the crap out of each other in martial arts practice, tried constantly to outdo one another in everything from marksmanship to barbecuing to winning at Halo—but when the bullets started flying, they had each other's backs, the tenuous connection that had been forged between them on that terrible winter's night having grown strong during Hunt's months on the force.

The day after Hunt's sentencing, Chief Irving had offered him a job as a SWAT sniper, then had fought like hell with the feds so that Hunt could carry a gun again—something his status as a convicted felon otherwise prohibited. Chief Irving's hard work had paid off when, during Hunt's second week on the SWAT team, he'd neutralized an armed bank robber who'd shot a security guard and taken a five-year-old boy hostage.

"One shot, one kill," the headline had read.

Hunt and Julian had been inseparable since.

"Oh, Emily, no, no! People have to sit there!" Back at the picnic table, Megan reached for the roll of paper towels and began to clean up the mess her daughter had made.

"Any news on her lawsuit against DOC?" Tessa asked.

With the help of John Kirschner, who'd taken Megan's ordeal to heart, Megan had filed a lawsuit against the Department of Corrections for failing to protect her and the other girls against Harburg and his buddies—and for whitewashing and burying the rape investigation. At stake were millions of dollars in damages.

"Still tied up in technicalities. DOC is pulling every slimy trick in the book, but there's no way they're going to win this one."

"That poor girl deserves every dime the jury gives her." Tessa burrowed her feet under the sand and wiggled her toes for her daughter to see. "Julian told me she's been to visit the other girls' graves."

Sophie nodded. "She said she needed to tell them what had happened, to let them know that Harburg and the others had been punished. Hunt and Pastor John went with her. Hunt said she broke down sobbing both times, and he almost had to carry her back to the car. Survivor's guilt, I guess."

"I can't even imagine." Tessa neatened the ponytail that held back her long, blond curls. "The preacher and his wife have been so good for her. She's like a different person."

"Hunt and I were just talking about that last night." Sophie pried Chase's sand-filled hand gently away from his curious little mouth. "Hunt thought he was helping her by taking the blame, but it turns out the thing that ate at her the most wasn't the rapes, but the fact that he was in prison for a crime she'd committed. She told Connie that the only time she could live with herself was when she was high."

"Well how about that? The truth really *shall* set you free."

Yes, the truth had set Megan free. But it had also given Hunt back his life. Yesterday—a year to the day after Hunt's sentencing—the governor had granted him a full pardon.

Today's celebration was a family affair. But last night they had celebrated at a formal party Reece and Kara had hosted at Denver's newest night club, Igneous Intrusion. It was, of course, Reece who had gained the governor's ear, armed with his damning probe of the Department of Corrections that had revealed rampant corruption and prisoner abuse. The legislature had passed three bills under his direction. One forbade the shackling of pregnant inmates in labor. Another defined any sex between a guard and an inmate as rape, even if it was supposedly consensual. "When one person is in a cage, and another person holds the key, there is no such thing as consent," Reece had argued powerfully on the Senate floor. The third bill set aside more money for medical care in prison, particularly for pregnant inmates.

Sophie had no idea how she would ever thank Reece for all he'd done. Because of him, Hunt could now live a normal life, free of the stigma of being a felon. Best of all, the chances that other inmates would suffer what Megan and Hunt had endured were greatly reduced. With Harburg losing appeal after appeal from his cell on death row and King sentenced to life in prison, this chapter in all of their lives was coming to a close.

And if Hunt was still occasionally haunted by his years in prison?

Well, she was there to pull him back from the shadows.

From behind Sophie came the sound of Kara's voice. "Oh, my God, is that it?"

Sophie turned to look—and there it was, just turning the corner. Chief Irving was right on time. The sight of it brought an unexpected lump to her throat. "Yes."

Tessa gave a squeal. "Julian is going to be so jealous!"

Holly and Natalie had noticed it, too, and were staring at something other than pecs and abs for the first time all afternoon.

Sophie stood, scooped Chase up, her sense of anticipation soaring. "Time for dessert."

And what she hoped would be the surprise of a lifetime.

MARC NUDGED A bit of ice cream into Chase's mouth and watched his reaction to the cool, sweet taste—a look of bewilderment . . . wide, innocent eyes . . . little mouth opening for more. "You like that, don't you?"

Marc pressed a kiss to the top of his son's downy head, scooped another small bite from his paper plate, and slipped it into Chase's mouth.

"I wonder what it's like to be a baby and to experience everything for the first time." Kat watched Chase with obvious fascination. "Every day must seem like stepping into a new world."

Marc nodded. "I imagine so."

A new world.

That pretty much described it.

He glanced around the table at the people who'd become his extended family—David, his fellow SWAT officers, Julian and Tessa, Reece and Kara, Holly, Kat, and Natalie. At one end of the table, Megan laughed over something David had said, while Emily dug her fingers into her cake, turning her dessert into an art project. Across from him Sophie chatted with Kara, a smile on her beautiful face, while Julian sat at the far end of the table, holding his sleepy daughter and flirting with his own wife.

This was his new world, a world that had once been as far from his reach as the stars. Instead of a living death caged by concrete and steel, he had a good job, a good boss, good friends, a precious baby boy, a wife he loved with the very breath in his body—and his freedom. A man couldn't ask for more than that.

Sometimes at night, he found himself watching Sophie sleep, a part of him afraid all of this was a dream. But then she would reach for him, the heat of her touch driving everything from his mind except for how much he loved her. And if somewhere inside he still worried that he didn't deserve her? Well, he was learning to ignore that voice.

Sophie had been his salvation, and he would spend the rest of his life loving her.

That's all there was to it.

He scooped up another small bite of ice cream and laughed as Chase opened his mouth like a hungry baby bird. "You like this even more than you like your mama's milk, don't you? Don't worry. I won't tell her."

Then Julian stood, tapping the blade of a pocket knife against an empty beer bottle. "I've been asked to say a few words, so I'd like to get it over with as soon as possible."

What the hell?

Marc hadn't seen this coming. "Sit down, Darcangelo."

"Shut up, Hunter." Julian cleared his throat. "A little over a year ago, we all had our lives turned upside down when Hunter here took Sophie hostage. Our lives got turned upside down again when we found out he wasn't quite the bad guy we'd all believed him to be—and that Sophie actually *liked* him. Well, I can't say I've ever understood women—"

The men laughed, while Tessa gave an indignant, "Hey!"

"Apart from my own lovely wife, of course."

More laughter.

"But yesterday, Hunter had *his* life turned upside down when, thanks to Mr. Senator, Governor Rollins gave him an official pardon."

Cheers and applause—and a big grin from Reece.

Julian raised his bottle. "Not many men have the guts or the skill to do what you did. You put your life on the line for the women you loved, and you prevailed. So here's to you, Hunter, for being one of the good guys all along."

"Hear, hear!"

"To Hunter!"

Holding Chase on one arm, Marc stood, met Julian's gaze, and raised his own bottle, emotion swelling in his chest. Across the table from him, Sophie beamed. "Thanks, everyone, for the support you've given us. We couldn't have gotten through this without you."

More cheers.

Then Sophie stood—and pulled a bandana out of her back jeans pocket. "Now it's time for your present."

"Present?" As if a full pardon weren't enough. "What present?"

"You'll see—in a minute. Sit." Sophie circled the table, covered his eyes with the bandana and bound it in place.

Shit!

He heard her cell phone key pad beep as she dialed a number.

"Okay, we're ready," she said.

Whispers. A toddler's fussing. Holly's unmistakable giggle. And then—a deep, purring rumble.

The sound grew nearer and nearer.

A car? Sophie had bought him another car? But—

The rumble drew right up beside him, seeming somehow familiar . . .

Holy shit! No, it couldn't be!

Sophie pulled off his blindfold. "Surprise!"

The breath left his lungs in a gust—and Marc could only stare.

It was.

An old shiny blue '55 Chevy Bel Air. *His* old '55 Chevy Bel Air. The Chevy he'd driven to the Monument that summer night.

At the wheel sat Chief Irving, a broad smile on his face. He climbed out, held out the key. "Sophie thought you might want your wheels back now that you're no longer a crook."

Feeling dazed and utterly blindsided, Marc stood, handed the baby to Sophie, and reached for the key. "But how in the hell . . ."

The cops had confiscated it the day of his arrest. The last he'd known, it had been sold at a police auction. He'd never in a million years even hoped to see it again.

He walked over to the car, slid his hand along the hood, taking in every beautiful inch of chrome and steel. Not a scratch from fender to fender. And the interior—the original two-tone interior—was still beautifully intact. *"Jesus!"*

"Chief Irving looked up the old records for me right after we got married. I spent the past year tracking the car down and negotiating with its former owner. It's yours now, Hunt."

Marc tore his gaze away from the car and found Sophie watching him, a sheen of tears in her blue eyes. He drew her into his arms, not even sure what to say. "I can't believe you did this."

"I want you to have your life back, Hunt."

Marc couldn't help but laugh. "You've already given me that—and more."

"Damn, this is one sexy vehicle." Darcangelo looked the car up and down, blatant lust on his face. "You used to drive this?"

Holly caressed the hood as if it were muscle instead of machine. "This is the perfect makeout car. Look at the size of that backseat!"

"I may need to borrow this from time to time." Reece leaned down and looked inside. "I hope you don't mind."

Marc chuckled, his mind on one thing and one thing only—being alone with his wife. "What do you say we ditch these losers and go for a drive?"

THEY LEFT CHASE in Tessa's care and drove up I-70 and into the mountains, parking at an overlook somewhere above Genesee, the city of Denver spread out below them, stretching to the horizon.

Sophie watched as Hunt set the emergency brake, then turned the radio to an oldies station, a feeling of deep contentment settling inside her. This was the great thing about loving him—it made her happy just to see him happy. If she lived a hundred years, she would never forget the look on his face when she'd taken off the blindfold and he'd seen the car.

"Come here." He reached over, wrapped his arm around her shoulder, and drew her close.

For a while, they sat in silence watching the lights of the city come on, his fingers stroking her hair, a cool mountain breeze carrying the scent of pine through the open windows, some romantic love song drifting through the speakers. One by one, the stars revealed themselves, the last tendrils of sunlight stretching pink across the sky, the moon a miracle.

He turned and nuzzled her ear. "I am the luckiest bastard on earth."

She tilted her head, bared her throat to him. "Why?"

He nipped her sensitive skin, sucked her earlobe into his hot mouth, then whispered. "You, sprite. Because of you."

She turned her face toward him, offered her lips, felt her breath catch when his mouth took hers, his tongue sliding inside, scattering her thoughts.

"There's no tire iron this time," he whispered. "What are you going to do? I'm warning you right now, sprite—I intend to have my way with you tonight."

"I sure hope so!" She arched into him. "Show me the stars, Hunt."

And he did.

GLOSSARY OF TERMS

Bitch up—To break down, to act afraid or subservient.

Bull dogs—Prison bullies

CO—A correctional officer, i.e., a guard at a prison or jail

CORA—Colorado Open Records Act: A Colorado statute that defines which documents are open to the public. Any citizen may request documents under CORA, but most requests come from journalists, investigators, and attorneys.

DEA—Drug Enforcement Administration: A federal agency charged with enforcing laws regarding illicit drugs and illegal drug use.

D-Seg—Disciplinary segregation: Isolation for prisoners who are being punished for bad behavior.

DOC—Department of Corrections: The part of a state's government in charge of running state prisons. Also responsible for inmate health and safety.

Fefe—A deadly mix of heroin and the anesthetic fentanyl. Also called "drop dead," "executioner," and "flatliner."

G-ride—Stolen car: the *G* is derived from the charge of grand theft.

L.W.O.P. (pronounced EL-wop)—Life without the opportunity for parole.

Kill—To end someone's life. Also to masturbate, i.e., "He likes to kill to porn."

Kill one's number—To serve one's full prison sentence.

Rip—To sodomize by force, to rape.

Shim—A slender piece of metal manufactured illegally in prison.

Shank—An illegal homemade prison knife.

Tango—A sniper's target.

Turn out—To sodomize by force, to rape.

GABRIEL ROSSITER BENT her over the back of her sofa and
pushed her skirt up over her hips, rubbing his hands over her
smooth, round ass, her impatient whimpers urging him on. He
slipped on a condom, then grabbed her hips, forced her legs
wider apart, and filled her with one slow thrust.

Oh, hell, yeah.

It felt so good, so damned good. He let his mind go blank
and drove into her hard, allowing himself to feel only the pulsing ache in his cock, holding back just long enough to hear her
scream. Then he fell over the edge, orgasm washing through
him in a white-hot rush.

"God, Gabe, you are the best."

He closed his eyes, giving himself a moment to catch his
breath, her muscles still pulsing around him, the musky scent
of sex filling his head. He slowly withdrew, then walked to the
bathroom, and tossed the condom in the trash, wiping himself
off with a tissue. When he turned to go, she was blocking the
bathroom doorway, wearing nothing but spiked heels and a
smile.

Samantha Price had the best body money could buy, from
her surgically enhanced tits to the tips of her polished toenails. She ran her fingers through her red hair, looked him up
and down. "Why don't you stay? We can do that all night
long—as many times as you like. I'll even let you tie me up."

He supposed he should take it as a compliment. He doubted
Samantha, one of Boulder's most expensive criminal attorneys, invited many men to dominate her. At another time in his
life, he'd have been only too happy to oblige her. Instead, he

felt annoyed. "That's not how it works, Samantha. You know that."

She tilted her head, an attempt at being seductive. "Things can change. We've been together for almost six months now."

"Together?" He couldn't help but laugh. "Fucking now and again doesn't mean we're 'together.' "

He zipped his pants, buckled his gun belt, and pushed past her, adjusting the weight of his sidearm as he went. He'd known it was going to come to this. It always did—the mutual exchange of physical pleasure ruined by delusions of attachment.

"It doesn't have to be just sex. I know that's what I said at first but—"

"Forget it, Samantha." He picked his undershirt up off the floor, slipped it over his head, then reached for his shirt, buttoning it and tucking it into his pants while she watched. "It won't work."

"What makes you so sure?" She picked up his winter uniform jacket, traced a finger over the badge pinned to the front, then began to search the pockets in a cloying display of possessiveness.

"Because I'm sure."

She drew something out of his pocket and held it up to the light. "What this?"

It was Katherine James's turquoise earring. He'd forgotten to give it to her before the chopper had taken off. He'd meant to track down her address and mail it to her afterward but hadn't. Even he couldn't explain how it had ended up in his pocket. Of course, he wasn't about to tell Samantha any of this.

"Is she your next destination?"

"We never agreed to be exclusive, Samantha—only safe."

She shoved the jacket into his chest, the earring still in her hand. "You're an asshole, you know that?"

"Did you enjoy what we just did?" He put on his jacket and held out his hand for the earring.

"Yes." She dropped it onto his upturned palm. "You know I did."

"Then what do you want from me?" He tucked it back in his pocket.

"More. Just more."

Christ, were those tears in her eyes?

"Sorry, Sam, but I don't have anything more to give you." He turned and walked out of the living room and down the hallway toward the front door.

"I know about your fiancée," she called after him, an edge to her voice. "I know what happened."

Gabe felt his stride falter, but he didn't look back. He opened the door and stepped into the night, knowing he wouldn't be coming here again.

A cold wind hit him in the face, carrying away Samantha's scent, taking the hottest edge off the anger inside him. He filled his lungs, walked down the icy sidewalk to his service vehicle, putting Samantha and her last salvo out of his mind and trying to ignore the pricking of his own conscience.

Why in the hell should he feel guilty? Samantha was an adult. She knew what she'd signed on for. He'd told her right up front that he wasn't interested in a relationship, and she'd told him all she wanted was good sex. So now she'd changed her mind and *he* was supposed to feel bad?

You are *an asshole, man.*

He climbed in behind the wheel, adjusted the gear on his gun belt so that it wouldn't jab him in the back, then shoved his key into the ignition. The digital clock on the truck's dash read 8:45—enough time to get in a few good routes at the rock gym before it closed. He'd turned onto Pearl Street when his pager went off. He pulled it out of it's holster and read the LED display.

"*Flames seen on Mesa Butte. On-call officer please respond. Police request backup.*"

On-call officer. Tonight, that was Gabe.

He flipped on his overheads, pulled a U-turn, and sped east toward the Butte.

KAT STARED IN disbelief and shock toward the open sweat lodge door, only to be blinded by a flashlight.

"Police!" a man's voice shouted. "Everyone out!"

Stunned, she shielded her eyes and looked to Grandpa Two Crows, who sat around to her left closest to the door. He looked amazingly calm, beads of sweat on his wrinkled face and bare chest, an eagle-bone whistle in his hand, its piercing song silenced.

"Come on! Move it! Out!"

Grandpa Two Crows leaned toward the door, spoke to the man outside. "You are interrupting the *inipi*, a sacred Indian ceremony—"

The police officer reached in and grabbed Grandpa by the arms. "Come on, old man. Out!"

Towel wrapped around his waist, Grandpa was hauled roughly forward, whistle clutched tightly in his hand.

"No!" Kat shouted, her cry echoed by the dozen women who'd come to Mesa Butte to pray.

This can't be happening!

Oh, but it was.

No sooner had Grandpa Two Crows been dragged through the small opening, than the same cop ducked down and took hold of Glenna, an Oglala Lakota elder from Denver. Her eyes wide, Glenna cried out for help in her native tongue, her towel slipping from her shoulders as the officer pulled her through the doorway.

Then the cop ducked down and shined his flashlight into the lodge once more. "Are the rest of you going to come out or do we have to drag you out one at a time?"

Pauline, a young Cheyenne woman and next in line to the door, looked to Kat, panic in her eyes. "What should I do?"

Kat swallowed her own fear. "I'll go, and you follow me."

She crawled around the edge of the fire pit toward the door, feeling trapped in some kind of surreal nightmare. When she reached the doorway, she ducked down to press her forehead to the earth as she would have done at the end of the ceremony had it not been interrupted. *"Mitakuye Oyasin."*

"Come on! Hurry it up!" the man's voice said.

She lifted her head and crawled forward another step, only to feel a fist close in her hair, the cop yanking her painfully upright, her towel falling into the mud. She tried to stand, but her weight came down on her right leg, which had been out of a cast for less than a week. Her ankle gave way, and she lost her balance, falling forward, clutching at the hand that held her hair, trying to keep it from being ripped out by the roots.

"What the *hell* are you doing?" A familiar voice, footsteps. "Let go of her! You can't just manhandle people like that!"

"They're resisting." The cop released her.

Scalp still burning, Kat landed on her hands and knees in cold mud, her heart slamming, tears of shock and rage and pain blurring her vision. Unable to stop her trembling, she looked up—and felt as if the breath had been knocked from her lungs.

There, striding toward her, was Gabriel Rossiter, the park ranger. This time he was dressed in his full ranger uniform—dark jacket with a silver badge on the front, gun on his hip, heavy boots on his feet. From the way he walked, she could tell he was angry.

"It looks to me like they're doing what you asked them to do, so why don't you stand back and give them some room?" He knelt down before her, his face cast half in golden light from the fire and half in shadow. "How's your leg? Are you able to stand?"

Kat nodded, confused to see him here, horrified to think that the man who'd saved her life, the man she'd thought about every day for the past three months, the man she'd just remembered in her prayers, could be a part of this . . . *desecration*.

"You know her?" the cop asked. Lantern-jawed and clean cut, he had a military look about him. "Better get her out of here before she gets herself arrested."

The ranger didn't answer. "I'll help you up."

Before she could tell him she didn't want his help this time, strong hands grasped her arms, lifting her out of the mud until she could get her footing. Her gaze met his, and for a moment all she could do was stand there, looking up at him.

He was taller than she remembered—and angrier. "I'm sorry, Katherine, but we have orders to put out the fire and clear the Butte."

"Why?" Cold November wind blew through Kat's damp hair, piercing the wet cloth of her skirt and T-shirt, chilling her to the bone.

"I'm not exactly sure why." He released her. "Apparently, the sweat lodge and fire violate city land-use codes that the cops have suddenly decided to enforce."

Land-use codes?

She started to tell him that federal laws protecting Indian sacred sites trumped land-use codes, but the cop had knelt down before the sweat lodge.

"I guess all we got here are squaws," he said, panning his flashlight over the women inside, a degrading tone to his voice. "Must be the braves' night off. Either that or the old guy has himself a harem. Come on! Move it!"

Inside, Pauline sobbed.

"No! Let me! She's afraid of you!" Outraged by the cop's insulting comments and his bullying manner, Kat turned to help, but the ranger held her back, his arm clamped around her waist, his mouth next to her ear.

He spoke quietly, his breath warm on her cheek. "You'll only get yourself arrested. I'll handle it. You go back to your car and warm up."

But right now Kat didn't care about being cold, and she wasn't about to leave the other women behind. Shivering hard, she rapped her arms around herself, took a step back and watched as the ranger bent down beside the cop and spoke to him.

She couldn't hear what he was saying, but after a moment, the cop stood, glaring at him. "Fine. Do it your way, Rossiter, but it's on your head."

Then the cop stepped back, making room for the ranger, obviously furious at the ranger for interfering and ruining his good time.

The ranger knelt before the sweat lodge door, hands in his pockets. "It's all right. No one's going to hurt you. Come on out."

Kat recognized that soothing tone of voice, and despite her anger, she knew the ranger meant what he said. She leaned nearer to the sweat lodge door and called out. "It's okay, Pauline. You don't have to be afraid. This one won't hurt you."

She saw the top of Pauline's head and stepped back to make room for her and the other women, looking beyond the firelight, searching for Grandpa Two Crows and Glenna.

And then she saw.

A dozen squad cars were parked down below on the access road, lights flashing. Three fire trucks stood nearby. The Butte seemed to swarm with law enforcement, two officers holding German shepherds on leashes.

Police? Firefighters? K-9 units?

All of this—to stop an *inipi*?

Everything but the cavalry.

Fighting tears with every breath, she spotted both Grandpa Two Crows and Glenna just beyond the firelight, talking with a uniformed officer. She might have walked over to them and tried to help, but then Pauline was there, trembling and crying, soggy towel around her shoulders, the other women emerging one by one behind her, their faces pinched with fear.

"Come." She met the ranger's gaze, then turned away, taking Pauline by the hand. "Let's get dressed."

GABE WATCHED AS Katherine walked soaking wet and barefoot through the snow, shepherding the other women around to the other side of a blanket that had been strung up between two saplings, her quiet dignity an indictment.

He'd arrived to find three fire trucks and most of the cops in the county parked along the access road to the Butte, lights flashing. With that kind of response, he'd expected to find a frat party turned homicide or perhaps even arson. Instead, he'd found nothing more threatening than a sweat lodge ceremony—the same kind of ceremony that had been going on up here every Saturday night since before Gabe became a ranger.

He'd hiked up the Butte in search of the officer in charge of this clusterfuck to try to minimize the damage, only to see Sgt.

Frank Daniels—one cop he'd never liked—dragging a woman out of the lodge by her hair. In a heartbeat he'd gone from irritated to fucking pissed off. And then he'd recognized her.

Katherine had fallen to her hands and knees, her long hair wet and hanging to the muddy ground, tears on her pretty face, the shock and fear in her eyes making him want to kick Daniels's ass, to knock his balls into his throat, to drag him around by the short hairs and see how he liked it.

He turned on Daniels. "Do you want to tell me what in the hell you were doing?"

Beneath his coat, the son of a bitch was wearing Kevlar, the knuckles of his black leather gloves lined with buckshot. He was strapped and ready to fight. "We got an anonymous complaint that someone had seen flames up here and found—"

"I know that!" Gabe glanced toward the blanket, making sure no gung-ho cop was headed in that direction. "What I want to know is why having a campfire without a permit merits the use of physical force. These aren't drug traffickers, Daniels. They're unarmed, terrified women."

"I'm under orders to vacate that little hut—or whatever they call it." Daniels jerked a gloved thumb in the direction of the dome-shaped sweat lodge. "If they resist, we have to take it to another level."

"It didn't seem to me that anyone was resisting, least of all the woman whose head you nearly yanked off." Gabe bent nearer, no longer masking his anger, his face inches from Daniels's. "This land is under Mountain Parks' jurisdiction. Knock off the Rambo act, got it? Now who the fuck is responsible for this mess?"

GABE PUT IN a call to his supervisor Chief Ranger Stone, then spent the next ten minutes trying to undo as much of the damage as he could, assuring Police Chief Barker that Indian people had always used Mesa Butte for ceremonies with the knowledge of Mountain Parks. No, Mountain Parks had never

required the medicine men who ran the sweat lodges to pay
for a permit because sweat lodges constituted a traditional use
of the land and were religious in nature. Yes, they occasionally
got phone calls from concerned citizens who saw the fire and
didn't know what was going on, but no one had ever filed a
formal complaint. No, there had never been any problem with
litter or property damage because the participants had always
been careful to clean up after themselves.

Then Chief Barker fell back on city land-use codes, reading from his notebook. "It says here, plain as day, 'No open
fires on open-space land without a permit.' Do you boys over
at Mountain Parks enforce the law or—"

But Gabe didn't hear another word. "Excuse me."

Katherine stepped out from behind the blanket, now bundled into a heavy fleece jacket, her towel rolled up and tucked
beneath her arm. She walked with the other women toward
several parked vehicles at the top of the access road, then split
off on her own, heading toward a big, black Dodge Ram.

He came up behind her. "Katherine."

She ignored him, unlocked the door to her truck.

"Ms. James, I'm sorry. This wasn't supposed to happen."

She looked over her shoulder at him, jerked her door open.
"No, it wasn't."

"Someone called an anonymous complaint to the police. If
the call had come in to Mountain Parks, this never would have
happened. The land is under Mountain Parks' jurisdiction, so I
expect there will be some shouting at city hall tomorrow.
We'll get it sorted out."

She tossed her towel across the street then turned to face
him. "While you're sorting it out, think about this: tonight was
a special women's lodge called so that we could pray for a
friend of ours who's in the hospital with ovarian cancer. The
police brought men with guns and dogs to stop our prayers.
How would you feel if you were in church praying for a friend
and got hauled out by your hair?"

"I'd be angry as hell." He didn't say that he hadn't set foot
in a church since grade school. "I'm sorry. I really am. But
I'm not your enemy."

"Then why are you here?" She crossed her arms over her chest.

"It's my night on call"—lucky him—"and I was paged. I had no idea what was happening up here until I got here. By then it was already too late to do anything beyond damage control. I'm trying to find out how this happened, and I promise I'll do everything I can to keep it from happening again."

She seemed to consider this. "Thanks for getting that cop to back off."

"I'm sorry he hurt you. I'm going to report it, for what it's worth, and you should, too."

"I will." She turned away, then hesitated and looked back at him. "And thanks again for saving my life."

Around them, the other cars were backing up, turning, driving away, their tires crunching on the snowy gravel road.

"Hey, I told you. You saved your own life." Then he remembered. "I have something that belongs to you."

He felt in his pocket for the earring, then held it out for her.

For a moment she stared at it as if she didn't know what it was. Then a look of surprise came over her face, and she took it from him. "Thank you."

"Have dinner with me."

What the hell? Have you lost your fucking mind?

Apparently, he had. Not only had he asked her out—he hadn't asked a woman out since he'd met Jill almost five years ago—but he seemed to be holding his breath while waiting for her answer.

"I'm sorry. I . . . I couldn't." She looked toward the line of red tail lights heading down the road. "I need to go. We're meeting at Grandpa Two Crows's to talk about this and finish our prayers."

"Then how about lunch, something really informal?"

She climbed into her truck, slid behind the wheel, and for a moment said nothing, obviously thinking it over. "Okay, but only if you agree to find out everything you can about why this happened."

Having conditions placed on an informal lunch date felt like more of a smack in the face than an outright rejection.

"All right. It's a deal. How about the Walnut Café at noon on Monday."

"Noon on Monday." She closed the door, and the truck roared to life.

And as Gabe watched her drive away, he wondered whether he truly had lost his mind.

PAMELA CLARE began her writing career as an investigative reporter and columnist, working her way up the newsroom ladder to become the first woman editor of two different newspapers. Along the way, she and her team won numerous state and national journalism awards, including the 2000 National Journalism Award for Public Service. A single mother with two teenage sons, she lives in Colorado at the foot of the Rocky Mountains. Visit her website at www.pamelaclare.com.

Discover Romance

berkleyjoveauthors.com

See what's coming up next from your favorite romance authors and explore all the latest Berkley, Jove, and Sensation selections.

Fall in love

- See what's new
- Find author appearances
- Win fantastic prizes
- Get reading recommendations
- Chat with authors and other fans
- Read interviews with authors you love

berkleyjoveauthors.com